THE

Good Liar

THE *Good Liar*

C.P. HARRIS

AUTHOR'S NOTE

The Good Liar is book 1 in the infidelity series. Themes include cheating (not between the MCs), possessive and jealous behavior, light kink including bondage, blood play, double penetration, and one scene involving somnophilia. This story centers around the off page death of a parent. As always, I encourage readers to put their safety above their curiosity.

CHAPTER 1

Jasper

YOU'D THINK THE television in the staff quarters of the rented estate was a roaring fire, and I in need of its warmth the way I huddled in close, intently listening to the financial news commentary with fists clenched inside my trouser pockets.

I'd only caught a portion of the ticker text gliding along the screen, but it was more than enough to paint a picture. Nexcom's star—as well as their stock—was on the rise. Now I couldn't walk away from the televised discussion on the company if I wanted to.

"Nexcom Global has bought out another major player in the tech industry. Its third acquisition of this kind in a matter of months," stated the burly anchorman seated in the center of the panel.

They debated what that would mean for the future of Artificial Intelligence, since Nexcom had dumped some of their smaller subsidiaries to focus their efforts on the big business of robotics engineering.

"Cole Kincaid has turned tragedy into a goldmine," the redhead on the left pointed out heartlessly. "No one can dispute the company has flourished under his control. He's done in a little over two years what his father—Franklin Kincaid—had tried for over two decades to accomplish."

"I'd argue," the stout, balding man at the other end interjected, "that Franklin paved the way for his son to steer the company into the stratosphere. Building something of this magnitude doesn't happen overnight. And I'm sure giving up the helm doesn't mean giving up total control. Not completely. Men like Franklin don't relinquish absolute control." His co-anchors conceded to his point.

I couldn't turn on a TV or radio station these days without being bombarded with news of another takeover by the tech giant. Daniel called it the Pac-Man effect. Nexcom ate up everything in its path, clearing the way for world domination. And apparently, New York was next on their hit list. Nexcom's headquarters had made the inconvenient move to my city.

The debate now moved on to whether Nexcom's founder should be heralded a modern-day genius, only rivaled by his son and predecessor, Cole Kincaid. I'd had enough, muting it once shallow phrases such as "broodingly handsome" and "world's most eligible bachelor" started getting tossed around. If only they knew how deep things could get when wading into Cole's waters.

"There you are."

I whirled toward the intrigued voice. "Jesus, Daniel, you scared the crap out of me."

My husband approached with a smile and two champagne-filled flutes, extending one in my direction. "I knocked before entering. *Twice.* I actually didn't expect to find you hiding in here, but it was the only place I hadn't searched."

I downed the drink in one go.

"Are you alright?" he asked, eyeing my empty glass with concern. "Exactly why *are* you hiding in here? It's your birthday. Your *twenty-eighth* birthday," he stressed, as if it was the milestone it wasn't. "You should be celebrating, not holed up in..." He scanned the sparse room with its wall of staff lockers and the tattered loveseat in the corner. "...in this...closet?"

"It's a room, and you know it." I chuckled, giving him what he wanted. "I'm fine. I promise," I lied.

Daniel wasn't domineering, jealous, nor possessive. None of the unhealthy things I occasionally craved but didn't need. He was ambitious, funny, smart, and generous with me. I should've loved him. I *did* love him.

"I still can't believe you threw me a party. Actually, make that a ball. Or a gala? A freaking concert, Daniel?" We both laughed, only his was genuine.

Thumbing my brow, I resisted the urge to travel my hand to my aching heart. The platinum band on my finger burned as a reminder he deserved better.

"A live band doesn't make it a concert," he said with uncharacteristic modesty, his hazel eyes shimmering with awed adoration for me.

"You rented out the Lincoln Center Orchestra," I deadpanned, straightening his bow tie. "Who are all these people anyway?"

"Colleagues, friends...potential contacts," he finished sheepishly, setting his glass on the table next to mine.

"I have two friends—including you. And I don't need you to help me find a job. I already have one I love," I said firmly.

"I know, I know," he said, smoothing his hands up my chest, calming me. "You want to defend the defenseless. Help those in need gain a fighting chance against the unjust, oppressive system, yada, yada..." He waved a hand vaguely, and I rolled my eyes at the theatrical spin he put on it. He splayed his palms along my waist, gently guiding me into his chest. Daniel did everything gently. "I love your tender heart the most, you know."

"Well, now the rest of me is jealous," I quipped.

"Don't be. Your lovely place comes in a close second." He squeezed my ass.

"My lovely *place*?" I fought my grin.

He shrugged. "Sounds more romantic than butthole, doesn't it?"

My grin won the battle.

"Seriously," he started, taking on his courtroom tone. "Your brilliance is sitting on a shelf collecting dust. Can't you do both? Be the powerhouse attorney negotiating corporate takeovers, who also happens to help the needy on occasion. You can be the lawyer equivalent of Robin Hood in your spare time."

Having been born into affluence and entitlement made Daniel an unintentional asshole sometimes. I'd spent enough of my childhood living in poverty before being catapulted into wealth. It had afforded me a healthy dose of empathy, and I was more connected to that side of myself. This world—Daniel's world—had never gotten its claws in me.

No one was perfect, though, I'd tell myself, and his good far outweighed the moments when his privilege went right over his head with comments such as the one he'd just made. "You're being an elitist dick again," I whispered, running my hands through his chestnut hair. It was what I called him when he needed reeling in. A reminder that having more-of didn't make him more-than. He'd flush and apologize sincerely, letting me know there was hope for him.

"I'm sorry. I meant to say the less fortunate." He kissed me sweetly. He always kissed me sweetly, and I always pulled away first.

"It's only been two years since I passed the bar—"

"Since you obliterated the bar." He pressed an elegant finger to my lips, cutting off my objection. "You're brilliant. And I want to make sure you have the best options available to you."

"Can we table this for another day?"

"Of course," he said, taking an apologetic step back, seemingly remembering where we were and what we were there to celebrate. Daniel flicked his wrist, hiking up the cuff of his dinner jacket to check the time on his Rolex. He grasped my hand, urgently ushering us out of the room. "Your surprise should be ready."

"Surprise?" I allowed him to tow me along the maze of halls. The music grew louder the closer we got to the ballroom.

"I've had the pleasure of loving you through three birthdays, and you've been somber for every one of them. You've been somber since the day I met you, Jasper."

We'd met while I was interning at his firm almost four years ago. I had a strict rule about not dating within the work-place—*because you're a man of high morals,* my hypercritical conscience mocked. Honestly, I'd had a strict rule about not dating at all, but Daniel was persistent, and I'd desperately needed a distraction. A few weeks after my internship had concluded, Daniel showed up to my law school graduation with an offer for dinner, and I'd hesitantly accepted. That was three years ago.

"What is it? Can I get a hint?" I asked. He stopped short, feet away from the ornate mahogany doors, partygoers jam-packed on the other side of it—most of whom I'd never seen, contrary to his claim of colleagues and friends. Concern rose in me like smoke as his nervous gaze bounced from me to the closed doors. "Daniel—"

"It isn't an *it*."

"What?" My brows pinched in confusion.

"It's a *who*," he said, and one by one the cylinders clicked into place. I didn't talk much about my past, but I'd finally given in to his prying last year. I'd given him a piece of me I gave to no one, because he'd gone above and beyond to surprise me with a grand gesture I didn't need, and my non-reaction to him renting out Cipriani for a birthday dinner for two had said as much. And because he'd deserved to know the problem wasn't him, it was me. Because... Because he simply deserved the truth, and his patience had been rightfully thinning.

I snatched my hand from his and retreated a step. "What did you do?"

His words faltered as he examined the terror I could feel carving itself into my face. He reached for me. "Jasper?"

"There you two are." The tight, exasperated voice belonged to Jessica, Daniel's assistant turned party planner, as she burst through the grand doors, chased by the harmony of a string quartet. "Come, come now," she said, shuffling over to loop her arms through the crooks of ours before leading us inside.

The chattering pretentious crowd made way for us as we sliced through the red velvet-draped room, heading for the center of it. My eyes roamed restlessly as pain pounded at my temples with a sense of foreboding.

There, standing beneath the Peloponnesian Battle depicted on the vaulted ceiling, standing right in the heart of it, loomed my heaven and hell.

Cole Kincaid.

Even with his back to me, engaging with the wide-eyed vultures swarming him, I knew. Even with the obvious changes to his body during our years apart, I *knew*. To hell with my mind, it was my body that would never forget him.

The music halted abruptly, and a hush fell over the room. My blood sped through me, the sound crashing against my eardrums like battering waves as my heart pumped recklessly, chasing the shore, chasing safety.

He turned unhurriedly, not the least bit surprised to find me standing there affected by him. He nodded once in a gesture of acknowledgement, his long, sleek fingers cupping his glass in ownership. The way they'd once cupped every part of me.

"Jasper," he said with all the arrogance and self-possession of a man who'd one day rule the fucking world.

"Surprise!" Daniel exclaimed from my side, kissing my lifeless cheek. If I wasn't so hyper-aware of the man in front of me,

I would've missed the subtle rippling of his jaw caused by my husband's easy display of affection toward me.

Within seconds, the partiers grew bored of us, the noise level heightening once again as the pointless drivel resumed its competition with the reignited orchestra.

I was supposed to do something. Proper etiquette called for me to at least say hello to Cole, and to offer my sincere thanks to my husband for making my nightmares come true. But I couldn't even find it in me to breathe. As I fought for air, Cole stood there as if there wasn't a pile of pain and rubble beneath both our feet.

He wore his dark hair slicked away from his face, his angular jaw hidden beneath his artfully constructed five-o'clock shadow. His icy blue eyes were backlit with a cruelty that had earned him the label of mysterious. I'd always joked that Franklin's obsidian eyes were wasted on him. Between him and his son, Cole wore the darkness well.

Cole took on the olive coloring of his South American maternal grandfather, while I'd been gifted with the paleness of my European father. He towered unflinchingly, statuesque, wearing the hell out of his black suit, whereas my tux wore me. In this room full of people who were supposed to be important, the controlling shareholder and CEO of Nexcom Global was in his element. He was the man Daniel wanted me to be.

"I'm sure you two have a lot of catching up to do," Daniel said, bursting our awkward bubble of silence. "The terrace is empty if you want some privacy."

Privacy was the last thing we needed. Cole and I needed to be supervised at all times.

"After you," Cole said, with a flourish of his hand.

I moved ahead of him, feeling his gaze fan me from skull to heels. We stepped onto the wide balcony overlooking the courtyard. Up ahead, the vast skyline silhouetted the river separating us from the city with an oil-like sheen.

Cole closed the French doors behind us and strode toward me as if he didn't have plans to stop. I shivered, placing the blame on the frigid fall air and the need for my coat, and not the man in front of me.

"You're cold."

"I'm fine," I insisted. "You could've said no."

"And why would I do that?" he asked.

"You know why," I bit out, irritated by the way my voice thickened from his proximity. I shuffled over to the stone railing, giving him my back. "It's been years. Why now? Why show up now?"

"I took Daniel's invitation as a sign—"

"As an excuse, you mean. An excuse to show up and throw my life off its fucking axis."

"I see New York has roughened you," he said in answer to my vulgarity. I didn't find him one bit entertaining, and the glower I aimed over my shoulder said as much. He sighed, coming to stand next to me, both of us staring past the bristling treetops and into the twinkling night sky. The cold breeze pile-drove his cologne into my nostrils. Against my will, I breathed in deeply.

"I was on my way here anyway," he said.

The move. How much of the blame for that could be shouldered by coincidence, I wondered, and how much of it was part of a calculated play to get to me. It'd been a little over two years—the news anchor had said—since Franklin took the company public, before handing over the majority stake to Cole, then stepping away. Could Cole have been planning this move since then? Before then? Biding his time? A company of that magnitude didn't spontaneously decide to move across the country overnight.

"And I missed my brother," he admitted, his tone held a vulnerability his stoicism would never betray.

"Stepbrothers," I corrected. "And we were never just that, Cole." We had been more. We had been sinful. And the high voltage of electricity sizzling through my veins warned me we were all those things still. Time and space would never change that. "But we aren't even that anymore. Any familial link we had died with my mother."

A hint of sadness flickered in the depths of his eyes at the mention of her, and then it settled into something more steady, more permanent as he said—as if only now realizing it, or only now wanting to face it. "You're married."

"Yes," I said, following his gaze to my hand. Daniel had asked after our fight last year, and in the heat of the moment, I'd agreed, giving him the security he needed. The truth was, if it wasn't Daniel getting the scraps of me, it would've been someone else, because my heart wasn't whole. I'd left the other half of it back in Seattle, and now it was here, right in front of me, staring into me as if nothing could keep us apart. Not even my vows.

"Why are you really here, Cole?" I spoke to him with more care than I had moments ago. Maybe because he'd dropped the aloof façade, reminding me I wasn't the only one hurt by the events of the past. Reminding me that what had happened wasn't his fault. "Is this your attempt at repeating history?"

"I gave you what you wanted. I let you go, and I stayed away. I didn't try to find or make contact with you. But I miss our friendship. Our brotherhood. I miss you," he whispered. "And not in the way you think."

Why did the latter hurt to hear? He'd reentered my life less than ten minutes ago, and already the old poison resting dormant in me began to unfurl, yawning to life. Already I was forgetting I was a taken man. My wedding band, suddenly feeling like a ball and chain, bit into my skin as a reminder. I needed Cole gone.

"What?" I asked after a chanced side-glance revealed his thoughtful inspection of me.

"I'm not used to seeing you in a suit." He gazed skyward as a stiff breeze rattled his perfectly styled hair. "Selene's probably gaping down on you in shock. She couldn't get you into anything but a ratty t-shirt and jeans. Not even bribery worked."

"Because I can't be bought." The mention of my mother thawed some of my internal ice. I hadn't spoken of her out loud in years. Not since she'd died. I fought the urge to reminisce with him, fought against wanting to let him in, even an inch. But how could I not? She was his as much as she was mine. And Cole was the only person in the world who *knew*. The only one who understood.

"She loved it when you called her mom," I said, unable to resist revisiting her memory, the words slithering past my guards. I could give him this, give myself this moment of reflection, and then be done with him. "You don't have to stop."

My mother and Franklin had married when I was eight and Cole ten. We'd both suffered the loss of a parent early on. He had been a closed-off kid, and my mother tried to get through to him for a long while without pressure or success. And then one day over breakfast, he'd said, "Can you pass the pancakes, Mom?" No one had made a big deal about it, and she'd hidden her tears well.

"Doesn't feel right anymore. Not after..." He stopped there, and I was grateful for it. Unlike Cole, I'd always addressed his father by name. Franklin was a good man, an even better stepfather to me—in his own way. I was unlucky enough to have known my real father long before entering the Kincaid household, and for me the word held a negative connotation of neglect and abuse, so I never used it. Franklin was emotionally mature enough to not take offense, and he'd cultivated a strong bond with me anyway. Real pain lingered behind losing him, but I mourned the loss of Cole the most.

"Daniel insisted," I said, tugging at the tuxedo cuffs self-consciously, taking us back to the reason my mother's name had been brought up in the first place.

Cole huffed. "I bet he thinks it makes you look more expensive."

I stiffened. "What's that supposed to mean? Are you saying without the finery I'm cheap? Nothing?" I demanded, facing off with him.

"You're priceless, Jasper," he said, seemingly perplexed as to how I didn't already know it. "It was a bad joke, made to imply something about him, never you."

I swallowed thickly and centered my thoughts around protecting my husband's character instead of counting the years since I'd truly felt worth anything. "Daniel's a good man, and I don't appreciate you showing up after all this time and insinuating differently. You don't know him."

Cole wisely let it go. "How much does he know?"

"I told him we were estranged." I tossed my hand in the air, running off the list of excuses I'd given Daniel on the fly. "Separated by a misunderstanding, the severing of family ties, and building our careers on opposing sides of the map." I worked my jaw. "I gave up your name in a moment of weakness." A moment when I thought I'd lose Daniel due to my lies and omissions.

"He was supposed to respect my decision to make amends with you on my own terms." Daniel had obviously assumed that day would never come, and that my dejection would always be the third wheel in our relationship, and so decided to take matters into his own hands. *I should love him more for it.* "Wait, what did *you* tell him?" Had our stories been conflicting? Panic surged, coating and burning the back of my throat.

"I told him I'd show up, but that our past history would have to be explained by you."

My shoulders loosened, and I turned to the view of the city again, giving him my profile as he leaned a hip against the ledge.

I braved another glance at him after a minute of tense silence, noting, again, how otherworldly well-bred he appeared. But Cole was an animal with a suit as his cage, and no forged piece of jewelry on my hand or legal document binding me to Daniel would keep him from what he wanted, if what he wanted was me. I couldn't afford to forget that. I couldn't afford to forget we were one and the same.

"My therapist thinks us being friends is a great idea," he said half-smiling, the stitching of his tailored suit straining as he crossed his arms over his broad chest. The pose added a bit of youthfulness to his stern exterior. To others he'd seem almost human, less intimidating. The stance reminded me of the one he'd take whenever I'd call him my Coley-bear. Only thing missing was the pout of his full lips.

My manic laughter rumbled through me. "Does she happen to know about the bodies we left in our wake? And not just the dead and buried one, because Franklin was added to the pile of the deceased the moment my mother took her last breath." According to the local papers and news outlets, Selene Kincaid had died from a failing heart. Cole and I knew the truth, though. She'd died from a broken one.

The mention of his father decimated the tiny speck of levity his comment had won him, proving we were in over our heads by being this close to each other. We needed mountains, oceans, fucking worlds between us.

"We can't see each other again. You leave now, and we avoid each other at all costs," I said anxiously. Shouldn't have been too hard. New York was a big city. And Cole and I didn't run in the same types of circles. He also wasn't the kind of man you'd bump into on the subway or out running his own errands.

"Didn't Daniel tell you?" he asked, genuinely taken aback. "Nexcom has retained Parker & Mitchell's services. The contract was signed this morning. It's tentative on Daniel sealing an important deal for us. One we haven't been able to effectively negotiate with prior counsel. One he promised he could make happen. We agreed to bring them in-house, if so."

Parker & Mitchell was the high-profile law firm Daniel worked for. Hiring them out was one thing, bringing them in-house meant they couldn't take on other clients. They'd take up office space with Nexcom. Cole would be their sole interest. "You can't possibly need their whole legal team under your roof," I said, flustered. Daniel's firm was one of the largest in the city. I had no doubt Nexcom needed a whole roster of attorneys who could and would provide the business with their undivided attention, but Cole didn't need them all.

"For now we only need one, but if Daniel makes this deal happen that will change. He'll then have the option to take lead on our account," Cole said, cutting down my rising hope that maybe after this deal had been buttoned up, Daniel would be cut loose. That someone else would be chosen from the firm's attorney pool to live and breathe all things Nexcom. But if the choice to stay on and oversee the team handling Nexcom's affairs would be up to Daniel, I knew what he'd be making.

The rest of Cole's words filtered into my brain through a vacuum as I turned to the party heating up through the glass doors behind us. I spotted Daniel through the viper's nest of "friends" and "colleagues" surrounding him in a tight circle, scenting his new upward trajectory.

With a look of jubilee, he raised his flute to the room in the gesture of a toast. It was then I realized the ostentatious party wasn't just for me.

If it was ever for me at all.

CHAPTER 2

Jasper

A RAGE HOTTER than lava erupted inside me as I stormed into the living room, aggressively rolling up my sleeves on my way over to the bar.

"I didn't want the good news to overshadow your night," Daniel said, hot on my trail but smart enough to maintain a healthy distance.

"Good news? *Good news?*" I scoffed, pouring myself a hefty drink before knocking it back. "You call being betrayed good news?"

"It all happened quickly," he proceeded to explain in that pompous way of his, like if I only listened for a moment, I'd see reason. It was a defense mechanism. One I wouldn't indulge him in. Not tonight. "I thought I'd leave a message with his assistant, and at best I'd get a return call or email from her stating he'd graciously declined my invite. You made it seem as if things were left irrevocable between you two. But I had to try. For you I had to try."

I guzzled my second drink as he continued, the brown liquor scorching everything in its path on the way down. I aimed to be numb before the completion of his excuse.

"I got a call from him instead, and he agreed to attend the party."

"Attend? You mean ambush."

"What do you want from me, Jasper?"

"I want you to stop meddling in my life!"

"Meddling?" His head snapped back. "Is that what you call wanting to get to know my husband?"

"You know me," I answered weakly, mulling over the time-saving advantages of drinking straight from the decanter.

"Do I? I learned more about you by Googling your long-lost brother—"

"Stop calling him that—"

"—than I've ever gotten directly from you in the last four years I've known you," he finished, speaking over me.

"Only three of those years count," I said, settling onto the edge of the leather wingback chair.

Daniel gaped at me from where he stood behind the sofa. "Are you purposely missing the point?" he asked.

"You did a search into my past the moment you gleaned the slightest bit of information about me. You chose to investigate me rather than wait for me to open up."

"That's a bit extreme, don't you think? I was able to pull up the official story about what happened to your mother, but I don't have the emotional backstory. I don't have the *truth*. I don't know what her death did to you, what it still does to you. I don't know why you changed your last name from Kincaid, or why you didn't attend her funeral. Christ, Jasper, the five-year anniversary of her passing was a week before we got married, and you didn't say a thing. And I had to pretend not to know, even though you were hurting, because you hadn't told me. Because I wasn't supposed to know."

Daniel had rushed me down the aisle like a fire was on our tails the moment I'd agreed to his proposal. He'd gotten pieces of my secrets and a promise he could have me for life. Yet it wasn't enough for him. It never was. To be fair, it *wasn't* enough. Not by a long shot, and he had a right to ask for more. But I'd given him all I could give, because the rest of me belonged to someone else. And I couldn't make the belonging stop no matter how hard I tried.

I set my glass on the coffee table, refilling it with a shaking hand, scotch splashing in a barrage of teardrops onto the wood. My mother had taken Franklin's last name immediately after marrying him. She'd allowed me to make the same choice for myself, which I'd eventually done. "I changed my name because I wanted my privacy. I didn't want to be shackled to the Kincaid legacy." That was only partially true, but it was all I could offer him.

"So you took your mother's maiden name," he said, revealing another tidbit of secrets he'd unearthed. I was naïve to think he wouldn't follow the breadcrumbs I'd felt forced to give him.

"What else do you know?"

"That's it. What else are you willing to tell me?"

I stared at him in silence.

"Right," he said tightly, charging for the stairs.

"You still haven't explained how you ended up working for him!"

He stilled with one hand on the banister, his shoulders going rigid, then relaxing. "Cole had done his own due diligence before calling me," he said calmly as he sauntered back over. "He knew who I was, and more importantly, who I worked for. Nexcom Global is in need of new legal representation. I saw my opportunity and made my sales pitch."

"And it never occurred to you to question why he would so readily get into bed with Parker & Mitchell?"

"How about giving both of us a little more credit, hmm?" he said, unable to mask his offense, coming around the sofa to sit across from me, our individual anger now at eye level. "Your brother and I didn't get to where we are in life by making rash decisions. Parker & Mitchell's sign-on is contingent on me successfully facilitating a deal. One I intend to deliver to your brother on a silver platter—"

"Stop calling him my brother!" I shot to my feet, whirling and pitching the glass tumbler with its contents into the fireplace. I screwed my eyes shut, willing my pulse to stabilize to something more manageable, or to still completely. I just needed the pain to go away.

"Jesus, Jasper. I've never seen you like this," Daniel whispered from behind me. We were mild men, Daniel and I. He made decisions he believed were right for us—right for *me*, and I relented on all with the exception of my job. Mostly I let him have his way, and I forgave him all too easily for everything. I never cared enough to fight. I'd left my passion burning next to my fractured heart when I'd run from my old life six years ago.

"I've done nothing but support you. *Spoil* you, even. I work tirelessly to make you realize your potential—"

"I've never asked you for any of that," I bit out tightly. "In fact, I've blatantly asked you to do nothing but love me."

"I thought that's what I was doing."

My defenses were weakening for his victim portrayal, as always. Any therapist worth their weight would've called it gaslighting. And maybe it was. If so, it was unintentional. One dinner with Daniel's family would've convinced anyone of that. Inside, he was a wounded kid. We both were. "Daniel..." I swung around to meet his expectant stare, but had nothing more to offer him. He would win this. I would let him get away with it. What was the alternative? Leave him? He'd fucked up, but he was my husband. And currently, he was the only thing standing in the way of history repeating itself, no matter how fragile of a barricade our marriage could potentially end up being in the long run.

"Instead of being upset, and accusing me of betrayal when all I've done is love you, how about you try being happy for me for a change," he seethed. I didn't stop him when he left this time. He ascended one stair before blasting me with his parting shot. "Oh, and you may want to consider the fact that I didn't have to sell him too hard on taking a chance on the firm. Cole practically reached through the phone and put the contract and pen in my hand."

I gritted my teeth and tugged my hair at the roots, blond strands curling around my fingers.

Cole. He'd wanted this as much as Daniel did. He'd wanted it even more.

◆ ◆ ◆

It'd taken some digging around, but by morning I had Cole's address. I should've expected he'd preemptively—and presumptuously—add me onto the approved guest list. I nodded my thanks to the concierge clerk, and then made my way to the elevator bank designated to the hotel's penthouse.

The doors swooshed open to a foyer made up of gray-veined white marble that poured through the expanse of the residence. The exterior glass walls throughout provided unobstructed, panoramic views of the cityscape, the Hudson River, and beyond.

Cole rounded a corner from the other end of the vast suite, padding toward me shirtless and barefoot, his hair dripping wet from a shower. I trained my eyes on the mischievous glint in his, and not on the inky trail of hair traveling from his navel into the silk pajama bottoms he wore, which did nothing to camouflage the imprint of his bobbing cock.

"Jasper," he started with a smile.

"Did you push for the deal with Parker & Mitchell or did Daniel?" I asked with zero patience for chitchat. I'd gotten minimal sleep last night, and the detour here would cause me to be late for work, but the confrontation couldn't wait for later.

"Can I take your things?" he asked, pointing to the trench I wore, and the leather satchel slung across my body.

"I won't be here long." My hands tightened around the strap of my bag.

"The hot water in this place is divine," a baritone voice crooned orgasmically.

Cole scratched at the crimson rising to his neck, peering behind him as a tall, willowy man, with blond hair a shade darker than mine, swaggered toward us, head lowered as he smoothed down his wrinkled shirt. Cole had obviously forgotten he wasn't alone. "Ah, Leland..."

"Yeah? Oh!" Leland said, startled, then brandishing what some may have called a roguishly charming half-grin. I wanted to punch him in it, whoever he was, and I didn't dare dissect the reasons why. "You've got company."

"This is my stepbrother, Jasper. Jasper, my *assistant,* Leland. He was just leaving."

"Ah, yeah. Sure was. Nice to finally meet you, Jasper." He snatched up the jacket slung over the oval table in the foyer. "I'll see you in the office, Co—er, Mr. Kincaid." The elevator doors closed, taking him down.

"Is following HR protocol below your paygrade?"

"Are you asking me if I'm fucking my assistant?"

"Are you?"

"Do you care?" he asked.

"Only as far as using your answer to build my case on your character—or lack thereof—goes."

His nostrils pulsed, signaling his upset, but he spoke with the utmost patience. "We were up late going over contracts and logistical matters related to the move from Seattle." He ambled toward an arched entryway leading to the living room. Folders and stacks of paper littered the coffee table and the white shag area rug. "He showered in the guest room."

I stopped a few feet past the room's threshold as Cole headed for the wet bar. With his back to me I released a quiet breath. I'd been jealous. *I'm still jealous.* Because although his explanation made sense, it didn't explain Leland's level of comfort with him. Cole and fucking weren't mutually exclusive. If he wasn't having sex with Leland, he was having it with someone else, and I hated that I cared.

"Answer me, Cole. Was this deal premeditated?"

He twisted the cap off a bottle of water, taking a leisurely sip before setting it down. "The move was imminent. We'd already signed the lease on office space, and most of our personnel were making arrangements to transfer here. Leland relayed Daniel's message to me, and I looked into his firm before getting back to him. As it happened, we were in the market for new attorneys."

"Nexcom is a big pond, and I'm not saying Parker & Mitchell are little fish, but they're not worth the trouble you're going through to get them."

"You're worth all the trouble, Jasper. And I needed a way in." The sunlight beamed down on him through the balcony doors at his back, removing all shadows, highlighting the raw honesty in his eyes. He wanted a place in my life, but I wanted to maintain what my life had been without him. Safe in its predictability. Reliable in its boredom.

"You could've knocked on my door—"

"And you would've turned me away," he argued.

"So you hired Daniel as a way to tether us together. You decided to make it impossible for me to get rid of you," I said around the lump of terror lodged in my throat.

"Impossible for you to ignore me," he amended without remorse. "I'm not here to make your life hard."

"Then why has it suddenly gotten harder? Why does it feel like it's about to implode?"

Cole inched closer, and I instinctively skittered back, shaking my head. "I'll play whatever role you want me to play, Jasper.

I just can't take being a stranger to the man who knows me best any longer. Please, let me in." His eyes pleaded with me.

My mind traveled back to a different time. A time when those three words had been innocent.

"Let me in. Cole, let me in!" I'd banged on his bedroom door again and again, my knuckles chafing, but I'd refused to give up until he answered. My persistence had paid off.

"What do you want?" he'd growled, face set in a hard scowl as he glared down at me through red-rimmed eyes.

"Why won't you play with me? We're brothers now."

"No, we're not. Leave me alone."

I'd slid my little palm into his much bigger hand, surprising him. *"No one wants to be alone."*

I snapped out of the memory, coming face-to-face with the scared boy from all those years ago. He wasn't scared now, though. He was confident, larger than life, *tempting,* and I was as defenseless to him now as I was then. "Are you still in love with me, Cole?"

"No," he said quickly. Too quickly. I should've called bullshit. It should've been a deal breaker for whatever I was about to concede to. My head knew better, but my heart had other plans. My heart would destroy us all. "What are your ground rules?" he asked, sensing my momentary lapse of good judgment. "Name them, and I'll abide by them."

My back met the wide archway's molding as I retreated. His hand spasmed at his side, probably tempted to reach for me before he lost me for good.

"Anything, Jas," he said desperately, using the nickname he'd given me as a kid.

"No one's called me that before," I'd said.

"It's mine. If anyone calls you that, you tell them it belongs to me. That you belong to me."

"You have to respect my marriage," I breathed, the organ in my chest beating a not-so-silent warning. "I love him." I narrowed my stare on him, tracking his every reaction, ready to call all bets off and run in the direction I'd come from at the first sign of his resistance. "I *love* him." *Who are you trying to convince here, Jasper?*

"I can do that," he said.

"Our relationship, or whatever this is"—I gestured between us—"shouldn't come between my relationship with him." *You're making a bad decision, Jasper.* My conscience kept pounding away at me.

"If you're happy, I won't interfere—"

"That isn't good enough," I snapped urgently.

"You can't expect me to sit idle and watch you be hurt. That's a promise I can't make. But if you're happy with him..." He drifted off on a swallow as if preparing for the pain of his next words. "If he's good to you, then you have nothing to worry about from me."

"We *are* happy."

"Okay, then," he said.

"And I *need* you to respect that," I asserted.

"Got it." His words were clipped.

"I gotta go."

"Where are you headed?" he asked, as if he didn't want me to leave just yet.

"To work," I said, to which he gazed dubiously at my distressed jeans and laced-up boots. "It's casual Friday," I explained absently, rubbing my forehead, trying to gather my wits.

He leaned against the balcony door, his entwined hands falling casually at the junction of his hips. "Yeah, except today's Monday," he said, laughing with his eyes.

"Right," I said, cheeks warming. "I guess it's always Friday when you love what you do."

"Not much has changed in that area, I see." He donned that cocky grin of his, the one that bordered on flirtatious and here-comes-trouble. "You were always big on doing what you love, and not what anyone wanted of you. I used to want to be just like you. Still do."

I shook my head in disbelief. How could it be so easy to go from wanting to punch him to wanting to comfort him? "You're making changes over at Nexcom. I'm guessing that means you're doing what you want."

"I'm doing what I have to do," he said pointedly. "I'm doing what's right."

"And what's right?" I asked.

"I want to develop a new and improved robotic heart. Make it more sustainable."

I took a step forward. "Is that even possible?" I asked with a breathless type of hope.

"I don't know, but it's what I plan on dedicating my life to."

And that quickly, something in me opened up for him, a small pocket of warmth not yet frozen over from the cold burden of guilt I'd carried around like a cross I had to bear. Cole slid right in, making himself cozy. "I'm going to be late," I said, weathering his haunted stare for a second longer than I should have, unable to take my eyes off him, unable to move.

The glue that bound us together when we were boys re-sealed us now, hardening. If I didn't rip myself away from him right then, the epoxy would dry, making a second separation from him virtually inconceivable.

"What is it that you do?" His question reached out like a desperate hand trying to hold me there. He rolled his eyes at my hitched brow. "I want to hear it from you, not read it from the printout my assistant slipped on my desk."

I sighed, relenting, but only because I didn't get to talk about my day with anyone. I didn't get to share details on the one area of my life providing me with purpose. With Daniel, the conversation would lead to his attempt at poaching me for Parker & Mitchell, or another firm equally as "respectable." And there was my best friend, Sofia, but she was in the thick of the fight right alongside me, pounding the pavement. Discussions with her were usually around strategies to implement change, proposals for new legislation, and how we could make more of an impact.

Sharing with Cole would feel like unwinding from a long day, like having a cheerleader in my corner. Like old times. "What I do depends on the day. My friend Sofia runs a non-profit organization that provides legal services to underprivileged communities. I take on cases when needed—which is almost always. And I help where I can with the many foundations she supports, which I in turn support. They're all geared around being of service to others in some way. And twice a week I teach a first-year criminal justice course at Columbia Law."

"Wow," he said, impressed, eyes bursting with his eagerness to hear more.

"Did your printout not mention all that?" I shoved my hands into my front pockets for something to do other than strangle the strap of my bag or hang stupidly at my sides.

"Yeah, but it lacked emotion. Passion. I'm proud of you," he whispered. My chest clenched, holding tight to his validation. "And which are you going to be late for today?"

"Class starts in fifteen minutes, and the train ride is twenty from here. So..." I hiked a thumb over my shoulder.

"Yeah, sorry. I've held you up long enough. Hang on." His long strides ate up the distance to his cell phone perched on the end table near the sofa. "I'll have my driver rush you over."

"Unless he has a siren attached to the roof of his car, I'm better off on public transportation. Thanks for the offer, though," I said, showing myself to the elevator.

"You forgive too easily," Cole said at my back. "Always have. Selene used to call you her big, bleeding heart."

"What's your point?" I asked, not unkindly, just short on time.

"Nothing." He shrugged. "Just, thank you. That's all."

It didn't feel like nothing, but with no time to spare on dwelling, I let it be. "I'll be in touch." I sagged against the cabin wall once the doors sealed me inside, pretending I hadn't heard his last whispered question, pretending it hadn't taken my breath away.

"Are you still in love with me, Jasper?"

◆ ◆ ◆

"You're late, Mr. D," Lorenzo, one of my younger students, said from the back row of the lecture hall. A few chuckles could be heard from all sides. Des Moines was a mouthful, so my students referred to me as Mr. D.

"Are you sure you all aren't just early?" I asked, hanging my jacket on the coat rack by the door before stepping up to the lectern and sliding my notes from my bag.

"Oh no, you don't," Sonia chimed in, wagging a finger at me. "You owe us one push-up for every minute you were late." She even mimicked my I-mean-business tone, earning a high five from her neighbor.

"How old are you guys again?" I asked.

"That won't work on us. If you're going to make the rules, you gotta live by them," Lorenzo said with an apologetic shrug as if he'd let me off the hook if he could. "I counted ten." He held both palms out, wiggling each finger.

"Everyone better have their textbooks out and open to chapter twenty by the time I'm done, or I'm pulling you all down here with me," I said, letting my own finger in on the action, waving it threat-

eningly into the crowd. Books thumped onto desks, and pages rus-
tled with urgency. I loved my job, and I loved these adult-children.
I descended into the pit and paid my penalty, my smile firmly in
placc as I thought, *Cole would get a kick out of this.*

♦ ♦ ♦

The smell of roasted tomatoes and fresh garlic bread assaulted
me when I returned home later that evening to Daniel's favorite apology-meal, from my favorite Italian restaurant. We hadn't
spoken since our argument the night before, and he was already
gone by the time I'd dragged my booze-addled brain from the
guest bedroom that morning. The fight had already slipped my
mind, but his attempt at making things right tugged at my heart-
strings all the same. This was good. *We* were good.

You forgive too easily. Cole's words from earlier came back
to taunt me.

I closed the apartment door heavy-handedly, making my arrival known, because Daniel would want to greet me as soon as
I walked in.

"You're home," he said brightly, appearing from the kitch-
en, a nervous curve to his lips. "And you're all wet." His forehead
creased with displeasure.

"Yeah, it started coming down out of nowhere."

"Here, let me take that before you leave a trail." He shook
the rain droplets from my coat over the doormat before isolat-
ing it to one side of the coat closet, and then scanned the hardwood floor with a sharp eye for signs of moisture. I left him to his
fussing while I removed my shoes and the rubber band holding
my damp hair together at my nape. The barely shoulder-length
strands twisted, falling into loose waves instantly.

Daniel, now satisfied his Brazilian wood hadn't been blem-
ished, moved ahead of me, halting my advancement on the food.

"Did you get the risotto, too?" I sniffed the air with enthusiasm for his benefit, and his timid smile rounded into one of contentment.

"I'm insulted. Of course I did." He leaned in for a kiss. Thunder rumbled, lightning lit up the darkening sky, and an obnoxious deluge of rain splattered the living room windows. "Remind me again why you wanted to live this high up?" He'd sold his apartment on a lower floor to purchase this one after I'd dragged him up for the open house out of curiosity, and then needed to be pried away from the windows.

"I can answer that," Cole said, his voice appearing from thin air.

"Fuck," I hissed, backing away from Daniel's lips with a hand to my pounding heart. Behind Daniel, Cole strode from the dining room, hands slung into the pockets of his gray, pinstriped pants, his shoes clicking against the hardwood floor as he languidly approached. His expression gave nothing away.

"Because the sound is magnified tenfold this high off the ground," he continued. "And because storms always get Jasper going. Some things never change, right? Brother," he tacked on, and I chose not to see it as an intentional afterthought.

"Oh, yeah. I almost forgot," Daniel said. "There was a slight mix-up. Cole and I were supposed to meet tomorrow evening, but his assistant had it penciled in for tonight." He lowered his voice. "Seemed rude to ask him to leave."

"I'll be sure to speak with Leland about the error. My offer to leave still stands. Feels like I'm intruding on something," he said, gaze shackled to mine.

"Nonsense," Daniel protested. "It's only dinner, and besides, you're family."

"Jas?" Cole asked, waiting for my approval.

"Wait," Daniel said, frowning. "He gets to call you Jas? You said you hated the nickname."

"I said I hated it as a pet name. There's a difference." Really, there wasn't. My lips flattened at Cole's amused expression, even as I prayed he didn't utter the other name he liked to call me. The one that had been reserved for our more intimate moments. "You're already here, and it's coming down pretty hard out there. Might as well eat. Wait it out," I said begrudgingly.

We ate by candlelight after Cole insisted Daniel do whatever he would have had he not been there. It was odd, but Daniel's need to suck up to Cole won out. I couldn't help feeling as if our relationship was being examined by Cole. Not our marriage—because that could be scaled down to a piece of paper, but how we worked together as a couple. The roles we played in each other's lives. What we saw in each other. Were we loving enough? Touching enough? Were we coming up short on his mental checklist of things two people did when crazy about each other? After all, he'd know.

Daniel loosened up after a few glasses of Merlot, idly caressing my nape from his seat next to me as he spoke about his day. It felt awkward having another man's hands on me in front of Cole, even if those hands belonged to my husband, but Cole didn't so much as bat an eyelash. Maybe he did want to be brothers, friends. Leave the past behind us and move on. Maybe we could successfully do it, because truthfully, I had missed him, too.

"How was class, Jas?" Cole asked, lowering his wine glass by its bowl, licking the crimson stain away from his blush-hued lips. He sat across from me, and the candle's flame made his blue eyes shine like a sun-filled sky. Fiercer than Daniel's shade of light brown. He'd removed his jacket and folded up his sleeves before eating, his forearms thick and veiny. Sturdier than Daniel's lean physique. My skin burned in all the places he'd touched before. I burned everywhere.

Maybe we couldn't be friends after all, I second-guessed. My feelings on the matter pinged back and forth by the nanosecond.

I shoved my own wine glass away, feeling shitty for comparing them, and faulting the alcohol for making me do it.

Not expecting to be asked to contribute, my brain processed the question with delay. Daniel typically did all the talking. "It started with a workout." I chuckled. Daniel stared in confusion. Cole waited with interest. "There's a 'one push-up for every minute late' rule."

"Jasper," Daniel chided, embarrassed on my behalf.

"So the lambs got retribution today," Cole said appreciatively.

"Yeah," I answered.

"Tell me more," he said in that eager, yet casual, way he had about him, slinging an arm across the back of the vacant chair next to him.

I hesitated for a beat, still unsure of him, of me, of my role at the table. But then Cole's beseeching stare met mine. *"Let me in,"* it said. I propped my elbow on the table, causing Daniel's hand at the base of my neck to fall away. "There's really only a few it ever applies to. A pack of younger kids. Ages twenty-one, twenty-two. Most of the students are closer to my age. A couple of them are older." I launched into our current course work: gathering evidence. I answered his questions with zest—even answering some he hadn't asked, and I delved, in great detail, into the mock trial we had going. "We've got a district attorney, a defense team, a jury—"

"And let me guess, you're the judge?" Cole said without an ounce of surprise.

"Well, of course," I answered smugly, easing back in my seat. "Someone's gotta keep them honest." We laughed, and I peered over to Daniel, who I'd forgotten about. He sat frozen, studying me with an odd look. Almost like he was searching for his husband.

"I've never seen you come alive like this before," Daniel said.

"I don't get to talk about this side of my life often is all," I replied, squeezing his knee below the table, feeling a strange need to apologize to him for my excitement. For letting my existence be known.

To that Cole sat straighter. "What do you mean?" He cut his eyes to Daniel. "Do you not ask him about his passions? His job?"

"Well, admittedly, I'm usually trying to sway him to put his knowledge and skills as an attorney to better use," Daniel said, now sifting his fingers through the back of my hair. He wasn't usually this touchy in front of people. I guessed public displays of affection was another side effect of him wanting to impress Cole.

"I see," Cole said slowly, his gaze growing more keen as he took in our relationship with fresh eyes.

"Look at that," Daniel said to me. "Even your brother understands." He actually believed he had Cole's full support.

"I take it you know what's best for him," Cole said to Daniel.

"At the very least I see what he doesn't."

"And what's that?" Cole asked with a feigned curiousness Daniel was too consumed with his own hubris to see.

"That he can be great, *if* he only applied himself," Daniel said, brushing a thumb down my cheek as if he'd just given me the highest compliment. I closed my eyes and internally groaned, because Cole wouldn't get it. He wouldn't get why I allowed Daniel to get away with this. He wouldn't understand Daniel meant no harm. And that above all, I was getting *exactly* what I deserved.

Cole methodically uncoiled his shirt sleeves, buttoning the cuffs. "My mother died giving birth to me. I spent a good deal of my younger years trying to reconcile with the fact that I'd killed the woman who gave me life. And then one day my father shows up with a beautiful woman he claimed was to be my new mother.

And she had a son, and therefore I now had a brother. He was blond with boney limbs, and eyes the color of pale emeralds."

I tried to get his attention with the force of my stare. Daniel sat riveted, while I strived to remain in my skin.

"I'd never met Selene or her son prior to the day they showed up at our estate hand in hand. My father had met her on a beach and proclaimed love at first sight. I didn't understand the concept at first, but then I got to know her," Cole whispered before finally gazing at me. "I was a surly kid in need of love and affection who didn't want anyone coming in and erasing the memory of my mother. Her pictures were removed from the walls shortly before they'd arrived. We no longer lived in a shrine to her. The last of her had been killed.

"I wasn't in the business of letting anyone in. I had no time for a boy who wanted to spend his days helping the staff prepare meals and clean the messes he'd made. A boy who thought handmade Christmas gifts meant more than something shiny from Tiffany's. A boy who'd sneak food to my bedroom door when I was ordered to go there without dinner for being rude to him. A boy who got two thousand signatures on a petition to name a fountain in the park after my mother. Jasper is relentless when he believes in something, and he believed in me. Without him I might have ended up like you, but because of him, I know what makes a great man. And he's the greatest man in this room."

When Cole decided he needed to be heard, everyone within earshot listened up. Even the thunderstorm had held its breath for him.

Cole left me flushed and speechless, and I didn't chance looking over at Daniel for fear he'd see everything I'd ever hidden from him written all over me. His cell phone rang from somewhere upstairs, interrupting the tense silence left over from Cole's less than subtle chastisement of him.

Daniel ducked his head and muttered a faint, "Excuse me," before his chair legs scraped the floor in his departure.

Cole and I were left alone with all our memories before the romantic firelight and arcs of lightning flashing across the night sky. His chest rose and fell rapidly with each angered breath, but he didn't eye me with judgment, only a raging need to comprehend.

"Why?" he implored. "You're too good for him."

"Don't." I looked nervously toward the stairs.

"Why do you let him demean you?"

"He grew up with expectations, too. You of all people should understand that. He didn't have me to save him like you did," I said. Cole had been groomed to one day take over Nexcom, and had nearly buckled more than once under the pressure. Franklin could be equal parts good and uncompromising. Gentle and hard. Nothing would stand in the way of Cole becoming his successor, but I'd been there for the more difficult days when the weight of his destiny had been too great a thing for him to shoulder alone.

"But he has you now, and he doesn't even see you," he said. "Even the way he touches you—" He cut himself off, sucking in a hiss of air through the seam of his lips.

"Keep going," I said, challenging him. "How does he touch me, Cole?"

"Like you're his," he said boldly.

"As opposed to yours?"

"No, that's not what I meant. You're property to him. A pet. Something he can train to his whims, even if he's doing it without malice. I'm not saying this because I want you. I'm saying it because I care. Because you would do the same for me."

I let up on the grinding of my molars. I *would've* done the same for him, under different circumstances, though. I didn't need him riding in on his high horse to fight my battles for me. A lot needed to happen before we got to a place where looking out for each other's best interests was merely that. We needed the luxury of time. Time to be something different to each other. I was in way over my head here, and soon I wouldn't care. "Cole," I sighed.

"Sorry about that," Daniel said, sticking a pin in our balloon.

"No worries," Cole insisted. "I need to get going anyway." He stood, and like a heartstring being tugged, I did, too.

"It's still early," Daniel said, checking the time. "I was going to ask about the storm reference you made earlier. I would love to know what trouble this one got up to." He waggled his brows and hugged me into his side.

"Some secrets are Jasper's to tell," Cole said, leaving the room in a hurry. Daniel and I trailed behind him.

"Well, he does seem to be more willing to share when you're around. I think your presence will be good for us," Daniel said. Cole ignored his comment.

"Can I give you a call tomorrow?" Cole asked me, getting his wool coat from the closet.

"Ah, yeah. Sure," I said.

"Daniel, I'll see you in the office bright and early."

"I'll be the one with bells on," Daniel replied, and I wondered how he could speak with his mouth hard-pressed to Cole's ass.

We were alone for two seconds before Daniel wheeled around on me. "I think I may have offended him."

"You *think*?" I asked, wondering if maybe the embarrassment I thought he'd expressed before leaving the dining room had been imagined. Did he think that much of himself that Cole's reprimand of him had gone right over his head?

"I'm overthinking it. Everything's fine." He bit his lip in thought, staring at the door Cole had exited through.

"Yeah, of course," I said, gently tugging his lip from his teeth. "I'll help you clean up so we can hit the sack." The housekeeper would be here bright and early, but Daniel wouldn't be able to sleep with dishes in the sink.

Daniel wiped down the counters while I loaded the dishwasher and pretended I didn't feel him staring at me. "What?" I asked in resignation, starting up the wash cycle and hitching a hip against the island.

Daniel tossed the dishtowel over his shoulder. "Are you going to tell me about your love of storms?" He pressed into my front, my lower back biting into the marble. Damn Cole for making this into something bigger than it needed to be.

I relaxed as he placed kisses along my neck. "Don't listen to everything Cole says."

"I kind of have to, because you don't tell me much."

I grabbed the sides of his head and kissed him as a distraction, sending my tongue as deep into his mouth as possible.

"Whoa, slow down." He pushed me back by my shoulders. "What's gotten into you tonight?"

"How about sex right here?" I hopped onto the island.

"We eat here," he said, mouth downturned.

"Okay," I whispered, fingers deftly unlatching his belt buckle. "How about the floor?"

"We walk on it. With our *shoes*."

I dropped my head to his shoulder, defeated, erection dwindling.

"How about we go up to bed? I promise I'll make it worthwhile." He pulled me off the island and led me by the hand upstairs and into our bedroom.

"Where are you going?" I asked, snatching his wrist as he moved toward the master bathroom.

"To grab a towel."

"How about we make a mess tonight?" With a hand in his hair, I nibbled seductively at his chin.

"All over my Egyptian cotton?"

"Right." I let him go, cursing Cole for reigniting old memories. Old passions. Old parts of me. For forcing me to relive cum-streaked handprints on walls, and nights of howling my pleasure into a thunderstorm while being fucked on my hands and knees as my tears scattered the earth alongside the rain. For forcing me to replay all the dirty, wicked things done to me at his hands, and forcing me to pretend they were being done to me tonight to survive making the sweet, neat, predictable kind of love with my husband.

The kind I didn't mind twenty-four hours ago.

CHAPTER 3

Cole

THE COLD GLOOMINESS from outside streamed into my office windows, its shadow staining the monitor I'd been staring at for the last half hour. Leftover nasty weather from last night's icy downpour. The bustling city streets were slicked with it, the puddles slowly icing over.

Not allowing the dismal weather to dictate my moods had always been a challenge. I tended to be more introspective on gray days, and overall bad company for anyone needing me to do more than just *be*. On rainy days, I gave myself permission to miss Jasper to the full extent of my capabilities.

An old cinema reel of flashes ticked through my mind's eye. Jasper's defined Cupid's bow, its rim a darker pink than the bed of his lips.

Instant replays swarmed me of his warm, timid smiles, now replaced with frown lines. The deep rumble of his enticing laughter, which now seemed elusive. Not even the incessant sound of my clicking pen could drown out the playback on his smoky voice, and how breathless it became whenever I handled him roughly.

I could almost feel the memory of his silky hair being abused by my unforgiving fingers. I could almost ignore the shadowy image in the corner of my mind invading those recollections, there to remind me that now Jasper was his.

Daniel.

Outside the glass double doors of my office, Leland circled his desk carrying a small stack of folders tucked under his arm. "Still haven't heard back?" he asked, entering and making himself comfortable in the chair across from me.

"No," I said, tossing my pen aside, watching it roll and crash into a paperweight. "I left a message a couple hours ago. Calling back now would make me seem too eager."

"Didn't you say he had like twenty jobs? He'll get back to you. By the way," he said, plopping a magazine onto my desk, "his friend Sofia is hot. Think she's single?"

"You're a womanizer, Leland. Stay away from her. The last thing I need is Jasper upset because you broke his best friend's heart—or her vagina."

"Ouch. You're crass when you're cranky," he said through a wicked grin, crossing an ankle over his knee.

Leland and I met at a bar shortly after Selene's death and Jasper's subsequent vanishing act. He'd served me drinks, listened to my ramblings, and called me on my bullshit all night. He'd had no prior experience as an executive assistant, but he was honest, and he didn't care about who I was, he just cared. I'd brought him with me when I took over for my father at Nexcom.

My moods didn't intimidate him, and he often pretended he didn't know I was having one, anyway.

I thumbed to the page he'd creased. An article on philanthropist and activist Sofia Rivera leading a protest on the steps of the Supreme Court. I'd asked Leland to look into her.

"She's big on social justice issues," said Leland. "A Columbia Law grad. Jasper's alma mater. Must be where they met."

"No," I said absently as I skimmed through the write-up. "They likely met before then. Jasper's ambitions were never lofty. The fact that he'd waited so long after completing undergrad to attend law school tells me something—or someone—came along and inspired him to do it. I'm guessing Sofia's that someone." If Jasper felt being an attorney would have a greater impact on the good they were doing, he wouldn't hesitate to see it done. I handed the periodical back to Leland.

"How'd the dinner meeting go last night?" he asked.

"I've been meaning to ask you about that. It was supposed to be today. It's not like you to make that kind of mistake."

"Because I didn't," he scoffed. "Someone from Parker & Mitchell called and asked to shift things around. I assumed it was a clerk or Daniel's assistant. You had an opening in your calendar, so I made the swap."

"Hmm." I planted my elbows on the arms of my chair and steepled my hands in front of me. "Strange."

"Want me to get a name?"

"No, it's fine. I'm sure it was a simple case of crossed wires."

"Does Jasper think you made it up?"

"Possibly, but it worked out. It was an eye-opening night," I said.

"Uh-oh, I know that look."

"What look?" I asked.

"I thought you agreed not to come between them."

"And I won't. But I won't sit back, though, and watch his life choices be insulted, or accept Daniel's belittlement of him. Jasper deserves better."

"He deserves you?" he asked meaningfully.

I dropped my head back on my chair. I wasn't above much when it came to Jasper. I also didn't want to show up after all those years and be a wrecking ball to what he'd built for himself. If we were only meant to be friends, then so be it. I'd meant it when I said I needed him in my life. I'd continue to swallow my feelings for him, smile and bear the pain of seeing him with someone else, if that was all I could have. Perhaps he and Daniel were happy. Perhaps I was searching for cracks in their foundation to ease some of my guilt behind wanting him anyway. Because guilt would be a hard emotion to come by when knowing I wouldn't be destroying something good to have what I wanted.

"If Daniel's as bad for him as you say, then the choice should be easy. So what if you two used to be stepbrothers? Bigger scandals have been overcome. I once got busted shagging my professor and his wife."

If only it were that simple, I mused to myself.

"If that's what's keeping you two apart, you're both idiots."

"Remind me why I thought it was a good idea to hire a friend as my assistant?"

"Because I keep you humble and I keep your secrets." He winked. Leland was innately flirtatious, had a sailor's mouth, and wouldn't know the meaning of monogamy if the word fell out of the dictionary and straddled his lap. If I was looking for someone to talk me out of playing a role in the downfall of a marriage, he was the wrong guy for the job.

"Thanks," I said sincerely. "Or maybe I shouldn't be thanking you. Thanks to your awkward exit the other morning, Jasper thinks I'm fucking you."

"Oy, yeah, sorry about that. You two reeked of sexual tension. It was either get out of there, or make an indecent proposal. Need me to do damage control? Shove my tongue down Sofia's throat? That'll clear things right up."

"Absolutely not, you heathen." I laughed. Jealousy was a dangerous emotion, and one I was more than capable of succumbing to. It had taken everything to maintain a neutral expression as Daniel ran his hands over Jasper at the dinner table last night. I'd wanted to clear the dishes away with a sweep of my arm. I had wanted to fuck Jasper right there and make Daniel watch. Wanted to show him how Jasper loved to be touched. How he loved to be taken not asked. School him on what it meant to bring his husband pleasure. And I had wanted him to choke on it.

"Alright, you're starting to look murdery, which means you've got visions of sex and violence in your head. That's my cue to leave." He left the stack of folders for me to review their contents but snatched up the magazine on his way out. "And stop looking at your phone. It won't make him call you any faster," he said as he went. I huffed a laugh and turned the device face down on the wooden desktop.

"Do me a favor," I called out. "Jasper said he teaches twice a week, can you—"

"Already did. He's got a class starting in less than an hour," he slung over his shoulder.

I checked my watch. I had a meeting in thirty minutes. "Can you—"

"Done. Your schedule's clear for the rest of the day." He grinned arrogantly, the door swishing closed in his wake.

◆◆◆

Class was in full swing by the time I'd snuck in through the rear door of the lecture hall and slunk into a corner seat out of view. Below, Jasper stood behind his lectern, gavel in hand. On the far right side, twelve students sat clustered in three rows, playing the role of jury, I assumed.

A couple steps down in the pit, two independent desks had been brought in, situated a few feet apart where the prosecution and defense teams held position. Court was in session.

Their voices echoed well enough in the amphitheater as the jury whispered restlessly, waiting for the district attorney to gather her notes.

"Order in the court," Jasper bellowed to the pool of twelve, banging his gavel with a childish glee. "Take your time, Mrs.

Baker," he said, to which a woman—whom I gathered to be Mrs. Baker—wobbled out of her chair, batting away the assistant DA's help, and demanding no special treatment from either of them as she rubbed her rounded belly.

They were all dressed for the part, showing how serious they took the exercise. The presence of lightness and humor was evident, too. They were learning while having fun.

As both sides made their closing arguments, Jasper would cut in to correct course and offer advice on working the courtroom. "Unfortunately, this *is* partly a popularity contest. You need to win the jury's regard as much as you need to present them with the facts. Eye contact, pauses for dramatic effect. Win them over, make them think. You can't do that if you're speaking with your head in your notes," he said encouragingly. He was beautiful, brilliant. They all were, but he was their fierce leader, and he led well.

I hadn't gone unnoticed after all. Once we reached the top of the hour, and everyone began filing out of the makeshift courtroom, Jasper's eyes immediately traveled to me. I desperately hoped he'd felt me there, which would mean the indescribable, intangible link once connecting us hadn't been broken along with everything else.

With my coat draped over my forearm, I made my way down the broad steps just as the last student bid him farewell and exited through the door. "That was impressive," I said.

"What are you doing here?" he asked in place of a thank you. I'd settle for the color tinting his sharp cheekbones as acknowledgement of my praise any day. It spoke volumes about what my approval meant to him. It would do.

"I had time, so I thought I'd pop in to see you in action."

"You run a multimillion dollar company. Time is the one thing you don't have."

"We make time for what's important to us," I said, a thrill jolting up my spine when his gaze wandered to my mouth. "You're good at this," I whispered. "Teaching."

He smiled in spite of himself. I knew him, enough to know a battle waged between his mind's instinct to be suspicious of me, and his heart's desire to be nice to me, for its need to let me in. He was scared, and he had every right to be.

"What does the rest of your day look like?"

"Why?" he asked, his paper-filled hand stopping halfway into his leather bag.

"Thought maybe I'd tag along." I shrugged nonchalantly. His brows met in a doubtful expression and held as he seemed to struggle internally.

"You want to tag along with me?"

"Is that so hard to believe?"

"Yeah. It is. What if I said I had grocery shopping to do?"

"I'd ask if I could ride in the front seat of the shopping cart," I joked. "Come on, you know you want to laugh."

"What I want is to not be constantly suspicious of you, Cole."

"Then don't be. Take it a day at a time. Do what feels right."

"That's what I'm afraid of," he mumbled under his breath. He sighed in resignation, shoving his things into his bag and closing the flap. "I'm free, actually. Thought maybe I could have dinner with Daniel, but he has this new client, or boss," he corrected, unsure, "who doesn't believe in acclimation periods."

"Sounds like this new client-boss is an important one. You probably should be more supportive of Daniel's hard work and dedication," I said with mock severity.

"Funny, he said the same thing." Jasper slung his satchel across his chest, then said in a more serious tone, "He wants to make partner at Parker & Mitchell. He thinks this is the way to do it. I hope you're not toying with him, Cole."

"I'm not," I said, matching his tone. "He's a great attorney." *A shitty husband, though.* "I wanted back in your life, but I would've found another way before hiring a mediocre firm to represent us, Jasper. I'm glad it didn't have to come to that."

That seemed to appease him. "Alright. I guess I'm all yours then for the night. Where to?"

His words, delivered innocently, sent a flare of something forbidden and hot to the floor of my gut. If only he were mine for the night. For forever. If only. "Let's go back to my place," I said, thanking everything holy I'd succeeded in making my tone airy. "We can order in. Catch up without the prying ears of neighboring diners."

"Prying ears might be best."

"Please," I said.

He blew out a breath, battling his decision. "Okay," he said to my bewilderment. "Let's go before I change my mind."

Outside, my driver tipped his hat to Jasper as he held open the rear door for us. Once inside, I made introductions, then we weaved our way through traffic in comfortable silence before picking up Chinese takeout, and then deciding to walk the short distance to the hotel I'd made home. It was bitterly cold out, but it would've taken Mark double the time to circle the block in the afternoon gridlock than to simply foot it to the penthouse.

"This living arrangement is temporary, right?" Jasper said, digging through the bags of food on the kitchen island.

"Why?" I asked, coming in behind him and plucking a fortune cookie from his hands. "They take care of every inconvenience here. Laundry, housekeeping services, there's a barber downstairs, *and* there's even an in-house chef I could hire if I so please," I said, breaking my fortune paper free.

"I see our years apart haven't negatively affected your humility at all," he said, heavy on the sarcasm.

"I'm humble," I protested. "But as you said, I'm short on time, so living here works out perfectly. Can you give me one good reason why I shouldn't?"

He waved a hand over the wet front of my suit. "For one thing, there'd be less yellow-cab traffic in a more residential area, which could potentially prevent you from being puddle-splashed head to toe when one nearly rides onto the curb for a fare." He'd been teasing me about it the whole walk and elevator ride up. And for a moment, I could almost pretend nothing had changed between us. My sentimental gaze hovered over him longer than it should have, and I cursed myself when his easy smile fell, a leery stare filling the void.

"I'm sorry," I said. "I was reminded for a second of how easy it used to be between us. I miss this."

"Me too," he admitted before averting his eyes to the containers of food, taking his and moving to the other side of the behemoth island.

"I should probably change out of these wet clothes before I eat." I excused myself, journeying straight to my bathroom to splash cold water over my face. Huffing uneven breaths into the basin, I pressed my weight into my palms, wondering what the hell I thought I was doing. I loved him, and regardless of the lie I'd readily told him yesterday, I was still *in* love with him. Madly so.

Jasper had a way of appearing helpless, even though he was the strongest person in the room. Handsome, pretty, even. A face so delicate had no business being atop a body so stringent. He was a slut, a virgin, the devil, and an angel rolled into one. A case study in contradictions, leaving my cock hard and my heart soft as putty. I wanted to break him, and then piece his fractured parts back together again. Nothing would ever change that, and I didn't know how long I'd be capable of sticking to my promise, of keeping my hands off him, of not ruining everything.

He's married, I reminded myself. *You've been gone, and he moved on, and you have no right to sweep in and turn every obstacle keeping you apart into collateral damage.*

I hadn't been completely honest. My therapist *did* think being friends with him was a good idea. I'd merely left out the "from a distance" part. And also the part where I'd fired her soon after she'd suggested it.

I tugged off my tie and expeditiously ditched the suit for a t-shirt and sweats before trekking back into the kitchen to find Jasper rummaging through the fridge.

"Water?" he asked, holding up two bottles.

"I need something stronger than that." I fetched a bottle of gin from one of the cabinets near the sink.

"Make that two," he said, shutting the bottled waters into the fridge. I lined up two shots of gin before downing mine. Jasper breathed deeply before chugging his and grimacing. "Fuck, that's not the cheap stuff, is it?"

"No, it isn't."

We ate until the cartons were clean and scarfed down shots in between bites until there was nothing to do but think or talk. Or both. Jasper played nervously with the thin, gold chain at his neck. It had belonged to Selene, but the small cross pendant dangling from it had been a gift from me. It had once belonged to my mother.

"I didn't notice you wearing that yesterday," I said, refilling our glasses.

"Because I wasn't. I woke up in the middle of the night and went through a box of old things I keep inside a loose floorboard in our closet."

"Sounds like a hiding place." Something he didn't want Daniel knowing about. "What other secrets do you keep in there?"

"It's more about what I'm hiding from myself, not Daniel," he said with a defensive edge. "You showing up made me think about her. More so than usual. I keep a few of her trinkets in there."

Some of mine as well, I didn't say.

"She wouldn't be happy knowing we were together, now. Here."

"I don't believe that for a second, Jasper. She loved us."

"Have you forgotten what happened?"

"She had a bad heart, Jas. Isn't it possible her heart attack stemmed from the shock of walking in on us together, and not the actual fact that we were together?"

"If we'd only waited. If only we hadn't acted on an impulse—"

He stopped himself. I knew he was referring to us making love the night I'd arrived home after completing my last semester of college. I'd finished high school a year ahead of him, but had taken a gap year so we could leave for Harvard together. The irony was that he'd ended up graduating a semester earlier than me. He'd gone home to help my father care for Selene while I'd completed school at their insistence. The night I returned home we'd made love in his bedroom. We'd stopped taking risks under their roof after high school, but Jasper couldn't wait, no matter how much I'd insisted we should.

I'd spent years on my therapist's couch working out how to let go of the guilt I'd carried. Some days it returned with a vengeance, but I had to believe she loved us enough to want our happiness, and Jasper and I had made each other happy once.

"If we had only waited," he repeated.

In a sick twist of fate, she'd made it to the top of the donor list. Twenty-four hours after she'd gone into cardiac arrest, we got the call we'd been waiting all year for. But she was gone.

I wanted to hold Jasper, rock him in my arms and place kisses to his temples while breathing love into him. I couldn't, though. I didn't know if I had the right to. I didn't know if it would've brought us closer or sent him running away.

He swallowed another shot, and then shoved the glass my way markedly. I plucked two tumblers from the dishwasher and poured us a heartier portion.

"It takes someone special to win the heart of Franklin Kincaid without even trying. To raise a man like you. I refuse to believe she doesn't approve of us. Can you try looking at it from that perspective, Jasper?"

He grunted, his equivalent to easier-said-than-done. "Do you miss her?" he asked.

"Yes," I said, reaching to brush a rogue strand of hair away from the plump vein at the center of his forehead. It protruded when he was angry or sad. Moved by the raw brutality of pain and love in his watery, green gaze, I gave him honesty. A different type. Revealing how flawed, how imperfect I was. It came from the dark place I'd only ever allowed him to see and touch. I said the thing others would warn me to think but not say. "I miss her, but sometimes, I miss us more."

"Me too." His words were slurred and whispered like the walls had ears. "Does that make us vile people?" he asked. *Begged.*

"Maybe," I answered. "Maybe it does." I didn't give him what he wanted to hear, I gave him what he needed. I gave him the truth. That we were the same. That I bore the same shame for how I felt, too. That I wasn't over it either. But unlike Jasper, the truth didn't make me want to run from him. I'd made it to the other side of denial. I'd made it to acceptance.

Seeing Jasper this conflicted, this unhappy, felt tragic, and I was at a loss for how to help him. It made me dislike Daniel even more, which made me want Jasper even more because someone needed to save him. I wanted that someone to be me.

If still wanting him, knowing the pain loving this version of him might bring me, made me an unapologetic sadist, then so be it. I'd do bad things with a clear head to have him. And then I'd do them all over again if it meant I got to have him in the next life, too.

We polished off the bottle of gin, and sat for hours talking, not talking, apologizing, and pointing fingers. All too soon the sun slinked below the horizon, and when he'd said he needed to get home, while remaining rooted to his stool with sorrowful eyes, only then did I tell him what he *wanted* to hear.

"Stay," I'd said. *"You're my brother. He'll understand."*

And so he stayed, and we laughed through our intoxication, listened to music, and for the most part we avoided the good ol' days in favor of the here and now. And then we fell asleep on the sofa.

At some point in the night I stirred, finding us too close to one another, finding him in my arms. I told myself it was in the spirit of being past brothers and now tentative friends, and only hoped if he woke he'd think so, too. Above all, I hoped he wouldn't pull away from me.

CHAPTER 4

Daniel

4 Weeks Ago

"SON OF A bitch," I bark angrily into my clenched fist, crashing onto my office chair. It's never enough. Nothing I do is ever enough for them.

Jessica, my assistant, hovers nervously outside my open office door. I wave her in.

"Not good?" she asks.

"Not good at all," I reply grimly.

"Is there anything I can do?"

I shake my head even as the cogs spin for a solution.

The photo of Jasper I keep perched on my desk catches my eye. I snatch up the picture frame, thinking. "How fast can you organize a birthday party?"

"Depends on the scale."

"The largest scale you can find," I say.

"How much time do I have?"

"A month."

"That's more than enough time, Mr. Ward."

"No expense spared," I say. She nods curtly, spine stiff with purpose. "And were you able to get the contact details I asked you for?" I murmur distractedly, running a finger over Jasper's tormented smile.

"It's waiting in your inbox."

"Thank you."

"I hope he knows how lucky he is to have you," she says.

CHAPTER 5

Jasper

I'D JUST UNLOADED the last box from the truck, and dumped it in the corner of the banquet hall when Sofia cornered me.

"Are you expecting Daniel to show up and help?" she asked, pushing her untamed, curly bangs out of her eyes and glancing at the door I'd apparently done a shitty job at covertly monitoring. "Manual labor doesn't seem like his kind of thing." As far as compliments went, that was the nicest thing she'd ever said about Daniel. Not that she had a tendency of trashing him, it was more in what she didn't say, or what her expressions or body language conveyed.

"No, I'm not, and he isn't," I said, dusting my hands off on the thighs of my jeans. I'd stopped by to help with the initial set-up for the fundraiser she was holding next week.

"Oh?" She made it a question, prying me apart with her brown eyes. They were the biggest thing on her petite frame, and quite terrifying when holding you under their scrutiny. "Then why have you been staring at the door like a skittish kitten since you got here?"

I considered lying, but I'd been doing enough of that to her, to myself, and to Daniel, too. Most of all Daniel. Maybe it was time to let someone else in on my secrets, some of them at least.

"My, ah, brother's in town," I said, circling her to count the boxes that didn't need counting. "He's moved here, actually." I readied to weather her reaction.

My whereabouts for the day were unknown to Cole. In fact, I hadn't spoken to him in days. Not since finishing a bottle of gin with him, then waking up the following morning with my nose lodged at his throat, and then sneaking out as his fingers twitched in his sleep from the loss of me.

It wasn't beyond his means to find me, though. The prospect agitated me, ensuring I constantly peered over my shoulders for his sudden appearance. Some of my agitation came from wanting to feel important enough to be hunted down.

"You have a *brother*?" she exclaimed, hands going to her hips. "No running in here, mijo!" she shouted to her eldest son who'd taken up position as ringleader of all the other teens who'd shown up to assist. The distraction earned me a two-second reprieve from her knife-like undivided attention. "How did I not know you had a brother? And you say I'm your best friend," she said derisively.

"You are my best friend, 'Fia." I squatted to open the flaps on one of the dozens of boxes lining the wall. Anything to avoid the look of hurt on her face.

"Feels really one-sided, Jasper."

I hung my head at her tone, then pushed to my feet, determined to give her the respect she deserved by meeting her stare. "He's my stepbrother, to be exact. My old stepbrother."

"He's old?" she asked, perplexed.

"No, I mean we used to be stepbrothers. Before my mother died. We're nothing now."

"So..." She dragged the word out, her mind working to make sense of the sudden stranger who stood in front of her. That was how I felt. To myself at the very least. "So that means you had a stepfather at some point."

Sofia was one of the first people I'd met when I moved to New York in search of anonymity. I had happened upon a small protest she was heading in front of City Hall, and after fifteen minutes of listening to her impassioned speech on gun violence, I found myself behind her picket line in full support. The rest was history.

She'd become an older sister to me. A mentor and a friend. She knew I'd lost my parents, but it ended there. I'd left Franklin and Cole out completely, and she never pushed for more than what I'd given her about my past. To discover I'd kept something this vital from her had to sting, especially after she'd shared so much of her life and herself with me. "It's complicated, 'Fia. Cole and I have been out of touch for years. He's the part of my life I wish I could forget."

"Uh-huh," she said, unconvinced.

Across the room, Cole's broad frame filled the double doorway, and I smiled faintly, forgetting Sofia watched me. She craned her head around. "Is that the so-called 'old brother but means nothing to me now' guy?" she drawled with sass.

"Ah, yeah."

She considered me with pursed lips. "You know, I've never once seen you smile when Daniel entered a room. Yeah," she said to my stupefied expression, "you've got a lot of explaining—and groveling to do. But later." She patted my cheek before strolling off.

Cole soaked in the chaos around him, narrowly avoiding being trampled by kids as he meandered over to me dressed like he'd teleported in from the boardroom. I should've been pissed. I should've felt violated, stalked even. I couldn't find it in me to be, though. I sighed internally at the lowering of my guards.

"Do I even want to know how you found me?" I asked.

"Don't you remember supplying me with your weekly itinerary? Dates and times. I even knew what you'd be wearing. Remind me to restock on gin." He winked, pleased with himself.

I vaguely remembered him weaseling my schedule out of me, now that he mentioned it. I held his comfy sofa responsible for my loose lips—deep enough to accommodate two men of our size, and the alcohol he all but jammed down my throat. I'd woken up with my nose pressed to his Adam's apple, like I used to, even before we were...*more*. It vibrated with his soft snores and never failed to drag me into a bottomless slumber. He'd slept with a proprietary fist in my hair, holding me to him, like he used to do, even before we were more.

We were forced to be brothers, then all too willing friends, then something else entirely. What were we doing now? What were we becoming? And who were we fooling with it?

"Three days." He wiggled his fingers to punctuate his point. "It's been three days since you left me asleep on my sofa without so much as a blanket thrown over me. And I haven't heard a peep from you."

"First of all," I said, "that thing is a cloud, not a sofa. Nothing has the right to be that comfortable. And secondly, it's been two days."

"So you've been counting," he said, his sea blue eyes bright with victory.

"I see you're still incorrigible," I quipped, unable to keep the zing from my tone.

Cole's gaze turned worrisome as he noticed the grime on my clothes and the folded tables and chairs stacked in the corners.

"Where do you want these, Mr. Jasper?" one of the youth volunteers from Sofia's organization asked. The box in his arms overflowed with table linens.

"Set it along the stage for now, Jimmy. Once the tables are up, you and Camille can work on dressing them."

"You're all responsible for getting this place together for the charity event?" Cole asked incredulously, taking in the scope of the rented hall once more. "Don't you have hired people who can do this?"

"The professionals will come in and add the glitz and glam before the red carpet is rolled out, but hard work builds character. A good lesson for the kids."

"Does hard work have to equate to *manual* work?"

"I don't expect you to understand, Mr. Businessman. The rest of us don't mind getting our hands dirty," I said, baiting him.

Without another word, Cole dramatically removed his expensive wool coat, tossing it carelessly onto the mountain of boxes, then began the process of removing his cufflinks and hiking up his sleeves. "Getting dirty is my specialty, *Mr. Jasper*. Or have you forgotten?" he said sinfully. My cheeks boiled from the inside out.

"You can start by setting up the tables and chairs," I said, clearing my throat.

"Easy enough," he mused. "You never did say which cause you guys were raising money for."

"Innocent Bystanders. It's a charity that helps pay for prosthetics and other medical services for families left physically and mentally affected by acts of violence in some way. Hit and runs, domestic violence, shootings..."

Cole circled slowly, only now registering the slew of young amputees pitching in however they could. "I'll have Leland move the rest of my meetings today," he said, getting to work, while I bit back the snarky remark on my tongue. I'd need to get over my issue with his assistant.

It was well into late evening when we finished, and I waited by the exit for Cole as Sofia spoke animatedly at him. She'd intercepted him on his way to me. Probably converting him to a serial activist, knowing her. Whatever they talked about, he seemed genuinely interested in the topic.

Daniel would've pretended to care while searching for a way out. It wasn't his fault, though. It'd been ingrained in him to see things in terms of mutual gain. Deacon Ward would've had a stroke to learn his son was volunteering. Daniel's father didn't see the benefit in helping others if it didn't in turn elevate your status in some way, professionally or financially. Daniel had told me on several occasions I'd made a great difference in his life. I'd seen the small changes over the years we'd been together. Patience and understanding were key with my husband.

Sofia finally came up for air, and allowed Cole to leave. Behind his back she made the throat-slitting gesture at me, then blew me a kiss. I'd need to get my knee pads ready for the level of groveling she'd require to gain her forgiveness.

"This is why you decided to go to law school?" he asked, striding toward me until we were only inches apart. I stepped away under the guise of needing room to slip into my coat. I wasn't strong enough to handle being so close, yet. Not while sober at least.

"Yeah. She tried to do both for a while, but all areas were suffering because of it. So now, I tackle the courtroom, and she spends her time laying groundwork."

He gripped my elbow, moving in close again, this time making sure I couldn't escape. "Thank you, again. For this," he gestured around us, "and for letting me back in. Thank you."

I couldn't say he was welcome, because I didn't want to let him in. I didn't want to love having him around. I didn't want to miss having him in my corner. I also couldn't fight him on it, because I lacked the strength needed to fight a connection so strong, which was ultimately why I'd ended up agreeing to hang out at his place the other day. I couldn't push him away if he was intent on pushing back for a place to stay, because I didn't hate him. I hated myself for what I did to him, for what I was still doing to him. For what I'd done to all of us.

It would've been so much easier if I had hated him. And after our talk the other night I realized I envied his ability to live in spite of his guilt. To go for what he wanted, consequences be damned, and not lose a wink of sleep behind it. Especially since the death of my mother had triggered the trauma he'd carried around for the tragic death of his own mother, and the role he incorrectly believed he'd played in it. It was obvious he'd taken the time and done the self-work needed to be okay in the face of what happened to us.

I'd never get there. My mother and I had been all each other had for so long, and I'd promised to always take care of her. I would never forgive myself, or give up my carefully constructed life of penance. I should've known better. The responsibility to know better rested on my back. So no, the fault wasn't Cole's, or my mother's sickness, or the universe, or even God.

It was mine.

◆◆◆

Daniel arrived home around midnight to find me brooding outside on our bedroom deck. It was freezing out, and I'd blindly gone out there with only my racing thoughts to keep me warm.

Didn't matter the temperature or the hour, the city still pulsed energetically fifteen stories below, the magnitude of it reaching me, crawling along my skin. Pedestrians skipped across streets without the right-of-way, horns honked at their stupidity, while I winced at their death wishes.

Daniel's warm hands skirted up my exposed arms, raising gooseflesh. I couldn't say if the tiny buds were sparked by repulsion, or the drastic change in temperature on my frigid skin. "You're freezing, Jasper. Come inside."

I swung round on him, tearing open his shirt, buttons pinging along the metal railing.

"Jas—"

I silenced him with my tongue, needing him to shut up, to not sound like himself. I backed him up. "I know this isn't like me." *Like the me you've come to know.* "But I need this. I need you to not be nice, to not watch where we land, to not calculate how long it'll take for our bodily fluids to permanently stain... Just...fuck me. *Please.*" If I could just get this from him, if he could just give me what I needed, then I wouldn't have to think about Cole in the ways I had been, and our marriage would be fine. He'd make partner at the firm, he'd be happy, content, even. He'd grow to accept me for who I was, and we would be fine. *Fine.* And Cole and I could be brothers, friends, fucking priest and parishioner for all I cared. I just needed *this* to be okay for *that* to work, or we were doomed.

Daniel relented, following my lead, and therein resided the problem. I needed him to take, to make me pay for whatever he could come up with, even if the transgression had to be imagined. I needed to choke on my breaths, and die a thousand deaths in his arms, at his hands. I needed to lose control, to have it stolen from me. I needed to be robbed of free will.

I was a ball of repression, of pent-up aggression, and he was pleasant, a tranquil sea, when what I needed was a fucking tornado to come through and rip everything down to its foundation, including me.

I needed him to be Cole.

♦ ♦ ♦

"Wake up, sleepy head," Daniel crooned, and I groaned, tugging a pillow over my face. The scent of coffee filtered through the goose feathers, and I lowered it, peeling an eye open.

Daniel chuckled, waiting for me to sit up against the headboard and accept the mug containing my other addiction. My brain fog cleared after my first sip, and the first thing I noted was our bedroom had been cleaned while I'd slept. It bore no signs of our lovemaking. Then I homed in on Daniel, fully dressed with a carry-on by his side.

"Where are you going?"

"Last-minute business trip. A meeting with the head of the company Cole wants a controlling stake in."

"What? When did you find out about this?"

"I got the email not too long ago. My flight leaves in a couple hours."

"Can't you do a Zoom thingy or something? Do you have to leave?"

"You're cute when you haven't had your first cup of coffee," he said indulgently. "No, this is too important. Cole thinks it'll make a stronger impression if I'm there. All senior level employees will be in attendance. I have to go—"

"Okay, I get it. How long will you be gone? You promised you'd make it to the fundraiser." Sensing I was in a mood last night, Daniel had volunteered to attend as my date. I hadn't planned on asking; he always magically had a good excuse as to why he couldn't make it to these sorts of things, why he couldn't support me. Him agreeing to go, without being asked, was a sign he was trying, and it meant everything to me.

"When's the event?" he asked.

"Saturday evening. *Five* days from now," I emphasized.

"That works out perfectly. I'll be back Friday evening." He kissed my forehead. "I really have to go. Maybe get some quality time with your brother while I'm gone?" It landed like a question.

"What?!" I asked as hot coffee spilled over the edge of the mug and onto the comforter. "I thought you said all senior staff members were going?" It didn't get more senior than Cole.

"He has something pressing he needs to handle here." His eyes widened on the quilt, but his phone chirped before he could go into a decent tailspin about it. "That's the front desk. My car service is here. I'll call you when I land," he shouted as he hastily made his way to the stairs. "Scrub that with a block of ice before it sets in!"

The front door clicked shut, and I was out of the bed in a flash. Face washed, teeth brushed, hastily dressed, and at the curb hailing a cab in under ten minutes. I hadn't been this pissed in ages. Actually, I had. The night Cole exploded back into my life like a fucking life-altering grenade.

I cursed the Manhattan traffic as I peered anxiously through the Plexiglas, urging my feet on an invisible gas pedal, needing to get to Cole's office yesterday. "I'll walk from here," I said, after the driver in front of us got out of his car to road rage with the guy who'd cut him off two lights back. I stuffed a bundle of bills into the payment slot and hopped out, holding a hand out for the driver in the next lane to slow so I could make it onto the side-walk. My palm collided with the hood of his car, and he laid on the horn before flipping me off.

I had to dodge a motorbike riding against traffic, and a lady walking her poodle by the time I rounded the corner and entered Cole's office building. The skyscraper took up one half of a city block.

I signed in, slipped my temporary badge into the rightful slot on the turnstile, and searched for the bank of elevators that went to his floor. I drummed my fingers against my thigh the whole ride up.

"Excuse me. Sir!" the receptionist called as I blew past her desk in search of Cole's office. It'd be the biggest one with the unfettered eastern view of the city. Couldn't be that hard to find.

Leland shoved to his feet as I charged for Cole's office doors but wisely didn't stop me.

"I'll call you right back," Cole said into his desk phone re-ceiver, sliding it into its cradle as he took in my appearance with concern. "Is everything alright—"

I slammed my palms onto his desk and hovered menacingly, cutting him off. I hadn't even combed my hair or bothered to confirm if my shoes matched. Thankfully, they did.

"Did you come up with this last-minute business trip to get Daniel out of the way?"

"Excuse me?"

"Don't play games with me, Cole."

He pressed a button on his desk and the glass doors frosted, giving us privacy. "Let me get this straight. You think I scheduled a meeting with a Fortune 500 company twenty states away, paid for travel arrangements for my entire senior staff—not to mention inconvenience them and their families, just so I could have you to myself?"

Well, when he put it that way...

"I'm not above sending Daniel away, but this secret operation you're accusing me of is on a whole other scale, Jasper. At the end of the day, I'm running a business. I can't not send your husband on a work trip in order to appease your suspicions. And your lack of self-control."

He's right. I pushed myself away and tried to pull it together. I was on edge ever since last night, ever since last week, last year. For more than half a damn decade! I scrubbed a palm over my face. "You're right." It pained me to say it.

"And you could've simply called," Cole said with a roguish grin.

I hit him with the full weight of my stare. "You find this funny?"

"Your expression right now? Yeah, I do." His eyes narrowed with cruelty that only I knew was actually jealousy. Hard and uncompromising. "What I don't find funny is you saturating my office with his scent. You might want to shower before you go charging through the city on a tear next time. Just a little friendly advice."

"Yeah, friendly. *Sure.*" My neck and ears heated from left-over rage and fresh embarrassment. "He said he'll be back Friday. Make sure nothing comes up to delay him. He promised to make it to the fundraiser." I gained less satisfaction than I thought I would when his self-righteousness took a nosedive. Cole hadn't outright said he wanted to attend with me, but I knew how to take a hint.

"I'll let you get back to what you were doing." I hurried for the door before I did or said something else foolish, like confess I was terrified of being in a city with him and no Daniel as a buffer or human shield. Without the constant reminder that what I deserved, not what I wanted, waited for me at home.

So I left without a backward glance. I would make my relationship with Daniel work, I swore. Because the alternative was to piss all over my mother's grave, and Franklin's broken heart by going back to the thing that had destroyed everything, even if going back meant a return to life for me. And I couldn't justify making Daniel or Franklin suffer simply so I could live.

CHAPTER 6

Jasper

SOFIA AND HER boys came flying around the bend of the ice-skating rink, and I perked up and waved from where I leaned on the opposite side of it, counting the seconds until I would gain a reprieve from faking my joy, if only to do it all over again on their next lap.

Afraid that with Daniel gone there'd be nothing holding me back from running headfirst into Cole, I took her up on the offer to play assistant chaperone. There was only her, her two boys, and Camille—who was old enough to babysit herself and had been doing so from the warmth of the café overlooking the rink.

The invite was a desperate attempt at getting me out of the house, and I'd clung to it like the lifeline I needed.

I couldn't face him yet. Not after I'd embarrassed myself and given so much away when I'd stormed his headquarters days ago.

My warm breaths were working to heat my cupped, bare hands when a set of leather gloves suddenly hung limp in front of my face, dangling from dexterous fingers I'd recognize anywhere. They haunted my dreams, brought me solace during my worst nightmares, and crawled down my spine like tickling spider legs during my every waking hour.

I straightened and turned to Cole, ignoring the olive branch he still held out to me. My need for warmth had miraculously been replaced with a dire need to shed my body of its layers in order to douse the fire now burning in me. "How'd you know I was here?"

Beside him, an older man and woman alternated between huddling tight and cheering as they hurried to snap pictures of their grandchildren circling the ice.

"Sofia invited me."

I searched through the crowd of skaters for the pink pom-pom atop her hat. "I didn't realize you two had gotten so close." Seemed my own invitation from her might have been more of a calculated move than the pity I'd thought it sprang from.

"Don't be jealous," he said. "I'm not trying to steal your best friend."

"I'm not jealous." Even I heard the petulance in my tone.

"Liar," he teased. "You never liked anyone else playing with your things."

Things sounded pretty filthy coming from his mouth. His full, deceptively sweet mouth. The things it could do, the tortures it could inflict, and the person those pillows of hell could make me become was anything but sweet. I averted my gaze, but not quickly enough. Damn him and his maddeningly knowing grin.

My tight stare collided with Sofia's guilty one, and I took an immature pleasure in her crash-landing on the ice.

Cole studied me, studied the wayward curl swaying across my forehead like a carrot on a string. The fine leather gloves he'd held out for me now creaked between one white-knuckled fist. I knew my rabbit. Knew his need to comb the curl away if only so he could touch some part of me.

There was a time when not touching him felt like dying. Back when sleeping with each other seemed innocent to watching eyes, and when bolting our door became a requirement when we were old enough to be judged for it. When as teens we walked each other to the bathroom hand in hand in the middle of the night, because we couldn't be apart for not even a minute. If that meant I'd have to hold his cock and aim, well then... We'd done what we had to do to remain connected. *Always.*

I couldn't say if I nodded with my head, my mind, or my eyes, but the lump at his throat bobbed, and he stuffed the stray hair under my beanie hat, his fingers tracing my cheek on their way down. *Fuck.*

"Hey, you two," Sofia said, gliding to a stop in front of us, the boys continuing on without her. "Are you just going to stand there all night?"

Night. When had the sun fully set? How long had Cole and I actually been standing there silently making the decision to touch and be touched? "Maybe I should check on Camille," I said, to which Sofia pointed behind me to where Camille could be seen through the glass of the rink café not even ten feet behind me.

"She's got hot cocoa and her phone. Kids, they can be on those things for *hours,*" she said in a you-know-what-I-mean tone. "In Picatuna, a teen actually killed her nana for interrupting her Candy Crush game. I don't think you wanna die tonight, do you, Jasper?" She was amused and I knew it. And not just because there was no such place as Picatuna, but because her other passion—besides fighting for the voiceless—was to drive me insane.

"I don't want you to die, Jas. How would we explain that to Daniel?" Cole said. If looks could kill, Cole would've burst into flames under my glare right then. Sofia snorted before pushing off, yelling for us to get on the ice.

"Don't encourage her," I said, taking his hand and weaving us through the crowd toward the skate rental booth. He was less familiar with Brooklyn than he was with the city. Prospect Park was big, and I didn't want him to get lost—so I told my brain when it shouted for me to let go of him.

Sure, he ran a successful company projected to double in size over the next five years. Yeah, maybe he did get himself to Brooklyn in the first place. Maybe it wouldn't take a genius to figure out how to stay within the skating area, but I didn't feel like having to search for him when it was time to go. And I didn't need better excuses when it was only the inside of my head hearing them.

"You don't have it in you to remain upset, do you?" Cole asked, changing the grip of our hands so our fingers were entwined. It felt more personal. Intimate. Less like guiding a child and more like lovers strolling through the park. I withdrew from it, but not instantly. Not until we'd needed to pay for and accept our skates.

"I wasn't upset with you," I said, handing the cashier our shoes, and then showing Cole to the benches off to the side. Keeping him at a distance, shutting myself off to him, was the kind of hard work my heart wasn't built for. Not when only a thin strip of cold air separated us.

We laced into our skates, and with a deep breath, I relaxed my shoulders. I wanted to smile. I couldn't wait to laugh at his attempts to make it around the rink. I wanted to feel the joy I had faked before he'd arrived tonight. He made me want these things without even trying. "Fair warning, if you fall, I'm laughing. Like laughing my ass off laughing." I pushed up and held out a hand.

"That'll be worth every hard blow I take to the ass," he said, accepting my hand and staggering to his feet. The innuendo went over his head. He'd been so caught up in the idea of seeing me laugh, of seeing me happy, that he hadn't even realized he missed his greatest punchline yet. I guffawed right then to his wide-eyed amazement. "What?" he said. "I haven't fallen yet."

"Just don't break your ankle before we get on the ice, okay?"

I'd gotten an hour of laughter in before Sofia called it a night. The boys, and Camille—who'd skated five minutes before deciding she was better suited for indoors—had school the next day. We'd never gone ice skating as kids, and I'd only learned from all the times I'd gone with Sofia, but I was still sure Cole had botched his first go at it so completely for my benefit alone. It was in the way he'd lie there on the cold surface gazing up at me in wonder as I folded over him, hands on knees, cackling hysterically. The way he'd make sure to let go of my hand seconds before his premeditated fall, so I wouldn't go down with him. It worked like a charm every time. I laughed so hard I knew my stomach would be sore come morning.

"Give me a minute to send my driver home," Cole said as we waited off to the side for Sofia and her boys to return their skates.

"Why would you do that? I asked.

"Well, we all can't fit. I wouldn't feel right if we rode off in luxury while they had to hike it to the train alone in this weather." He tightened his scarf around his neck. Why did he have to make it so hard to push him away? I was struck once again by how different he and Daniel were, even though they'd both been born with silver spoons in their mouths. Nexcom may have been a seedling of a company, maybe even just an idea, when Cole was born, but he came from old money. Then I remembered something Cole had told Daniel at dinner that night.

"Without him I might have ended up like you, but because of him, I know what makes a great man."

He'd given me too much credit. Cole was good, with or without me.

"No, you go ahead. Sofia drove, and I'm staying the night at her place anyway." I wasn't, but leaving with him after enjoying the time I'd spent with him, and without the excuse of needing to go home to Daniel... There'd be no telling where I'd end up tonight. In whose arms, in whose bed. Happiness still zapped through my veins, cracking the walls I'd built, rebounding off them and zipping through every dark chamber of me again, letting light in. It wouldn't take much for him to convince me the night didn't have to end.

He masked his disappointment well. "Okay."

Sofia tapped on the glass window of the café. Camille raised her head from her phone sharply, a look of murder in her green eyes. Maybe there *was* a place called Picatuna.

Her annoyance cleared at the sight of us standing there, and she squealed, jumping from her seat when she spotted Cole. Practically cartwheeling through the doors, she threw her arms around him.

"Mr. Kincaid! I didn't know you'd be coming."

"Sofia wanted to surprise you," Cole said, returning her embrace.

So Sofia hadn't invited him for me? Of course she hadn't, I thought, reprimanding myself. She was married, and believed in the promises made before God. She'd never actively take part in the tarnishing of a marriage, not even one she didn't approve of. *Another person I didn't deserve in my life.*

But why would Camille be interested in seeing Cole? I'd spied them conversing while we'd completed the first phase of setup for the upcoming fundraiser. He must have made an impression.

"Look," Camille said, unzipping her coat. Cole stopped her with a hand on her shoulder.

"It's freezing out here, and Mrs. Rivera's in a rush to get you guys home. Something about school tomorrow," he said from the corner of his mouth, and they both rolled their eyes, spurring a giggle from her. "I just wanted to pop in and say hi. You can show me next time."

"Alright," she said, conceding to his point before going over to where the boys waited with their faces inches from their phone screens.

Cole bid Sofia and me a goodnight before I could ask him what that was all about. Beyond the bare branches and thin bark of a baby elm tree, a black SUV waited for him.

"What was that about?" I asked, moving out of the way of a passing family.

"Oh, Cole sent one of the prosthetists consulting with Nexcom's robotics department to meet with the amputees of Innocent Bystanders. Got them all fitted for upgraded, state-of-the-art prostheses. Camille's prosthetic arm came in first. He delivered it to her himself but couldn't stick around while the doctor got her fitted. Said he had a last-minute meeting pop up."

My mouth parted, and I looked between the taillights of the retreating vehicle and Camille, who I only now noticed worked her left arm with equal confidence as her right. He'd done this in a matter of days?

"She begged me to invite him so she could thank him. I didn't think he'd come, honestly. I'm sure he had better things to do than trek to Brooklyn in the cold on a weekday. But he agreed." She finally looked up from digging to the bottom of the suitcase she called a purse for her car keys. She observed my stumped expression. "Didn't he tell you?"

"No," I said, smiling so hard I'd have sore cheeks to match my sore abdominals. "That isn't his style."

$\blacklozenge \blacklozenge \blacklozenge$

Sweat beaded my hairline as I strolled swiftly down the hall of the Grossman School of Medicine, hoping I'd gotten there before the keynote speaker—a renowned cardiologist—stepped onto the auditorium stage. Cole had offhandedly mentioned during our dinner of Chinese and gin the other night that he sometimes attended these types of conferences when time allowed. I'd spotted his solitary ticket on the foyer table as I'd slithered out like a thief in the night the following morning.

"I don't know why I subject myself to being in a room full of people who make me feel inadequate," he'd said. *"Most, if not all of the medical jargon they sling around goes right over my head, and I never have anything brilliant to ask during the Q & A segments. I sit there and let everyone else around me contribute. But it keeps me on track, keeps my goal front and center. Keeps her at the forefront of my mind."*

It wasn't until last night at the ice-skating rink when I'd learned from Sofia what Cole had done for Camille and everyone else that I'd decided to attend. To be there for him. I thanked my lucky stars tickets were still available last minute.

A rotund, middle-aged man wearing a toupee approached the microphone as I slid inside, careful not to let the door bang shut behind me. I peered down the rows of stadium seating until I spotted a head at least six inches above the rest in his section, whose trimmed, dark mane gleamed with vitality. Even his hair was a turn-on.

I removed my hat and sliced impatient fingers through my own hair, noting it could do with a cut, but knowing I'd let it grow to my ankles because Cole liked it long.

What are you doing, Jasper?

I descended the LED-lit steps, giving my mind something else to focus on, distracting it from having to answer the grave question I'd just posed.

I folded myself into the seat next to him, trembling with amusement when he did a double take on me.

"Jas?" he asked two octaves above a whisper. That earned him a backward glare from the people seated in front of us, and a chorus of shushes from behind. I kept my eyes straight ahead, but allowed my legs to fall open, my knee coming to rest along his.

When we were boys, we'd link our pinkies under the dinner table. I'd had to learn how to eat left-handed. When we were near it had been impossible not to touch, not to hold, not to love.

The keynote was already a few minutes into his speech before Cole collected himself, peeled his eyes off me and focused on the stage.

An hour later when the projector went off and the lights came up, signaling the start of intermission before the Q & A portion of the conference began, I slipped a square of paper into his hands.

"A few questions I thought of for you," I said.

He unfolded it, reading while absently shaking his head in confoundment. "You did this for me?"

"You say it like no one does anything nice for you." It was just a few questions. The idea was absurd. He had drivers and assistants and chefs and maids. *Lovers,* I was sure. Anything he wanted could be obtained with a beckoned call from him.

"It's not the same," he said. I thought about Daniel and all his gifts and expensive trips and our fancy apartment in the sky. *His* fancy apartment in the sky. And I got it. It wasn't the same. Those people were paid to take care of Cole. Even Leland, who appeared to have more than a working relationship with him, was on his payroll. I'd done something for Cole simply because. Something I didn't have to do.

I shrugged it off as nothing, terrified by the open look on his face. The unveiled love and appreciation. "It's just a few questions."

"No," he said. "It's not." He was the first to raise a hand when the time came, his voice booming to be heard down below, and he reached over to squeeze my hand, mouthing *thank you,* after having been told his question was a good one.

After the conference let out, I treated Cole to his first New York City pretzel. We stood near the hot dog and pretzel cart on the corner, attempting to keep warm as the steam billowed from the boiled water compartment where the hot dogs were stationed. It was a pretty busy corner, but we managed to not get our heads bit off by the passing pedestrians.

I was tempted to buy another one, but time was ticking, and Daniel's flight was scheduled to land at any moment. I couldn't stall any longer. "Look, about the fundraiser..." I started. I felt horrible for not inviting him, but with the inevitable craziness of the night, and Daniel being in attendance, I didn't want to add the anxiety of being in the same room with them onto my plate. Not during a night when the attention shouldn't be on me and my messy life. Cole probably deserved to be the one to go, but Daniel said he'd come. He'd promised. I couldn't pass that up.

"It's alright," Cole said, saving me. "Leland and I have plans, anyway."

"Is it wise to hang out after work hours with your subordinates?" I snapped. Thankfully, Cole didn't comment on my irritation. My *jealousy*.

"Leland and I are friends, first. He was there for me when—"

When you weren't, I finished internally for him. I wanted to ask how things were after I'd left. After I'd abandoned him. That would have to wait for the next round of Chinese and gin, though. I wasn't brave enough to ask for that truth uninebriated.

"I'll call you," he said, before leaving me there in the cold. His departure felt like a film being paused, like we had unfinished business. I stood there confused, not knowing if I needed to wait or go. Not knowing who he'd left me to run to.

I went home to Daniel, and while he made love to me that night, I imagined all the ways Cole could be fucking Leland, wondering if he was taking his body in the same ways and positions he'd once taken mine.

I was so caught up in my envy, caught up in the way it was killing me, I missed the moment when Daniel left my body and our bed.

The shower came on, and I blinked at the tufted headboard, my jaws aching from the tension I'd placed on it in my anger. I felt...nothing. If it weren't for the slight ache in the place Daniel had been seconds ago, and the empty condom wrapper on the bed, I would've thought nothing had happened. *We were done?* I thought stupidly.

I peered down my chest, and my cock stared back at me angrily, hard and unsatisfied. And the towel Daniel had placed between my hands and knees was bone dry.

I swung my disbelieving gaze at the cracked bathroom door. *Daniel* was done, but I had been forgotten.

In all fairness, he'd been forgotten, too.

CHAPTER 7

Cole

WORKING FROM HOME had always been too much of a distraction. I preferred the stillness of an abandoned office space, and
the lack of personal effects. Made me work harder and faster to
get things done and get out.

I'd needed to go over some urgent paperwork before meeting up with Leland, and so killing two birds with one stone, I'd
gotten my workout in by running the four-mile route from home
to the office that Saturday morning. So much for getting in and
out. It was five in the evening., behind me the sun was fading
fast, and I had an hour to get showered and dressed for my ap-
pointment to get smashed at the first bar in sight with my friend.

The notes of "Clair De Lune" sifted through my phone. Jasper's favorite piece. He'd said it reminded him of the calm before
a storm, and then being at the apex of it. The analogy wasn't lost
on me.

I tapped the screen to silence the alarm, then rubbed the
tiredness from my eyes, which had little to do with lack of sleep
and more a weariness of the soul. I'd considered going as is, but
then remembered I still wore my workout clothes. The sweat had
long dried up, but the stench remained. "Shit." I hurled my face
away from my raised armpit.

Shutting down my computer and scooping up my phone
and keys, I bolted for my office door while pulling up the Uber

app because I hadn't had the sense to have Mark waiting outside for me, and there was no time to wait for him now.

Hustling past the row of offices and through the labyrinth of cubicles to the reception area, I skidded to a stop upon seeing Daniel studiously at work in his temporary office. With Parker & Mitchell's headquarters being on the other side of the city, and our need to work closely on this deal, it made sense for him to split his time between both locations, so Nexcom provided him with office space.

What the hell?

"Shouldn't you be getting ready for the fundraiser?" I asked in lieu of a proper greeting.

"Cole," he said, jerking upright. "I didn't realize you were here."

"Yeah. I prefer getting work done in the office when possible."

"Same here," he said. "I hope you don't mind me being here after work hours. With the marathon happening so close to the Parker & Mitchell office building, it was more convenient getting here. I made some leeway with the negotiations. I'm reviewing their counteroffer and making minor adjustments of my own before sending it off to you for approval." He continued typing, caught up in what he was doing.

"Daniel," I said, markedly, to which he peered over the rim of his reading glasses, flushing at having realized he'd dismissed me without another word. "Does Jasper know you're here?"

"Yes, the fundraiser," he said, removing his specs. "I told him I'd meet him there after I got this squared away."

From the number of stacked legal texts, piles of paper, the steaming cup of coffee, and the hairs standing on end atop his head, it seemed more like he was just getting started. I checked my watch, and he should've been hailing a cab or meeting his driver at this very moment if he expected to get to Brooklyn on time, yet he was decked out in wool trousers and an argyle sweater.

"He promised," Jasper had said with childlike hope. He'd be devastated, and while I should be celebrating Daniel disappointing him, all I could muster was my own heartbreak for what this would do to him. Not like this, I didn't want to win him like this. I didn't want him more broken than he already was, because I loved him more than I wanted him.

"It's okay," I said. "This can wait. I appreciate all the hard work you're putting in, the extra mile you're willing to go, but tonight is important to Jasper. You should be there for him."

"He'll understand," he assured me. "He wants to support me in this. He knows how much this position means to me."

Of course he'd make this about him. I wanted to punch him right between his unibrow.

"I'm your boss." One of them at least. He still answered to Parker & Mitchell, but Parker & Mitchell answered to me. "And I'm telling you, you can go."

Daniel found himself in a weird position working for me. I was the man he needed to impress, I held his professional future in my hands, so to speak. But I played a pivotal role in his personal life, too. Walking the line between treating me with the utmost respect, and telling me to mind my damn business couldn't have been easy.

"With all due respect, Cole. I know Jasper in a way you don't, and I'm telling you, he'll understand. Please respect my decision to stay." He'd said it with an assuredness that made him a stellar attorney. A powerhouse, even. I had a line to straddle as well, and Nexcom couldn't afford the lawsuit it surely would receive if I scratched the itch on my knuckles with his face. Their relationship shouldn't be my concern. Not when we were within company walls. And maybe not even when we weren't.

I nodded, jaw nailed shut, as I marched back to my office.

Exploding into my office, I punched Leland's number into my desk phone, listening to it ring on speaker as I tore open my closet door, examining the tuxedo hanging within. I'd have to thank him for convincing me having one on hand here made sense.

"You never know when you might need to rush last minute from the office to some pretentious business mixer, or whatever it is you rich folk do," he'd said.

"Do I even want to know why you're calling me from the office?" he asked upon answering, music blaring and car horns honking in the background.

I frosted my office door, carrying the tux into my personal bathroom. "I need a raincheck and a favor," I said, flicking on the standup shower.

"That sounds like two favors to me," he deadpanned. The city ruckus died down, and a second later he was asking for a beer. *Shit*. He'd already made it to the bar.

I hit the speaker icon on the bathroom wall phone. "I'm sorry," I said, "but I don't have much time." I stripped down to nothing. "I need to hurry to Sofia's fundraiser."

He was silent for a moment, understanding exactly what that meant. "What do you need me to do?"

"Make some calls. See if you can get some friends to show up with their checkbooks." "Friends" was a term used loosely in the business world, but under the rules of quid pro quo, I was owed a few favors. I inched under the spray before the water had warmed.

"How soon?" Leland asked.

"Within the hour."

Leland cursed and hung up, and I prayed Jasper seeing my face instead of Daniel's didn't do more harm than good.

♦ ♦ ♦

I hid in the rear of the banquet hall behind the tall, stone pillars that overflowed with white floral arrangements. I surveyed Jasper's table, the seat to the right of him empty, and every few seconds he'd cast a hopeful glance at the doors in between appearing interested in whatever Sofia spoke vivaciously about. A tall man, who I assumed to be Sofia's husband by the strong resemblance to her boys, slouched in his chair on the other side of her.

I remained stuck there for a good while, until the crowd of attendees bustling about thinned as everyone seemed to pick up on some unheard signal that things would soon begin.

Jasper appeared to remember there was a back door, where I'd been standing, at the same moment I stepped into the open. His nervously optimistic expression tumbled the moment he spotted me, and when he stretched his neck to get a look behind me and saw no one else, his eyes questioned me, asking me if Daniel would be there. It hurt like hell to have to shake my head no. He turned away sharply, probably blaming me, even if it'd be misplaced, because Daniel was busy with Nexcom.

I claimed the seat next to him, scooting in close to the table as Sofia glanced between Jasper and me, no doubt guessing why I was there, before introducing me to her husband. We shook hands around the floral centerpiece.

The lights dimmed, and the waitstaff poured into the expansive space wearing all white, matching the table linens and seat covers, hands laden with plates of food. Sofia and her husband now leaned into each other, chairs angled close, whispering and quietly trembling with laughter while Jasper ignored my presence.

"I hope it's okay that I came," I said. "I ran into Daniel at the office, and when it was clear he wouldn't make it, I figured I'd show up for you instead."

We pressed back into our seats, allowing our waiter to place our food in front of us. Jasper reached for his napkin, setting the utensils aside to drape the cloth over his lap. "Was he sorry?" he whispered. "Was he at least fucking destroyed he couldn't make it?" He finally met my gaze. His hair was gelled back into a sleek bun at his nape, and the sharp points of his cheekbones were tinged pink with either anger or embarrassment, and his eyes were round pools of bleakness. I wanted to send him to his knees, I wanted to get down on mine, I wanted to kiss every aching part of him right then.

I should've told him the truth, but I wanted to relieve his pain, not add to it. "I'm sure he was," I said. Jasper grunted, inhaling the glass of champagne set in front of him before devouring mine, too. His hands disappeared under the table just as everyone else started in on their food.

I picked up my fork, moving the potatoes and peas around, my stomach a ball of knots and blades. I wanted to storm Nexcom's offices, hoist Daniel to his feet before laying my fists into him, consequences be damned. Instead, I focused on what I could do to help Jasper right then, and discreetly slid the hand closest to him under the table, searching out his fingers, then hooking my pinky around his and squeezed.

A ghost of a gloomy smile played around his lips, and with a sigh, he rolled his shoulders back, and held on when I attempted to pull my hand away. He picked up his fork. "Good thing I learned how to eat with my left hand," he said.

Jasper took to the stage after we ate, giving a moving speech about how much the cause we were there to support meant to him. I enjoyed seeing him in his element. I felt a pride that went beyond brotherly, beyond what a friend felt for a friend, and beyond even the pride of lovers. I loved him as a person first and foremost. No matter how imperfect he believed himself to be, there was no denying just how perfect he was to me.

How could Daniel not see that? Not appreciate it? And how could Jasper accept that for himself? Had Selene's death, had the circumstances in which she'd died, truly sent him into a spiral of self-loathing he couldn't pry himself out of? I felt the weight of it on my shoulders, because I didn't know how to help him. The more I down talked Daniel, the more Jasper would dig his heels in, the more he'd profess his love for him. Hurting Daniel would win me no points with Jasper. Not as long as he was intent on only seeing the bad in himself. Until that changed, he'd continue to believe himself worthy of what he was receiving, which was nothing.

He introduced Sofia, passed her the microphone and retook his seat and my pinky as he continued to drink the night away.

♦ ♦ ♦

Jasper wasn't ready to face Daniel, so we went back to my place. I dragged myself over to the piano, adjacent to the fireplace, and took a seat on the bench, loosening my bow tie as I gazed over my shoulder at him.

Jasper watched me from his drunken lean against the archway. I hadn't bothered with the light switch; the moon and city lights would have to do.

"Your Steinway," Jasper said with a slight slur. "I didn't notice it the last time I was here."

"Leland surprised me. Had it shipped here from Seattle." I had no intention of going through the trouble. I hadn't played it in years. Not since Jasper up and disappeared from my life, removing my source of inspiration. It had only served as a reminder of all we'd lost. A reminder of the times I'd made love to him on top of it or up against it. Times when our parents would jet away for a romantic weekend, leaving us to our own devices. We'd send the staff home and take our pleasure out in the open.

No hiding, no hands over mouths or teeth clamped around fists to catch our screams, to soften the blow of our mutual climax. I could still smell the phantom scent of my cum as it trickled from his snug hole onto the shiny black surface of the Baby Grand.

And now, to soothe the yearning in me, I smoothed a finger over the scratches he'd made with his nails, digging them in as I took a belt to him, or fucked him too long and too hard out of jealousy—his or mine, it didn't matter.

"Leland," Jasper sneered drunkenly with undisguised resentment. Sharper than the tempered version of the emotion he'd let slip over salted pretzels after the medical conference. My fingers faltered on the lowered fallboard. "What other services does he provide for you?"

I inhaled his jealousy, swam and danced around in it, letting it stroke my loneliness. It wouldn't cure it, though, and I needed more than a temporary fix. I needed him. "Leland isn't my type," I said, my back to him as I stared unseeingly into the night.

"Why not? He's handsome enough."

Leland was gorgeous, the son of a model, but he'd want to top me from the bottom, then slip from my bed and into the streets in search of round two. Two qualities that clashed with my need to dominate and possess. We'd be a match made in hell. "I like my men submissive with only the occasional flare of temper in bed for those moments when I'd rather take than be given. Because sometimes, I like to fight for what's mine."

Jasper's hitch of breath was the only sign he'd been affected by my declaration. He didn't come closer, he didn't move a muscle. Probably remembering the time he'd innocently accepted a ride home from Matthew—a high school classmate who'd been interested in him. It had ended with my knuckles bruised, Matthew scraping himself off our front lawn, and me tackling Jasper to the floor behind my locked bedroom door before conquering him. Our relationship had already progressed to something more than sexual by then. We were hungry for each other, our need unquenchable.

I raised the fallboard and stretched my fingers, wondering where to start, wondering if I still had it in me. I let love guide me. I let my love for *him* guide me.

My fingers floated over the keys self-consciously, but with every note I landed correctly, and with every click of Jasper's shoes announcing he was drawing near, I became more confident. More secure.

"Claude Debussy," he said, settling next to me on the bench, resting his head on my shoulder. "My favorite."

I played like the song didn't have an ending, restarting before the moment had a chance to slip away from us. I played through every uttered, "Again," that escaped his lips. I played until my fingers hurt, until the ebony and ivory keys were slicked with sweat, or blood, or tears. Until finally Jasper placed a hand over mine, until harsh panting and impending truths filled the air.

"He says I don't support him." His voice trembled. "And he's right."

I wanted to smash something with my bare hands. I wanted to force him to take those words back. But more importantly I wanted to listen, because he needed me to.

"He's right," he repeated, voice labored and soft with sadness. "He's got this great opportunity, and instead of supporting him, I secretly hope he fails. Because then I wouldn't be tied to you. I could walk away from you, again."

But he's the one who didn't support you! I wanted to bellow. *I told him he could go. I told him how important the fundraiser was to you. And he'd chosen himself when work could've waited until tomorrow.*

"You scare me," he said in a small voice, putting an end to my mental shouting. "The things you make me want to do to him scare me."

My brows nudged each other. "Like what?" I asked. What could I have possibly made him want to do to Daniel? *Leave him?* My lovesick heart supplied. *Cheat on him?* A more sinister part of me said. The part that knew he wouldn't leave Daniel, and that I'd do anything to have even a tiny piece of him.

"I love him," he said, and someone stabbing me in the gut would've hurt less. Would've angered me less. "Not like I loved..." He swallowed, and then settled on, "He's misunderstood. He wants to be a good man. He *is* a good man. He's good." He nodded. "He's better than me."

I pressed a kiss to the top of his head to keep from barking out the crude words clogging my throat. I breathed steadily, winding myself down. "No one's better than you, Jasper. No one."

His laugh was vicious, aimed inward. "You wouldn't say that if you knew—" He stopped himself.

I shifted us so we faced each other. His sluggish eyes spotlit by the moon's glow. I should've cut him off after the fifth drink, but he was in a mood, and I hadn't wanted to make a scene. "Knew what, Jasper?" *Did* he want to have an affair?

"I manipulated you to have you. From the very beginning. From the moment I met you all I could think about was what I could do to have you. Not in *that* way. Not at first. But I wanted you. Always in some way."

"I knew that, Jas. All your subtle and shy attempts at seducing me when we got older didn't go unnoticed. You weren't the clever little mouse you thought you were." I tapped my forehead to his.

He sliced one hand through my hair, and used the other to situate my palm at the base of his skull. I moaned, my forehead rolling against his. It'd been so long since we'd touched like this. "I hate it when your hands aren't on me. Always so hu–hungry. Starving for–for your touch, Cole." His words were disjointed, a mash of feelings brought on by too much alcohol digested in too short a time span, and by whatever sat here with us, eating him alive.

"Jasper," I rasped, "you're drunk." And he'd regret this come morning.

He hummed ambiguously. "How were things after I left?"

This was safer territory, although still heavy to discuss. "It was lonely," I said at last. "My father was a ghost. I'd had to learn the business quickly and eventually take over much of his day-to-day tasks."

"I ran and left you there with him. How did he treat you?" Jasper hadn't even stuck around for Selene's funeral. He couldn't even meet my father's stare. Other than Maggie, Selene's childhood friend, visiting whenever she could, it had been my father and Jasper taking care of Selene those months I was off finishing school. My father hadn't put up a fight when Jasper announced he was leaving. If anything, he seemed relieved. One less reminder. Me, on the other hand, he was stuck with.

Jasper's guilt took him away from us, mine kept me there. I couldn't abandon my father after killing his wife, even if he didn't know it. One of us had to stay behind, and I understood why it had to be me. Most days he found it hard to stomach me. It wasn't in what he said, or did. It was in all the things he didn't say. The times I'd catch him watching me, only to turn and leave without saying a word. I'd assumed Selene's death triggered recollections of his first lost love. My mother. I'd assumed it rekindled the memory of how she'd met her end. By giving me life.

I applied pressure to the back of Jasper's neck, while his fingers scraped across my scalp, and something close to a purr rumbled in his chest.

"I understood my father's feelings toward me. I had never resented him for it. Losing you is what crushed me, Jasper." I'd let him go. I'd given him what he'd begged for, because how could

I not? After what we'd done, how could I have expected him to stay with me? And I was looking for ways to punish myself, too. I'd killed my first and second chances at having a mother. What better way to pay penance than to sacrifice the one thing I loved most. Why did our love get to live when his mother, and my father's second chance at life, had died at our metaphorical hands?

"If only we'd waited." The memory of Jasper's words knocked around in my head. But he hadn't been able to wait. That night in particular he was uncharacteristically the aggressor. We hadn't been apart that long since he and Selene had moved in when we were boys. I understood his need because it matched my own.

"Did you lock the door?" I'd asked.

"Yes," he'd said between kisses, settling onto my erection with tear-streaked cheeks. But he hadn't.

"I'm sorry," Jasper said, jarring me from those old thoughts. He shuffled his body closer to mine, the warmth of his sorrow fanning over my mouth. "I'm sorry."

I couldn't say if he collided into me, or if it was the other way around, but something snapped in my head the moment our mouths fused. I hauled him to his feet with both hands wrapped around his throat, kicking the bench aside and wheeling him around so he sat flush on the piano's keys. The blare of crushed notes screamed in offense, battling with the sounds of our moans and the cold, harrowing wind rattling the balcony doors, searching for a way in to stop this madness.

I tore through his dress shirt, buttons assaulting the marble floor as I gripped his belt buckle and hefted his waist up until his cock connected with mine. We worked our hips in tandem, dicks hard and ravenous, threatening to do damage if unleashed.

Our kiss turned violent, painful, toxic, even, as one of us spilled blood. The smell and taste of vodka on his tongue pierced through the delicious coppery tang sliding down my throat, smacking a bit of sense into me. I wrenched my face away from him. "We can't." My voice sounded monstrous.

Jasper sent both legs around my middle, his toned ass pressing against the piano keys once more, the sound worked like a stiff wind, clearing the last of my haze. "I need you," he whimpered, bucking up into me.

"Not like this. I need you to make the choice with a clear head." I pried his digging fingers from around my neck. "Not like this." I was giving up my opportunity to have him, but in his current frame of mind, taking Jasper would only serve to prove I was a better lover than Daniel. It would do little to prove I was a better man than him.

Jasper sagged, breathing recklessly. He tilted forward, his forehead settling on my stomach, and I tore at the elastic holding his hair before spearing my hands through the thick curls that sprang up instantly. "Can I stay?" he asked. "I can't go home to him tonight."

He could stay, he could never leave. One word from him and I'd make it so he'd never have to lay his beautiful eyes on Daniel again. Whatever the cost may be. There was no price I wouldn't pay.

I helped him to his feet, catching his elbow when he veered to the side.

"It's so damn dark in here," he said accusingly.

I chuckled lifelessly. "Yeah, blame it on the darkness." I guided him onto the couch, helped him remove all but his boxer briefs, and watched as he instantly fell asleep. I kicked off my shoes but could do no more as I perched on the other end, feet planted on the cushion, a hand slung over my knee as I gazed into the starless night sky. Sleep wouldn't be in the cards for me.

Jasper reached blindly for me, and I crawled over, letting him cling to me like a magnet, his nose searching out the spot below my chin. I held him there, cradling him by a fistful of his minty hair.

"I'm going to be sick tomorrow," he murmured incoherently, gentle snores chasing the end of his statement.

"Don't worry," I whispered into his wispy curls. "I'll take care of you." *I would do anything for you.*

CHAPTER 8

JASPER PASSED THE bar exam, and we're at my parents' house celebrating. More like me rubbing it in their faces. They've never been accepting of our relationship, and certainly not our recent marriage, and they don't even try to hide it. Not even for Jasper's benefit.

But he's an attorney now, and that should make him respectable in their eyes. It should make me respectable in their eyes.

"Daniel," my father sighs from behind me, my mother surely by his side. I stare through the patio doors to where they left Jasper in the backyard alone, following me into the kitchen. I cut the sink water off, drying my hands on a dish towel before facing them. "He's going into *civil rights law?*" he asks incredulously. "He still wants to devote his time to *those* people?"

"*Those* people" meaning poor people. The marginalized, as Jasper calls them. I hoped he'd change his mind. I'd thought that all the subtle urging I did every opportunity I got would've worked by now. "He'll come around, Father. He's just starting out. Give him a little while to see great effort with little to no reward will come from his humble ambitions. It'll only be a matter of time before he comes running to me with arms open begging me to use my connections to elevate him."

My father folds his arms over his burly chest, deferring to my mother who brushes imaginary lint from the front of her Chanel sheath dress before raising her nose haughtily into the air. They were a pair. "Clifford's oldest, Maxwell, has completed his residency. All Clifford ever talks about is how his son is going to be the country's leading neurosurgeon one day. And Maxwell's fiancé runs a hedge fund. They'll be the power couple of the century," she mocks in Clifford's lofty, melodramatic tone. "You're thirty-two years old, Daniel. We expected you to be further along in life by now."

"Yes," my father cuts in.

"I graduated from the best schools, at the top of my class, and am arguably the best damn attorney at my firm, and yet it isn't enough."

"Your name should be on that plaque by now!" my father bellows with barely enough restraint to keep his outburst within these walls.

"We just want the best for you, Daniel," my mother says, laying a calming hand on my father's arm.

No, they want what's best for their reputation, and unfortunately, they'd passed that trait on to me at inception. I want what's best for me, for my social status, for my future, for the alliances I'll form, the powerful people I plan to be seated at the table with. I was behind, as my mother pointed out, constantly overlooked.

"You don't have to be what they want you to be, Daniel. You're good enough as you are."

I pinch my eyes shut on Jasper's voice filtering in through my cracks. "I know, Mother."

I gaze at Jasper who sits studying the eclipsed moon with fascination. I'll never understand why it takes so little to please him. Why he lacks imagination. My parents are right, I think, standing straighter, toughening my spine, sealing all the cracks.

"Don't worry," I say into the room. "I know what I'm doing."

CHAPTER 9

Jasper

"MY HEAD IS killing me," I complained, my bare feet slapping against the floor as I joined Cole in the kitchen. He pushed a steaming mug of coffee and a bottle of pain pills my way, but otherwise remained silent, drinking from his own ceramic cup. His beard, which he usually wore close to the skin, had grown exponentially since yesterday. Heavy bags dragged below his eyes, and he still wore his clothes from last night. "Did you sleep at all?"

"Not a wink," he said. "How much do you remember from last night?"

"Snippets. And thinking hard about it hurts," I said. Cole set his mug down, hugging it between his palms. "I remember Daniel not showing up for me, but you did." I'd sent Daniel's call to voicemail a little while ago, still not ready to deal with him. "I don't remember how my shirt lost its buttons." Vague flashes of a piano and a passionate kiss assaulted me, clearing that mystery up. I cut the memory off, compartmentalizing the guilt it summoned. My body didn't bear any of the love wounds Cole liked to leave as souvenirs, and it didn't feel used, so I knew things hadn't gone further than a kiss. Cole wouldn't have taken advantage of me in the state I must have been in, anyway.

I gazed at the t-shirt and sweats I now wore. They had been waiting on the bed for me when I got out of the shower. Cole and

I were close enough in height, but he was broader, bulkier, so the clothes hung off my frame a bit. "I'll get these back to you."

"Keep them," he said.

Asking him why he couldn't sleep might have been the polite thing to do, but ignoring the elephant seemed to be the pain-free option. I chose pain-free over polite. "'Fia called. She said the remaining tickets were sold last minute. We had a full house, and some of the donors were ridiculously generous. She reached her goal. You wouldn't happen to know anything about that, would you?"

"No," he said, blowing into his coffee, reminding me about my own.

"Thank you," I said sincerely. He nodded, and we drank and thought in comfortable silence. "So what are we doing today?" I asked, surprising him. "It's Sunday. I don't have plans, and I don't want to go home yet." *And I don't want to leave you, yet.* "Thought maybe I could be your tour guide for the day." I kept my tone light, cheery, even. An easy breezy invitation he could take or leave.

"I'd like that," he replied.

While Cole showered, I dug through his walk-in closet for a pair of jeans to wear. He strode in, a towel drying his hair and one tucked around his hips. "You don't own a pair of jeans?" I asked, patting myself on the back for containing my drool. A light dusting of silky hair coated his forearms and rock-hard abs, vanishing beneath the terry cloth dangerously close to hitting the carpet. I hadn't been blessed in the body hair department. The blond peach fuzz licking up my calves and the slim trail of it below my navel were too fine to see with the naked eye.

"I spent the last six years of my life preparing for meetings, attending meetings, and leaving meetings. Denim didn't fit into my schedule. Besides, I've been told I look sexy in suits." The full force of his cocky grin came out to play. I had once told him he looked sexy in suits. Nothing had changed.

My eyes widened on his. "So does this mean you only have dress shoes?"

"Yes." He laughed, his eyes and mood lighter than a mere hour before. "Aside from my sweaty running shoes. You'll have to walk the streets in a suit and wingtips today."

"Don't joke like that," I said horrified, to which his laugh turned fuller, darker. He went into the bedroom and came back with his phone.

"I'll have something brought up for you from one of the shops downstairs."

"*Us,*" I said. "Have something casual brought up for us both to wear."

I thought he'd argue with me, but he gave an indulgent grin instead and made the call.

Thanks to the hotel staff's efficiency, we were dressed and out the door in no time. Cole wore a slim-fitting heather gray sweat suit with designer sneakers, the hood untucked and draped over the neck of his navy pea coat. He looked like he'd hopped out of a fashion billboard. I wore my usual uniform of jeans and a t-shirt.

I took it upon myself to give Mark, who'd waited out front, the rest of the day off. "You and I are riding the subway today," I said.

He breathed in the cold November air, and with a smile full of white teeth, he said, "You lead, and I'll follow."

We did the cheesy touristy stuff like take in the breathtaking views of the city from the Empire State Building observatory deck, then ran to catch the departing, red Big Bus Tour out front. We rode the open-roofed second level of the double decker, because you haven't lived until the frigid bite of fall cuts into your cheeks at a mind-bending speed of twenty-five miles per hour. Even less when caught in a cramped pocket of midtown traffic.

We ended that part of our day eating hot dogs topped with sauerkraut and mustard while taking on the Herald Square crowd. Cole was astonished by the sheer amount of people overwhelming the sidewalks. I pointed toward the windows of Macy's department store. "You should see how many people show up when they unveil their Christmas display. It's done right before Thanksgiving. I hear this year's theme is going to be A Charlie Brown Christmas," I said with a mischievous grin. Part of the excitement was actually not knowing what the display would be until the unveiling, but teasing Cole with a not so fond memory for him was fun.

He groaned, no doubt remembering the times I'd watched *A Charlie Brown Christmas* on repeat with the volume on high just to piss him off. Cole had always been a grouch around the holidays, and I'd made it my mission to change that, even if I'd nearly lost a limb in the process.

"Are you thinking about—"

"Yes, I am," he said. "You were so damn irritating."

"And you were so mean," I shouted to be heard over the saxophone player performing for tips a short distance from us.

Cole swallowed his last bite of hot dog, and I swiped a glob of mustard from the corner of his mouth, licking it off my finger without thinking, sending us into a freeze-frame not even the two squealing kids pushing between us could interrupt.

Cole snapped out of it first, wiping his mouth with a balled-up napkin. "I'm still mean," he said, keeping the conversation rolling.

"You're such a pretender." It was meant as a joke, but ended up hitting too close to home, because the award for pretending went to me.

"Where to next?" he asked.

"Now we visit the city's hidden treasure. Do you have room for some of the best Dim Sum you've ever had?" I could've sworn I heard his stomach say yes. "Come on." I caught his hand, steering us out of the fray to walk the dozen or so blocks to Dim Sum Palace.

The street was fairly residential, the restaurant itself sat below a three-story apartment building, and the inside wasn't much to write home about. I knew the owners, though, and had considered it my lunch sanctuary ever since stumbling in there for directions my first week in New York. I hadn't brought anyone there before. It was my something-for-me, but I couldn't wait to share it with Cole.

We were in luck, my usual table by the window was available, so we showed ourselves over with a nod from Mr. Yan.

Cole rubbed his cold palms together to generate warmth while I shrugged my coat over my shoulders. Without thought, and as natural as it had once been, I covered his hands with mine, providing added friction. "You were always more warm-blooded than me," he said.

"That was a lie I told so you'd let me into your bed at night," I confessed. Franklin hated the heat, and for him, anything above freezing was a degree too hot. We'd survive below mountains of quilts and roaring fireplaces at night. During the day, we took advantage of his absence by turning the house into a tropical oasis with the heat set to maximum combustion. Mom would join in on the action, too.

"You think I didn't know that?" Cole snorted, picking up his menu. "I'd end up being the one keeping your lanky limbs warm."

My phone vibrated on the table with a text from Daniel. I powered it down and shoved it into my pocket. Cole's cell phone chimed next, and at the shake of my head, he turned it off, too.

He relaxed in his seat, drumming his fingers on the table as he worked out what to say on the topic. "Don't you at least want to let him know you're alive? You're going to have to face him eventually."

"I sent him a text earlier saying I was with you. The rest will have to wait."

"Alright," he said, "but I get the feeling the silent treatment is more about punishing yourself than Daniel."

"What makes you say that?" I asked. Cole waited until the server had filled our kanto mugs with hot tea before continuing.

"You were always harder on yourself than other people. You make a mistake and you can't seem to let it go, but you'd brush aside my wrongdoings with such grace." He folded himself in closer. "You remember the kiss last night and you feel bad about it, don't you? Is that why you're avoiding him?"

In all honesty, I didn't feel bad. Maybe because I hadn't truly faced the kiss yet. That would change once I forgave Daniel. Once I forgave him, I would then be the one needing to be forgiven. Letting go, forgiving him, would have to wait. I wanted to feel good just a little longer. "He could've shown up just this once. I mean, he could've even called."

"I can't argue with that," Cole agreed. "But if he had shown up, I wouldn't have, and I don't regret a thing about last night." His gaze turned predatory, and my insides clenched around a knot of hunger having nothing to do with needing to be fed, at least not with actual food.

Our waiter returned to take our order, buying me precious minutes needed to divert my thoughts away from the images coming back to me from last night. Of the darkness, both his and the night sky. Of his rough handling of me, and the way my heart had skipped a beat because of it. Of the admissions I'd made, *and the one I hadn't.*

"Do you remember that time Dylan came over to study with me?" Cole asked once we were alone again, forearms pressing into the table. "And you'd come up with every excuse to barge into my room and interrupt us?"

"Yeah, because the only studying happening in that room was the study of your tonsils."

Cole shook with laughter. "You were such a brat about it. Popping your head in to remind me my company had to leave before dinner. And showing up every fifteen minutes after that to let us know how much time we had left."

"And when you locked your door, I climbed the tree outside your window and knocked on the glass so hard it webbed." I must have been twelve, and it was the first friend he'd ever brought home. I hated it from the start, because until Cole had started high school, all we'd needed was each other. Our two-year age gap didn't matter. And when Dylan came over, it felt like Cole had forgotten about me. Catching them kissing through the window had raised the stakes. I'd been equal parts angry, sad, and murderous. I'd thought the fire roaring in my gut, and the tears budding behind my eyes came from believing Dylan was taking my brother—and my best friend from me. In reality, it had been so much more than that. *So* much more. It had taken a while longer to understand that, though.

"He never showed up again after that," Cole said.

"Yeah, I'd scared him off," I replied, feeling the same measure of accomplishment I'd felt back then.

"No," he said solemnly. "He'd called you weird, and I told him no one was allowed to speak about you like that."

I smoothed an invisible wrinkle out of the tablecloth. "Well, if it's a battle of the crazies you want, how about the night you stormed in and cut the phone line in my room with a razor blade because I'd made another friend." I was fourteen, a freshman in high school by then, and scared of my ever-shifting and intensifying feelings for Cole. Figured I needed some other friends. Jeremy was cool, too. We'd shared a lot of the same interests.

"I was jealous," he said, stating the obvious, like his jealousy was the good answer for everything. It normally was with us. I'd purposely keep Jeremy on the phone late, laughing loud enough to be heard from Cole's bedroom next door.

Jeremy was a victim of my obsession with Cole. And maybe Dylan was a victim of Cole's obsession with me, but neither of us understood that at the time. We were just boys, then young men, trying to hang on to what we had for dear life, even while what we had was changing.

My mother could be added to the list of casualties. And Franklin. And maybe Daniel, too.

I peered at Cole from beneath my lashes, careful not to let the neighboring tables overhear. "You were my first, but I wasn't yours." I could tell by the way he'd moved inside me once he'd finally given in. So sure, so confident. Joy and rage had made a potent cocktail in my veins as he'd taken his time with me in bed. "I'd racked my brain trying to figure out where you even found the time to be with someone else like that, because we did everything together. The free period you had after biology? Boys' locker room? The private, wheelchair accessible bathroom next to Mrs. Delaney's classroom?"

"All of the above," he said, which of course I'd eventually found out. Needing to know had driven me insane. I didn't speak to him for days after that. Not until he'd told me who, when, and where, and swore to me it was over, and that from then on it would only ever be me.

"We were more than brothers. More than best friends," he whispered. "And then something changed, and not just for you. Our hugs were different. Holding you stirred a different response in me. The difference between us was that I didn't want to go there with you. I wanted to get those feelings for you out of my system, but you were a flame ready to burn everything down. Not only did I not want to fuck up what we had, I didn't want to ruin our family, because if Mom..." He licked his lips. "If *Selene* and my father had found out, it would've ruined everything."

"You can keep calling her Mom, you know," I said for the second time since his return. "It's okay."

"Took me two years of therapy to realize calling her Mom only amplified my self-hate. Now," he shrugged. "I'm used to the shift. I don't want to imagine what going back would do."

The acidic burn of guilt scorched my tongue. I wished I'd been there for him. Wished he hadn't needed the therapy *I* so desperately needed but refused to seek out, because I didn't deserve relief. The pain for what I'd done would forever remain front and center, as it should. But I should've suffered in this alone. Not him. Never him. "I'm glad you're better."

"What about you, Jas?"

Our food arrived. *Saved again.* I dug in, faking starvation. Cole speared his chopsticks and did the same.

It wasn't until my stomach was too full to move that I struck up conversation again. "So, you uprooted your company for a city you'd never been to," I said, pushing my empty steamer bowl aside.

"I've been here before," he said after a brief pause, kicking the wind out of me. He'd been here before? We'd been in the same city, and he hadn't looked for me? My mind knew it'd been for the best, but my heart refused to get with the damn program.

"Oh," I said, unable to contain the weird sense of betrayal I felt. "So today," I made a circling motion with my finger in the air to encompass what we'd been doing. "The awed tourist performance. Was it all for my benefit?"

"No. I'd flown in twice for business meetings. In and out the same day. I didn't allow myself to linger," he said significantly. "I'd been considering it for a while. And yes, it had a lot to do with you, but not everything. Took a couple years to get Nexcom's affairs in order for the move." He dropped his napkin on the table. "Let's get out of here."

We paid the bill and bundled ourselves up, the sun had vanished, taking about ten degrees with it, so we kept our heads low, collars up, and hustled the few blocks to the train where a panhandler held the station door open for us. Cole dropped a large bill into his outstretched cup.

It smelled of urine and steam, and I'd had to save Cole from leaping into the tracks when a furry rodent scurried along the platform. "We could be in the back of a warm, roomy SUV right now," he complained over the sound of steel raking steel as our train approached, but I spotted the upward tug of his lips as we boarded the front car and snagged a double-seater in the corner. He was enjoying himself.

We got back to Cole's place and made it as far as the darkness of his living room before he pulled me to him for a hug. It was natural for us. Not touching meant not breathing when we were alone. Brothers, friends, lovers... It didn't matter. We'd always been affectionate. We'd always needed it. We could be the same without being the same, couldn't we?

Even as I posed the question to myself, I stepped in impossibly closer, my hands gliding up his spine from where I'd slipped them under his coat. His breath against my neck came at a faster and faster clip, and I inhaled with my nose pressed against the spot beneath his ear.

"Would you ever leav—?"

I pulled away, bringing an abrupt end to his unfinished question. The lines tightening his mouth said the action hurt or angered him. Probably both.

"I love him. He's not perfect, but neither am I," I said to him, and then to myself I gave the whole truth. *Because I'm scared to leave him, because if I did, there would still be things holding me back from you. Things I don't want to deal with, like forgiving myself. It would eat away at us, and then you'd leave me, and I'd have nothing while alone. With Daniel, I get to have nothing with someone.* How was I able to look at myself in the mirror?

"Then why are you here with me, right now?"

Because I'm in love with you, I wanted to scream. *Because I'm selfish, and I can't stop doing evil things no matter who they hurt. Because I just want to go back, I want to take it all back. Make my wrong right again. But I can't, because the only other person I'd ever loved more than I love you is gone. Gone because of me.*

"Because I want you…" I said instead of all that, and then tacked on like a coward, "in my life." I didn't want to say *it*. The thing we both understood right then. I didn't want to admit why my hands were suddenly roaming up his chest. I didn't want to later have to face the choice I was making. I wanted deniability. Even from myself. "Aren't you the one who came looking for me?"

He hummed in the back of his throat, retreating further into the room, leaving my hands to fall and dangle at my side. "It wasn't too long ago you wanted me on the next flight out of here."

"Where's this coming from?" I crossed my arms defensively.

"The truth is, I want you, and there isn't anything I'm above doing to have you. But I don't want to risk losing you completely once you wake up and decide to use whatever happens between us as a weapon to push me away, again. I don't want you pretending you didn't make a clear choice tonight. I…" He let the vowel hang until it was gone.

"Say it. What are you thinking?" I asked.

He removed a hand from his pocket to ruffle his hair, filling his cheeks with air before releasing it into the quiet. Returning his hand to his pocket, he said, "I'm thinking you should talk to

Daniel. I'm thinking you may not be drunk tonight, but you're still operating from an unclear head because you're upset with him. I think you need to be *damn* sure about this, because I won't turn you down a third time."

He needed me to be sure. He needed to know I wouldn't use this to hate him. And because I wasn't sure of anything right then, I said goodnight, then backed up and turned to leave. I peeked over my shoulder before getting on the elevator. Cole had perched on the arm of the sofa with his head in his hands.

Had I really been considering an affair? Would I have gone through with it if Cole hadn't just stopped me—again. What would that even look like? Cole would never be able to share me, and would that leave the door open for him to do as he pleased with whomever while I watched paralyzed, unable to do anything about it? Did I really want to damn us all to hell? Would it be worth it? Would the lies we'd have to tell, and attempting to fight against our possessive nature be worth it?

We were crazy to consider it. And I was the crazier of us two. I needed to leave Daniel, do things the right way for once in my life. But then the cold claws of fear tapped at the mounds of my shoulder, reminding me this couldn't end with my happiness. I could accept a temporary form of happiness, but I'd forfeited my right to anything more.

This could end badly. *Would* end badly. *No, I could handle it,* I thought anxiously. *I could do this, and Daniel would never need to know.*

But what if it didn't work out that way? What if I ended up scorching everything around me because I couldn't let sleeping dogs lie? Because I couldn't get over Cole.

Would. It. Be. Worth it?

The doors eased shut, caging me in with my rambling conscience. The tiny voice whispered up the line from my heart and into my skull. *Yes,* it said. Having him in some way would be worth everything.

CHAPTER 10

Jasper

ENDING THE NIGHT in the ER, being treated for hypothermia, wasn't my idea of a good time, so after stalling for a few hours on a cold park bench, I went home to face the music.

Tiptoeing through the silent apartment, I was relieved to find Daniel in our bed, fast asleep. I sailed my hands through my hair, backing away just as quietly, beyond grateful for the reprieve from our confrontation.

The relief was short-lived, but at least when he found me an hour or so later in the darkness of our home library, I was already a quarter bottle deep into my scotch and could barely feel anything. As it turned out, barely wasn't good enough.

I stood at the window, staring into the bottom of my glass, feeling his eyes scrape along the rear of me. "Are you going to say something?" I asked, raising my gaze to his reflection. Daniel leaned against the doorframe, backlit by whatever faraway light he'd switched on during his hunt for me.

"When did you get home?" he asked, voice bogged down by sleep, expression blank.

I didn't answer. It was one of those preliminary questions you asked before getting to the good stuff. The fight icebreaker. It didn't matter in the grand scheme of things. "I couldn't make it. I tried—"

"Did you?" I interrupted coolly, finishing my drink and setting the tumbler on the rolling ladder rung next to me.

"It's about me right now, Jasper—"

"When has it ever not been about you, Daniel?"

"You mean in between all the time I spend on you? On wanting better for you? On doing everything in my power to put a smile on your face? Because let's face it, trying to make you happy is a full-time job," he snapped, and there I went, doubting myself, doubting my right to be disappointed, upset. "And your brother was there with you. It's not like you were alone," he said softly.

"You don't get it, do you?" I whispered dejectedly, counting the rows of holiday motif lights strung from light post to light post along the street. "You *promised* me." Through the window I caught sight of him throwing his hands up and marching over to the corner table with the tidy stack of law books for a coaster.

"Did you ask him to take your place? Did you think about me enough to make the conscious decision to ask him to be there for me?"

"No. My firm is contracted to Nexcom at the moment. Tenuously so. I'm not going to ask him for favors. Certainly not personal ones," he said, coming to place the coaster under my empty glass, scowling at the circle of condensation already soaking into the wooden rung. "But I hoped he would," he said. "Would that be so bad? At least it means I was thinking about you, and what my no-show would do to you. Can I get some credit here?" He waited expectantly. "I'm going back to bed. I've got an early start tomorrow."

"No. It's not so bad." I had to meet him halfway.

"I'm close, Jasper," he said, snatching the lifeline I'd just cast him. "Hopefully in the next week or two I'll have made Nexcom infinitely richer, and that much closer to achieving their goals. Life can go back to normal between us. Or as close to normal as a newly minted partner life can be."

"So it's really going to happen?"

"Mm-hm. They promised. All I have to do is deliver on this. Then we sign something more binding with Nexcom, and the thanks will be to me." He smiled sleepily.

"That's great, Daniel. I'm happy for you." I embraced him. Daniel wanting to make partner had been the one constant since the day I met him. He could've left Parker & Mitchell, although they were highly prestigious. Daniel had the resources to start something on his own if he wanted to, but for some reason he needed this validation. Needed *their* validation. He had a point to prove.

I may not have been thrilled about this new work arrangement, but I'd always supported his goals, contrary to how he made it seem. "We should celebrate now."

"How much have you had to drink? It's two in the morning, Jasper," he said, amused.

"Well not *now*. I just mean it's a sure thing. I believe in you. We don't need to wait for the ink to dry on the dotted line to celebrate." My mood turned contagious, and excitement split across his face.

"Well, I have a big break in the afternoon tomorrow. We could grab lunch at Rinaldo's."

"Tomorrow..." I trailed off, working through my own work schedule. "I have closing arguments on the Board of Education case tomorrow. You should come, sit in the gallery and watch with some of my students. You've never seen me in action. We can grab lunch right after." My grin matched his now. We were fine. *We are fine.*

Suddenly his smile dried up, causing everything inside me to ache. "Let's see how things pan out tomorrow. You never know what might pop up last minute. I don't want to break any more promises." Sounded reasonable enough, but his excitement was gone, leaving behind this awkward discomfort.

"Yeah, sure. Okay." I nodded.

"I ordered in. I wasn't sure if you were coming home, so I put it away."

"Thanks. I'm not hungry, though. I'll come up in a minute."

He yawned and disappeared out the door. I refilled my glass, flicking the coaster rebelliously, watching it bounce off the ladder rungs until it splattered onto the floor. I kind of empathized with it.

I resumed the mindless job of counting the lights again, of telling myself it would be okay, again. Of thinking about Cole. Again.

♦ ♦ ♦

Closing arguments were in and court was adjourned for deliberation. Sofia and I reassured Tyson and his grandmother things couldn't have gone better. "With any luck, we'll have a decision soon, but I wouldn't worry," I said, placing my hand over her nervous ones.

We sat huddled at the defense table as the courtroom emptied. I checked behind me to confirm Lorenzo and Mrs. Baker were still seated in the gallery, and to see if Daniel ended up making it. I didn't expect to see Cole sitting there giving me the thumbs-up. I offered him a half-hearted smile before returning my attention to my clients.

"Thank you so much for all you've done, Mr. Des Moines. And you too, Mrs. Rivera," Mrs. Wallace said.

"No need to thank us," Sofia assured her. "Tyson had every right to attend that school, and by the time we're done here, you'll be able to afford to send him anywhere. His siblings, too."

"Tell the nice people thank you," Mrs. Wallace said to Tyson who sat shyly next to her.

"Thank you," he said shyly.

I excused myself, leaving Sofia to answer any remaining questions. I held a finger up to Mrs. Baker and Lorenzo, asking them for one minute as I pushed through the short swinging door and strode for the back of the gallery. "What are you doing here?" I said to Cole, my tone light. "Do I need to file a restraining order?"

He stood, buttoning his blazer and checking the room around us before lowering his voice. "I got all the juicy details on your schedule, remember? And only if that order means I get to restrain you." He winked playfully. "You were brilliant in there," he exclaimed.

"Shhh. We're in court." I chuckled quietly, relieved by the absence of tension after how we'd left things last night.

"Court's no longer in session. The judge said so himself," he said adorably, which was a rare feat for Cole. On the spectrum of adorable and dangerously handsome, the pendulum tended to swing toward danger.

Lorenzo and Mrs. Baker came up from behind, thanking me for the invite and congratulating me on a job well done. We said our goodbyes, and they left as I turned my focus back on Cole.

"God, you were made for this, Jas. You had the jury eating out of the palm of your hands. And I like your hair," he said randomly. I wore it blown straight and tied back when in court. It helped with being taken seriously. "Tell me I can take you to lunch?"

"Lunch... Um," I checked my phone. No texts or missed calls from Daniel. I looked to Sofia, who was now walking our way with Tyson and Mrs. Wallace. I said my goodbyes to them, and then it was just the three of us.

"Did I hear lunch?" Sofia blurted before side-hugging Cole. "Please tell me I heard the word lunch. And yes, I will be third-wheeling it. My stomach is eating my spine at this point."

As far as Sofia knew, Cole and I were merely estranged stepbrothers. I still hadn't gotten around to spelling everything out to her and begging for her forgiveness.

"You heard right," Cole said. "My treat."

"I don't understand why this idiot's been hiding you," she deadpanned. Cole barked a laugh and held open the door for her.

We ended up at the deli across the street because Sofia was short on time. She used her sharp, courtroom skills to get all the familial details from Cole. How old we were when our parents married. How long it took for him to warm up to me. How I was as a child, and then as a teen. What kind of son I was, what kind of father was Franklin...I sat playing with my food as Cole maintained his cool under her pressure. He'd provided the truth, equipped with enough endearment and personal information to satisfy my best friend's appetite, without going *there*.

"Why didn't your dad ever adopt him?" she asked Cole. "And why didn't your mom adopt him?" she asked me next. "Seems like the logical thing to do. You'd technically still be brothers if they had."

"The subject came up once, but Cole wasn't ready," I said, without going into details about the tantrum Cole had thrown when he thought Franklin and my mom wanted to totally erase his birth mother. I also didn't mention the second time the topic came up. We were teens and lovers by then, and neither one of us were excited about adding another hurdle in our way. We'd told them we didn't need a piece of paper to know they were our parents, but that we'd let them know if that ever changed. They didn't push back.

"Well, one thing's for sure. In all the years I've known him, I've never seen him as content as when you're around. I love seeing him happy," she said, her eyes misting.

"'Fia," I whispered, tucking her hair behind her ear. "You're such a marshmallow." That was our inside joke. She was tough as nails, but sentimental as heck and could cry at the drop of a hat.

"Now tell me more," she said, and Cole launched into the story about his study buddy Dylan and his cracked bedroom window. He weaved it so I came off as the sweet younger brother who didn't want to share his sibling, which I had even believed at the time.

I wasn't sure how that segued into him speaking about my mother and what she'd meant to him, but Sofia had a way of disarming whomever she came in contact with. For a moment, I forgot about her existence, reaching over to sink my fingers into his hair and bring our foreheads together. All I could think about was consoling him, of making his sadness go away. We both seemed to remember her presence at the same time. We separated, clearing our throats.

We went through the motions of finishing our food, but I couldn't taste a thing. All my energy went into resisting the urge to look over at Sofia, whose stare hadn't moved from the right side of my face. Cole's phone rang as the waiter came by and asked if we needed anything else. "Just the check," he said, answering the call and excusing himself from the table.

"Well," she started, staring at me pointedly, "I think we're long overdue for a pal's night, wouldn't you say? Let's make that happen real soon."

"Yeah," I sighed.

"Okay. I'm going to be late for my meeting if I don't get out of here now." She shrugged into her ankle-length puffer coat, wrapping her scarf around her neck, and tugging on her gloves.

"Are you warm enough?" I asked.

"Make fun of me now," she said, "but there's a cold front coming, and they're even predicting snow."

"I'm pretty positive they said we'd *possibly* see flurries." It was still too early for snow. Then again, the summer had felt brief, and so far, the fall was colder than usual.

"Well, I had the boys salt the steps just in case. These meteorologists are all quacks." All zipped and buttoned up, she eyed me with concern. "Love you." She pinched, then patted my cheeks before dashing for the deli door, waving bye to Cole as she went.

"How much trouble are you in with her?" he asked, retaking his seat.

"Depends."

"On what?"

"On our next move," I said gravely. Sofia didn't ride-or-die blindly for anyone. She was a "right is right and wrong is wrong but I love you anyway" kind of friend. She wouldn't lie or cover for me in any way, shape, or form, but it was her respect I feared losing the most.

♦ ♦ ♦

Daniel ended up leaving on another impromptu business trip. I'd won my case, which freed me up, and Cole shifted things around on his schedule so we could enjoy quality time together. We were inseparable. And not in the clichéd sense, meaning we did everything together during those four days, but more in the Siamese twins way. We hugged even when the moment didn't call for it, like when I left his dinner table for the bathroom and ended up swallowed up in his arms instead.

"Sorry. I just miss you already," he'd said.

Or during our ridiculous snowball fight on his oversized balcony—because Sofia had been right, temperatures dropped drastically, and we did get a few inches of snow. We wouldn't release each other's hands so we could run for cover, so we just ended up pounding one-handed misshapen snowballs into each other's faces from an arm's length away.

"Let go of me, idiot," I'd laughed, blowing snowball tendrils out of my nostrils.

"You let go first," he'd demanded, coughing as I caught him right in the mouth.

We behaved like three-year-olds, but we didn't cross *the* line. And that's what mattered, right? I asked myself before falling asleep across his chest every night. We were brothers, and brothers could act this way. It could mean nothing if we didn't want it to.

We never spoke again about our kiss, or a possible affair, or me leaving Daniel. We just lived each moment a second at a time, regaining something pivotal, something I never wanted to lose again, something I was also terrified of re-obtaining.

I moaned in the dark. "What keeps ringing?" I asked, my words muffled by Cole's neck.

"Ignore it," he whispered. It was hot. I was sweaty, my throat dry, and I couldn't remember where we'd fallen asleep—or where *I'd* fallen asleep because Cole sounded wide awake. The ringing started up again, and this time I registered it as my phone.

"What time is it?" I asked, twisting my head away and blinking my eyes, trying to adjust to the darkness in the room. We were on the couch, Cole on his back, one leg thrown over the back of the sofa, and I sprawled over his chest. I vaguely remembered Chinese and gin shots again.

"It's four in the morning." He stroked my hair. Who would be calling me at that hour? *Daniel.* "Ignore it," he said again when I tried to push off of him.

"It might be important, Cole." True worry took over.

"What if I told you it's not?" he said, and between the phone ringing, the brain fog from the alcohol, the disorientation from the darkness, and his ominous tone, I began to get agitated.

"What aren't you telling me, Cole?"

He sighed, his own phone clutched in his other hand. "Daniel and the team made the deal. The contracts are signed. I'm sure he didn't stop to consider the time difference before calling you. He'll be home tomorrow. He knows you're safe and with me, so just ignore it."

"I... Okay." I didn't know what difference this made for us in the grand scheme of things, but Cole's behavior made it seem as if this would be our last night together. He stripped me out of my damp shirt, then pressed my face to the lump at his throat again.

"Sleep," he said, rolling us to our sides and locking his legs around me.

◆ ◆ ◆

Cole's mood wasn't any better by sun-up, and his stress-beard was in need of a serious shave. I finished packing the few items I had littered about, and buttoned into one of Cole's shirts since mine were all dirty. "Leave it all here," Cole said, stepping into the closet. "I'll have it dry-cleaned."

"It's okay—"

"Leave it," he said sharply, snatching the overnight bag off the island and placing it in a corner. We watched each other from opposite ends of the closet until neither of us could take it anymore and had made the silent decision to get closer. "I'm sorry," he said, hugging me. "I just need to know you'll be back."

"Are you ready to tell me why Daniel making this deal happen is a bad thing for you? I thought it was what you wanted."

"It is," he said, leading me by the hand to the kitchen where coffee waited. I settled onto a counter stool, and he took the one next to me, swiveling so we faced each other, our legs touching. I blew an impatient breath over the top of my coffee before taking a sip.

"Damn that's good," I said.

"Heavy on the cream," he said in a way that made my body tingle all over.

"Yeah. There's no such thing as too much cream," I tossed back before thinking. It was what we used to playfully say to each other over coffee years ago. He was then supposed to say, *"Is that a challenge?"* But he didn't, because we weren't those young college guys anymore, and because the privilege was no longer his. "Daniel and I use condoms," I blurted out, because I couldn't stand the loneliness wafting off him, or the obvious jealousy he was trying to hide. Brothers and friends spoke about these sorts of things, I told myself. "He's peculiar."

"Why am I not surprised," he said, in a relieved sort of way. We'd both gotten halfway through our coffee before he spoke again. "I shouldn't be telling you this. Daniel wanted it to be a surprise—"

"Tell me anyway. I'd rather not be surprised than to see you like this, Cole."

"Daniel wants to whisk you away for a few days. Sounded like he wants to get your marriage back on track."

"Oh. I mean, that's a good thing, right?"

"Yeah," he chuckled darkly, shoving off his stool and exiting the kitchen. "It's the fucking best, baby brother."

CHAPTER 11

Cole

LELAND SHOT HIS arm out to keep the elevator from closing on me. "Are you coming or what?" he asked, forehead creased in concern.

"Ah, yeah," I said, getting off on our floor, nodding to the receptionist before bearing left. We were approaching Daniel's open office door, and I was surprised to find him studiously working. Not only did I expect him to still be on vacation, but he'd successfully delivered on his promise to us and was no longer shackled to our offices. His name would be added to the gold plaque over at Parker & Mitchell's headquarters, and they'd send us a group of reputable replacements now that we'd be moving full steam ahead with their firm.

Daniel would have the option to stay on as our lead legal representative, if he wanted to. He'd earned the right to decide.

He was probably here tying up loose ends. Whatever it was had him so absorbed he hadn't noticed our advancement. Not even with Leland obnoxiously yapping away next to me.

"That's it," Leland said, fed up with my sour mood. "We're going out tonight. I hear Club Bale offers the best there is in the city."

I didn't bother asking the best of what. There was little I cared about these days.

Pushing through my office doors, I unwound my scarf, hanging it and my coat on the standing rack as Leland did the same. "Why doesn't he have a tan?" I asked.

"What?" Leland stared at me like I'd grown an extra head. I'd gotten accustomed to the expression over the past few days. Ever since Jasper left for his tropical getaway with Daniel.

"Daniel," I said, short on patience. "He spent the weekend on the beach, he should be tanned, or preferably burnt to ash."

"I don't know." Leland shrugged a shoulder and moved to the loveseat in the lounge area of my office, removing his laptop from his bag and setting it on the short table in front of him. "Mind if I work from here today?" he asked. In other words, did I mind if he kept an eye on me.

His sudden nonchalant demeanor on the matter of Daniel didn't fool me. Leland loved a grand conspiracy theory, and gossiping was his main hobby—only trumped by fucking. Any other time he'd jump at the opportunity to play detective.

"If you had to guess," I said, settling across from him and slamming his laptop closed to get his attention, "why do you think he doesn't have a tan?" Maybe things didn't go so well on their trip? Maybe they never made it? Maybe Daniel spent the whole trip locked inside their suite working?

"*Or,*" Leland interjected, letting me know I hadn't been speaking inside my head after all, "maybe he spent the whole trip locked in his suite fucking his husband."

I exploded to my feet, and if my steps could have burned a trail to my desk they would have. My chair creaked as I fell onto it. I flipped open my notes for an upcoming meeting without another word.

"I don't like what he's doing to you," Leland whispered.

"He isn't doing anything to me. I knew the deal before I got here. I'm the one with the problem." I didn't want him disliking

Jasper. They were both important to me, and I didn't need Leland working against us.

"You want an affair with him." He raised a palm to halt my argument. "Yes, I know you want more, but you're not going to get it, so you'll take anything. Even an affair you know you can't handle."

"I want him happy more than anything."

"It's time you stopped lying to yourself," Leland said. "You want him to choose you, but for whatever reason he won't, or he won't *yet*. I know what it feels like to want something over nothing, Cole, but have you considered what seeing him leave your bed to return home to his husband will do to you?"

I'm already living it.

"We're going out tonight. End of discussion," he said, re-opening his laptop.

"Something feels off," I said.

"Getting laid will fix that right up."

"I'm serious, Leland," I said, exasperated.

"It's all in your head, Cole. It's also ego driven. You want what you can't have, so something must be wrong with everyone else."

"Does your shady uncle still do private investigative work on the side?" I asked, not allowing his spot-on assessment to deter me.

"Uncle No one? Yeah, the fucker still owes me money, too. Why?"

"I have a job for him."

"So, you're going to have your stepbrother's husband looked into?"

"He's technically not my stepbrother anymore."

"*That's* the part you choose to address?" he asked. "Jasper may seem tame, but I remember the glare of death he gave me when I stepped out of your guest bathroom. He's a jungle cat with sharp claws. Do you think he'll just show you his belly and say thanks for invading my douchebag husband's privacy? He won't fall to his knees and thank you for uncovering Daniel's secrets. He'll see this as you trying to control his decisions."

"Just do it, Leland. I'll figure out how to handle whatever answers we find."

He blew an exaggerated breath, his longish blond bang flying away with it. "And what if we find nothing?"

"Then I'll deal with that, too." I grabbed a pen, getting to work, effectively ending the conversation.

◆ ◆ ◆

On behalf of Nexcom Global, Leland accepted the invite from Parker & Mitchell to attend the impromptu office celebration in honor of Daniel's new partnership with the firm. A more glitzy affair was scheduled to take place the following week, but they were eager to make the official announcement.

"They move fast," Leland said as we exited onto their floor. *Parker, Mitchell, & Ward Esq* read the gold engraved plaque on the wall of their reception area. "We don't have to stay for the whole thing, do we?"

"No," I answered, not looking forward to spending time in close proximity to Jasper and Daniel. I couldn't help feeling like I hadn't heard from Jasper because he'd decided I was bad for the health of his marriage. Perhaps our time apart, and their time together vacationing, had helped Jasper to align his priorities. And maybe I wasn't one of them.

"Good," Leland said, checking his watch. "There's plenty of time to schmooze it up here, then head to your place for a quick change before dashing over to Bale."

I'd almost forgotten about his plans to see me debauched before the night was out. I didn't bother mentioning all his hard work would likely be for nothing. "I need a stiff drink." I straightened my spine, preparing for the torturous hours ahead.

Leland remained a figure at my side, interjecting in the midst of conversation whenever my attention diverted to seeking out Jasper, or artfully steering discussions away from anything too personal when it seemed I lacked the brainpower to, because outsiders didn't know about my connection to Jasper Des Moines.

"Excuse me," I said, disentangling myself from the group. After pilfering a champagne flute from one of the passing servers hired for the evening, I weaved my way through the rows of cubicles draped in gold tinsel and garland and found a quiet spot near one of the windows overlooking midtown.

The snow had melted from the tree branches, leaving them bare, and the sidewalks and streets were coated in dingy slush. And if the ominous clouds tightening into gray fists were any indication, rain would be coming, or with any luck, more snow.

My heart began drafting the perfect picture of me chasing Jasper in from the cold after another snowball fight on my balcony, and tearing his clothes off in front of the raging fire as he panted, helpless to me. I'd then have him in my bed, because his preference for falling asleep on my sofa didn't go unnoticed. And while I couldn't argue against its comfort, I also knew it felt safer than the bedroom to him; he could tell himself what we were doing wasn't wrong so long as we weren't doing it between my sheets.

None of that mattered as I then counted the exact hours, minutes, and seconds since I'd last heard from him. A reminder of how unlikely my heart's fantasies would become a reality.

I suddenly regretted turning him away. Regretted saying he needed to be sure before we crossed the line. When had I ever needed him to be sure? And when had he ever wanted to be?

"Get a grip, Cole," I muttered to myself. "He isn't even speaking to you." I flagged a server down and took two flutes off his hands this time. "Anything stronger around here?" I asked. He gave an apologetic shake of his head before sauntering off.

A commotion came from the front. Raised voices and clapping hands crashing together in a melee of cheer and excitement. The guest of honor had arrived.

My hands warmed and prickled around the flutes, and I guzzled the champagne before setting the glasses on the windowsill. I couldn't see them from my vantage point, cowering and licking my wounds out of sight, but I was extremely aware of him. His aura, his soul, the air he breathed… It all acted as stimuli to my senses.

Things tended to revert to being strained between us whenever he spent a significant amount of time with his husband. I hated when he had to leave me, even for one night, because it meant I'd have to fight to climb over his walls again. Had Daniel changed overnight? Had he convinced Jasper he could? Would I at least get to hold on to him as a sort-of-sibling, or friend? Like I'd claimed I wanted in the first place.

I faced the city, which had gone dark on me. The shade of its bleakness matched my disposition, and I shut my eyes to it, willing myself together so I could do my job, remain professional, and congratulate Daniel on all he'd accomplished. All he'd won.

"Hi," came a smoky, breathless voice from behind, resurrecting me, reigniting the heart I only now noticed hadn't been beating. Not really. "What are you doing back here?" Jasper asked gently. I knew if I opened my eyes and turned to him, I'd be met with a beautiful blush along his cheeks, and eyes so penetrating and sharp they could cut through steel.

"You're such a beautiful contradiction," I whispered.

"What?" He rested a hand on my arm, urging me around.

"Nothing," I said, breathing deeply, preparing to meet my doom. He wore his hair straight, parted down the center and swept behind his ears. Although he looked delectable in a suit, I preferred him in sweats or threadbare jeans. "You look handsome." I couldn't help myself. I never could when it came to him.

"Thanks." His eyes roved me from head to toe, the hairs along my body standing at attention. "So do you." Jasper loved me in black.

"Why haven't I heard from you? I get you were on vacation, but I saw Daniel in the office today. I figured I would've heard something from you. A text saying you'd gotten back okay. Anything." I sounded needy, but if the shoe fit...

"We actually didn't end up going anywhere," he said. I'd noticed his lack of tan also, but Jasper tended to redden under the sun, and did everything in his power to avoid the effects from it. I'd hoped he'd sat under the biggest umbrella, sporting the largest sun hat, slathering on copious amounts of SPF. I'd hoped it wasn't because they'd spent the whole weekend locked in their suite like Leland had suggested. "Our flights were canceled. A tropical storm hit the island. We decided to make it a staycation."

I swallowed audibly, because a staycation was equally as bad as the nightmare Leland had implanted in my head.

"Daniel ended up working through most of it," he whispered, as if sensing my distress. "To be fair, we both did."

"Good," I said, my filter malfunctioning. It still didn't explain why I hadn't heard from him. We were too far from each other, even though his breath fanned my lips, even though I could count the three nearly translucent freckles on his perfect nose.

"Well, there you two are!" Daniel's grating, pompous voice knifed its way through our sphere.

"Daniel," I said flatly, wanting to reach out and hold Jasper in place when he backed away from me. "I didn't get to properly thank you. Thanks to your hard work, Nexcom Global is now the proud majority owner of Medtech International. We now have access to the best scientists, and one of the largest laboratories on the continent. Congratulations on making partner. I hear it's been a long-time dream of yours."

"It has been," he said with unmasked resentment in his tone before perking up again. "But thank you. And I look forward to our continued working relationship."

"I'll leave you two to talk business," Jasper said, heading to rejoin the party. My gaze followed his retreat—beyond my control, and I turned back to find Daniel watching me inquisitively. I offered him a stiff smile.

"We've amassed a list of our finest attorneys for Nexcom, but I'll take the lead, if that's alright with you. And I'd prefer my base be here," he said with all the confidence of a man who felt we were now equals. But he still needed me. Men like him always would, because Daniel was only as good as the company he kept. He didn't stand out on his own, no matter how hard he tried.

I moved in close, and never had I been more grateful for my breadth and height as I did when it forced him to crane his neck to meet my eyes. "Deliver the portfolios of your top twenty to my assistant by morning. I'll review and make my own selections. And I'd prefer you relocate to my headquarters. At least part time. I'd like to keep you close," I said, letting him know who held the real power.

"Sure, Cole," he said, amicably enough, even if it was said through clenched teeth. "I'll have my assistant put together—"

"I need your keen eye on this, Daniel. I need your best. I need more than a couple clicks on the keyboard and a printout. I need men and women who possess something that can't be drilled down to a wins and loses column."

"I'll...have a list to you by morning."

"Excellent." That should keep him busy tonight. "One other thing. I know the lines between us can easily become blurred with me being your firm's most valuable client, and also being family. I'd prefer it if you addressed me as Mr. Kincaid when in a work setting," I said before strolling off.

I spent the rest of the evening pretending I didn't notice the way Jasper's gaze stalked me. Pretending I didn't know it was because of his irrational jealousy when it came to Leland. The latter who ensured he leaned into my ear to whisper nonsensical things whenever Jasper pivoted our way, or steered me in the opposite direction with a hand to the small of my back whenever he spotted Jasper advancing on me. Leland laid it on extra thick when from the corner of my mouth I ordered him to stop it, and he laughed dark and seductively as if I'd said something highly inappropriate to him. That snagged everyone's attention, including a red-faced Jasper.

"I don't need anyone thinking I'm fucking my assistant, Leland," I said as we went in search of the men's room.

"No one's paying us any attention. Well, one someone is, but that's the point."

"I didn't ask you to torment him. Knock it off," I said as we entered the single-occupant restroom.

"Oh dear," he said, taking in our lack of privacy, and completely ignoring my order.

"Wait outside," I said, but he just brushed me off and faced the door.

A few minutes later we stepped out together and came face-to-face with Jasper, who looked anything but pleased. "I didn't realize there was only one stall," I said.

"But he did," Jasper said through tight lips, "because I saw him go in there less than a half an hour ago."

"Oops," Leland said innocently.

The sound of metal clinking against glass drew our heads around, distracting me from pummeling Leland. Robert Mitchell stood atop a makeshift podium, drink in hand, calling the room to order. It was time for the toast, and Jasper rushed off to be by his husband's side.

"You'll have dust for teeth if you keep grinding away like that," Leland said, covering his grin with the fresh glass of bubbly he'd just been handed. I declined the server's offer for another drink and stretched my jaw, teeth aching. "And you think you can handle an affair?"

"Has it ever occurred to you that maybe if I had *something,* I wouldn't be so irritable?" I whispered angrily.

"Never once," he said unperturbed. "Because you have something, and you're still a miserable twat. What happened to the promises you made to him, hmm? The ones he so badly wants you to break?"

"What is it you want to hear me say? That the thought of Daniel's hands on my stepbrother makes me want to draw blood? That I'd never be able to settle for an intimate affair with Jasper if it meant he'd be going home to be fucked by *him?*" I pointed a scathing finger in Daniel's direction. "But that I'd do it without hesitation and pay whatever life-altering consequences and emotional penalties would come of it later because I'm fucking obsessed with him and was a fool to think this could end any other way," I hissed, so close to him I could feel my breath rebound off his skin.

"Hey," Leland whispered apologetically, grabbing my hand as I shoved past him. "I'm sorry. I just hate seeing you like this."

"Then stop contributing to it," I said unfairly. He was only being honest, but I'd had enough of his brand of honesty. It forced me to see myself for what I truly was. For what I was willing to do. It was either walk away, or run my fist into the nearest wall.

I didn't need to look behind me to know the flame scorching my neck was coming from Jasper's hot gaze on me. On us. I tugged free from Leland's hold. "I'll be back. I'm going to get some air." I exited through the stairwell door off the reception area, needing to exert some of my frustration, and figured a thirty-floor descent would do the trick. Mitchell had reached the punchline of his joke, and raucous laughter chased me until the door closed behind me. Daniel's scabrous guffaw could be heard in the mix.

The stale air greeted me at the side of the building where the law offices shared an alleyway with a pizza shop, its dumpster overflowing with trash and oozing a liquid substance from beneath.

A bike messenger nearly swept me off my feet as I cleared the corner to stand on the more busy street of Broadway, in front of the office building but still off to the side. A mere few feet away an older man curbed his dog—closer to the building than the actual curb.

"Oh, hi, Mr. Kincaid," a woman's voice chimed minutes later. I craned my head to the side to see Daniel's assistant walking over, the revolving lobby door still spinning in her wake.

"Dog excrement everywhere, bike couriers gone rogue, disobeying traffic laws," I complained. "Aren't they supposed to ride in the street?" I flipped up the collar of my blazer to combat the wind. I'd escaped without my coat.

"New Yorkers make their own rules," she said nervously, my presence probably unnerving her. She'd obviously come down for a smoke, based on the gold tin and matching lighter in her hand, and she was unlucky enough to run into me, a grumpy Cole Kincaid.

"I can walk further down," she said, indicating the corner furthest from us and the door she'd swung through.

"It's okay," I replied. "The wind's blowing west anyway."

She cupped her French-manicured hand around the lip of the tall, slender cigarette, turning her back on the stiff breeze to spark an ember. She took a deep drag, exhaling like it'd been way too long of a day. I'd have been okay with silence, but it turned out she was the type to fill awkwardness with words.

"I really should quit," she said. "What's your excuse for braving the bitter cold without a coat?" Her red bun sat high and tight at the center of her head, pulling her expression into one of mild surprise.

"Just needed some fresh air," I said, sniffing, and then adding, "although I'm not sure New York City is the place one goes for that."

Her phone rang from within her shoulder bag, and balancing her cigarette while searching through the considerable purse proved to be too difficult, so she groaned, chucking the freshly lit smoke, nearly setting a passerby aflame. "Three voicemails?" she said, speaking to herself now. "I only heard it ring once. The service here is dreadful." She brought the phone to her ear, listening to the messages. "Darn it," she grumbled, pulling up her contacts and tapping at the screen. A phone rang audibly on the other end. "Pick up, pick up," she chanted, peering up the stone façade of the building as if wondering if she could scale it, or toss a message to the thirtieth floor.

"Is everything alright?" I asked.

"That was my mother trying to reach me. She thinks she's having a stroke," she said with a roll of her eyes like her mother's claim was nothing but hyperbole. "She's on her way to the emergency room." To herself she added, "I mean, who makes phone calls and drives herself to the ER if they're experiencing a stroke?" She frantically dug around in her bag again, balancing the phone with her shoulder. She withdrew a flash drive, then cursed, quickly sending another glance upward.

"Do you need something from up there?"

"I was calling a colleague to see if she could check my desk for this." She held up the flash drive. "I was hoping I'd left it there. Mr. Ward *has* to have this tonight." She chewed on her lip, confirming the time on her phone. "Maybe I can rush it upstairs and still make it to the hospital by the time my mother arrives."

"Don't worry," I said. "I was about to head up anyway. I'll make sure he gets it."

"Oh no, I've bothered you enough, Mr. Kincaid."

"Really, I don't mind."

"Thank you," she said, already backing away. "Check his office. He was headed that way when I left." She turned, her heels kicking up slush as she sped toward the parking garage across the street.

Leland was too busy flirting with a male intern to notice my reappearance, so I was able to seek Daniel's office out uninterrupted. I'd gone down two corridors and peeked into three empty rooms before stumbling across Mitchell and asked him for directions.

"Let him know Parker's looking for him, will you?" he said.

I agreed and retraced my steps to the other side of the office, stopping in front of the room with Daniel's name on the door. Muffled moans could be heard coming from inside, and it'd just occurred to me I hadn't seen Jasper during my walk through. Fury coursed through me, and I barged in without so much as a warning knock. "What the hell are you two doing in here?" I barked, and Daniel, who stood with his back to me as he kissed Jasper, flinched, spinning and covering Jasper with his body.

From over his shoulder, I could make out Jasper's disheveled hair, his puffy lips, and his eyes, which now held relief. Or maybe that was wishful thinking.

"What are *you* doing here?" Daniel countered breathlessly, more in a confused than angered manner. I had the wherewithal to at least pretend at some semblance of remorse.

"Sorry. Your assistant had a family emergency. She asked me to give this to you." I handed off the flash drive. "And Parker's urgently looking for you. Apparently, there's a fire in need of dousing," I said with an edge of coldness, my pinched gaze fixed pointedly on what I could see of Jasper.

Daniel hesitated, twisting his neck to look at Jasper who from the sounds of it was working on his belt buckle.

"It's okay." I moved aside so he could exit. "I'm his brother. Nothing I haven't seen before, right?" I said as if we were old pals.

He chuckled in that smug arrogant way of his, like we were boys discussing secrets over shared drinks. What I wouldn't have given to knock the smirk from his face.

Daniel left with a promise to return, and then there was just the two of us, our combined rage, and the heat rising up the walls to smother us. "Seems out of character for him, doesn't it? And not the fucking you over his desk where anyone could walk in part, but the dirty part. The environment doesn't seem..." I trailed off to look around, to search for the right word. "*Sterile* enough for him."

"Fuck you," he spat.

"Now you're talking," I said, ripping his hand away from his lowered zipper and reaching in to withdraw him again. I let his cock stand between us, but not before sweeping a finger over its glossy crown and bringing it to my mouth. We shivered in unison. "Why would you do this?" I asked. "Why here, when you know it would break me?"

"We're just brothers. Friends. It shouldn't matter—"

"Cut the bullshit, Jas. You *know* it matters. You *know* it does."

"You want me to turn down my husband's advances?"

"Yes," I said without a moment's pause. Fuck how insane it seemed, fuck the promises I'd made. I'd nearly been a witness to their indecency, and mad didn't begin to cover how I felt about it.

"The way you turn down Leland's?"

So that was what this was about. *Damn you, Leland.* "Leland and I are nothing more than boss, employee, and friend."

"Yeah? Does he know that?" He moved to slip his hard cock back into his pants.

"Leave it," I snarled, roughly unbuttoning and removing my blazer before flinging it over Daniel's desk.

"What are you doing?" Jasper asked, staring over my shoulder at the closed door.

"I'm not sending you home with him like this," I said, licking a stripe up my palm before wrapping my fist around his erection. He stifled a groan, gripping my forearm. Not with enough pressure to make me stop, but enough so he could say he tried.

Eventually his hand tumbled away, and I added more saliva to my palm and began working him in earnest. The smooth, warm, silky feel of him caused my own hardness to thud against my zipper.

His eyes glossed over, and his lips parted on a small *O*, but he defiantly refused to give me anything else.

"You're upset with me for coming back," I said jerkily. "You're upset with yourself for wanting this. For needing it. But please," I begged. "Don't be mean. Let me know when you're coming, Jasper."

With my free hand, I fought to get his buckle undone and his pants unbuttoned so I could slide in and fondle his balls. "Look at me," I said when his panicked gaze went back to the door. "The only thing you think about right now is me, is this moment." I didn't give a damn if we torched the world that very instant with our lies and disloyalty. "You're mine. This was inevitable. And I never want his fucking hands on you again."

More wishful thinking? Probably. But when I had him like that, in the literal palm of my hand, I lived with the belief that wishes came true every day. His testicles rose close to his body, and mine followed suit, all it would have taken was a whisper against my cock for me to blow.

"I—I'm coming," he breathed, gripping the edge of the desk. I was on my knees as the first jet shot through him, my mouth taking over for my hand as I choked him down whole, pumping my face back and forth relentlessly. "Shit," he cried with some restraint for the situation we were in. He clamped his hands over my head, undulating into my mouth, no longer being a passive participant.

Voices filtered in from a distance, and I fully expected him to pull away, but his orgasm was beyond his control, beyond his need for self-preservation.

All too soon he finished, clumsily backing away and falling from my lips. "Fuck," he said, fumbling with his pants as the voices of Daniel and Leland drew closer, Leland's booming louder than necessary as a warning to us.

I got to my feet, tangling my hand in his hair again, holding him still as I licked what spilled from him off my hand, making a sloppy show of it.

"Cole," he whispered urgently, but not before swallowing thickly. His clothes were situated now, and the smart thing to do would've been to release him, but I had to taste his pouty lips. I had to erase Daniel's mark there. I smashed our mouths together, tonguing him ruthlessly, spreading the taste of him, of us, over his gums. My heart sang when he gave in for a split second before forcing me away.

He worked on fixing his hair while I buttoned back into my blazer and adjusted the brick in my pants.

"Who's going to take care of you?" he whispered worriedly toward my dick.

"You were right, they are still here!" Leland said with fake cheer as he entered ahead of Daniel, sniffing the air, and then eyeing me with scorn. He held my coat out, and I quickly grabbed it, slinging it over my arm and covering my front.

"Sorry to be gone for so long," Daniel said to Jasper, leaning in for a kiss that landed on Jasper's hastily turned cheek.

"Well, we've gotta get going," Leland chirped in. "Long night ahead of us."

Jasper perked up at that, but Leland was ushering me out with a hand to my back before I could assuage his concerns.

It was a race for the lobby elevators. I didn't want to be stopped by anyone. Not in the state I was in.

"What the fuck?" Leland asked when the elevator doors shut.

"It's your fault. No more making him jealous."

"Come again?" he said.

"I caught him and Daniel kissing in his office, Leland! On their way to doing more. He thinks you and I are sleeping together."

"So he thinks you're fucking me, and in turn he almost fucked his husband? You do realize how absurd and twisted you two are, right?"

"I don't care," I growled. "Stop it or you're fired."

He held his hands in the sign of surrender. "Okay. I promise. Can I still take you out to get laid?"

"Have you always been this determined?" I laughed at his absurdity. "Let me get showered and changed first."

"Of course. Wouldn't want you dragging the scent of sex to the club. It would defeat the purpose."

I'd left the offices of Parker, Mitchell, & Ward convinced that stopping Daniel and Jasper, and then having Jasper's cum slide down my throat, meant I'd won something. Thinking I'd use Leland's forced night out as a celebration of my win. Didn't take long for the euphoria to subside, or for hollowness to return.

They'll be going home together, I'd thought. What then? I wasn't the only one who'd been left unfulfilled from our ordeal. My mood had blackened further, and all I could do was hope that Daniel kept his hands off his husband.

CHAPTER 12

Daniel

3 Years Ago

THE GRADUATION CEREMONY is over, and I patiently wait off to the side near the arena exit closest to Jasper. By the stage, a dark-haired, petite woman fusses over the tassel on his cap as he smiles down at her warmly.

I must look like a peacock angling my head this way and that way, but as family members and friends come down from the stands and converge on the graduates, it gets harder to see Jasper through the mayhem.

"Finally," I murmur as Jasper and the woman, who looks to be a few years older than him, make their way arm in arm toward the exit doors I stood next to. My hands are full with the gifts I now feel foolish for purchasing, but it's too late to question my choices now.

Jasper's steps falter when he notices me, and I brandish my best disarming smile. "Mr. Ward?" he asks hesitantly, then peers behind him as if maybe I'm here for someone else. "What are you doing here?" His friend drops his arm to answer her phone, then points to the doors, mouthing that she'll be right outside. He nods and continues his approach until we're close enough to hear ourselves over the ruckus of voices without shouting.

"I came to see you," I say.

"Alright." His brows lower as if he can't understand why I'd go through the trouble, and then we both wait for me to say something else.

"These are for you." I gesture with the flowers I hold in one arm, and the expensive bottle of scotch—equipped with a bow at its neck—in the other. "You'll have to forgive me. I've been married to my work for so long; I'm out of practice when it comes to courting someone. I wasn't sure if flowers were the way to go, or something a bit more masculine like a twenty-year aged single malt."

"Hmm, sounds pretty sexist to me," he says good-naturedly, and not for the first time I'm struck with how fierce yet delicate he is. It's definitely the bright hair and even brighter eyes, I tell myself. The long lashes and well-defined long limbs. The lost look he wears well. With the proper guidance, he'd be great in the courtroom.

"Did you just say courting?" he asks with delay, as if that part took a while to filter into his brain. Or perhaps he's teasing me for my choice of phrase. I blame my prim parents.

"Yes," I laugh, tugging at my collar. "I seem to remember you telling me you don't date within the workplace. Well, your internship ended two weeks ago, you've graduated law school—with honors, I might add." I take a step closer. "So, are you free for dinner?"

He looks to the door his friend went through, maybe hoping to be saved.

"It doesn't have to be today," I say, transferring my gifts to him. The move should remind him of all the trouble I went to, and hopefully it'll make him feel like he owes me something. I was a great attorney for a reason. I needed a yes from him.

"I'm not dating material, Mr. Ward—"

"Daniel," I say.

"I'm not what you're looking for, Daniel."

"Why don't you let me be the judge of that."

He bites his lip, and I know he's searching for a better way to let me down.

"One meal. At best we fall in love and run off into the sunset together—"

"That's highly unlikely," he says with a soft grin.

"Well then, let me distract you for one night."

"Distract me from what?"

"Whatever's always bothering you, Jasper." I've studied him enough to pick up on his ever-present melancholy. There's sudden interest in his eyes, but fear, too. I wonder if I should say more, or if less would win him over.

"One meal," he says reluctantly.

"I'll give you a call," I reply, concealing my triumphant smile before departing.

CHAPTER 13

Jasper

"**I BELIEVE YOUR** *brother and his assistant mentioned going to Club Bale tonight,*" Daniel had said once the office party came to a close. He'd overhead them discussing it in passing earlier, so he'd said. This was his way of getting rid of me. Of getting me out of the house so he could devote his attention to his mistress. *Work.* I immediately regretted the thought, because the only adulterer in our relationship was me.

I took the bait willingly. Of course I did. Cole's neglected arousal consumed my every thought since he and Leland had left Parker, Mitchell, & Ward. Lust might cool off, might take a back seat, but it didn't diminish completely until spent. It hung right below the surface, where even a tame image, or an innocent touch from a stranger reminded you that sooner or later it'd need to be addressed.

So, showered and encased in the tightest jeans I could find, and letting my hair have a mind of its own—the way Cole liked it, I left home with the intention of intruding on their party without a care for how it'd look. I was past caring. At least where Leland was concerned.

Didn't matter if they were having sex or not. I hated how close they were. I didn't enjoy being reminded of how available, how craveable Cole was, because I didn't want anyone having him but me. Nothing had changed in that aspect.

The gray sky had finally opened up after days of looming menacingly, bringing more snow. The cabbie's windshield wipers were no match for the thick flurries rushing groundward, and that, coupled with the police activity on the bridge, made traffic into Brooklyn slow for this time of night.

"There's an accident up ahead," the driver said, and I cleared the condensation fogging my window to get a better view.

Police cars and fire flares sealed off the far right lane, their sirens silent but flashing blue and red in the night.

It'd have been much easier for me to hang at home for a few hours then go straight to the club, but I needed to see Sofia first. I needed to say the words I'd never spoken out loud before making the decision I'd already made from the moment my eyes locked with Cole's at that estate.

Took a couple hours to pull onto her street, and due to the tightly packed cars parallel parked along the curb, I was left having to exit at the corner. I paid the driver, yelling for him to keep the change as I slammed the back door and eyed the long row of nearly identical homes.

Sofia's brownstone stood out. It was the only one with the three-headed, whimsical light post in the front yard, and the dancing Santa in the living room window on the parlor floor.

I avoided the black ice on the uneven pavement as I walked the short distance to her place. The curtain twitched at the garden-floor apartment she rented to old lady Tilder, and the muted bark of a small dog could be heard from within. I hurried up the stoop and jogged up the sandstone steps before she could investigate me further, or call the cops, which she was famous for doing.

It wasn't extremely late, but I knew her boys were in bed, so I shot her a text saying: *I'm here,* rather than ring the bell, then turned my back to the door so I could take in the beauty of the snowscaped park across the street and the couple shivering on the bench, smiling with their palms out and up, catching the gargantuan flakes.

People moved with purpose in the city, like they had somewhere to be since yesterday. At least that was the case the closer you ventured to lower Manhattan. The Brooklyn temperament was different. More relaxed, as if everyone here was already where they needed to be. It was what Sofia loved most about it. There was community here, she'd said. Something she wanted for her kids.

The front door opened, and with mother-mode engaged, Sofia waved me in and helped me out of my cold, wet things, even rubbing her warm hands over mine. She eyed my attire, the nearly sheer black V-neck that clung to my chest, the way my jeans strangled me, and the fancy shoes I kicked out of, but she didn't address any of it. Probably momentarily more concerned with our impending discussion about my past. About Cole.

"Come," she whispered, tightening the sash on her pink, fleece robe, "I've got a fire going in the living room." The rest of the house was silent and dark.

"Maybe this wasn't such a good idea," I started, feeling terrible about disturbing her when clearly she'd been ready to call it a night.

"Don't be silly," she said, falling onto the sofa and handing me one of two mugs she had situated on the coffee table. "I was about to binge-watch *Grey's Anatomy*. Hubby had the boys out all day, tiring them out. Little did he know he'd be out for the count, too. I love it when that happens," she said secretly.

I mirrored her position at the other end of the couch. My back to the arm, one leg bent and resting on the cushion, and started on my coffee. "Mmmm. How did you know I'd need this?"

"Because one of the few things I do know about you," she said, her voice reverberating into her cup, "is that nothing gets you more relaxed and inclined to talk like a hot mug of Joe. Now, start from the beginning and leave nothing out."

I finished my coffee and requested a refill while I worked on getting my thoughts organized, and she waited patiently. I started with how close my mother and I were. *The love bandits,* she'd call us. I'd stood up to my father for her—whenever he'd decide to come around. And she could never quite get me transitioned to sleeping in my own bed because she was a heavy sleeper, and all I'd have to do was wait for her to drift off before crawling back in. She'd wake up with me tucked into her side, and her nightgown fisted between my little hands. That continued until she married Franklin, until I was able to trust she had someone else who would take care of her like I had, and then I'd set my sights on Cole.

"She was tough, but didn't hide her vulnerability either. She could get riled up when the moment called for it, and she could be bullheaded when it came down to two things—her causes, and her family." I set my empty mug on the coffee table. "But there was a softness to her that outweighed it all. It made you want to protect her, to promise her everything."

"Sounds like someone I know," she said with a warm smile. I huffed, setting a throw pillow in my lap for something to do. "It's true. You come alive in the courtroom. And you don't stand up to Daniel, like ever, *unless,*" she emphasized, "it has something to do with your work—and maybe your hair. But you won't allow anyone to stand in the way of your work. And with Cole you morph into this content puppy." She shrugged. "I can't explain it. It's like you forget you're supposed to be sad. For years, I've tried to tap into you. Tried to get to that place where your happiness lives, but one glance in his direction, and poof!" she said a little too loudly, wincing as she waited for a sound of disturbance to come from upstairs.

"I was happy."

"Maybe. The work we do certainly brings you some measure of joy, but it isn't the sustaining kind. You were missing something. At first I thought it was because you needed family, and I felt bad for not having enough time in my day to be that for you." She stopped me before I could argue. "But it turns out it was more than that."

I blew a breath toward the ceiling, searching for a spot in my life story to continue from. "We didn't come home at all during our first year at Harvard. Finally, we didn't need to sneak around, didn't need to pretend to be stepbrothers when really we were more, and didn't need to run the risk of upsetting our parents. We weren't ready to give that up, yet. Not for a couple weeks in the fall, and not for a whole summer at the end of spring semester. Instead, we took winter courses, and studied abroad that first summer.

"My mom and Franklin had been ecstatic. Supported us completely. It was easy enough to get away with it at Harvard. We looked nothing alike, shared an apartment off campus, and never made any friends. We didn't need any. And college life was much different than high school. Everyone had their own lives, trying to find and make their own way. No one cared about us and what we were doing." I hadn't noticed I'd created a huge lull in the conversation until Sofia's hand brushed over mine along the back of the sofa.

"Our second year we came home more often, but it was when we visited during spring break at the end of our third year that I saw signs that something was off, but they weren't glaring, red flags, you know? My mother slept a lot that week but blamed it on all the overtime she'd been putting in on getting a new charity off the ground. I remember Franklin hovering over her more than usual." I cursed, ducking my head in shame for being so blind. "I told Cole we had to come back for the summer, and he agreed.

"Her legs were swollen when we returned, frighteningly so, and she didn't have enough energy to smile. I lost my fucking mind. They were lying to us, and I'd never been so upset in my life, not even after taking a beating from my birth father."

"Oh, honey," she said, scooting closer until our knees touched.

"Dilated cardiomyopathy. It's a condition where the heart's main pumping chamber is enlarged. As the chamber grows, its walls stretch, becoming weaker and thinner, affecting the heart's ability to pump enough blood to the rest of the body. Everything we tried was short-lived. In the end, she needed a new heart." Thinking back on my mother's decline wasn't easy. Her death left an unfillable void in me, and being the cause of it, on the eve of receiving the call about her transplant, left me seeking ways to self-sabotage my happiness, left me running in the opposite direction of joy, and flailing with arms wide open toward pain.

"She made us promise we'd finish school. She didn't want us hovering over her and waiting for her to survive, because in my mind that was the only possibility. So we went back, and I doubled up on classes with the goal of getting the hell out of there and back to her. We flew home every chance we got. Long weekends and short ones. We took online classes when we could in order to wring every free moment with her we could get." There were moments where she was okay. I called those life's small cruelties because they never lasted long, and each one sent me into an even deeper black hole. I ventured to Sofia's bay window, which was so rich with snow and clouded with frost I couldn't see through it. It meant I couldn't see my reflection either, so maybe there was a God, and maybe that was his small mercy, because the last thing I needed to do right then was face myself.

"I finished school ahead of schedule, and left Cole behind so I could be with my mother." I'd reached the sweat-inducing part of the tragic story. My stomach flipped in on itself, and I gasped through the nauseating, freefalling sensation, breathing and counting well beyond ten.

"I was alone with my mother the night she died. Or I was until Cole arrived from Massachusetts later that night. Franklin had been working late at the office." His way of coping with the bleakness of our ordeal. "And Maggie—my mother's friend—I wasn't sure where she was for most of the day, but she was there when the ambulance arrived." I realized I'd jumped ahead, so I backed up a few beats in the story.

"I had this urgent need to give my mother my truth. I was tired of hiding from her. I hated myself for it, because no matter how positive I tried to be for her benefit, it felt like I was losing my chance to be honest with her. I didn't want her dying and not knowing. I wanted to experience her happiness for us. So I told her about Cole and me," I whispered, dragging a shaky hand over my mouth. "She started wheezing in a panic, and I had to restrain her hands when she began tugging on her oxygen cannula." I was selfish even then. "Couldn't I have just hidden it for a little while longer?" I balled my hands at my sides, and exhaled deeply when Sofia circled my waist with her slender arms, pressing her cheek to my back.

"We were her sons. Of course she wouldn't have approved. *Of course not...*" I faded off hoarsely. "What was I thinking?"

"You didn't know. You couldn't have known. You were under a lot of stress, Jasper. Have some grace for yourself."

"You're a mother," I said, turning to face her. "Would you accept the unacceptable? He was her child. We were her children. My mistake was thinking the absence of shared DNA mattered to anyone but us. That it wouldn't matter to a woman like her."

She backed away, conceding with a nod and tightening her robe's sash again.

"She begged me not to break Franklin's heart. She said he wouldn't be okay with it. Said it would destroy him, and he was already losing so much. She *begged* me. And... And I promised." I promised I would end it. I'd have said or done anything she asked of me.

"Does Cole know?"

"No," I said. "Bad enough he had to believe he'd played a role in her death. I couldn't tell him she didn't want us together. He believes she's looking down on us with open approval. He thinks she wants us together." I chewed on my lip. "I could never take that from him." So I lived alone with the truth, and it took everything nowadays to look heavenward and not feel her disappointment.

I paced to her mantel, fixing the angle of one of the Christmas figurines before shoving my hands into my back pockets and gazing unseeingly into the fire. "She'd calmed and had fallen asleep under my reassurance I would fix things, and with the added fatigue, she slept even deeper those days. I'd often slip into her and Franklin's room in the middle of the night just to watch her chest rise and fall." I shot a glance over my shoulder because Sofia had gone so quiet and so still I'd thought maybe she'd judged and left me stranded with my shame.

"I'm here," she said, standing where I'd left her, arms wrapped around her middle. "I'm not going anywhere."

"I went over how I would tell Cole as I waited outside for Franklin's driver to pull in from the airport with him. How would I break him when he was already breaking? We all were." My chest caved in as I shrank smaller and smaller, the pain resurfacing and eating a hole through me. "No," I warned, when Sofia made a move to get closer to me. I didn't want to be consoled. "It'll only make me feel worse."

"Okay," she said, eyes pooling. I averted my stare because I couldn't stand to see her love for me. Couldn't stand that she was sharing in my agony. Things were much better when I suffered alone because I hated to be reminded of what I missed most.

Being loved.

"He was out of the passenger side door before the sedan came to a complete halt. He ran to me and didn't stop until he'd collided into me. He was what I was missing. *That* was what I was missing. I–I couldn't do it. I needed him too much. I needed him right fucking then."

"Where is she?" he'd asked, taking my hand and pushing inside the house.

"She's asleep."

"I need to see her—"

"Wait!" I'd said. At his puzzled expression I added, *"She had a hard night. She needs her rest."*

"I was a coward. I didn't want her waking up by chance and saying anything to him. Not until I'd had one last night with him." My mother and Franklin's room was on the other side of the house, and she couldn't walk more than a few feet unassisted without gasping for air. We were alone and safe and *I needed* him.

"Are you sure we shouldn't wait, Jas?"

"I can't," I'd said in a distant voice, pressing my back against my closed bedroom door, feeling the resistance of all the unfair things waiting on the other side to deal with us. *"It has to be now, and please, don't take it easy on me."*

I shook my head clear of the memory. "I don't know what drove her from sleep, or how long it'd taken her to get to us, or even how long she'd stood there horrified, watching us, *dying* because of us..." Cole and I had been so caught up in each other, so wholly lost in ourselves, in our desperate, fevered love, that neither of us had noticed her until it was too late. "What she must have thought *seeing* us like that." Panic filled my voice, and I stumbled back over to the couch just as the ceiling and floor switched places on me. "You don't know how we can be, 'Fia. You don't know how we can get. She saw *everything*. And it tortures me every day—"

"Breathe," she cooed, sitting next to me on the edge of the sofa and rubbing circles into my back.

"It kills me to know she died thinking she needed to save me from him. Thinking he took something he had no right to, when in reality he had my blessing. He *always* had my blessing."

"Mom!" I'd scrambled off the bed, tripping over the sheet to get to her.

"Mom?" Cole repeated, falling in beside me.

"Cole, get help," I'd said, but he'd sat there on his knees frozen. *"Cole!"* I'd screamed, and he jumped into motion.

"I'm so—sorry," she mouthed through blue-tinted lips, her sluggish stare moving over my shoulder to where Cole could be heard shouting into the phone.

"No. No, no, no," I'd begged. Her breaths came through in tiny whistles, and I scanned the room for answers.

"What's she saying, Jas?" Cole had cried. *"What's she saying?"*

"Jasper?" Sofia asked, bringing me back from the past with a hand in my hair. I swiveled my head in her direction, my elbows still planted on my knees. "What do you mean by 'took something he had no right to?'" She wanted to understand, she wanted clarity, an explanation for what I'd inadvertently revealed, but I'd given her enough for one night. And some things couldn't be explained with words. Some things could only be understood by the people involved.

I kissed her forehead, lingering there a beat before standing.

"It's getting late. Thanks for listening."

"O-okay," she stammered, confused by my complete shift and shutdown. Out in the hall I slipped into my shoes.

Sofia leaned with arms folded against the open entrance of the living room, tossing another glance up the staircase before whispering, "Do you want to leave Daniel for him?"

"It doesn't matter," I said, shrugging into my coat. "There's no future for Cole and me. I won't break the only other promise to her I can keep. I won't break Franklin's heart any more than I already have."

"Well, what about Daniel's heart? I may joke about it, but I don't actually believe he doesn't have one." One side of her mouth kicked up, but the atmosphere remained heavy. "He deserves the truth, but *you* deserve more than him." She said it as if a bandage were being ripped off. Like she wouldn't be able to live with herself if she didn't for once say it in plain terms.

I exhaled, searching for the will to pretend I didn't know who Daniel was. To spew the words dressed in denial about his character, and how good he was, and how he wanted nothing but the best for me.

He loved me, and I could see his potential to be a better man. I could almost touch it. And I understood what drove him. And some days I did love him. It was usually the days when I could find the strength to love myself. Those days didn't come by often and were fleeting when they did. Truthfully, Daniel was the protective shield standing between Cole and me. The one thing I couldn't ignore, the one thing keeping me from cementing myself to him again. It was the truth when I agreed to marry him, and it was even more so true now. It made me an even lesser man than him.

I couldn't admit to any of that ugliness living inside me, though. Not to Sofia. No one as good as her could fight the instinct to condemn me for it. "Daniel just wants what's best for me," I said mechanically, and she hummed her disappointment.

"At least that makes one of you," she said sadly. "I believe two opposing things can be true at the same time. I believe you can be good even while doing something you know is wrong. I believe you can love Daniel—in your own way—and love Cole, and love yourself, even while hurting all of you, because let's face it, no one will be spared in this," she said, already guessing at what my decision would be. "But I love you, anyway. I am not too good to love you, anyway," she said resolutely.

I closed the gap between us, and she stepped into me, sending her short arms around me as her head met my chest. "I love you, too, 'Fia." And before she could say anything that would call the good in me to the surface, I left, racing through the bitter cold for the subway station two blocks away, racing to make the second biggest mistake of my life with eyes wide open.

CHAPTER 14

CLUB BALE RESIDED a few blocks west of the river in the Meat-packing District, a name adopted from the hundreds of meat-packing plants and slaughterhouses that used to inhabit the area. The neighborhood sat sandwiched between Chelsea and Greenwich Village. And although the now lively enclave was no longer a major hub for meat wholesalers, a handful still remained, aiding in maintaining a feel of authenticity.

Hustling down 14th street, cold and out of breath, I began to wonder if maybe Daniel had gotten it wrong. The streets were eerily empty and quiet, with the only noise being the wet, crunching sound of car tires rolling over salted, melting snow.

My pulse kicked up a notch when while waiting for the traffic light to turn red at the two-way intersection, the club doors opened, momentarily flooding the dismal street with music. Leland exited, upturning the collar of his jacket before rushing for the waiting taxi. "Shit," I cursed when a city bus pulled into the bus stop near me, cutting off my view. By the time I'd gone around the rear of it, and braved the oncoming cars to cross the street, the cab was already u-turning and speeding in the direction the bus had now gone.

Cole hadn't been with him. At least I didn't think he was. I hadn't heard the music seep through the doors again, signaling it had opened once more, and I wanted to believe Cole couldn't have slipped through the club entrance and into the backseat with Leland in such a short amount of time. Plus, Cole had a driver. Was he still inside? Could he have already left? *Maybe he never came.*

I was maybe thirty feet away when a black SUV pulled up, and Mark hopped out of the driver's side to run around to the back door. My steps faltered, and I'd been about to shout his name when Club Bale's doors burst open again, and a coatless Cole, dressed in a black turtleneck and matching trousers, rushed to the SUV. His coat was draped over the shoulder of a ginger man who laughed and raced in behind him. They were speeding away before my shock wore off.

I hurried into the cobblestone street, watching as the taillights faded into the distance.

I should go home to my husband. I should cut Cole out of my life completely, tell Daniel the truth about us, and insist he no longer work for Nexcom. For once rational thoughts were spinning around in my head. Daniel had made partner. He'd gotten what he wanted. He no longer needed Cole. *I* no longer needed Cole either.

But I was angry. And I was *jealous. So* very jealous. And I felt entitled to him. "How fucking dare he—"

A car honked behind me, and I whirled on it, not even realizing I'd been marching in the middle of the street in the direction Mark had driven off in. I held my hand up to protect my eyes from the bright headlights, whispering an apology only I could hear before maneuvering between two parked cars, a puddle and an empty beer bottle to get back onto the sidewalk.

Because of the weather, hailing a cab proved to be impossible as they were all occupied, and using the app on my phone wasn't any better, which was why I'd taken the train there from Sofia's house.

My socks were damp and my fingers numb, but so was the rest of me now. I hoofed it back to the subway station, rushing down the platform steps to catch the waiting train, the only other occupant a sleeping homeless man. I skirted past his trash bags full of empty soda cans, and took up a seat at the other end of the car. My leg shook uncontrollably as I sat there fuming and terrified of what I'd find once I got to Cole's place.

♦♦♦

What felt like an eternity later, the conductor announced my stop, and I'd slipped sideways through the parting doors before they'd fully opened, ascending the platform steps two at a time and charging through the turnstile at breakneck speed.

Pushing through the hotel revolving doors like a madman, I banged Cole's code into his elevator keypad, my breaths sawing in and out of my flared nostrils as I imagined the worst.

The elevator dinged, announcing its arrival to the lobby, and I backed away from the opening doors, suddenly too afraid to face what potentially awaited me upstairs.

The doorman and front desk concierge eyed me cautiously, so it was either get inside, or be escorted off the premises.

Once inside, I shoved the flaps of my coat aside to brace my hands on my hips as I paced a tight circle, squeezing my eyes tight, trying to shut out the dread.

Heartbreak, rage, and guilt trampled my insides. I should've been in my marital bed, in my husband's arms, not concerning myself with who Cole could be fucking. But I *was* concerned, and I didn't know what I would do, what I was capable of doing, or who I'd become once these elevator doors opened.

And through it all, through the trembling in my limbs, the imaginings of what I would find, flashes of the ecstasy they both were experiencing right then and maybe not for the first time...

Through it all I wanted him anyway. Wanted him, *still*. With a need so hot and melting my veins erupted with it.

One step onto the marbled foyer and the soles of my wet shoes squeaked. I removed them slowly along with my coat to buy time, but also not wanting to make my presence known. I needed to see them in all their glory. I needed to see the look in his eyes as he had someone who wasn't me. As sad as it was, I needed to know if someone else could make him feel the way I once had, because if I was going to break, I needed to break completely. I couldn't take the in-between any longer.

Romantic music streamed through the penthouse surround system. Low and sensual. The kind of music that lacked words, the kind you made love to, the kind that turned the scene into something unsettling, macabre even, once that lovemaking escalated to uninhibited, unadulterated fucking. It was the kind of music he'd loved to take me to. The kind he'd orchestrated with his bare hands and eyes closed, imagining how our bodies moved together with every strike of the chord he played. It was a symphony put together of *our* lovemaking. I knew every note by heart. And he was playing it for someone else.

A scent that wasn't his stained the air, and the turtleneck and shoes he'd worn created a trail toward the living room archway, like he was too worked up to wait any longer or go any further. But other than the sounds of music, the palatial suite was serene.

Cole sat behind his piano in only his dress pants, bare shoulders and head slumped forward, an empty tumbler and a bottle of whiskey—still mostly full, perched on the closed lid. The flames from the fireplace turned the amber liquid gold.

Out of nowhere his hand shot up, smacking the tumbler away, sending it skidding across the shiny black top to crash at the feet of the fireplace.

I flinched, sharply intaking air and drawing his attention. Cole wheeled his upper body around, grabbing the edge of his bench to keep from falling. His lip curled. He wasn't happy to see me.

Whatever this was. Whatever had happened here in the time it took me to get to him, he blamed me for it. And he had every right to. All the bad things we'd faced had started with me.

"Are we alone?"

"What are you doing here?" he finally asked, his icy rage slicing against my skin.

The coffee table had been upended. Hopefully a result of his current bad temper, and not a consequence of unrestrained sex.

Two unopened foil packets lay on the white, shaggy rug, and a tube of lubrication rested on its side up against the sofa leg as if it'd rolled there.

"Did you fuck him?" I asked.

"Why. Are. You. Here?" he repeated, each word spoken clearly, threateningly even.

"How many people have you fucked since you showed up here?" I had no right to ask, given the stipulations I'd made him promise to in this very room. But right then, my heart didn't care about anyone's rights. It wanted answers, and my anger rose to the occasion. "Answer me! Did you fuck him? And how many others?"

He laughed bitterly and mockingly. "How many times have you fucked your husband since I arrived in town?" he countered, spitting out the word *husband*. He wore his cruelness on his sleeve tonight. "How many times have you fucked your husband wishing it were me?" He stood now, kicking the bench aside. It flipped and screeched across the floor, one of the legs cracking when it made impact with the back wall.

His pants button was undone, the zipper only partially closed, and how sick was it that I took pleasure in seeing him hard, seeing his cock flexed and punching at the inner seam along his trouser leg. My ego assumed that meant he hadn't just had sex with anyone, or at least that it meant he hadn't had enough. Hadn't been satisfied.

I remembered too late not to let my stare linger, and when I met his eyes again, they had darkened knowingly.

The music came to a grinding halt. The silence heightened my awareness of him. Of his height, his width, his might... Of what I could gain and lose in one single breath if I didn't get out of there. I twisted my head toward the elevator, then back to him.

Without taking his eyes off me, he reached out and pressed a button on a tiny remote I hadn't noticed next to the aged bottle of Balvenie, and the music started up again, this time louder than a whisper, but still too low to drown out the sound of rushing blood in my ears.

It was as if he knew he needed to soften the predatory impression he made or risk losing me. Even if his appearing human right then, or of us being able to talk or verbally fight our way through our issues without crossing that final boundary, was all an illusion. Smoke and mirrors.

"I should go—"

"I didn't fuck him," he said.

"I don't believe you."

"No," he answered, "You don't want to believe me because you want to talk yourself out of why you're here in the first place."

"Maybe you didn't fuck him tonight. That doesn't mean you haven't—"

"None and no one!" he shouted. "I haven't fucked anyone since I've been here. I've wanted no one but you since I've been here!"

His words poured into my cup, but I still felt empty. Still needed more. "Does that mean you wanted someone else *before* you got here?" It killed me to be this pathetic, this needy, this unfair and irrational. After *everything,* I should've wanted him happy and content, but I could only muster up the imperfect part of me who wanted him stagnant and mine. Even if I couldn't give him the same. I wanted him to say he'd never wanted anyone but me, *ever*.

He remained silent, and I swallowed around the pain in my esophagus.

"When Daniel makes love to me," I started, and his face contorted in pain, "he doesn't ask for anything, and I give him less than nothing, because I have nothing to give. It's all with you. But when you make love, Cole... You leave a piece of your soul on the table. You can't help but give so much."

"Trust me," he breathed. "That only applies to you."

"You've never been touched the way you touch me. You'd never understand."

"And you've never been loved the way you loved me, not even by me. *No one* is capable of the kind of love you give. So you wouldn't understand how impossible it would be for me to move on. Or to give anyone even a fraction of what I gave you," he promised.

Our anger had been replaced with something softer, something more vulnerable, and it was wreaking havoc on me. "I shouldn't be here," I said so quietly I couldn't confirm if the statement was for me, for him, or God.

"But you are!" he shouted in frustration, rage returning with a vengeance. I stepped back, not in fear of him, but in fear of how aroused his outburst had made me. Cole reached me in three strides, yanking me to him by my sweater. "You don't get to run from me tonight. You face me and tell me what you're doing here. Because we both know you're aware of why."

He was right, and we were wrong, so wrong for this, but God help me I wanted it. No more running, no more pushing him and this thing brewing between us away, no more pretending the decision to risk it all was a hard one.

I lunged for his mouth, and he groaned, more like wailed in relief as he moved us over to the sofa.

"God, you fucking taste like him," I said, thoroughly pissed. He tasted like fine scotch and the citrusy scent cloying up his foyer. They'd kissed. They'd fucking *kissed*. With everything going on, I'd forgotten there was a host of other things that encompassed sex besides penetration.

He forced his kiss on me again, tearing my thin V-neck down the middle.

"What else did you two do?" I asked, no match for his swift tenacity. "Cole!" I yelled once he'd taken me down to the floor and rolled me onto my stomach, the condoms resting near my head veiling my vision red.

Cole wrestled my torn shirt down my arms, tying it around my wrists, turning the fabric into shackles. I kicked back, but he'd straddled me, making it impossible to land a kick with any meaning behind it. He finally flipped me to my back, hovering over me, the mop of hair he wore longer at the top now sweaty and flopping over his forehead. "Did you suck his dick?" I panted, wriggling my arms behind me to no avail. "Did he suck yours? Tell me!" I'd fucking kill him, kill them both if he answered yes.

He scooted lower, unthreading my belt from its loops. I tried to buck him off me, but he was stronger.

With my pants undone, he shimmied them off me, my cock springing free to slap my belly. The jeans were too slim-fitting to wear underwear underneath. "Cole!" I said, using my legs to propel me back on the rug, grimacing as the fibers scraped along my upper back and shoulders.

He was afraid and emotional; I could feel it. And everything was happening so fast. He lashed a hand out, securing an ankle and tugging me toward him, his heated stare never abandoning my stiff length.

Cole relaxed on his haunches, spreading his knees wider, his other hand rubbing along his erection through the thin layer of his pants.

Falling over me, he started up a dry hump while chasing my lips, growling in frustration and securing a fist in my hair to keep me still, stealing the kiss he wanted. "I love you," he said over and over between kisses and taking a second for air.

My body was a live wire, my mind unable to settle on one thought, my voice unable to spit out a coherent sentence. I bit his lip, sending him snarling away as I wheezed, the taste of copper filling my mouth. Perspiration beaded my skin, the heat from the fireplace bumping up against the flames bursting free from within.

"Did he suck your cock?" I needed this resolved before I handed myself over to him. Before I allowed him to take what he wanted from me.

"No," he said. "We kissed. And I couldn't go any further. I promise, angel."

Angel. It had been too many years since he'd called me that, and I could no longer fight the urge to bend, to give him every-thing, all of me right then, to be his good fucking angel.

Cole traveled down my body, the loss of his cock on mine sent signals of confusion, relief, and grief scraping along my mind's sensors. "Cole." I didn't know what I wanted to say, I lacked the time needed for reasoning. He was like an earthquake in the middle of a tsunami. Rattling and drowning me in his in-tensity at the same time.

My hands were useless and growing numb wrapped in the confines of my shirt. "Fuck!" I gritted out when he threw both my legs over his shoulders, then slid his palms beneath my ass and raised me to his opened mouth.

He ate me greedily, making lewd lapping sounds, praising the taste of me, shaking his head like a rabid dog as he buried his nose between my cheeks and inhaled like someone breaking the ocean's surface after being held under for too long.

"Please," I said, voice breaking on the word, unclear of what I wanted it to mean, the result I wanted it to garner, but my hips worked in a gesture that said I wanted more, or don't stop.

"You taste like heaven," he whispered, his words spoken directly into my asshole. "Christ, I've missed this." He spread my globes, opening my split a fraction more, then sent his tongue in. I keened loudly. He flicked his rapacious eyes to mine as the tip of his tongue fought to go deeper.

Cole ate until his heart was content and his cock could no longer wait to be inside me. He straightened, lowering me slowly as I fought to breathe.

Precum mingled with the sweat running in rivulets down my chest. My cock ached to be touched, my hole needed to be filled. "Cole," I whimpered, swallowing around a parched throat. "Please."

He made a show of lowering his zipper, rising to his knees and dropping his pants below the curve of his ass before sitting back on his calves again. "You remember our safeword, right?" he asked. My knees fell to either side of me, and I watched raptured as he pinched the purple crown of his dick, a bead of precum spitting from its slit to tremble down the veiny surface of it, thinning and fading the further it traveled the long distance to his nut sac. I nodded once because saying the word might have activated it.

"Say it. I need you to say it," he said.

"Yes," I gritted out.

"Yes," he repeated. *Yes.* That was our safeword, because we both loved it when he ignored my *no's.*

Cole helped me onto his lap, still not willing to free my hands, our cocks grazing each other as he searched my face, his hand running through my hair. "Look at me," he whispered, and I released a shuddering breath before doing so. His thumb brushed away the moisture at the corner of my eyes, his gaze soft, his voice was anything but. "This won't be easy, and I plan to take you all night."

I beat back the whine of fear clambering up my throat. It wasn't fear of him, but fear of what would happen once we were through. Fear of my guilt being compounded. Fear that it wouldn't matter enough to stop me, to stop *this* from happening again. Fear that he'd want me to choose him once it was over. Fear because I didn't know if I could. Or that I wouldn't, even if I wanted to.

The click of a bottle's lid sounded, and then our joint moans rose louder than the music playing as he cupped our cocks between a slicked hand and stroked with the sole purpose of getting us ready.

I mourned the loss of his hand when he let go, but then a wet digit skirted down my cleft before sinking into my hole. I gasped and clenched at the intrusion.

"Fuck, you're so tight, angel." His hand holding me up by my hair spasmed. "I can barely get it in," he said, working his finger in slowly. "How long has it been?" He tugged my hair when my lips thinned defiantly. "How long."

"Weeks," I said as the pain in my scalp and the fullness in my ass formed a potent shot of pleasure throughout my body.

"What kind of man leaves you unsatisfied for weeks?" he growled, sending another finger in. My chin dropped to my chest, my forehead meeting his lips. He worked me open for longer than needed, occasionally fanning a hand over my cock, the touch so light and teasing it left me feeling faint.

Cole liked it when I whimpered, when I cried for an end to his torture, when I begged for him to start, or to stop. And I loved it when he apologized for being unable to, because it meant I was special. It meant I had something he couldn't resist.

"It's out of my hands, angel," he'd say, as he fucked me into the bed, or the ground, or the wall. *"This is what you do to me."*

No amount of begging or bargaining or promises would get me what I didn't really want in the first place. He wouldn't stop. Wouldn't ease up on the gas. Wouldn't apply the brakes until I lay in a heap so well fucked I was broken in two.

It was as if I wasn't even there. As if I didn't have a voice, or a say. It was like it used to be during times like this. For him it was needing a feeling of complete possession, a feeling of "this is mine." Of fulfilling whatever fantasies he'd dreamt up since the last time he'd had me. *Taken* me. And it felt good to be needed that much. To see him lose his mind with wanting me, wanting *in* me. To give him the freedom to let go. Nothing could penetrate our orb when we were like that. We had no concept of the outside world, of boundaries, or walls. We were all sensation. All pleasure. All his and all mine.

With his pants still halfway down his thighs, his hands on my hips, and my feet planted on the carpet, he held the full weight of my body up, his dick poised at my center. "Is this what you want?" he asked, biceps bunching.

I could've said yes. I could've made this train stop. But it would've been a lie. "No," I said, so close my lips caressed his.

"Thank, God," he wept, lowering me onto his dick.

"Fuck," I groaned as he plunged into me. I shouted nonsensical words, trying to stay upright without the use of my arms, as he tugged me up and down on his large cock.

"You're mine when you're with me, do you hear that?" he asked, controlling the impact and speed in which I accepted the fucking. My ass clapped against his bare thighs as he chanted *"you're mine, you're mine,"* repeatedly, passionately, warningly. I lost my breath and mind.

How had I ever taken him before? How was it that I was receiving him now? "Too much," I said, teeth clashing from the force of his pounding.

"Fuck that," he said, body quivering beneath me. "This is what a real cock is supposed to feel like inside you." He held me down with one hand, grinding into me as he unknotted the shirt from my wrists with his other. Blood flowed immediately to the spot, leaving my hands tingling, and my head spinning. "Fight back," he said, reaffirming his hold and pumping me on and off him faster, harder.

I gripped his hair, curling my toes into the rug and bouncing onto him incessantly. "Fuck, fuck, fuck," I persisted as my cock beat at my belly, tempting me to reach for it between us.

"Don't touch it," he warned, taking me to my back and placing his full weight on me. His pants restricted his movements, but I wrapped my legs around him, my breaths punching through me as he fucked me so hard and so thoroughly.

It felt like he was purging years of pain, asking me to take it away from him, and I hitched my legs higher, opening myself up more for him, letting him know I could take whatever he needed to force into me.

"I fucking love you," he said, out of breath. He kissed me before I could answer him, or maybe before I could *not* answer him.

Cole pulled back, holding himself up on one forearm as the fingers of his free hand grazed my collarbone. A question lurked behind his eyes.

"No," I said, giving him permission. His hand crawled higher, bumping against the gold necklace and cross pendant I hadn't taken off since he came back into my life. "No," I said louder, jerking from his unforgiving thrusts, which had slowed but hadn't lost their powerful kick.

His big palm clasped around my throat, applying a subtle pressure at first, then squeezing with purpose. My fight or flight took over, and I clawed at his forearm, even while pressing my heels into his lower back, asking him for more.

Black spots dotted my peripheral vision, and my balls shriveled up tight. "That's it," he praised, sounding as if he'd spoken from under water. I dug my blunt nails into the mounds of his shoulders, one hand slipping to fall to the carpet as my vision blurred, and as he propelled in and out of me as if my life wasn't on the line. And then I came so hard I blacked out.

I came to still on my back, coughing, Cole still inside me, but unmoving, and he'd removed his pants. I couldn't have been out for more than a few seconds. "Cole?" My voice wobbled. This type of play always left me emotional and disoriented.

"I've got you, angel." He kissed me slowly this time, his hips moving at a compatible speed to his lips, being mindful of my sensitivity now that I'd come.

Cole had the virile will to last as long as needed, and I preferred him inside me than not, so I used to live for these more tempered moments, too, when his cock rolled in and out of me patiently, waiting for me to swell again.

We continued our languid kiss as Cole possessively stroked my cock to firmness, all while letting me know it belonged to him, until I was ready again.

This was lovemaking. It was sensual, passionate, a coordinated dance routine we easily fell back into. And when he was ready to unload inside me, and when I was more than ready to spill again, he sent me to my hands and knees, his chest to my back, one hand under me, reaching for my dick, his tongue exploring my flesh.

"No marking," I pleaded, fisting the rug, the light of the moon glinting off my wedding band. Or maybe it was the condemning eyes of God shining down on me.

"You don't get to tell me what to do to you," he growled into my neck, teeth locking around my skin as we came, his cum temporarily washing the guilt away.

Moments later, I rested on my back as he stared down at me, transferring the cum leaking from my hole to his lips as I struggled to keep my eyes open. "I'm safe," he whispered, clearing the sleep haze away. I turned to the unwrapped condoms. Daniel and I never went without protection, and I trusted Cole, but it just went to show how completely we lost our heads when together. Our status was something to be addressed before, not after.

Cole pressed a palm to my chest when I went to sit up. "You're staying with me tonight," he said firmly but gently, plucking a strand of hair from my lips. "Tell him you're staying with me tonight."

"Okay." I exhaled, leaving tomorrow in the future and taking what I wanted right now.

We made love on the piano, and with my cheek pressed against the cold balcony doors, my breaths smoking up the glass. I trembled on my hands and knees as Cole played with the mess he'd made inside of me, fingering and licking me clean. I knelt between his spread legs and sucked his cock as he sat on the edge of the sofa, hands hanging loosely over his spread knees, back as straight as a god's, while I played shy and naïve, allowing him to instruct and guide me, while praising me on how good I was doing.

"Yeah, just like that. Take it all the way. I love it when you gag on it. I love that it's too much for you. You're perfect, angel."

Then he defiled my face, fingering my curls and feeding me the cum splattered on my nose and cheeks, and taking some for himself as I blushed.

He bathed me and washed my hair, and when it was my turn to take care of him, I did so tentatively as if it were my first time touching a man, touching anyone, and Cole hardened.

"You're so easy," I laughed before ditching the soapy sponge over my shoulder and backing him under the spray of water. I

kneaded his shoulders and chest as the suds washed away, feeling great satisfaction from his agonized groan.

Cole reached blindly behind him for the bottle of lube on the shower shelf, knocking the soap dispenser to the tiled floor in the process.

I nibbled on the corner of my lower lip, watching transfixed as he lathered up his cock while advancing on me until my back had met the glass shower wall. His sizable crown rubbed against my tensed abs as he reached a hand past my hip and around to open me. He then hiked me up by my ass, my legs circling him as he spread me apart so his dick could cruise through me.

Even after all the rigorous sex we'd had that night, taking him now was still an effort. He stood motionless, happy with the simple pleasure of having his cock in me, at having it surge impossibly bigger and harder as I flushed while swearing I couldn't handle him.

I'd obsessively studied Cole from the moment I walked through Franklin's estate doors. We worked because I gave him what he needed even when he hadn't known it was a need. And I didn't judge him for any of it, and he returned the favor because it worked both ways.

I'd always needed to be the source of Cole's happiness. The sole object of his affection and desire. Even when we were apart. Even when I wouldn't admit it to myself. And he'd always needed to feel like he was corrupting an angel, dirtying me up and stealing my innocence from me.

When the fullness became too much to ignore, Cole made love to me in the shower, taking his time with me as we kissed and hugged each other tight the whole way through. And when we dried off, and I headed for his living room, Cole caught my hand.

"No more sofa. No more pretending we aren't doing exactly what we're doing. You're sleeping in my bed tonight."

Leave tomorrow for the future, I reminded myself before falling asleep all over him, his arms and legs securing me in a vice grip, my nose tucked into his neck.

CHAPTER 15

Cole

WAKING WITH A racing heart, and shielding my eyes from the blast of morning sun, I

sighed in relief when the reason for my panic proved unwarranted. Jasper was here. It was real. It hadn't been a dream.

I generated an excessive amount of heat when asleep, and I'd kept him cocooned to me most of the night until it was either let him go, or drown in a pool of our combined sweat. At some point he'd found his way into my side anyway. Now he slept on his stomach, hairline sweaty, cheek flushed.

With a rough hand I grabbed his bare ass, my fingers so close to disappearing between his cleft, and he didn't stir. Jasper could sleep like the dead if I exhausted his body enough. I trailed my gaze down the hickeys on his back, to the matching deep purple bruises I'd sucked onto the curve of his ass in between rimming him as he prayed for mercy on the lid of my Steinway.

I'd gotten carried away. I could've used the alcohol I'd barely drunk as an excuse, but the weak attempt at justification would've been transparent. Jasper's body now reflected years of grief, of anger, resentment, betrayal, and love set free. I'd let it all go last night. I'd punished him for what the loss of him had done to me, and what not having him, even now as he slept peacefully in my bed, still did to me.

Fear tightened its claws around my heart because once Jasper woke up to what I'd done to him, with the night sky now behind us, and the lust cleared, he'd end this. Whatever *this* was. I couldn't send him home in his current state.

"No marking."

"You don't get to tell me what to do to you."

I'd wanted to do more.

My gaze sought out the gold rope tieback holding the curtains apart at the window, and then the pale skin at his ankles and wrists, and suddenly I wanted him again. I'd need him often now.

My need would have to take a back seat to something more pressing. Careful to not jostle him, I slid from the bed, slowly closing the bedroom door before working my way to my office. I made some urgent calls, shifted a few things around, and told Leland to make sure the company jet was fueled and on the tarmac within a couple hours.

Hanging up, I stared at my erect cock, which hadn't abated since leaving Jasper in my bed. Making my way to the living room for the bottle of lube I'd left there, I lathered my demanding erection, and then strode impatiently back to my bedroom. Jasper hadn't moved from his position.

I kissed the backs of his thighs, moving closer to the place I hungered to feast from, spreading his plump mounds and inhaling him, leashing a hand around my base. He slept through it all, which only increased the level of my arousal.

I drizzled lube over his hole, watching him for signs of waking, but he continued to snore softly.

With one hand planted on the pillow next to his head, and the other drawing his ass cheek to one side, I entered him with restraint, knowing he had to be sore from last night.

He grunted, his lower half twinged, and I paused, balls hanging in the air.

Once his breathing evened out, I plunged in halfway. My thrusts were excruciatingly slow and fractional, withdrawing and re-entering, moaning softly and vibrating with the need to fill him absolutely. But the moment my pelvis tapped against his soft skin, this clandestine act of making love to him without his knowledge would end, and fucking him like this was almost as good as taking his ass while he shouted *no*.

Jasper's breathing quickened as his body became aware, but his eyes remained closed as if his brain hadn't computed this wasn't a dream. I buried my nose in his hair, barely scraping his scalp with my teeth as I savored these final few seconds.

He whispered my name groggily into his pillow, and I changed my angle, adopting a sideways motion as I sank in all the way, clenching my ass and jamming up against him, shoving him higher up the bed. I wanted everything in him, and I pried his ass apart further just to be sure he'd gotten every piece of me, that there was nothing holding me back. My toes scraped along the sheets, trying to find purchase as I fed and fed and fed him all of me.

I moved my head away in time to escape a headbutt as he came awake on a gasp and pushed to his palms.

"It's okay," I whispered, increasing my rhythm as he clenched around me. "Hold on," I said, helping him to his knees and placing his hands on the headboard.

"Cole," he said, adrift, arching his back and dropping his head between his shoulders.

I ran my slicked hands over his chest, through the trimmed, tight curls surrounding his cock, up his muscled back, and up and down his straining, extended arms. "It's almost over, angel."

"No," he groaned, taking me so good I could've cried. I placed my hands on top of his, leaving him responsible for keeping his hips in place as I bore into him.

"Are you sore?" I asked, biting gently on his earlobe.

"Not sore enough," he answered, his voice sleep-heavy.

The bed rocked, and I focused on speeding up my climax so his body could get the rest it needed. "I'm about to come," I said between gnashed teeth, getting in a few more thrusts. "Fuck." My spine locked as my orgasm blew through me.

I ground against his ass, making sure every drop of my cum found its way home, found its way to the deepest parts of him. In the process, I gained a sick, superior satisfaction from knowing my seed was the only one being planted in his garden.

"Cole," he whimpered.

"I've got you," I said, slipping out and turning him around. He fell bonelessly onto the bed and was coming into my mouth before his weeping crown had tapped my tonsils.

Jasper urged me up his body by my hair, tonguing me and moaning from the taste of himself.

"Were you really asleep?" I asked as he dropped kisses along my jaw.

"Maybe," he said, laughing when I poked him in his ribs, and then rolled us until we hit the floor.

◆ ◆ ◆

Gripping the molding above the bathroom door frame, I watched with trepidation as Jasper—now showered and fully alert, took in the handprint at his throat, and the love bites surrounding his nipples like petals blooming from a pistil. My fingers dug in to the point of aching when he met my eyes through the mirror over the sink.

"Daniel's on his way to the airport. Something came up last minute, and we need him to help negotiate a contract. I told him I'd let you know. He'll be out of the country until Friday morning. More than enough time for those to fade."

"What?" he asked in disbelief. "The answer isn't to invent business trips to ship him off to whenever you feel like losing your cool in bed, Cole. We need to be more discreet, or this won't work."

Or you could leave him, I didn't say, because he was already getting worked up, and Jasper on an anger-bender wasn't something you willingly contended with.

"I'll be more careful with you." It killed me to say that.

The concern didn't entirely evaporate from his expression, but thankfully the regret had. I closed in behind him, smoothing my palms over his flanks and cupping his pectorals lovingly, already mourning the impending loss of the bruises cascading over them.

"And I didn't *invent* a business trip. I shifted some things around so I could up the timetable drastically on this one. Let's not fight." I groped and squeezed his pecs as if milking them, my cock ballooning at the crease of his ass. "Now come eat," I said, moving away and tapping one of his bruised cheeks lightly. "Your coffee's getting cold." I sauntered off, feeling his eyes on my nakedness as I went.

Jasper entered the kitchen wearing one of my t-shirts and a pair of my sweats. A protective barrier he'd be foolish to think I couldn't get through if I wanted or needed to, but his message was clear: the fun and games were over for now. And I'd respect it. For now.

He held a pair of plaid pajama bottoms out to me, and I legged into them without argument.

"Wish you could take it back?" I asked, sliding the milk across the island to him.

"I could lie and say yes," he said, "but I'd need at least two cups of coffee first. Right now I don't have it in me. I'm trying not to feel bad for something I did with a clear head, but this is so messed up, Cole."

"Do you want to stop?"

"No. But this isn't fair to him. I don't want to hurt him, but I'm not leaving him, either," he said conflicted.

He could be stubborn when he wanted to be, and I toyed with whether or not to address the unsaid thing between us, knowing facing it could potentially help him, and save us. "Do you plan on avoiding my father forever?"

He coughed around a mouthful of coffee, setting his mug down. "Where did *that* come from?"

"Just answer me, Jas."

"It's been working so far."

"That was before."

"Before what?" he asked.

"Before I moved here, and before we were back in each other's lives. I think seeing him may help—"

"No." The word was a slammed door, and now wasn't the right time to kick it down. I dug into my eggs, and he bit into a strip of his bacon. How had we gone from last night, to this morning, to this? It'd be up to me to bring us around.

"What's your week look like?" I asked.

He tore a sheet of paper towel off the holder on the island, wiping his mouth with it. "'Fia's got a case she wants me to look at. Nothing urgent, though. And classes are following an alternate schedule this week, so I'm free."

"I've cleared my calendar for most of the week. That means I'll be booked solid next week, but as of now, I'm all yours."

"What should we do?" he said, the mood lighter.

"I was thinking about Christmas tree shopping," I answered. Selene had implemented the family tradition. Prior to her, my father would hire the hassle out. She even managed to secure his participation in hunting down the perfect tree, even if he grumbled through the whole ordeal.

We hadn't had a Christmas tree since she died, and from the unease written on Jasper's face, neither had he. "You could come. Help me decorate it along with the rest of this place. Please," I added.

"We haven't even made it past Thanksgiving yet."

I hadn't mentioned Thanksgiving because I didn't want to draw attention to the fact that he'd be spending it with me, not Daniel. Not so soon after his upset about the marks I'd left on his body, and then shipping his husband away to cover it up. I didn't want him seeing what I had done as a premeditative way to have him to myself for the holiday, because it wasn't. But I was ecstatic about it and already working plans out in my head. And maybe by some miracle, I'd get him for Christmas, too. "Since when did that stop us?" Christmas season started when Selene said it did, which was usually any time after Halloween.

"True enough," he said, surprisingly not making his Thanksgiving without Daniel a talking point. "Okay."

We were too far apart, and when I prowled to his side of the island, he followed my advancement with a leeriness I hated seeing. One I helped put there with my disregard for his wish to keep our affair prudent. In my defense, I didn't know how to touch him in a nonproprietary way. I didn't know how to mate with him and not brand him, too. And he'd loved it. Wanted and needed it as much as I had. His body would always betray his denial. But in the light of day and thinking with a lust-free head, he needed to pretend I was the bad guy. He needed someone to share the burden of blame.

He spun around on his stool, his gaze falling between my legs and the tent pitched there. I crowded in between his thighs, directing his stare to mine with a hold on his chin. "Ignore it," I said. "It can't be helped." I examined his neck, angling his head accordingly, then kissed the angry scars. "I'm sorry," I said, nailing myself to the cross for him.

He bowed his head, releasing the tension he'd been storing in his shoulders since leaving my bed. "I wanted it," he admitted unnecessarily. "I still want it. Fuck, I want *more*. I want you to do whatever you want with my body and...my heart. But I won't let myself have you, Cole." He looked at me, then, a sorrowful expression mingled with his beauty. Pure innocence and vulnerability. The two things my fantasies of him were built on. "This is the best I can do. But I can't rein you or myself in when we're like that, Cole. You've always been the one in charge of the control."

I forcibly locked him into a smoldering kiss, agreeing without words, leaving us both short on air at its conclusion.

"And don't ever tell me to ignore this," he said, slipping his thumbs into my waistband and skimming the soft cotton below my ass and balls. He stared at me from below lush brows, blinking lazily.

"Do you remember what to do with it?" I asked.

"I think so," he said timidly, standing and then getting to his knees. My head sloped to the side as his mouth wrapped me up in its warmth. *Of course he remembered.*

◆ ◆ ◆

Mark found us a tree farm upstate, and we spent the long, snowy drive entertaining him with stories of our childhood Christmas shenanigans.

"...he vandalized Christmas!" I said, ending the story of how Jasper's first holiday with us went. Mark laughed, meeting my amusement in the rearview mirror.

"You're so full of it," Jasper chimed in, elbowing me.

"So you're saying you didn't sneak downstairs in the middle of the night and tear apart every gift looking for your own? *And* ate Santa's cookies?"

"Okay, maybe that much is true, but I grew up poor. Our Christmas tree was a potted plant my mother nearly suffered an aneurysm trying to keep alive. We'd hang these macaroni earrings I'd made for her in class one year on it as ornaments," he said nostalgically. "I was overwhelmed that first Christmas at Franklin's house—"

"Our house," I corrected, and he squeezed the hand I kept secretly pressed to his thigh under the coat I'd artfully draped between us. To Mark we were nothing more than reconnected family. To the rest of the world we weren't even that. No one in New York, other than Leland, Daniel, and Mark, knew of our connection. And only Leland knew the truth of it.

"Just the sheer size of that tree," he said in wonder. "I might've gone a little crazy."

"You think? The least you could have done was read the name tags to ensure it was your gift you were opening. Poor Mom turned beet red at seeing the skimpy lingerie my father had gotten her dangling like an ornament from a tree branch." The car went silent, and Jasper smiled at me. I retraced my words, catching my slip. "I loved her, you know."

"Yeah, I know," he said.

I often worried he believed I got over her, as if I ever could. Or that my pain couldn't possibly match his. I'd lost two mothers, and had a hand in both of their deaths. The pain had nearly killed me.

"I smartened up after that," he said to Mark. "Not only did I check the tags, I'd open my gifts so carefully, making sure I didn't tear the paper, that no one even noticed they'd been rewrapped and taped."

"Are you kidding me?" I doubled over laughing within the confines of my seat. "You thought you were getting over with those botch jobs? We were three years into his antics by then, Mark. Everyone gave up. Stopped caring. Why do you hate surprises so much?" I asked, but he shrugged, his mossy green eyes shining animatedly. Without thought I dragged a thumb down his top and lower lip, then withdrew it as if the plush pink pillows contained flames. Our eyes flashed to Mark, who'd been too busy making a left turn to notice us.

Jasper's face heated from the innocuous touch, his perfect row of teeth peering through his parted mouth, his body so responsive to me. He looked so scared and so innocent, and I'd have given up anything to take advantage of that right then. To seat my cock inside him while whispering he had nothing to be afraid of.

"So how did your parents meet?" Mark asked, folding down the sun visor. "Doesn't sound like they ran in the same circles."

"My mother won an all-expense paid, five-star beach vacation in one of those women's magazine raffles," Jasper said, collecting himself.

"And my father had finally decided to deal with the death of my mother. He took a much-needed break from work. The first vacation he'd taken since I was born. He saw Selene lounging by the pool, and the rest was history."

"Not many people are lucky to find love twice," Mark said, his gray eyes and gray hair populating the rearview mirror again.

"My father wasn't an easy man to love, Mark. I'd only known him to be broken, and that I was the one who'd broken him. He was dedicated to his job, and spent most of my childhood running away from me." *Running away from the reminder.* "Selene made him worth loving, though. He tried for her sake. She was his everything." I regretted speaking the honest words the instant Jasper pulled away from me; but then seeming to understand he wasn't the only one entitled to pain, he slid his palm back under the coat and retook my hand.

"Should we tell him about the apple picking incident?" I asked Jasper, changing the subject. Willing to say and do anything to bring a smile—or in this case a grimace—to his face. Mark looked intrigued.

"Let's just say I used to love green apples, and now I don't." He shivered from the memory of eating so many of them at the orchard that he'd puked all over my father's new car the whole ride home.

We arrived at the tree farm and spent about an hour debating over what size tree to purchase.

"We don't need something that big for just the two of us," Jasper argued when I pointed to a twelve-foot stunner. It warmed my heart to hear him consider the tree ours, even if it was said without thought. Maybe it meant I'd get him for Christmas, that he'd carve out some time for me. He'd mentioned spending his last couple Christmases with Daniel's family. Maybe this year it'd be him and me. *Our* family.

"Doesn't matter. I saw the way your eyes gleamed when you spotted it. It's an exact replica of the one we had that first Christmas together. We're getting it." I waved an attendant over to assist, stealing a side-glance at Jasper, fully expecting a scowl but finding whimsy instead as he stepped closer to the tree.

"Will this fit?" he asked, staring adoringly at the tall fir.

"Have you seen my ceilings?" I asked.

"Well what about the elevator?"

"We'll make it work." I wasn't leaving there without that tree. If it would've taken a crane to get it through the penthouse windows, so be it.

We helped Mark strap the whopper to the roof of the SUV, and then we were off. I'd had the concierge send one of their shoppers out for decorations, so we drove straight home and spent the rest of the evening decorating, making the penthouse a home for the holidays.

Jasper sat on the floor of the living room, staring up at the lit tree. Between its golden sparkle and the city lights filtering in through the wall of windows, we didn't need the interior lights on at all.

I left the room and returned with a wrapped present, sitting in front of him and handing it off after he'd pushed up from his palms and secured his hair into a bun. "Figured it didn't make sense putting this under the tree with you around. Open it."

"You could have hidden it until Christmas," he said, all while snatching it from me and ripping the silver paper to shreds. I chuckled, carding a rogue curl behind his ear.

"What is this?" he asked, turning the framed document right side up.

"It's a patent for this piece of technology," I said, producing a glass encased t-shaped object the size of a jellybean from my pocket. "This is going to help us succeed in making the artificial heart something close to permanent, not transitional. One that can sustain the host's life well beyond a handful of years."

"Stupid question, but we're not talking about immortality, are we?"

"No, it's not meant to last forever, a transplant will still ultimately be needed, but it provides the recipient more time. And it will allow for a relatively normal existence in the interim. And with any luck, anyone in need will be a candidate." Selene hadn't been a good candidate for what had currently been on the market.

"Will it work?" he whispered, daring to hope.

"We have the largest laboratory, top scientists, and engineers in the country who all believe it's possible."

"How long will it take?"

"Time," I admitted, regretfully. "Things like this take time. Right now all we have is the design and the technology to make it happen. And hopefully I'll get the call from Daniel or my team shortly telling me the necessary paperwork has been signed to get the prototype underway. There will be trial and error, and a lot of red tape to go through before getting the final product approved for testing. It'll be worth the wait, though."

"Thank you," he said.

"It's only a copy—"

"I'm not thanking you for the document, Cole."

I nodded. "Where will you hang it?"

"Maybe in my office," he said, chewing on his lower lip.

"Your home office?"

"No. I've been thinking about starting up my own firm."

"What?" I relieved him of the frame, setting it aside so I could send him to his back, my hands plastered on either side of his head as I held myself above him. "When did you decide this?"

"I haven't decided yet. I said I've been *thinking* about it." But he was breathless with anticipation. He wanted this; he just needed to know he had a right to go for it.

"You get to be excited about this, Jasper," I said, tugging his lip free and watching a smile split his face. "You never have to hide or downplay your happiness with me. *Never*," I said again with emphasis. "I'm not him."

"It'll be costly. But there's loans, and I've got a little savings—"

"You've got more than a *little* savings," I said. "You have enough company shares to fund a small country. And you haven't touched your trust—"

"That money doesn't belong to me."

"My father—"

"Would snatch it away in a heartbeat if he knew the truth. I'd have donated every cent of it by now if it were mine to give."

I sank my fingers below the turtleneck he strategically wore to hide my handprint and stroked the column of his throat. It would do me no good to argue with him. It wasn't how I wanted our night to end. "How can I help you?"

"You can't," he whispered, and I knew he was talking about more than the firm, the same way he probably knew my question had gone far beyond that, too.

"Okay," I said. "Have you told anyone else?"

"You're the first to know. You'll always be the first to know, Cole," he said, reading my need well.

I ran his lower lip between my teeth. "What should we do with the rest of our night? How should we celebrate?"

"I'm tired, to be honest," he said, raising his head to graze his soft lips up and down my stubbled chin. "Someone kept me up all night?"

"Well then, will you let me bathe you, take you to my bed and massage some fading cream into your bruises, and then hold you?"

"Do you really need to ask?" he said, stealing a kiss.

CHAPTER 16

Daniel

3 Years, 8 Months Ago

"MR. DES MOINES is here." Jessica's voice sounds through my office phone's speaker.

"Send him in." I press the disconnect button, and quickly stand to stretch into my blazer, buttoning it as my office door opens.

Jasper Des Moines steps in like a soft breeze, but something about him also screams chaos. His features are gentle, striking, even, with the juxtaposed clash of his obviously masculine body beneath the suit he seems uncomfortable in. One can't help but to take the time to notice him.

"Mr. Ward," he says, his bashful smile and baritone voice adding to his polarity. He holds out a hand, and I take it, his grip is firm but not challenging in the slightest, confident but willing to concede power.

"Interesting," I say.

"Excuse me?"

It's clear his perfect balance of demure charm, deference, and self-assuredness isn't a façade, a means to win me over. No, he's oblivious to his intrigue.

Something moves in me, then, but not enough. Not enough to make a difference.

"Please, call me Daniel, and welcome to the internship program."

CHAPTER 17

THE SCENT OF hazelnut breached my nostrils, snapping me from my thoughts of the past. "Mmm," I moaned, accepting the mug Cole held under my nose from behind.

"What were you thinking about?" he asked, coming around to rest his back on the bedroom window he'd caught me gazing unseeingly out of. "Whatever it was has got you leaking bigtime." He fingered the pearl-sized bead of precum from my stiff cock before letting it fall into his own coffee. He chanced a gulp of the steaming liquid, his eyes closing as he groaned in ecstasy. "Who knew a pinch of salt made everything better." He drank as he stroked me off with a spit-slicked palm, and I tried to drink as I orgasmed almost immediately, already having been on the cusp of it due to my travel back in time.

Cole licked his hands clean, adding a few more drops to his coffee. "So, what were you thinking about?"

"The time we came up with our safeword," I said, walking on shaky legs to the nightstand where Cole had placed the framed patent he'd given me four nights ago. I set my coffee down and strolled back over to him with the intention of getting to my knees and returning the favor.

"No," he said, grabbing my wrist. "I'm saving it for tonight." He offered me a sip of his cum-laced coffee to ease the bite of rejection. "Things changed after that," he said in reference to the implementation of our safeword. "We started experimenting more."

We'd found our rhythm—our kink, little did we know—and with every sexual encounter afterward, we began to understand more of what the other wanted and needed. We grew bolder. Judged ourselves less. Gave less fucks. I'd gotten that euphoric feeling back during these days spent with Cole.

"This doesn't end tonight," Cole said, reading my mind. Daniel would return tomorrow, and while Cole and I weren't ending things, we were ending our vacation. I'd be returning home, returning to how things used to be, in a way. *It's for the best. How it has to be.*

"I know. It won't be the same, though. You won't have the same access to me." I knew Cole well. Knew no matter how much he claimed he could manage this, chances were he couldn't, and I found myself subtly reminding him, or more like preparing him, for how things would be. We'd need to proceed with caution.

"We spend a good deal of time together whether he's around or not. You've spent nights here before."

"Yeah, but we can't play house," I said, gesturing to my bags and the clothes strewn all over the place, some whole, some ripped to shreds by his hands. Setting up boundaries was more for me than Daniel, because I was getting attached to the idea of how it could be, and it absolutely *couldn't* be.

He stood tall, drawing my chin up, laying a chaste kiss on my lips, his free hand soaring through my hair and tugging pain-fully. "Will you have sex with him?"

I'd already lost track of the days—possibly even weeks—since Daniel and I last had sex. We'd both been busy, and he'd never had an overactive sex drive to begin with. Going a few weeks here and there without sex wasn't outside the norm for us. I'd honestly been grateful for the lulls whenever they'd occur. I'd thought maybe something had died in me along with my mother and my relationship with Cole. Turned out I was fine, or if something had died, Cole's presence had resurrected it. Again I found myself overwhelmed with the mess I was making of our lives.

"He's my husband," I said, wondering again which of us I aimed to convince. "Cole," I said, reaching out when he backed away from me, but he dodged my hand.

"Will you enjoy it?"

"No." I'd avoid it at all costs, and chances were I wouldn't need to try hard. I couldn't tell Cole that, though. Admitting it would've served as false hope. Yet, I didn't want him with anyone else. "If you ever need me when we're not together... If it gets so bad that you can't wait, text or call. I'll try and get to you."

He huffed, shaking his head at my audacity. After the longest pause, he said around a tight smile, "I've got a whole day planned for us. No more talk about Daniel. You and I are the only ones who exist until tomorrow. Deal?"

It didn't escape me he hadn't agreed, and if his goal was to make me jealous and alarmed, he had succeeded. It'd need to go on the backburner for now. "Only if you promise we're not going to another medical conference," I joked, or tried to at least, fully on board with living in denial for the next twenty-four hours. Denial was where I thrived best.

"I thought you enjoyed learning about the atriums and ventricles of the heart," he said, feigning hurt as he looped his pinky through mine and walked us over to the bed.

"I'll always support you, but warn me before dragging me to a six-hour conference next time, okay?"

"*Dragging?*" he asked, setting his mug next to mine.

"Okay, maybe dragging is too strong a word," I conceded. The morning after he'd given me the framed patent, I'd personally gone online and found a conference in Brooklyn with tickets still available. I'd had them printed before he woke up. My way of saying thank you.

"You literally planned the whole thing. I *always* check to see how long those things run before biting the bullet." Our smiles were a tad more genuine now, our problems dissolving into the future as he sought to restore our connection.

"I need to taste you. I need my tongue and fingers deep inside you," he whispered, licking his lips in preparation. "And I need it now." I spread out on my back at his directive, spacing my heels far apart on the edge of the mattress. I bunched the sheets between my fists, undulating my hips as he got to his knees and fucking devoured me whole, leaving himself dripping and wanting.

♦ ♦ ♦

"Nothing but the clothes on your back." Those were Cole's instructions when I'd asked what I should pack for the night. He was tight-lipped otherwise on our plans. He'd given Mark the holiday off, and it felt good not having to pretend we were anything other than what we were today.

We rode in the back of a sleek, tinted sedan with the partition up as our driver maneuvered through the congestion caused by the Thanksgiving Day parade street closures.

I had been upset with Cole for not being discreet about our lovemaking. Upset with him sending Daniel out of town as a tactic for hiding our affair. I was terrified of being caught, of Daniel growing suspicious if Cole and I weren't careful. There was real guilt behind what I was doing to my husband. He didn't deserve it, just like my mother hadn't deserved what I'd done to her. I truly didn't want to hurt him, even though my actions said differently. My actions always seemed to say differently.

I hadn't made the fact that he'd be gone for the holiday an issue because honestly, I was relieved I wouldn't have to spend it with his parents. It was no secret they didn't approve of me, and they never let Daniel forget he could do better. Dinners with them usually involved his father scowling at my hair, and his mother reminding Daniel that his financial success was primarily due to the trust they'd established for him at birth, making him feel like he was living off their dime.

Attempting to forget about all that, and remain in the moment with Cole, I kept my eyes glued to the world outside my back seat window, trying to predict where we were headed. "Brunch at the top of the Empire State Building." I pursed my lips. "Then a Broadway play. *Hamilton*, because you know I've been wanting to see it since moving here," I said, and he laughed, because I hadn't ever mentioned that to him, but on the off chance we weren't going to see *Hamilton*, he now knew I wanted to. "Then dinner at Le Bernardin," I said with perfect pronunciation, proving my French tutoring hadn't been a complete waste of Franklin's money. "Because you're in the mood to throw your money around. Then," I finished in triumph, bringing an end to my ridiculous, one-man game of Clue, "we end the night in a suite atop the Riyodahn overlooking the twinkling city."

"Shit. Is it too late to change our plans to *that*?" he asked, hitting me with a crooked smile. "Stop squirming," he reprimanded.

"Stop enjoying it," I said, trying to find a position that didn't put so much pressure on the narrow plug he'd inserted in me. Due to its size, the low-level arousal was mostly easy to ignore, but this was only the beginning of his torturous plans.

Cole laced his fingers through mine, rolling his thumb over the deserted spot where my wedding band should've been.

"'You and I are the only ones who exist until tomorrow,'" I reminded him.

More than an hour later, we ended up at the heliport at Pier 6 along the East River, a short distance from our starting point at Cole's place. "Was keeping me on my toes *that* important?" I asked.

"Yes. Plus we had some time to kill before the pilot arrived. Let's go."

The island of Manhattan was majestic from that high up, but we spent most of the ride staring at each other. We landed on the helipad of a palatial estate, a good distance from the city, close to noon.

Lit fireplaces were the focal point of every room. Their stone craftsmanship rode the walls they were built against, tapping the ceilings. The estate manager provided a full tour, and then we were shown to our room where tuxedos hung in unzipped garment bags, and robes and other essentials were neatly draped over the velvet-lined brass bench at the foot of the king bed.

My heart rattled when I spotted the cold weather equestrian gear.

"Do you still ride?" Cole asked, sneaking in behind me as I lifted up a pair of riding breeches. His breath at my neck sent my toes curling in my boots, and I gripped one of the bed's four posters to keep my balance.

"Not since leaving home," I said.

"There are stables on the other side of the property. I made sure to instruct them to leave the tacking to us. I knew you'd want to make your own selection and do a little bonding first."

"Really?" I loved riding, but I never allowed myself to do it here. Leaving the city always felt like such a task, and riding reminded me too much of home. Too much of my mother shouting embarrassingly from the bleachers every time I cleared a hurdle in competition.

"Really," Cole said. "And I'll even let you beat me in a race."

"Let me?" I said doubtfully. Cole had been riding for years before I came along, but by the time I hit my teens you'd never know it.

"You've been out of the saddle for a while now. Don't get too cocky."

It never occurred to me he'd still be riding. I wasn't the only one Mom lost her mind and her voice for yelling in the stands. But he'd worked through what still triggered me. "How's Warrior?"

"She's fine. In serious need of a name change, but she's fine."

"Warrior's the perfect name for a horse. Better than Lightning."

"Hey, she's got a stripe of white in her mane. Lightning makes perfect sense. My horse was destined to have that name," Cole said with a finger pointed.

"Is she getting enough exercise?"

"Someone rides her a few days a week."

"Someone?" I asked, because Warrior didn't like just anyone riding her.

"It was me until I left," he admitted. Warrior hated him, and he'd taken care of her anyway. I didn't need another reason to love him, but the universe seemed intent on giving me one regardless. "Took us a while to reach an understanding. Bribing her with carrots did the trick, and she eventually stopped trying to throw me to my death. She never gave up the eye-of-scorn, though. It was like she knew you weren't there because of me."

"Do they know—"

"That she likes to be brushed before and after every ride, but only for a short while after a ride, because she prefers to mostly be rubbed until she settles down? Yes, they know." He bit my thumb as it weaved a path across his lips in gratitude.

"The snow's gone, and it's unseasonably warmer than it should be today. Mother Nature's holding her breath so we can have this moment. Let's go before we lose it," he said, stroking his knuckles over my cheek.

The estate sat on over thirty acres of land, and we rode for hours, laughing through our exertion, losing track of time, and our problems, too. My borrowed horse was named Sable—after the color of her coat. She could've been a direct relative of Warrior.

"You can come visit her anytime," Cole said, as I brushed and talked to her after our ride. He leaned against the stable door watching me, his own horse already tended to. I liked to linger.

"Only if you come with me," I said, chuckling at his pleased expression. I felt different there, with him. Changed somehow, but not yet clear on in what way. He'd returned a piece of me, though. A piece I'd been terrified to reclaim.

"Hungry?" he asked, twilight spreading over the property behind him.

"Famished," I admitted.

"Let's get cleaned up for dinner."

Our suite's shower had a whirlpool tub in its corner, which was already heated and bubbling when we got back to our room. Cole had rented out the place for us, and other than the stablehand, who'd kept a low profile, and the estate manager who'd given us the tour when we arrived, I hadn't seen anyone else. He'd planned this night perfectly, predicting what we'd need and when, and making sure it was ready.

We slipped into the tub first, the jets massaging the muscles that would be sore from riding come morning, then we headed for a hot shower.

Cole kneaded my skin with soapy hands, examining and kissing each fading bruise he'd given me, mourning the loss of them, as if they were the only thing making us real. What was left of them could easily be explained away if noticed by Daniel.

"If only I could take my hands to you," Cole murmured from down on his knees, nose against my plug-free pucker. "If only I could spank you hard." He smacked my ass cheek lightly, his palm and the water sluicing down my skin creating a beautiful song, echoing through the marbled enclosure. I moaned, holding myself up with a hand to the glass wall. His palm landed heavier, faster, in the same place and then not, with just the right amount of hurt to make my cock perk up, but not enough to cause damage. Not enough to make my ears ring as I came.

He'd need to be the one to stop. He held the control for a reason, and I was the victim to his dirty deeds for a reason. We were both helpless to the roles we played. "Cole," I begged, rubbing my asshole against his nostrils, knowing he got off on it.

I bruised easily; we had maybe one more level of intensity before the proof of what we were doing here would be written all over me. I'd let him, I couldn't stop him, I didn't want to—

He stopped, standing and dragging his flattened tongue over my fluttering hole on his way up. "Careful," he whispered into my ear, biting a line down my neck. "I promised to be careful." He turned the water off and grabbed a thicker plug and lubricant from off the shower bench.

"That's it?" I asked, staring at our hard dicks.

"Dinner's getting cold," he said, adding a generous helping of lube to the monstrosity in his hand. It was still much smaller than him. I could take it. "Bend over," he whispered.

♦ ♦ ♦

Dinner turned out to be a four-course meal in the grand dining hall, all served and fed to me by Cole. He'd vanish after each course into what I assumed was the kitchen, and return holding a fancy tray, something decadent hiding beneath its silver lid.

After turning away from the last forkful of dessert he held out to me, Cole took my hand, leading me down winding corridors until we came to a glass-enclosed atrium overlooking the expanse of the south lawn.

The lights were off, and the grand piano in the center sat directly under the spotlight of the moon and stars. He left me to trail behind him in wonderment as he settled onto the bench, warming up his fingers before jumping into "My Immortal" by Evanescence. The lyrics, which spoke of pain, wounds, and time apart, danced through my head as I fought to hold on to this moment and not revisit old hurtful ones.

He finished, extending the outro, then walked to where I stood watching the night sky, holding two flutes and the bottle of champagne that had been chilling on ice next to the Baby Grand.

I plucked one from his hand by its stem, and studied his attractiveness as he filled our glasses. He'd worn all black, had removed his tie and undone the top two buttons on his shirt, revealing his smooth, tanned collarbone. And he'd slicked his thick, jet-black hair away from his chiseled face. "You're so *fucking* sexy," I said.

"*Especially* when I'm fucking," he replied, his brows dancing. He walked the bottle back to the ice bucket, and then returned on a loose gait to clink his glass against mine. His confidence in what he could do with his body, with his cock, was the biggest turn-on. I was lucky enough to have been his blank canvas when we were younger. To be the body he'd improved his art upon. To see and feel the changes as we both grew into our sexuality. There was power that came with that. A possessiveness, too. His abilities belonged to me.

I drank to keep from launching myself at him.

The fireworks started in the distance then, and I nearly choked on my drink as the exploding lights flooded the sky in fiery colors. Cole rocked back on his heels, a hand going into his pocket. "Happy Thanksgiving," he said, taking my breath and my heart away, too.

CHAPTER 18

Jasper

AFTER THE FIREWORKS ended, Cole suggested a late-night swim in the indoor grotto. We kissed under the waterfall until our lips were raw, then he laid me out on the decking, giving me a teasing two strokes of his cock, before plugging me again with something bigger.

"You're almost ready," he said.

"Ready for what?" I asked in annoyance, gnashing my teeth through the burn of insertion. He pretended to not hear me, calling me into the pool instead, and treading around lazily while I reclined along the stone edge watching him.

"I spoke to my father before we left this morning. He didn't sound himself. Well, he hasn't sounded himself in years but this was different," he said thoughtfully.

"Different how?"

"Well, first of all, the call had nothing to do with business." He'd mentioned before that Nexcom was the only thing they shared since my mother died. "He said he was *personally* doing his Christmas shopping this year, and then asked me what I wanted." He seemed puzzled by this.

"Are you sure it was Franklin? Franklin hates Christmas shopping more than he hates organized activities," I stated, scooting over to reach my forgotten tumbler of scotch. We'd moved on to the hard stuff.

"I know. I almost demanded a video call to prove someone wasn't literally holding a gun to his head."

"What did you ask for?"

Cole disappeared below the water, reappearing in front of me, nearly causing me to spill my drink. He reached for his own from over my shoulder, tossing it back and setting the empty glass down.

"Nothing. I told him I wanted nothing. But it was a lie. It's just... He'd caught me off guard." He pressed in close to me, securing my legs around him from under the water, checking to make sure the plug hadn't moved. I was committed to not begging for him to fuck me. Not yet. And mutual arousal aside, because his dick was hard and currently using mine as a crutch, this conversation was important to him. He'd always been a superb multitasker.

"What if he hadn't caught you by surprise? What would you have asked for?" There was some selfish intent in my question. Cole had always been hard to shop for, and I still hadn't gotten him anything.

"For him to be okay. It hit me how much I wanted him to be okay. Whatever that looks like."

Franklin hurting didn't sit well with me. All the more reason why he could never learn the truth. I turned Cole's response over in my head, searching for the right words to comfort him. Up until then, I'd diverted all discussions away from the topic of Franklin, for self-serving reasons. But Cole was worth whatever it would cost me emotionally to revisit my past with his father.

"At the end of the night, after Mom was settled and sleeping, sometimes Franklin and I would share a beer on the porch or while walking the grounds. Or while sitting across from each other in the kitchen like two sad puppies who didn't want to be alone with their pain." I'd never told Cole this because he was away, and if he'd thought I wasn't okay without him, he would've ditched school and caught the first flight home. "Somehow, he knew when I needed someone. When I needed him." Because he was living the day-to-day with me, and he understood me then in a way maybe Cole couldn't have. "It was like that with him from the beginning. He never pushed himself on me. He just always appeared when I needed him."

"Like when it was your turn to make introductions on bring-your-dad-to-school day, and you sat slumped in your chair, the whole class watching, the chair next to your desk empty—"

"And then Franklin slid into it. Homerun," we said in unison, because I'd come home, hyped up and animated describing how him sliding into that seat at that exact moment was like the homerun that saved the game. He'd walked out of an important meeting to be there after my mother had taken the balled-up notice out of my bedroom trash bin and immediately called his office. His assistant knew to pass through all calls from his family, no matter what. He was that type of man.

"What did you two talk about over beers?" Cole asked, interrupting my surprisingly non-painful memories. The light from the water reflected off his blue eyes, they were wide and sparkling, his tone eager for more details.

"Nothing," I said. "Absolutely nothing. But the commiserating silence made me feel better." There had been enough people giving us their words. Doctors, well-wishers, friends... All of it useless drivel that didn't change a thing, and I got to escape it for a couple hours with Franklin.

Cole cupped water into his palms and let it run over my collarbone, coming in for a chlorine-flavored kiss. "Give me a fond memory of you and your father," I asked.

He dipped his head back, staring at the cavernous ceiling in thought. "Probably every time I'd catch him watching you, me, and Selene play board games. He'd stand outside the great room sporting a smile both heartbreaking and hopeful."

"I never knew he did that."

"Yeah. I'd hoped it meant that while our new family had made him think about the one he'd lost, he was grateful for what he had then, and not upset with what I'd taken from him by being born."

"I don't think Franklin ever blamed you, Cole."

"But you think he'd blame you?" He urged me to calm with a raised hand when my face hardened. And instead of addressing my defensiveness at him using my words against me, he moved on. "I mistook his grief for blame. I know that now."

He waded toward the pool stairs with me still wrapped around him, careful to hold me by the ass and keep my cheeks closed, and I groaned from the extra bit of plug it sent into me.

We kissed sloppily as he walked us to the lounge chairs, planting a knee on one and taking us down. He unwound my legs from his hips, spreading them over the armrests and swiping up the lube from the square drink table. He lathered his crown as my own dick strained to reach past my navel.

I'd been about to ask why he was only working the head of his erection, but before the words could form he'd removed the plug, fallen over me, and directed his tip inside my needy hole. "Cole," I panted, sweat beading across my nose and upper lip, but he kept his cruel eyes on me, promising he wouldn't be swayed.

I canted my hips as best I could from my prone position with my legs dangling over the chair arms, but he jerked back, taking his cockhead with him. "It's not enough," I complained as he eased that scant couple inches inside me again. I tugged restlessly at my hair.

"It's gonna have to be, angel."

The whole day had been one long edging session. From the thorough rimming job that morning, to the seductive glances while riding horseback, to him cantering up alongside me to cop an aggressive feel through the front of my riding pants before trotting off. Not to mention the scene in the shower, and now this.

"No touching yourself," he said sharply, and I shoved my traveling hand back into my hair, drilling my eyes shut and concentrating, trying my best to reach the finish line with the little I'd been given.

"Fuck, Cole. Just a little more," I begged in frustration, and he fell away, leaving me lost, empty, and reaching for him to stay.

"I need you in a bed," he said, breathing raggedly, finally exposing how much his need matched mine.

We were alone on the estate now, and would be for the rest of the night, so we didn't need to waste time or lose momentum by getting dressed before heading to our room.

Cole charged with purpose through the labyrinth of hallways with me in tow. I did my best to keep up with his longer strides. "You're moving too slow, Jasper. I need your body beneath my hands."

If I moved any faster, I'd be running. He whirled on me, bending at the knees and tossing me over his shoulder, my breath whooshed out of me in surprise.

One forearm banded behind my knees, as the fingers on his other hand disappeared inside my lubed hole. I sank my teeth into his ass to stifle my moan. "I want to hear you," he said, finger fucking me deeper.

"*God,*" I called out.

"I'm here, angel," he crooned, his fingers working me. "I'm here."

He blew through our suite's doorway, padding across the beige carpet before pitching me onto the center of the bed, and then leaping on top of me, assaulting me with a kiss.

Heat and sweat licked over my body, turning parts of me crimson. "Look at you," he whispered in wonderment, spreading my hair around my head, and fingering the blush crawling over my face.

"Cole," I said shakily, my skin pebbling in spite of my warmth. "Do something."

He knelt over me, salivating as he raked me with his deviant gaze, then swatted my hand away from my cock when I chose to take matters into my own hand.

I curled upward, latching my mouth onto his, and was swiftly pinned to my back by the throat for my trouble. I couldn't swallow past the compression of his palm.

I batted him away and scurried backward, irritation graduating to fury. "I'm not a fucking toy."

Cole's hand locked around my ankle and tugged until my legs bracketed his kneeling form again. He was in a mood tonight. A predator playing with its meal.

My chest heaved, my balls ached for release, and I was losing my grip on my humanity.

He climbed my torso to reach for a padded cuff attached to a length of chain hooked to the bedpost. I snapped my head to the other post, breaths punching through me harder when I spotted the other manacle. *When did he have time to do this?*

"These are padded," he explained, holding it up for my inspection. "They won't leave a bruise." Not like the three-stranded hemp rope we'd used in the past. I'd worn the marks on my wrists with pride back then, showcasing his dominance over me. I nodded, and he secured the cuff, mindfully leaving enough slack.

The other post was further away, requiring him to scoot higher, bringing his cock in close proximity to my mouth. My tongue darted out wickedly, thieving the precum drenching his extra-thick crown.

"No," he said sharply, slamming my head to the mattress with a fist in my hair. I lapped at my lips, fucking the air.

Cole made quick work of buckling up my free wrist before retaking his position, his fingers probing along my groin area, seeking the razor thin scar tissue hidden beneath the short thatch of curls there. "Do you remember?" he asked, fondling the wound he'd tapped into so many times the lesion had become permanent.

"Yes," I said, as he used his nose to sift through my pubes, dipping under my testicles to noisily inhale along my taint as if it were a line of coke. His middle finger voyaged inside my sticky hole.

"Mmmm," he moaned into my skin, sniffing twice more before coming up for air. His eyes shimmered; he was high off my scent, hair disheveled. My knees dropped to the mattress as I arched my back, all while lowering my lashes in embarrassment. I could never fully kick the shame that came with being turned-on by his perversions. "You know exactly what you do to me, don't you, angel?" he asked, caressing the heat I could feel along my neck.

He left the bed to haul my ass to the edge of it, then cuffed my ankles, looping the chain around the top of the post, where the canopy began, until my legs were spread wide and raised at a ninety-degree angle. I was strung up and at his mercy.

We'd both softened to a degree during his preparation, and he used the opportunity to fit us both with cock rings. "Cole," I said in warning, tugging uselessly at my restraints. "I need to come."

"And you will," he promised. "You know what to say to make this stop, right?"

Yes, I said in my head, afraid saying it out loud would trigger his brakes. I bobbed my head once instead.

Cole inched back the bench at the bed's footboard, giving him room to slide in and fold over me. He buried his fists into the mattress, lewdly kissing me until our erections towered at full mast again. The outward restriction of blood flow caused by the cock ring made his dick more pronounced, and I was suddenly thankful for the stretching he'd been giving me all day.

He stepped away and returned with a brand-new bottle of lube, upending it over his hardness and the fingers of his free hand, then jerking himself off while driving and scissoring wet digits inside me. My chains rattled as I tensed from the pleasure and rising swelter attacking my hole.

"Where can I hurt you tonight?" he said, eyeing me apologetically as if the need was out of his hands. "Tell me you need it, too?" He lined his cock up at my apex, breaching me with half of it, but half of him was nothing to scoff at. He gripped two handfuls of my hips, holding me down when I began to tremble with overwhelming need.

The words *fuck yes* couldn't be used, so in place of it, I lifted my head and nudged my chin toward my straining dick. "There," I said throatily.

"Here?" he asked to be sure, swirling the pad of a finger through the pre-ejaculate at my slit, his breath quickening at the possibility.

"There," I confirmed, grains of perspiration spilling over my trembling ribcage. He withdrew from me, and my heavy head fell to the bed, lolling to one side. My nerves were frazzled, anticipation and lust driving me insane.

Something hit the bottom of the mattress, and I struggled to heft my head up again to get a visual.

Cole situated three dildos side by side according to their size, medium, large, and colossal, before withdrawing a custom, pearl-headed needle from its sterile sheath—one of three, I remembered, each eye thicker than the other, and he'd chosen the thinnest. So thin that under normal circumstances it wouldn't have called blood to the surface, but with so much blood filling my dick and looking for a way out, it'd be enough to satisfy his craving, which in turn would satisfy mine. If careful, I wouldn't scar, and any reddening would be a thing of the past by morning.

From between my spread legs, Cole licked around my cockhead, and the bedposts creaked as my body spasmed in my chains. "So sensitive," he said.

I gritted my teeth at the first prick of his needle, my ass cheeks clenching around the medium dildo he'd simultaneously slid inside me to the hilt. He chased the sand grain-sized speck of blood, his taste buds absorbing it before it had a proper chance to breathe. "Relax," he whispered so low it had to have been a warning for himself. His body quaked with the need to be savage.

He kept his mouth over my dick, thirsty for my blood. A string of saliva stretched from his shiny bottom lip to my glistening crown. "God, I've missed you," he said to my cock, his choppy warm breaths adding fuel to the flame, and with every nick of his needle, and swipe of his tongue, he steadily fucked the dildo in and out of me.

It became a cycle of disjointed, labored ramblings, and sharp hisses as he injured me, then sucked the pain away. By the time we'd escalated to the next dildo, my sweat-slicked body had soaked through the sheets, and Cole was loosely hanging on to his control.

"God damnit, Jasper," he said unevenly, needle slipping from his fingers, his ass hitting the padded bench behind him.

"*Please*, just fuck me," I tried again. "I'm fucking begging you."

"Almost there," he said, wetting his lips, before withdrawing the dildo, separating my ass cheeks and faceplanting into my hole.

"Fuck!" I screamed through a raw throat as he ate me with vigor, swearing and spitting and moaning obscenely into me. "I–I can't."

"You can and you will," he said before shoving off the bench and fitting his dick into me next. "Shit," he cursed, like that wasn't the plan but he couldn't resist. He got a few pumps in, then retook his seat and worked in the biggest of the three this time, its shaft curved and veiny, and much darker than the others. "Unclench yourself," he instructed, twisting in the lubed edifice steadily. I thrashed my head, the drenched strands of my hair blinding me. "That's it," he said with pride, sweating through the patience it took to hold back. "If you can take me, you can take this, angel."

That became our new loop. Cole would make a meal of my hole and cleft, then stand—shouting filthy words, and take me with his cock, then sit and drill me with the dildo.

Eventually needing more, he straightened, the stubble surrounding his chin as luminous as a pool of tar. Cole inserted a finger into my mouth, and I weakly suckled on it. "I'm dying right alongside you, angel," he said, finally freeing my balls and cock, then removing his ring as well.

Cole was a vibrating, pupil-blown mess of desire, proof that one can be both in control and utterly unraveling at the same time.

"Cole," I croaked through a hoarse voice and chapped lips, unsure of what I wanted from him, but knowing I needed whatever it was *now*. I felt the cold head of the dildo at my entrance again, and then something warmer, something *real* bump up alongside it. I popped my head to the side, casting my eyes downward to see the largest dildo missing from the lineup. "Fucking impossible," I breathed, shaking my head as the dual cockheads crossed through me and waited just inside. "It's too much," I whimpered.

"I once got a fist and half a forearm in here, angel. Nothing's impossible," he said gently, coaxing my retreating erection. "That's it," he praised when I began to reharden against the graze of his palm, a slave to my need. To him. "We've been preparing for this all day. Loosen up for me. Let us in."

Cole took his time, complimenting my cock-taking skills as he made his way home in small increments, ebbing and flowing, all while fisting my cock leisurely, occasionally clutching me at the base when my lack of breathing gave away my approaching orgasm. "Look how well you take us," he said, "and how wrecked you look while doing it."

At one point in time my body had been conditioned to take Cole's cock regularly. Conditioned to accept whatever he had to give me. And although we'd been fucking pretty heavily for several days now, taking Cole's dick with grace after so many years of going without it was not like riding a bike. Accepting double his size at once was downright unthinkable. But I wanted his pride, his acclamations, his demons and whatever else he had to offer.

"How do you feel, Jas?" he asked.

"Fu–full," I stuttered, muscles aching and rigid.

"Not full enough," he said jaggedly, neck stretching away from his shoulders. "Just a little more."

I was splintering apart, feeling more vulnerable than I'd ever felt in my life, my heart beating uncontrollably against its cage. There was too much of everything, and yet not enough. There was the calling for my orgasm by his hand, yet not enough squeeze to force an answer. There were one too many cocks fighting for entry, yet I didn't have all of either of them. I needed more, I needed less, I needed to come undone.

So I surrendered the sliver of control I hadn't known I was holding on to until then. I relaxed in my chains, trusting them to hold me, and I opened every part of me resistant to granting Cole total entry. My mind, my heart, and my body. I let go of the fear.

"Yes," he said, dragging out the syllable, bottoming out and going motionless. "Look at me, angel. Stay with me." Cole and the dildo became one, giving and taking pleasure in synchrony.

"More," I mouthed, hooking my eyes to his, fighting to see past my tears. "More, Cole."

He released my dick to hold me steady at the hip, his other hand remained between my legs, securing the dildo. They fucked me long and hard, fast and slow, erratic and certain, sending me spiraling face-first into a sexual vortex.

Cole shifted his angle, hitting my bundle of nerves, and with a reserve of strength and sounds born from a rapid influx of overpowering stimulation, I wailed his name.

"Feel that? That's me. What you're feeling right now is all because of me." He punctuated his irrational jealousy with sharp, concise jabs, needing me to know that of all the cocks at our hedonistic party, it was his driving me wild.

Cole removed the dildo, his expression smug when I remained a blubbering, gaping mess. *"See?"* his gaze said. *"I'm the reason."*

He revved up his thrusts, his body undulating erotically as he bent over me, his now unoccupied hand tangled in my hair.

The bed posts whined, the headboard aggressively thumped against the wall, and my right leg lowered as the chain holding it unwound a fraction. And Cole fucked me like he didn't notice the mayhem he was causing, as if nothing outside the joining of our bodies and souls deserved his attention.

I met the whipping of his pelvis as best I could, head craning, lips parted and slightly puckered, demanding his mouth on mine. Cole met my demand bruisingly, hand hardening in my hair, cock belting into me punishingly.

Our heads lurched in competing directions, both fighting for a kiss we'd already won, for a passion we already had.

Cole reached out blindly, unclasping the chain from one of the cuff's eye hooks. My hand immediately shot to my dick, and he threw his whole body into fucking me now, rattling the whole bed and sending the dildos toppling off the mattress.

The chain holding my right leg out and up abandoned the post completely, sending my foot crashing to the floor from where Cole fucked me along the edge of the bed. He was too far gone to stop and investigate the disturbance, his tongue still piercing my mouth, his fingers still clutching my hair.

Pins and needles bolted through my leg as blood flow returned to the numb limb. I hitched it over Cole's lower back, urging him on, encouraging him to lose his fucking mind, to break me open.

"Fuck, fuck, *fuck,*" he breathed down my throat before devouring my tongue again. "Work yourself harder, angel. I'm right—" he paused to groan, "there."

It was what I'd been unknowingly waiting for. His permission, him chasing me as I exploded into microscopic fragments, only to be pieced back together again by him.

Cole roared through his climax, body going stiff as a board as he rutted into me over and over and over, forcefully emptying himself and flooding me with his thick seed.

With vocal cords stripped from endless begging and screaming, all I could manage was a wide-mouthed rasp of his name and all that was holy.

My harsh breathing canceled his out, and vice versa, until we were just one breath, one entity, one orgasm.

Without pulling out of me, Cole unhooked my other wrist and leg, sliding an arm under my back, and hoisting me to the top of the bed.

His cock was still full, but not with lust. Sometimes it took him a minute to come down, and he enjoyed spending that minute drowning in his own pool of cum. So he gently nestled in, scooping my release from our chests and mopping it off his fingers with his tongue as our bodies cooled.

Once he slipped free, he massaged life back into my extremities, then examined my opening for injury. Cole removed the cuffs and checked for bruising before planting me on top of him and offering me shelter at his neck. I inhaled him in, eyes drooping shut.

"Tell me the truth you've been holding back from me, angel," he whispered. "Just this once. Just for tonight. And I promise to never use it against you." His arms became steel bands around me. His heart thrummed fiercely against my skin. *"Please."*

I debated pretending I'd already fallen asleep, but Cole had given me so much, had *always* given me so much, wasn't it time I gave him something in return? No matter the emotional cost to me? "I still love you, Cole. And I can't make it stop," I said, words shattering like glass, the shards stabbing at my heart.

He kissed the top of my head, smiling against my scalp. There was something unexpectedly freeing in my selfless admission, almost as if facing the elephant meant I no longer had to hide from it, no matter how temporary the mutual contentment gained from it would be.

"Thank you," he said sleepily, taking us to our sides and drawing the quilt up and over our shoulders, letting our love, and our last few hours of ignorant bliss, lull us to sleep.

CHAPTER 19

THE PENTHOUSE WAS cold without him, and every surface I'd taken him on had been scrubbed clean in our absence. The cum-stained sheets we'd left behind had been replaced with silks that smelled of a fragrance too soft to be him, yet too masculine to be him either. Jasper landed somewhere in between Heaven and Hell, angel and devil, and without even trying, even when he believed he was doing exactly that for my benefit. It was all him. Rare and lovely.

I'd scoured the place I called home for any traces of him ever since returning hours ago from our Thanksgiving night away. The piano lid I'd eaten him like a delicacy on while he shook on all fours now sparkled. And even the smudge on the window from where I'd sent him to his knees to lick clean after he'd orgasmed against it now shined immaculately. And all the clothing he'd left thrown about had already been taken to be laundered.

They didn't come any messier than Jasper, and it had thrilled me to see him let loose and turn this place into a disaster zone the few days he'd spent here. It couldn't be easy for someone like him to live with someone as rigid as Daniel.

My last hope was the living room area rug, and I shamelessly sniffed its center and its circumference searching for Jasper. Any hint of him. There was nothing.

I fell to my ass, reclining against the loveseat, thinking about the weighted silence we'd maintained as we showered and departed for the real world that morning, now wishing I could get that time back, do things differently. I'd kiss him one last time, make plans for us to see each other soon. I'd steal the shirt off his back.

Instantly, I rose to my feet, remembering something important. I disregarded the ringing of my cell phone; Leland could wait, and headed for the master bedroom closet.

Balled up in the back of my top dresser drawer was the t-shirt Jasper had discarded on my bathroom floor before showering with me the last night we were here. I'd decided on a whim to hold on to it because I needed some part of him, some kind of link to him whenever he wasn't here.

Bringing the cotton to my nose, I fiendishly inhaled, sagging against the shoe shelves behind me. After the week we'd had, hell, after the *night* we'd had, being without him for a day would feel like a century, and two days *would* be an eternity. I knew this because I'd gone through it before. We were, in a way, repeating the past.

It wasn't that I needed him near me at all times. Our individual lives were too full for that level of obsession. It was the access to him I needed like my next breath. I needed to be the one who got to see the sun rise in his eyes every morning and set over nightly dinners. I wanted our schedules to be built around the time we set aside for each other, instead of having to shift things around to be together. I wanted him to surprise me at work in the middle of the day because he missed me, and simply because he could. I wanted the privilege of holding his hand around friends and strangers, of letting the world know he was mine. I had Jasper's heart, but Daniel got to share a life with him out loud, and it was killing me. I'd been a fool to think it wouldn't.

With the shirt white-knuckled to my chest, as if daring any-one to try and take it from me, I grabbed the bottle of gin I kept in the kitchen, then swiped my phone off the foyer table to return Leland's many missed calls.

"Cole?" he answered, before the completion of a full ring. "Where are you?"

I dragged my feet back to the living room and placed the call on speaker, letting the phone fall and rattle onto the piano so I could uncap the bottle, Jasper's shirt now tucked under my arm.

"Cole?" his voice lowered.

"I'm fine, Leland," I said, pouring the alcohol directly down my throat and wandering to the window.

"If you were fine, you'd be at the office attending the board meeting. They're in the conference room waiting for you." His whispered words lacked heat. The meeting wasn't his priority right then, he was fishing for the truth of my well-being. "Talk to me, Cole," he said with enough care to make it hurt. "I can reschedule the meeting. Make up some excuse about traffic—an accident even. Maybe a car swerved into a divider trying to avoid a runaway puppy," he joked without humor, his way of getting something out of me.

Fuck. I'd forgotten about the meeting. "Whose bright idea was it to set this meeting up right after a holiday? No one's even in the office today."

"It was *your* bright idea for that reason exactly."

To my credit, I'd *suggested* not mandated it, but the share-holders had agreed. For some it was as simple as making it across town. The others would be joining in virtually. "Say what you have to Leland. I can't make it in."

"Okay," he said. "How'd your night go?" He knew about my night away with Jasper. He'd helped with some of the arrange-ments.

"It went as expected," I said dully, staring blankly toward the frigid river in the distance.

"I'll come over—"

"Don't," I said, swinging my torso around to the phone. "I know you want to help, Leland, but you can't. Clear my calendar, reschedule the meeting for Monday, and I'll see you in the office then." The silence returned, feeling like a pinched breath, but so much was communicated through it.

"Call if you need me," he finally said, and I nodded as if he could see me.

I didn't have the strength or interest to walk the short distance needed to end the call. He would have to do it. I gave my back to the window, winced at the burn the booze caused on its way to my liver, and slid to the floor. I didn't move for the rest of the day, and I couldn't say how long Leland's breathing kept me company before it was gone, before leaving me to my misery.

♦ ♦ ♦

I'd kept myself numb all weekend, and a roaring headache waited for me Monday morning along with numerous missed calls, ten voicemail messages, and a text from Leland that read: *Turn on the fucking news and call me. Now!*

I patted around the blanket and sheets for the missing TV remote before giving up and staggering to my study. Clicking on the television over the mantel, I sank to the edge of my desk, listening to the business news station in horror. An investigation had been launched into sexual harassment claims made by multiple women against the CEO of Delnewik—a recently acquired tech subsidiary of Nexcom. *"Shit."*

My phone vibrated in my hand. Another text from Leland: *The board wants to meet at 9 a.m. instead of 10. Think it has anything to do with Delnewik?*

I was certain he was being sarcastic, but I replied anyway: *Of course it does. Get a hold of Daniel. Tell him to be ready in an hour. I'll pick him up on my way to the office.*

I needed to discuss how this would legally impact us before the board descended on me. Daniel and I could prepare for the new direction of the meeting—which he would now be a part of—on the drive in.

Twenty minutes and two painkillers later, and I was climbing into the back seat of the SUV, begging Mark to take it easy on the potholes as I cradled my head. He reached back without a word, steaming cup of coffee in hand. I thanked him profusely, promising him an end of year bonus as he pulled away from the curb.

"Your check cleared the bank already, Mr. Kincaid," he said around a chuckle. "And thank your assistant. He told me to get the largest cup size they offered."

The morning traffic made the journey to Daniel and Jasper's place arduous, but I needed all the time I could get to collect myself if I planned to get through the tidbits of Daniel's homecoming he'd likely share, or to stomach a simple offhand comment about how Jasper was still tucked into their bed, or in the shower, or sad to see him go after having just gotten him back. Daniel's small talk almost always included Jasper; it was like he thought any mention of my *brother* served as a reminder that he'd made our reunion possible, which in turn meant I owed him, or at the very least needed to make Jasper happy by seeing his husband as valuable to me.

Way too soon we were approaching their high-rise apartment building, but Daniel wasn't waiting in front like his response to my text said he'd be. I checked the time, then squinted past the morning mist to where the doorman held the entrance open for someone—not Daniel—exiting.

No one kept me waiting. And certainly not Daniel, I thought with a superiority birthed from jealousy. And then on the heel of that were the many sickening reasons why I might've been waiting. He'd said he was on his way down, did he decide he needed another minute with Jasper before he left? Did they get caught up in a kiss? Did one thing lead to another?

I called and got no answer. "I'll be back," I said to Mark as I got out of the vehicle and tipped my head to the doorman before stepping into the festively decorated lobby. I gave my name and identification to the woman behind the desk. She verified I was on the visitor's list, and then directed me unnecessarily to the bank of elevators that traveled to their floor.

My palms grew sweaty, my thoughts moving at lightning speed as the elevator ascended, and my haggard expression met me in the mirrored control panel. I hadn't had time to shave or dry my wet hair, and the whites of my eyes were red from all the alcohol and lack of sleep. *What a difference a few days could make.*

The elevator opened in front of their ajar apartment door, and my heart pumped harsher. He'd obviously turned back on his way out, and in such a rush he hadn't fully shut the door. Maybe he went back for his hat, or his gloves, or phone. *Anything* except Jasper.

The elevator doors began to close me in as I debated whether or not to punish myself with what waited beyond their door. I then questioned what I would do if I found them in a compromising position. I whipped my arm out, triggering the sensors before schooling my expression and entering their home.

Ahead of me, Daniel bounded down the stairs, his coat thrown over his arm, and Jasper trailing behind, his shirt askew. "Oh, Cole," Daniel said, his ascension slowing. Jasper halted completely, his hand tightening on the iron banister. "Sorry to keep you waiting. I got to the door and realized I'd left my coat upstairs." He held it up, presenting it as evidence. Only Daniel's coat never made it past the third hanger from the left in the coat closet near the front door, the one that stood partially open now.

He was habitual and compulsive about his rituals, that much about him was glaringly obvious. He turned an office work lunch into a meticulous ordeal of table wipe downs and napkin bibs, and he was the reason for the bare shelves in our cleaning supply closet. According to him, a coat should never make it more than a few feet past the front door of any home. Not unless he'd slipped out of the front door and then became so consumed with need, with missing his husband, so out of his mind with lust that he'd charged back upstairs to have him one last time before leaving for the day. Would that have been worth breaking protocol for him? It would've been for me.

"I called you," I said, prying my teeth apart.

"Sorry, I didn't hear the phone ring."

I got the sense he was lying and an even stranger feeling that he'd wanted me to know it. I couldn't rely on my intuition right then, though. Not when my jealousy was running the show. And I'd never needed proof or proper reasoning for something to be true when jealous.

"Ready?" he chirped.

"Yeah," I mustered, my eyes clinging to Jasper's.

"Sweetheart," he then said to Jasper, oblivious to the war happening right in front of him. "Make a reservation at the Italian restaurant you love. I'll be done with work before dinner." With his coat now on he smiled, gesturing for me to exit ahead of him.

"Yeah," Jasper said, his reply lagging, "Okay."

Out in the hall, the elevator waited, and we got on. "Actually," I said, holding the doors open. "I need to use the bathroom. Mark's waiting outside. I'll meet you down there."

"Sure," he said accommodatingly, then gave me the keypad code to get into the apartment.

Jasper was nowhere in sight, so I crossed the living room and mounted the stairs two at a time and hunted down their bedroom.

He faced the deck doors in the all-white room. Through the reflection of the glass I could see him hugging a coffee mug, deep in thought. "Did you let him fuck you?" I asked crudely.

Jasper whirled around, biting off a curse as a small tidal wave of coffee crashed over the rim of the cup to land on his hand. He discarded the mug on the mahogany nightstand. "What are you doing up here?" he asked in a panic, his gaze darting into the hall behind me. He dried his hand on the fitted pajama joggers he wore, and the matching navy Henley hung off his shoulder. The collar had been stretched. Like a fist had taken a hold of it and pulled.

"He's waiting in the car. Now answer me," I said impatiently, advancing further into the room. The bed separated us, and my insides churned from how rumpled it was, how slept in, how used it appeared. How much it smelled like Jasper, reminding me of how little my place smelled of him. I subtly inhaled, my jealousy heightening when punched with a second scent belonging to Daniel. My cheek twitched involuntarily.

"No," he said. "We didn't have sex."

"Then why does it look like someone's had their hands on you?"

He crossed his arms defensively, his biceps poking at the waffled fabric of his shirt. "He was jetlagged all weekend, re-acclimating after the huge time difference. We talked about his trip a bit, what little he could legally share. Then we mostly slept or did our own thing at different ends of the apartment. I was exhausted, too," he said significantly. "This morning he promised to make me coffee for having woken me up so early with his call from Leland. I guess he forgot it was brewing and ran back to bring it to me, as I was still in bed. I was walking him to the door when you showed up."

"That doesn't answer my question," I said, stalking him to his side of the bed. Again, Jasper's stare fixated on the hall, then back to me. "Where did he touch you?"

"Cole," he cautioned, still not answering me. "Not here. We can't have this conversation here."

My shoes bumped up against his bare toes, and I palmed his nape, rubbing my thumb over the soft hair there. His breathing turned jittery, and he brushed a finger over the bags under my eyes.

"Did you sleep at all?" he asked.

"No. Not really," I said before dipping my head to his exposed shoulder and inhaling up to his ear. He smelled like coffee. Like someone had taken a sip before tugging his shirt to the side and laying their mouth on him. I bit him there, replacing the last memory of what had happened in that spot. Now when he thought of it, he'd think of me.

Jasper stiffened, crying out, and I withdrew my teeth before breaking the skin. "Don't worry, my mark will be gone long before *dinner.*" My words dripped with venom. A venom I'd never had toward him before. I cupped his cock and noted nothing else—besides the cotton joggers—stood between my hand and his semi-erect length. Was it swelling for me? Or was it left over from whatever Daniel had started but hopefully couldn't finish?

"Maybe if you didn't walk around with your dick swinging in these pants, he wouldn't need to lay a hand on you." I'd heard myself. I understood how unlike myself I sounded. How irrational my argument was. I didn't care. I didn't care that I could be blowing his marriage to smithereens if Daniel walked in on us now. Right then, I only cared about whether or not my hands, my mouth, and my cock, had been the last thing to touch him intimately.

My behavior lit a fire behind his eyes, and the soft, submissive version of him began to melt away. "Get out," he said firmly. *"Now."*

"No," I growled, fighting a hand into the back of his pants and down his cleft to see how tight or loose he was. He let me in, his lips pale and flat, but he seemed to understand what needed to be done to get rid of me. He was dry, no signs of morning sex, and honestly, he should've been too sore for sex after the last night we'd had together—which had been partially the point.

While he complied with my inspection of his opening, he drew the line when I reached around for his cock. "Don't," he said, taking a hold of my wrist and yanking my hand out of his bottoms. My fingers moved to his throat as I caught him up in a brutal kiss. "Cole," he said, breaking away only to be pulled back in. "Stop."

I couldn't. I needed him. I needed him *immediately*. I needed him on the bed he shared with his husband. I needed Daniel to charge in and make the executive decision Jasper couldn't.

He backed away, and I followed, never relinquishing his lips. Jasper bumped into the nightstand, knocking something over, his coffee, maybe. And I wrestled to get his pants down while he fought to keep them up.

"Yes," he panted, then again more pointedly, *"Yes."*

I leaped away as if splashed with fire, eyes expanding. He'd used his safeword.

"You don't come in here and demand to know what's going on. You don't get to fuck my life up, no matter how fucked up you think it already is. Not here, Cole. You can say and do what you want anywhere else, but you leave any destruction that may happen in my home to me." His words hissed like steam.

I'd never seen him so upset. He stared at me as if he didn't know me, but there was hurt there, too. Hurt for me, for us both, and I held on to it as I tried to pull my shit together.

Dragging a hand over my beard, I aimed for the bedroom door, stopping to lean against the jamb, to recoup some strength. "You said to call or text whenever I *needed* you," I said with meaning, my back to him.

"That hasn't changed," he said in a relieved tone, ready to forgive me now that I'd put a few feet between us.

"Keep your phone close at all times." I shot him a look over my shoulder. "I'll be needing you often." And with that I left, calling on my professionalism, and years of experience in dealing with individuals I disliked for the sake of business, in order to survive the ride into the office with Daniel.

◆ ◆ ◆

Leaving Daniel to answer a call in the vestibule outside the elevators, I pushed through Nexcom's glass doors, intent on making it to my office without being stopped. Becca bolted up from the receptionist desk, sticky note in hand. "Mr. Kincaid—"

"Pass the message along to Leland, Becca," I said, working hard not to come off irritable as I breezed by.

"Oh! Cole—"

"Send it in an email, Mr. Glover." I turned the corner before getting the head of marketing's affirmative.

Phones rang, papers shuffled, staplers stapled, and the pain pills I'd taken earlier had lied. They didn't last four to six hours. They hadn't even kicked in.

Waltzing past Leland's desk without a word, I strode into my office, tossing my coat in the general direction of the sofa before circling my desk and taking a seat. I flipped through the paperwork left there for me, pretending I hadn't heard Leland come in and that I didn't notice him glowering near the closed door wearing a cocktailed expression of rage, concern, and pity. "Get it off your chest, Leland," I said eventually. "I've got ten minutes until the board meeting."

"You've survived years without him, and now you're back in his life and this is what one night apart does to you?" He flung his hand toward me, and I smoothed down my tie. There wasn't anything I could do about the rest of me.

"It's not that simple, and you know it."

"Did you think he'd have a come-to-Jesus moment and leave his husband?"

"I'd hoped," I admitted.

"Why would he? Because he loves you? They never leave, Cole," he said with conviction, stopping my senseless clicking of my pen.

"Are we still talking about me?" I asked, to which he scratched at his nose and shifted uncomfortably on his feet. "Who hurt you, Leland?"

"Everyone who mattered. But enough about me. What can I do?" He'd closed himself off to me. It was what he always did when the conversation turned to him and his past.

"You've been a great friend, Leland. When will you let me return the favor?" I implored, searching his eyes for an opening.

"You can return it by telling me what I can do for you."

It was always about what he could do for me, which was why I didn't miss an opportunity to pay him back in other ways. "Tell me your uncle found something on Daniel."

"No. I believe his exact words were 'squeaky clean, neat freak boy scout.' Couldn't turn up so much as a parking ticket. Although, he did win the overachiever award four years in a row back in high school. If that isn't a crime, I don't know what is."

I slumped in my chair, the day wearing on me already and there was still so much of it left. "What about phone records? Emails?"

"Everything sent and received has been aboveboard."

"How long have you known all this?" I asked, observing him carefully.

"All week," he said. "You were having a good time, so..." He trailed off with a shrug. "I didn't want to ruin it."

"There has to be something," I said to myself. "Have him look again, or find me someone else who can."

He agreed, checking the time on his watch. "Your ten minutes are up. It's showtime."

"Leland," I called before he could leave, he waited with raised brows. "You actively seek out lovers who are unavailable. You of all people should understand me on some level here."

"I understand you aren't built for this life. Maybe I didn't take it seriously before. Maybe because I genuinely thought he'd leave him—despite my claims of it never happening. I'd hoped for your sake this was different. But I've had a front-row seat to how this is playing out. It's like watching a car crash in slow motion. And I hate it," he said. "Oh, and speaking of favors, stop paying my rent or I'll quit." And without another word he was gone.

Two hours later I was back at my desk, crisis averted. Daniel had brilliantly presented our options to the board in dealing with the Delnewik scandal, assuring them that legally we had nothing to worry about, but if we wanted to uphold our reputation, we'd need to act swiftly in getting the CEO removed, and show our unyielding support for the victims. For now they were mollified.

I went online and booked a suite at The Sharai Hotel down the street. I reserved it for the next few weeks as my work calendar was cramped and unavoidable due to all the things I'd been pushing off lately. Now, there'd never be a missed opportunity for Jasper and me to see each other in the middle of the day when his schedule allowed for it. We could meet up at the hotel for lunch and other things. I could've asked Leland to book it, but after our talk I'd decided to keep my stupidity to myself.

I took a look at my planner and saw a small gap between meetings in the evening, so I texted Jasper the hotel details and told him to be there.

◆ ◆ ◆

"I'm sorry about earlier," I said, lying back on the pillows amid the crumpled hotel sheets.

"It's too soon to forgive you," he said jokingly, buttoning into his shirt near the window.

I climbed off the bed and ventured over to him, taking his face in my hands. "You already have." I'd left a key for him at the front desk, and had only provided him with a time and place. He'd entered the suite equally worried and confused.

"What's going on, Cole?" he'd asked as the door swung shut behind him.

"I need you," had been my reply.

I'd been careless with his clothing—per usual, wrangling his pants to his knees and taking him against the entryway wall before having him just as urgently again on the bed.

"Talk to me," he said, rubbing his cheek against my palm like a love-starved cat. "The last thing I want to do is hurt you."

Leland was right, I wasn't cut out for an affair with Jasper. For being the *other man.* With him I needed to be the one-and-only man. I couldn't blame him, though, and yet I felt myself leading up to doing exactly that. He didn't ask for me to come barreling back into his life. In fact, he'd asked me several times to leave. He wasn't the one who broke a promise to not come between him and Daniel. That was all me. And I was the one who arrogantly, or naïvely, believed I could fix him, heal him, and in turn fix and heal us. He'd told me what he could offer me, and I didn't believe it. It was all on me.

Or was it? Wasn't he the one who kissed me first? Wasn't he the one who forced my hand and my cock?

I didn't know. All I knew for sure was the situation was changing me, or better yet I was regressing to the me I had been fresh after losing him six years ago.

"It's not your problem," I settled on, dropping my hands to my sides.

"Tell me anyway."

How could I tell him that Daniel's disappearance after the board meeting—and after I'd booked the suite, had sent me into a tailspin, making it virtually impossible to get anything else done, too obsessed with where he could be. I'd made multiple needless trips to the copy room merely so I could pass his office, checking for his return. Was he still somewhere in the building? Was he handling non-Nexcom business for his firm? Had he taken the rest of the day off? If so, why? And where was Jasper? With him? Waiting for him? Heading to meet him?

Jasper hadn't responded to my text by then, and my call to him had gone to voicemail, so I'd caved and made up some silly excuse to phone Daniel just so I could listen to what was happening in the background of our call. No, I couldn't tell Jasper all that.

Suddenly, I needed him again, so instead of answering his question, I undid the buttons he'd worked closed and tugged the fabric over his shoulders.

"I thought you had a meeting this evening?" he asked, allowing me to back him into the chest of drawers. I freed him of his jeans and underwear before lifting him at the hips and seating him on the dresser, feeling around for the lube I'd set on top of it. He sent his legs around me, his hand pulling my cock and balls through the opening in my boxer briefs.

"The world can wait," I said, sinking into his slick and wanting hole.

CHAPTER 20

Daniel

3 Years, 10 Months Ago

EVERYONE'S GONE BY the time I return to the office around ten at night. Gold and silver streamers hang from every doorway, and the "Congratulations, Mitchell!" sign still dominates the wall in the reception area. I'd had my own party to rush to at my parents' house, or I guess I should say the party I rushed to end before it could embarrassingly begin.

"You said it was a sure thing, Daniel," my father had mocked disappointedly for all in attendance to hear.

"I secured the firm its largest account this year," I'd whispered, hoping to maintain some modicum of respect from those who'd come out to celebrate me. *"And Parker hinted at news that would change everything for me. How was I supposed to know Mitchell was the one he'd decided to make partner?"* I'd had to break the news to everyone, before leaving without my dignity.

Returning to my purpose for coming back to the office at this hour, I withdraw the small silver key from the breast pocket of my suit and unlock my desk drawer. Removing the three files within, I spread their contents over my desk, surveying the information inside for the second time that week before making a final decision. I dial my assistant next.

"Mr. Ward?" Jessica answers, flustered, but at least she sounds wide awake.

"Sorry for calling this late, Jessica, but something came up and I need to urgently head to Nebraska for a couple days. I'll need you to reschedule all upcoming meetings this week. And unless it's a dire emergency, my trip is not to be interrupted." I wait for her to agree before hanging up. I send a quick email to Parker, making up some emergency for my short notice time off, then leave posthaste for the airport.

CHAPTER 21

Jasper

I STUMBLED OUT of Cole's elevator, using the foyer wall for balance, gasping as I caught my breath. He moseyed toward the kitchen like we hadn't just run a gazillion miles in the bitter cold.

"You were saying?" he asked, pleased by my suffering, returning with two bottles of water and handing one to me.

"Only crazy people run outdoors in the fall. Or winter. Or the spring. Or summer," I said, finishing the sentences I was unable to a minute ago.

"Yeah, well, not all of us hit the genetic jackpot," he said, gesturing to my body.

"I work out," I said, slightly offended. Cole laughed around the mouth of his bottle.

"You hit the university weight room twice a week after teaching your class. *If* you're in the mood." He cocked a brow daring me to challenge him. He was right. The one good thing my father had ever given me was his ability to pack on muscle mass without much effort. I'd gained my speedy metabolism from my mother. I mostly worked out because I thought I should, and since riding was no longer an option, I took advantage of the perks that came with being a Columbia Law School alumni.

"Next time I get to pick how we spend a free morning." I rested my now empty bottle on the foyer table, kicked my shoes off in different directions, and peeled out of my jacket before dumping it on the floor. "What?" I asked, following Cole's gaze to the mess I'd made.

"Nothing." He closed in, kissing me before retracing his steps to the kitchen. "I promised you coffee."

I trailed him, cardio-induced crankiness forgotten, and hopped onto the island as Cole bypassed his fancy French press to pop a pod into the Keurig he'd purchased just for me. He then eased my legs apart, slotting his body in between.

"You can't keep doing this," I said, munching lightly on his neck. Daniel had hit the ground running after the announcement of his partnership. There were more business dinners and rubbing-of-elbows than usual as he worked to up the firm's clientele, and poach the top tier attorneys from competing firms, which meant I had to play arm candy. As a result, Cole and I hadn't had an evening alone in the almost two weeks since Thanksgiving. Our time together had come down to stolen moments, when our busy schedules allowed, at the hotel.

But this morning, Daniel, along with Parker and Mitchell, had left for an overnight legal conference. Somehow, some way, I knew it was Cole's doing. Nexcom was their largest, highest profile account, and therefore Cole had sway over them. If he'd made the suggestion for them to attend, they likely would have. The firm would bend over backward for their star client, and he wasn't above taking advantage of that.

"I'll send him on horseback to fucking Siberia if I have to," Cole whispered, roughing me up by my hair, his hard gaze flickering over my suddenly scalding face. I shouldn't have found his constant harsh treatment of my body erotic. Shouldn't have reveled in feeling like a piece of meat, or property. But I did, and I was helpless to do anything about it.

"Tonight," he said in response to my arousal. "If I take you now, I won't want to stop, and I want more than sex today." *I want you,* he didn't say, but didn't have to because there wasn't much his heart could hide from me. I was grateful he didn't vocalize it, though. Grateful I didn't have to ruin things with a reminder of what couldn't be, especially when day by day I was finding it harder to hold on to the reasons why not.

"Coffee's ready," I said huskily, and he reluctantly backed away, searching the fridge for milk. "So, where are we going?"

"It's a surprise," he said, voice echoing inside the fridge.

"A surprise for you, or for me?" I asked, spying the symphony tickets poking out from under a vase on the island. He must have forgotten he'd stuck them there.

"For you..." His voice faded, lengthening the *you* as he spun, fridge door slamming shut behind him.

"The New York Philharmonic," I read aloud, the tickets now pinched between my two fingers. "*Who's* the surprise for?" I asked again, my lips twitching as his mouth gaped and closed repeatedly. As a pianist, and an okay cellist, Cole loved music, and especially symphony music. In fact, I'd just purchased him tickets for Christmas to see their New Year's Eve showing. I'd need to think of another gift for him now.

"You used to tag along with me to see the Seattle Symphony. I figured—"

"I'd love to go with you, Cole." I held him back with a hand to his chest when he moved in enthusiastically. "Coffee," I reminded him.

We spent the rest of the morning into late afternoon alternating between cuddling on the sofa, crunching numbers and drafting a business plan for my maybe-firm, and napping on and off as Beethoven played ambiently throughout the penthouse.

"I'll need to travel a bit next month for work," Cole said later that evening as we were getting ready. "You can come with me, you know," he said, casually adjusting his sapphire cufflinks. "They're brief trips, really. Spread out over six weeks or so. One's for a write-up in Modern Medicine Magazine. Where AI and science meet," he said dramatically. "They even want to take pictures of me." He frowned. Cole hated taking photos. I'd had to get him in a chokehold earlier just to get a selfie. He said they made him look brooding. I said he did a good job of that all on his own.

"We'll see," I said, non-committedly, inserting my arms into my shirt sleeves. "I have this case I've taken on for 'Fia, and I need to prepare my syllabus for spring semester. I should be able to get away here and there, though," I said, because I hated the fear overtaking his eyes, the worry they conveyed: *If I'm gone, and he's here—with Daniel, what would happen?* He seemed momentarily appeased.

"Don't think I don't know you're taking your sweet time because you don't want to get into that suit," he said, removing his blazer from its hanger and crossing over to the mirror.

"Or maybe it's because I can't take my eyes off you long enough to get dressed," I shot back. "You know how I feel about you in all black."

"Good excuse—I'll give you that, but we need to hurry or we'll be late. I'll wait out there." He motioned toward the hall. "As to not disturb you further with my sexiness."

I sulked, and he laughed, the dark, rich texture of it skimming along my skin.

Fifteen minutes—and ten attempts at aligning my bow tie—later, and I was ready to go.

"Wow," Cole said as the soles of my suede loafers clicked against the marble floor. I strutted his way, turning his hall into a catwalk.

The hunter green suit was new. It complemented my eyes, and I'd had it custom made to fit me like a glove. I was muscular, but not nearly as imposing as Cole. Tall, but my bearing didn't intimidate the way Cole's did. I'd been told my approachability won me the hearts of jurors. I'd also been told I was striking, in an ethereal sort of way, not in the Satan personified way of Cole's desirability.

But I knew what I had to offer. I knew I was alluring even though I rarely tried to be, even though I couldn't verbalize what made me that way.

"It's in your blood," Cole would say as he made love to me with an awe-stricken expression. To me I was simply being myself. But I also knew how to play up that provocative side of me when needed, and so I fueled all my confidence into my strut, and I didn't stop moving until my lips were on his, until my hands were firmly planted on his chiseled ass.

"Ready?" I said smoothly.

"Ah, yeah," he replied, shaking his head clear and prompting me to get on the elevator first.

There were secret touches from the backseat on our drive to Lincoln Center. Fingers sent fluttering over the part of my throat Cole loved to sink his teeth into. A hand fondling my clothed cock, a thumb running along my waistband, tugging as if saying, "I need this the fuck off *now*..." And all those torturous touches made to my body were made by my own hand as I pretended Cole wasn't suffering as he watched from the seat next to me.

I kept at it in the dimly lit audience, my eyes fixed on the performance. At one point I turned to Cole, who couldn't keep his eyes off me, and seductively bit my bottom lip while nudging my head toward the stage. "Pay attention," I mouthed.

He went to the restroom during intermission, probably expecting me to follow, but I didn't. When he returned, those vicious eyes told me I would pay for it later.

With pleasure.

It took everything we had to remain neutral as Mark made small talk on the way home. If he could sense how charged things were between Cole and me, he did a good job of not showing it, and by the time we fell into Cole's entryway, most of our clothes were missing or in tatters.

The closing elevator doors jammed on something, and I tore from Cole's kiss to see my shoe caught in its path.

"Leave it," he breathed, unhooking my pants. From somewhere my phone rang, starting right up again after it had stopped, and then the text alerts began.

"Hold on," I said, turning in circles, picking up my suit jacket but the pockets were empty. I hurried into the elevator, feeling around my coat pockets for my phone, checking the messages and exhaling. "It's Daniel. He's heading home."

"Tonight?" Cole said disbelievingly. "It's a four-hour drive. It's already after ten."

I didn't mention the part about him missing me. About him wanting to wake up next to me. The conference ended hours ago, but the plan was for them to leave after the event-catered breakfast in the morning. Another opportunity for them to mingle with the right people.

I returned to the foyer. "Cole—"

"You're not leaving. Stop seeing every move you make as an admission of guilt and tell him what any normal, loving husband would. Tell him it's late, and you're already half asleep on my couch. Tell him you'll see him tomorrow."

"Cole—" I tried again.

"Did it ever occur to you *why* he'd want to drive four hours in the middle of the night to get to you?" he asked, getting increasingly worked up. "How long did you think this 'no sex' thing would last? It's a phase. They say all married couples go through it. He was overwhelmed with work, focused on making a good impression—"

"Cole!"

"You're not leaving! I'm not sending you home with my cum running down your legs all so he can attempt to fuck you and make it like this night never happened. Like we never happened." His admission brought with it a grave silence. This was about more than this moment. It was about every second of every minute I wasn't his. It was about the promises I couldn't make but wanted to.

I shot off a text to Daniel. The one I'd intended on sending from the beginning. Cole set his shoulders back, preparing to keep me there by force if he had to. "I never said I was leaving, Cole." I flattened my palm against his heaving chest, then pushed his shirt down his arms while angling my head to kiss the vein leaping angrily at his neck. "And your cum isn't running down my legs," I whispered.

"But it will be," he said gutturally, rectifying that problem immediately.

◆◆◆

I'd been sitting in the closet, going through the box of knick-knacks I kept stashed under a loose floorboard when the front door of the apartment closed. I returned the seashell my mother had given me from the beach vacation she'd won. She couldn't afford a proper souvenir, so she'd spent hours exploring the oceanfront for the perfect shell. That became our thing, and I looked forward to seeing what she'd unearth from the sand every getaway taken thereafter. She'd find ways to get her hands on a seashell no matter where Franklin whisked her off to. As I got older, I'd suspected she'd started ordering them online.

I tucked that, along with every birthday card she'd ever given me, back into the box, only holding on to the item I'd gone in there for in the first place. "Be right down!" I shouted when Daniel called my name inquiringly.

"You're home early," I noted, jogging down the stairs. The closet muffled Daniel's griping as he leaned in to reorganize things. I'd probably hung my jacket in his assigned area.

"We've been invited to the Smithen brothers' holiday party tonight."

"Tonight?" I said. We'd been to a function three nights in a row now, and I had plans with Cole, who I hadn't seen in days, not even at the hotel, due to our busy work schedules.

"I know it's last minute, but it's the *Smithen* brothers, Jasper. I'll be a god if I can secure a contract with them." The idea made him giddy.

"I've already got plans with Cole," I said as relaxed as possible. He was my brother, after all, according to Daniel. "He got us tickets to see *Hamilton*."

"For which showing?" he asked.

"The last one."

"Well, we won't be terribly far from the theater. You can spend a couple hours making me look good, then meet him there before the show starts," he said, problem solved. I'd left out the part about the dinner reservations Cole and I had beforehand.

"I'm not a trophy, Daniel. You can't bring me out of your display case whenever you need something shiny to distract potentials with all so you can bait them to your cause."

"Of course not," he said, stunned. "But tonight is important, Jasper." His hazel eyes begged for me to do this one thing for him. It made me think about all the ways I was secretly destroying him. Made me feel guilty for wanting to choose a night with Cole over an important opportunity for my husband.

"Fine. I'll get ready."

"And wear that green suit of yours," his voice followed me upstairs. "It does something majestic to your eyes."

That suit had been left in ruins on Cole's foyer floor. "I think I'll wear the maroon one," I shouted back.

◆◆◆

It had taken Cole a half hour to reply to my text informing him of the unfortunate change in plans, which wasn't like him. And while his texts weren't usually verbose, the one worded: *Okay,* coupled with the response delay, did concern me.

To top it all off, I'd rushed out of the house, at Daniel's frantic insistence, and forgotten my phone.

"I could've sworn I slipped it into my coat," I'd said from the back seat of the chauffeured sedan, checking and rechecking each pocket. *"We need to go back."*

"There's no time for that, Jasper. Especially if you plan on leaving early to meet your brother," he'd dangled over me. *"You can use my phone to call him if you need to."*

That was the last thing I needed to do.

The Smithen brothers dominated their sector of the hospitality industry, and were in the market for new legal representation. Since Daniel was the only gay, married man of the three partners, and both Smithen brothers were gay and happily married, it was decided he'd be sent in for the kill, so to speak.

Alcohol flowed, and Daniel had effectively snagged and held their attention. Jacob Smithen's husband had taken an interest in my work, and for once, Daniel didn't mind me doing more than looking pretty. Things were going well, too well, and so it came as no surprise when the brothers begged me to stay.

"Cole is a successful businessman. He knows how these things work. He'll understand," Daniel had said from the corner of the event space he'd hauled me to, smiling and waving as the brothers watched on from the bar. *"This is important to me,"* he'd stressed for the second time that night before closing my hand over his phone and cheerfully making his way through the crowd, accepting the drink Jacob offered him. It was already

late. The show would've started by then. I called Cole, but he didn't answer.

A few hours later, I arrived home to no missed calls or text messages, and somehow that felt much worse. It felt like resignation.

"You found your phone," Daniel said, yawning on his way to the stairs.

"I don't remember leaving it here," I said, staring questioningly at the coffee table.

"Tonight was a success," he said from the landing, "But I'm exhausted. Are you coming to bed?"

"Yeah. In a minute." I waited until I'd heard our bathroom sink cut on, then dialed Cole. I got his voicemail and hung up. I spent the next hour gazing over the city from the living room, thinking, knowing I needed to do the right thing, because we couldn't go on like this, and I was held prisoner by a promise and by guilt, and I didn't see that changing anytime soon.

Daniel was fast asleep by the time I got to our bedroom, but I knew rest would evade me if I didn't go to Cole tonight. So knowing what needed to be done, and hating it, I went to him.

◆ ◆ ◆

Cole wasn't home when I got there, and I fought the temptation to call again, to text him my location, because a twisted part of me wanted to lurk and see if he'd show up with someone. The same part of me that would see the act as a betrayal, irony be damned.

I wanted to know how easy it would be for him to replace me, now that he'd need to. Or maybe I just wanted him to be as wrong as me. Either way, the idea that he might try to bring someone else here, again, made me violent.

My bones were cold, giving me a sneak peek of what life without him would be like. What life without him *was* like. I took the liberty of starting a fire, and then waited near his balcony doors.

His footsteps sounded a lifetime later, and then stopped at what I assumed was the archway to the room. With my back to him, I wasn't left to imagine his shock at finding me there, because I could feel his anger pounding at my spine. Could almost taste his need to cut me open, to rip me apart. *What have I done to him?* I'd swallow the blame for it all.

"Do I even want to know where you've been?" I asked, knowing I had no right to. There was the sound of fabric, and then a thunk as what I guessed was his coat hitting the sofa. I couldn't turn to him. Couldn't even face his reflection in the glass doors. I kept my gaze downcast.

"I could ask you the same," he said, "but I'd rather not know." His tone was limp, tragic, deserving of its own ballad, and my chest constricted from the pain of hearing it.

"It's always the worst at night," he said, getting straight to the excruciating part. "When I don't have a busy day to distract me. When I don't have your busy day, or Daniel's, to bring me comfort, because then I know at least he doesn't have you." He exhaled. "But at night, I imagine him holding you. His arms around you in bed, testing the waters to see if you're in the mood. I tell myself you're not, because I've been more than taking care of your needs. But still he holds you, and I imagine you pretending it's me, and while that soothes my ego, it does nothing for my fracturing heart, because whether you're pretending to want him or not, whether it's my face you're seeing instead of his, he does in fact have you. And the sad part is, he doesn't even appreciate it."

I was breaking apart, my fingers digging into my ribs from where my arms crossed over me protectively. "You said you could handle this," I tried, finding his reflection in the glass.

"I lied!" he roared, throwing his hands in the air. I flinched. He slapped his hands at his sides, and then echoed in a whisper, "I lied. But you knew that, didn't you?"

I did, but I'd hoped. *God* did I fucking hope. I dropped my chin, because even seeing a faint image of his heartbreak through a sheet of glass was too much. But then I turned to him, because I owed him. I owed him full absorption. I owed him more than this.

"And then I think," he said, facing the fire, hands drifting into his pockets, "I never should have come here. But chasing that thought is the realization that I've experienced more happiness here, even during moments of private misery, than I have in all the years I've spent without you." He nodded thoughtfully, and I stood there willingly bleeding for him.

"I don't blame you. We've all gotta heal in our own way," he said, as if reciting some piece of advice he'd heard before. I wanted to throw myself at his feet. Plead for his forgiveness and vow that from this point on I'd choose him. But then Franklin flashed into my mind, and the vision of my mother taking her last breath on my bedroom floor, and I just couldn't do it. I couldn't say the words to make him okay, because *I* wasn't okay. Not by a long shot.

"You know what hurts the most?" He took a beat to formulate his words, and I braced for the next blow, wanting it, even. Wanting all his pain to be piled on top of the hill of mine, because as much as it would hurt, as much as I was already weighed down by my own pain, going through my day knowing I hadn't given him closure, or something close to it, would destroy whatever was left of me, which wasn't much to begin with.

"What hurts the most is that I can't make things right for you. That my love isn't enough to make you want to try. Hell," he started, "you tried to warn me, but I wouldn't listen. I'm listening now, angel. I'm listening now."

"I'm sorry," I said, angrily wiping away a lone tear. I *was* sorry. Both apologetically, and pathetically. Sorry was all I had to give.

He moved closer, ferrying the scent of expensive booze with him. "Don't be sorry," he gritted out, hands combing through his hair as he stopped an arm's length away from me. "How can you stand it?" he asked, begging for me to provide an explanation he could work with. "You don't love him. There's no room left in your heart for him. It's filled to capacity with loving me."

"What would we tell your father?" I asked, hoping to make him comprehend the impossibility of us.

"Nothing!" he snapped without thinking, then sighed, intertwining his fingers at his nape. Franklin was not vanquished on some forgotten island with no means to return. He was one of the richest men in the world who still held influence and power, and Cole wasn't just an unknown paper pusher or businessman either. If Cole and I brought our love out of hiding, Franklin would know. Everyone would. "I don't care what he'd think," he amended. "Why do you?"

He didn't know, because I'd been trying to spare him. To spare them both. He didn't *know*. Maybe telling him would bring him closure, because then he'd understand.

"Say something." He was so close now, too close, and his hands were on me, his palms cupping the sides of my neck, cupping my hastening pulse, and all I could do was latch on to his forearms to stay on my feet. All I could think was *yes,* he's finally touching me. *Yes,* his touch still held love. "Please," he begged brokenly.

"She knew." The confession came from the deepest parts of me, contorting my voice as it traveled through my churning gut and past my shattered heart to break free of me. "She *knew*."

"What?" he breathed, his face leeching of color. I glossed a hand over his cheek, the sharp hairs there abrading my skin.

"My... *Our* mother knew. And she didn't approve."

"That isn't true," he said, unknowingly moving forward until my shoulders met the balcony door.

"She couldn't conceive of her kids being with each other in that way. She hated it. She was also afraid of what it would do to Franklin on top of everything else." *On top of her dying.* "Afraid of what it would do to you and me. Afraid our family would be irrevocably ruined and broken apart. She made me promise to end it right then. Made me promise not to tell Franklin, not to hurt him with this. And I gave her my word on both accounts. Only I broke one promise, and it killed her. *I* killed her, Cole." She was my cool breeze on a dry summer day, my stars guiding me in the dark, and my sun through the gray clouds. We'd run through the rose garden during a spring rain shower. I'd take her riding on Warrior to reconnect whenever she felt guilty for being too preoccupied with her charity work, or she'd take me driving through the valley with the top down as the god-awful "Love Is A Battlefield" blasted through the speakers. And I killed her.

"All she had to do was hold on for one more day. All *I* had to do was hold off on loving you one more day, at the very least, until she had her new heart. *That's* what hurts *me* the most, Cole," I cried. "She would be here. She *should* be here."

"Jasper," he breathed, searching for his next words as if gearing up to make things okay for me.

I shook my head vehemently. "My plan was to end things with you that night, but all that would've changed once we'd gotten the call from the hospital the next day about her new heart. That would've bought us time to convince her. It would've given us all more time." I blinked away the moisture budding behind my eyes. "I don't deserve you. I can't have you. And Franklin can *never* know." Besides Cole, my mother was my everything. She was everything to all of us, and more.

"It wasn't your fault, Jasper," he tried, jostling me in his conviction, his hands tightening at my neck. "How can I make you understand that?"

He couldn't. And I knew he wanted me to choose him. To choose us. To believe our love could conquer anything. But choosing him had cost me. Had cost us. Choosing him again would cost Franklin. And what would she think of me then? What was she thinking of me now? My thoughts must have been screaming too loudly, because a hopeless melancholy settled over Cole's face. It hurt me to see the look of defeat. To watch as he came to terms with the fact that he couldn't save me from this. But it didn't hurt enough to make a difference.

"If anyone knows what it's like to feel responsible for the death of a parent, it's me. I had to battle that nightmare twice, Jasper. If I hadn't gotten help when I did, our story would've had a much different ending," he said, making a last-ditch effort. "Believe me when I say it's not your fault."

I shook off his words. "I won't ever believe that. *I can't.*" I tried to break away from the hug he was determined to wrap me up in. I was too raw for compassion, for love, and suddenly I didn't want his understanding or forgiveness.

We tussled for a bit before my forehead tapped against his shoulder in surrender, anguish clawing at my insides as he rocked me, the back of his shirt balled between my fists.

"I don't regret any of this," he whispered into my ear. "Yes, I want more than you can give me right now. Yes, it kills me that it isn't my ring you're wearing as I make love to you in *our* bed. But there isn't anything I can't love you through, Jasper."

I pinched my eyes shut, flattening my ear to his shoulder, hoping it would prevent me from hearing his parting words.

"One day, you'll grow tired of being broken. You'll rightfully give up on holding yourself accountable for the worst thing that ever happened to you. And I'll be there to pick you up," he promised, kissing my hair. "I'll forgive every imaginable sin against me that your martyr's heart will conjure up. I'm telling you this now because I know how your mind works, Jasper. And when our time comes, I don't want a moment of it wasted on you beating yourself up. There isn't anything I couldn't forgive you for. There is nothing to forgive."

I raised my head, my stare connecting with his red-rimmed eyes, drinking in all of him, all of his unconditional love.

"I'll be here when you're ready. Because one of these days you're going to realize you deserve all the happiness I can give you."

"I'm sorry," I said, again, lips quivering. I fluttered my hands over his face, down to the spot at his throat I'd miss, the place I loved to fall asleep.

"I know," he said, smiling sadly, kissing my lips softly. This was goodbye. We were over before we had even begun. "I can't compete with your pain, angel. Your wounds are too deep for my love to reach. Too deep for my love to heal. You have to find a way past it. But *something's* gotta give because I can't do this, and I know, right now, that something won't be you."

CHAPTER 22

COLE AND I had held each other for as long as we could last night. Until staying a minute longer would've meant entering the cycle again.

The ending of our affair mirrored a death. My own this time. I was an empty shell, a rotting corpse tasked with the job of making sure my husband couldn't tell. I pretended to wake up ready to take on the day, when really, I hadn't fallen asleep at all, I'd stared at the wall while Daniel snored peacefully at my back.

I drank the bland coffee he'd set on the bathroom sink as I gazed into the mirror seeing nothing, then smiled artificially when he'd angled his head, giving me an evaluating look.

I cooked and picked at the tasteless breakfast I'd nearly burnt when something as simple as eggs sent me into a paralyzing flashback of Cole. He loved eggs.

I showered, because it was what I always did after coffee and breakfast, and I needed to keep up appearances, but then the water went cold, and Daniel poked his head in chuckling, checking to see if I was still alive. I wasn't, but I smiled and told him I'd be right out, anyway.

All things considered, I thought I was handling things well, until late afternoon when Daniel asked if I was okay.

"You don't seem like yourself," he said, coming up behind me to massage my shoulders as I sat hypnotized by my blank laptop screen.

His touch made my heart jitter, and I stood sharply from the dining table, knocking him back with my chair, not caring how erratic it made me look. I just needed to get from underneath his hands.

"How can he love you when he doesn't even know you?" Cole had asked once.

"He knows me," I'd shot back at him.

"No," he'd said. *"He knows who he wants you to be, but I know how beautiful you already are."*

Maybe his point wasn't valid after all, because as the antique sideboard behind Daniel broke his fall, he observed me as if I were an uncaged animal, and in that moment, it felt like he knew all of me. Like he knew *everything*.

Or maybe this type of ache simply couldn't be concealed. Maybe it pressed at the very air around me. Maybe it stank up the walls.

"What are you working on?" he asked, redirecting things, pointing to the screen with his chin. It was no longer asleep, but open to the trademark website I'd pulled up over an hour ago.

To try and take my mind off Cole, I'd decided to further research opening my own firm, but in this case, distractions weren't working. "I ah..." I hadn't mentioned my plans to Daniel. The dream was still in its infant stages, and I wasn't yet sure I could make it work. One negative comment from him would ruin everything. "I'm playing around with the idea of starting my own practice."

"Really?" he asked, seemingly excited, which surprisingly added some light to my dark mood.

"Yeah," I said, my tone more confident. "I know it won't be easy, but..."

"Yeah, well, nothing worth having ever is," he said absently as he leaned over the table to read the business name I'd entered into the site's search bar. "No other hits. It pays to have an uncommon last name," he said. "What field are you considering?"

I swallowed. "Civil rights."

"Ah," he said, "of course."

I wasn't in peak fighting condition. Everything in me hurt, and my heart was sensitive to the touch. Right then, it wouldn't have taken much to destroy the one thing I had left.

"Helping others has always been your passion, Jasper. I'm sure you'll continue to be successful at it."

"Thanks," I said from the bottom of what remained of my heart.

Daniel ambled for the stairs, head lowered, pinching his top lip in thought. "And hey," he said, twisting my way, one foot on the first step, hand on the railing, "at least when you can't keep the lights on, because defending lowlifes who can't afford to pay you doesn't cover the bills, you can always pull at your brother's purse strings."

I could've been a test study on how fast an already fleeting light could be snuffed out completely. Daniel jogged upstairs, his voice cheerfully informing me we needed to get ready for his parents' annual Christmas Eve party, oblivious to the mess he'd made of me. I collapsed lifeless onto my chair, closing my laptop, shutting away my dreams, and sank my head to the table.

My sulking didn't last long because I'd remembered Cole's Christmas present to me sat waiting in my coat pocket. After leaving his place, and exiting into the cold, I'd bundled my hands in my pocket to find a long, slender wrapped box waiting inside. He must have put it there when I went to the bathroom to splash water on my tear-streaked face. I didn't think I'd ever open it, as denial seemed to be my go-to when dealing—or not dealing with things. But I needed a pick-me-up. I needed to be reminded of what made me great even if I felt the complete opposite.

Cole's gifts are always meaningful, I thought as I played with the gold cross at my neck, his mother's pendant. He'd given it to me at a time when he wasn't yet strong enough to let me into the hole left behind from losing a mother he never got to know. The pendant was his way of saying: here's something of her until I'm able to share the rest.

At the closet, I dug in my coat pocket until my fingers banged against the box, withdrawing it and admiring the silver wrapping and red ribbon tied into a bow. I ripped the metallic paper away before I could talk myself out of it, and inside the velvet-padded box sat a sterling silver fountain pen.

I turned the pricey pen over in my hands, marveling at the gold piping along the edges of the felt tip. There was an inscription along the barrel. I brought it closer and whispered the fancy script aloud. *Don't ever quit your daydream. Love always, Cole.* And on the other side it read: *Jasper Des Moines Esq.*

I recapped the pen, a ghost of a smile playing across my lips, and reopened my laptop.

♦ ♦ ♦

I gazed over the holiday-infused city with my coat on waiting for Daniel to come downstairs, my fist tightened around the pen in my pocket.

"Pierre's stuck in traffic," he said, closing in and pecking the column of my neck, the place designated for Cole's punishing grasp. I spun away and faced him, counting down the seconds until I could wipe away the moisture he'd left behind before it evaporated into my skin.

"I didn't hear you come down," I said, hoping he'd see my reaction as shock and not rejection.

"I can believe that. You've been preoccupied with your thoughts all day. I know being around my parents isn't always easy, but they are the way they are because they care." He stepped in closer to the window, taking in the barricaded street corner due to the holiday parade happening on the block intersecting with ours. "I sure hope Pierre finds a way around this."

Because God forbid we'd need to ride the subway with those lowly human creatures, or have to walk two blocks north to meet his parents' driver instead of forcing him to maneuver in this madness. He'd need to reverse down our street to meet us out front.

"You can take off your coat. It might be a while," he said, walking toward the kitchen. "Oh," he doubled back, "don't mention any of this civil rights firm stuff at the party tonight, okay, sweetheart? I don't want to ruin my parents' holiday."

I stood there appalled, wondering had he always been this vile? Had he always served passive aggressive jabs with a side of airy smiles, and then pretended to be the recipient of my victimization whenever I fought back against his stabs at my career? Had I explained away his behavior time and time again as well-meaning, seeing him as a byproduct of Deacon and Caroline's loveless parenting? And did I forgive him for it all too quickly? Yes, I did. But this was the first time I'd allowed myself to see the cold truth. That there were no excuses good enough, and that all the actions I'd excused away as unintentional, were something else entirely, and I hadn't cared enough about myself to see it. I rubbed at the engraving on my pen.

"Screw you, Daniel," I said, astounding even myself. I didn't know if it was the pen bolstering me, the fact that I not only woke up on the wrong side of the bed, but also *in* the wrong bed, or the fact that I'd carved out the heart of the only man who truly loved me enough to accommodate my guilt and fear, but suddenly, I didn't feel so deserving of Daniel's bullshit.

"Where are you going?" he asked, baffled.

Already on the other side of the apartment door, I said, "I think I'll skip out on the phony family party this year. Give your parents my best." I shut the door, got onto the elevator when it arrived, and didn't take my first breath until I was gasping out in the cold.

I looked to both ends of the street and headed in the direction opposite the block party. I moved on autopilot, unsure of where I was heading until I'd gotten to the train station and remembered Sofia's annual toy drive. I typically missed it or showed up in time to help with clean up, because of Daniel's traditional family party of torture, but not this year. I got on the train heading south to Brooklyn.

◆ ◆ ◆

"Jasper!" Sofia's voice rang as I entered the rented storefront, but I couldn't see her past the ocean of excited kids and grateful parents trying to rein them in. A tiny arm shot in the air as a beacon, jazz-hand waving, and I cut through the crowd and around the long table she was stationed behind.

"Couldn't someone get you a stepstool?" I asked.

"Very funny," she said, slapping my arm. She was first on the assembly line they had going, and with a nudge from the person next to her, Sofia snatched a backpack from one of the many stocked shelves behind her, placing notebooks in it, then sending it down for other supplies and toys to be added.

"How can I help?" I asked as a little girl squealed, pointing at a doll on the top shelf before a person Sofia had called Jasmine stuffed it in the bag, and passed it to the person at her left, keeping the line moving.

Sofia called her son over, and I ruffled his hair as she asked him to take her place. "Follow me," she said, powerwalking to the back.

"This is a pretty huge storefront," I said from the open door of the stock room.

"Yeah, we got lucky this year, but the turnout is growing," she said, sighing toward the new wave of families piling in. It was a good sigh. It was her I'm-complaining-but-I'm-so-happy sigh. "Anyway, what are you doing here? You said you'd be at Daniel's parents' house."

"Yeah, not this year. What's wrong?" I asked as she chewed her lip, head snapping toward the entrance every time the bell hanging over the front door jingled, announcing someone had left or arrived.

"Um," she started. The rest was lost between "Sleigh Ride" playing through the store speakers, and a loud shriek of excitement coming from amidst the fray of people. Sofia tried to close the stockroom door, but I caught it in time to see Cole enter, and Camille race over to give him a hug, nearly knocking him off his feet. "She wanted to invite him. Apparently, they're on speed dial status now," she said, taking a stab at lightheartedness. "Jesus, Jasper, you're white as a ghost."

I'd texted her this morning letting her know Cole and I would be avoiding each other as much as possible. She didn't need to know any more than that. And I'd only told her that much to circumvent situations like this, because he'd gotten involved with some of her charities and would likely be around at times.

Cole and Camille had moved from the door to a high table off to the side where she seemingly tried to challenge him to an arm-wrestling match using her prosthetic limb. Cole laughed, and I wanted to crumble to the floor. How could he be okay? How could he laugh, how could he look so damn handsome and well put together, when I was nothing but an apparition of myself moving through the world.

"I didn't know you were coming," Sofia whispered, resting a palm on my forearm.

"It's okay," I assured her. "But if you don't mind, I think I'll go. Is there a back door?"

"Where are you going to go?"

"Home. Honestly, I could use the alone time." With Daniel breathing down my neck all day, I hadn't had the opportunity to properly mourn.

"Okay," she said, unsure. "But you call me if you need me. Promise?"

I kissed her cheek, done with making promises, then fled for the door she'd pointed at.

♦ ♦ ♦

As if my day couldn't have gotten any worse, I'd been met with icy rain as soon as I cleared the subway station near our apartment. Standing in our doorway, I deliberated what to do with my wet coat and shoes, because Daniel hadn't laid out a mat, or towel, to dry my coat before hanging it in the closet. The weather app hadn't mentioned rain or sleet.

I exhaled, searching inside myself, trying to determine if I actually cared about the hissy fit he'd have when he got home if I didn't handle this the right way. Turned out I didn't have it in me to give a damn. I dropped my coat to the floor, and then marched for the kitchen leaving wet footprints behind.

K-cup in place, I ordered some food, and called downstairs to let the lobby clerk know I'd be expecting someone, then took a hot shower.

The ringing of my phone shook me from my one-tracked thoughts, and thinking it could be my food delivery, I cut off the water, snagged a towel from the rack, and shot into the bedroom.

"Hello," I said, hitting the speaker phone icon and dropping the phone to the bed so I could dry off.

"Good evening, Mr. Des Moines. You have a um, ah, er, food delivery guy here wanting to come up."

"Yes. I'd called down, letting Nancy know already." Nancy's shift must have ended, and she'd forgotten to fill him in. I slipped on my boxers and sweats.

"Yes, she told me," he said. "Just wanted to double-check. Sending him right up." The call ended, and I stared at the screen perplexed before remembering my coffee, which had likely gone cold by now because looking at the time, I realized I'd been in the shower way too long again.

There was a knock at the door before I'd made it to the kitchen. The knock was oddly precise and commanding, and my brows dipped as I kicked my coat out of the way to open it, freezing in place, and fully understanding the lobby clerk's apprehension.

The man holding my food was no delivery boy. He was tall, imposing, and could make you feel equally loved or hated with one cutting glance of his obsidian eyes.

"Franklin," I breathed.

♦ ♦ ♦

"You've done well for yourself," Franklin said, his measured voice traveling from the living room. I chucked the food he'd intercepted from the delivery guy in the building lobby into the fridge. I didn't have an appetite anyway.

"It's my hus... It's Daniel's." The apartment and every piece of ostentatious furniture belonged to him. There was nothing of me there, and I hadn't cared. Maybe until now.

I grew uncomfortable under Franklin's probing stare, because he was good at seeing to the heart of things.

"I'd forgotten how much you look like her," he said before turning his pained expression away and venturing closer to the windows. "You're probably wondering why I'm here. Why I hadn't come sooner, or why I came at all." He clasped his wrist at the small of his back, much like Cole did when deep in thought. "I'm here to apologize, son," he whispered, cutting to the chase.

My breath left me on a ragged exhale. Hearing him call me *son*, hearing him say I probably wondered why he hadn't come sooner, made me feel like a child. Like someone's unabandoned child. And I hadn't felt like either of those for so long. It hurt in the best way. "You don't have to—"

"Yes, I do." He pivoted to me, his eyes showing me more than they ever had. Showing me what he already knew.

Oh God.

"I knew, Jasper. Not before that night, but certainly after. I lacked the finer details, but she was found on the threshold of your bedroom, and seeing the way you and Cole consoled each other when you thought I wasn't looking..." His voice petered off as he took a second to collect himself. My nails pierced the fabric of the sofa I stood behind as I waited.

"Nothing was more telling than how broken he was when you left. I let you leave, and I became cold to the only blood relation I had left. She would be ashamed of me. *Is* ashamed of me." He looked over his shoulder and into the night clouds.

"You—you *knew*?"

"Did you think I would have allowed you to leave so easily had I not known? Did you think I cared so little for you?"

I'd cared so little for me that it hadn't mattered how anyone else felt. I couldn't see or feel anything through the drip-feed of pain I'd been hooked to.

"I let you leave because I was in too much pain to deal with what I already knew."

"That I killed her," I said around the fist in my throat.

He shook his head. "No. That it wasn't your fault."

I shuddered then, grip tightening on the couch back. I had so much to say, so much to refute, but it occurred to me that this visit wasn't for me. Not really. This was every bit of Franklin releasing his aches and pains as it was about freeing me of mine. I wouldn't tarnish this for him by telling him his feelings were a lie. I'd let him say his peace. I'd let him find his peace, too.

"I know she didn't approve," he said. "I know this because she'd written her thoughts down. It was her final journal entry." He blushed as if ashamed to admit he'd read her private thoughts. "It helped. After she died...it helped."

"I'd never judge you for that, Franklin."

"My guess is she couldn't sleep. Not with the way things were left. And so she went looking for you that night." He scratched at the gray strands along his hairline. That and the slight wrinkles at the corner of his eyes were the only things betraying his age. Cole got his eyes from his mother, but every other physical attribute was a carbon copy of his father.

"I'm..." I searched for a better word than sorry, so sick of being it and feeling it and speaking it. "I didn't mean to hurt you."

"She wasn't perfect, you know. Children often expect parents to be ideal, forgetting we're human, too. We're flawed, too. Selene had a temper, and an aptitude for wanting things her way." He gave a slanted smile. "The latter was my fault because I'd formed a habit of never saying no to her. The former might've been my fault too for the same reason." He placed a hand over his heart, as if indicating it was what currently ailed him. I was looking at an upgraded version of the stoic man I knew. He might as well have been touching his sleeve, because right then that was where his heart had taken up residency.

"I loved both her temper and her sometimes non-compromising way. But you boys didn't see that side of her, because as a mother, she constantly strived for perfection.

"My point is, she was afraid. She thought she was running out of time, and wanted to reduce the heartache and suffering left behind. She wanted our family intact. She didn't want me hurt and lashing out. She didn't want you alone in the world with no family if things went bad. Sure, she was also your and Cole's mother, so she had that to battle with, too. But she made a mistake, and by the looks of it, you're holding on to that just so you can hold on to her."

He sauntered closer to the window, staring at the cold, wet street below. "I bet she feels closer, doesn't she? With you constantly reminding yourself of the pain, sharpening it so it never dulls...it keeps her near," he whispered, speaking more to himself now. "I understand it. But we've gotta let it go."

"How?" I asked, and he glanced back at me as if remembering I was there.

"Forgive her," he said. And never had two words torn me so irreversibly apart.

CHAPTER 23

Cole

"ONLY CRAZY PEOPLE *run outdoors in the fall. Or winter. Or the spring. Or summer."* I thought back on Jasper's words as I pushed my legs harder and swung my arms faster to counterbalance the momentum. Crazy was exactly how I felt as I hit the sixty-minute mark on my run, and showing no signs of letting up.

I rounded a corner, startling a flock of pigeons and sending them flying from the sidewalk when my gaze smacked against Jasper's building. I slowed to a jog before stopping completely, winter smoke billowing from my mouth as I panted through my exertion and pain.

Backing under the awning of a bakery that hadn't yet opened for the day, I peered to the left and right of me, ensuring neither Jasper nor Daniel weren't somehow walking the streets this early in the morning and would spot me.

When the hell had I decided to take the route to him? I hadn't. At least not consciously, but he was all I could think about since we ended things last night. I couldn't help feeling like I'd given up on him, although that couldn't be further from the truth.

Ending things didn't end my mental turmoil, though. As I gazed up in the vicinity of their apartment, jealousy still plagued me. Was Daniel holding him? Consoling him without even knowing it? Would Jasper now do everything in his power to make his marriage work? Did I subconsciously break things off hoping it would force him to pick me?

"*Fuck*. I can't do this." I tugged the hood of my running jacket over my head, and jogged off in the direction I'd come from, suddenly anxious to get home so I could lick my wounds in private, because I was terrifyingly close to falling apart on the street.

"*She knew.*" Jasper's voice spirited through my mind, and I cursed again, picking up my pace.

"*She didn't approve*" filtered in next, leveling up the panic to the point I darted into the street without looking, the blare of a horn waking me from the replay of my nightmare.

"Shit!" I jumped back just in time to narrowly miss being run over. The driver cursed at me through his cracked window as he sped past. I gestured for the oncoming car to proceed while I waited in the middle of the intersection before cautiously getting to the curb and hailing a cab. I wasn't fit to be outdoors.

After Jasper had left, I'd sat at the piano and played until the sun poked its head over the horizon. I played *Moonlight Sonata,* Selene's favorite, and thought back on the many recitals she'd sat front and center at, and the tears she'd cry into my father's handkerchief. I tried to reconcile that image with the woman who wanted Jasper to sever our relationship. Tried to reconcile the woman who once told me she'd love me through anything and everything, with the woman who disapproved of our love.

I'd played as my tears flooded the keys making my fingers slip and the song go out of tune. I'd played as I whispered the self-love mantras I'd accumulated over the years, needing them badly right then because I'd felt myself toe-dipping into a pit of self-hate again. The one I'd crawled out of with the support of Leland and countless hours of therapy.

At one point I'd stopped playing, needing the quiet to apply the rationality I'd gained on my therapist's couch to my current situation.

Selene had every right to disapprove of us. Or to have needed time and space to come to terms with who Jasper and I were to each other. What I knew for sure was she loved us, and she would've found a way to move past her own ideas for our lives, past her discomfort. She would have found a way to accept us. And then she would've been our advocate, even if it meant going up against her husband. Selene was love and light, and she would have discovered a way to meet us where we were. I had to believe that.

"Sir?" the cabbie said a bit aggressively, as if it weren't his first attempt at getting my attention.

"Sorry," I said, paying him and exiting in front of the hotel I called home.

"This living arrangement is temporary, right?" Jasper had asked during his first visit here. Maybe it would've been if leaving meant getting over him.

I thanked the doorman and then slid onto the elevator.

As soon as the doors opened onto my foyer I was hit with his scent, sparking a sort of grief-rage. There was a time I'd searched this place practically on hands and knees praying to find a trace of him. A sock under the bed, deodorant left behind, a dirty coffee mug with the imprint of his lush lips on the rim. And now that I wanted no reminders, reminders were all I had.

I snatched a trash bag from the kitchen pantry, charging through the house on the hunt for anything Jasper. I tugged the dresser drawer so hard it crashed to the floor, the t-shirts unfolding onto the closet carpet. Rummaging through it, I struck gold, coming across the black wide-armed tank he loved to lounge around in. It showed off his defined arms and rib cage. It was mine, but it had to go.

Next, I dug around the cabinet under the bathroom sink, spilling its contents onto the marble floor in search of the lotion he favored, then tossed it into the bag, too. I'd have to start wearing something new.

The hazelnut coffee he loved went next. Then his favorite mug. If I could have, I would've ripped away the kitchen island I'd laid him out on countless times just to taste him while seated on a stool with his legs thrown over my shoulders.

I roughly rolled up the fluffy living room rug I'd made love to him on, flashes of him gripping it as his cum soaked into the fibers sent me to my knees. While there, I scanned the room for what would be next. *My piano.*

An ache of a different kind took up residency, then, because that instrument was more than its shiny lid littered with Jasper's seed, more than his tongue cleaning up the mess he'd made—with my help, and more than the place we'd first kissed upon my reentry into his life.

It was also the place Selene loved to watch me get lost in from her curled up position on the bay window bench. It was also the only place I could get Jasper to venture to when he was sick. I'd promise to play "Clair De Lune" if he'd only get out of bed and stretch his legs. He'd sit with his head on my shoulder as I played, fingers tapping away on his thighs because he'd memorized each note of the song by then.

I sat then, with my back against the sofa—the one we'd notoriously fall asleep on intertwined like vines. By my reasoning, nothing short of burning the place down with everything in it would do. And that's when I noticed the gift tucked under the Christmas tree.

Crawling over, I snagged it before returning to my spot, turning the badly wrapped item over in my hand. It wasn't from Leland. He hadn't been by for a while.

Jasper. He must have snuck it under there while waiting for me to get home last night.

Christmas was still a day away, but I couldn't tear the red and gold paper away fast enough, convincing myself it was so I could throw the gift away even faster, be done with him and this thing causing my heart to fold in on itself. Be done with love.

Functions of the body normally done subconsciously escaped me as I stared at the item in my shaking hand. I didn't blink. I didn't breathe.

The clay bowl was big enough to store a set of keys that were always lost, a wallet that could rarely be found, and the pocket change that would sometimes make its way into the wash cycle. I knew what it could hold, because it was perfectly crafted for me for all those reasons.

I brought it reverently to my nose, expecting to find a trace of her there, the lingering scent of her favorite perfume, but there was nothing. The best I could do was close my eyes and think back on that day.

"Come on, Coley-bear!" Selene had called from the front door, wrapping her favorite tattered scarf around her neck.

My father bought her a new cashmere scarf every Christmas, a not-so-subtle hint if you asked me, but she'd always worn the one Jasper had saved his allowance to buy her before they came into our lives. The thing was atrocious.

I'd bounded down the stairs, checking behind me to be sure Jasper wasn't trailing. *"Don't call me that,"* I'd said sulkily, slipping into the jacket she held open for me. *"It'll only encourage him."*

"But it's so cute," she'd said, before kissing the tip of my nose. *"Just like you."*

"I'm fourteen," I'd grumbled, secretly loving the way she nurtured me as if knowing there was a lot of that to make up for.

I pushed the memory away, examining the bowl once again. Selene made sure we did things as a family, but she also gave Jasper and me our individual time with her. She'd signed us up for a pottery class that day. I'd wanted to see the new Tom Cruise movie, but she was big on bonding activities.

Moving from the floor to the sofa, I steeled myself before turning the bowl over to read the barely legible inscription.

"You'll always be my Coley-bear. Love, Mom."

The bowl had sat on our entryway table for years, way into my adulthood. Then I thought back on a conversation I'd had with Jasper shortly after crash-landing back into his life.

"I combed the house from top to bottom looking for it after she died."

He'd taken it. Probably to have something that was both a piece of her and a part of me.

Hauling myself over to the foyer, I situated the bowl on the table. I no longer had a need for keys, but I retraced my steps, eventually finding my wallet on the bathroom floor, and then placed it inside.

Jasper's gift—or return of my stolen property—had temporarily eased some of the pain, allowing my exhaustion to take the focus.

The sofa was as far as I could go, and after a few hours of dozing, a reminder ping jerked me awake. *Camille.* I'd made her a promise before having my heart torn out of me, but I couldn't disappoint her. I expelled a deep breath, and then got ready for Sofia's annual toy drive.

♦ ♦ ♦

"Cole Kincaid without a suit," Sofia said, rubbing the material of my charcoal-colored sweater between her thumb and forefinger. "Cashmere. I'll have you in jeans and cotton in no time, my friend." The tightness around her eyes betrayed her casual tone, but it warmed me to hear her refer to me as a friend, because I was down one as of last night.

"Many before you have tried," I said, failing at returning her feigned lightness.

"How are you?" she asked, gesturing for me to follow her to the back where she'd been with Jasper when I walked in. I hadn't seen him, but I'd felt him. We were like opposing atoms in that way, searching for our counterpart when near. In that same vein, I felt stripped, bereft when he'd vanished. It had taken everything I didn't have to keep my composure for Camille. To not disregard her happiness in search of my own. In search of him.

"I've been better," I admitted. Sofia was keen, and also Jasper's best friend. Lying to her would've been pointless.

"What's going on with you two?"

"Nothing," I said, huffing a hollow laugh. "Absolutely nothing." After a brief pause, in which Camille and one of Sofia's boys came into the supply room for more toys, I asked, "How is he?"

Sofia straightened her Santa hat before crossing her arms. "I thought Daniel would be as bad as it got for him, but now—"

"So you hate him too?" I asked, hoping for an ally.

"Well, hate is a strong word. Do I think Jasper can do better?" She pursed her lips and tilted her head side to side in a so-so gesture. "Certainly."

"Then why haven't you told him that?" I asked accusingly.

Sofia's hands dropped to her hips in frustration. "Have you met your stepbrother-slash-no longer brothers-slash-friend-slash-lover-friend?" she asked. "If he doesn't want to see something, he won't. It's a freaking superpower, I swear." She mumbled words in Spanish before swiping her hat completely off. She was right. Jasper could be stubbornly obtuse at will. "I'm worried about him," she confessed. So was I, but I couldn't be the one to be there for him. Jasper and I couldn't be friends. We hadn't even gotten the science down on how to be brothers. Our romantic love would get in the way of all of it. It was either everything or nothing with us. Something we'd understood but lied to ourselves about this go-round.

"Come on," Sofia said as families kept piling in. "Help me reel this circus in."

◆ ◆ ◆

Leland was waiting for me when I got home, leaning against the wall with his feet crossed at the ankle as he investigated his cuticles, completely pulling off the "you haven't returned my calls, but I'm so not worried about you" look.

"I was going to call you back," I said as I hung my coat on the hook. "It was crazy down at the toy drive."

"I got your message," he said, straightening. "The one asking me to cancel the standing reservation on a suite I knew nothing about. I canceled Jasper's flight on your upcoming trip, too."

"Thanks," I said, gunning for the gin I'd left on the coffee table.

"Where's your rug?" he asked, entering the living room behind me.

"Had to get rid of it," I answered, keeping it simple, but nothing's ever simple with Leland.

"Why?"

"It was stained."

"What kind of stain?" he asked roguishly. I gave him a look conveying how much I wasn't in the mood for his ill-timed humor.

"Sorry," he said. "Look, I figured you might not want company, but I'm here anyway. Figured we could do our Christmas gift exchange early. I even made my famous chicken Florentine you love so much. It's keeping warm in the oven."

God bless him and his *horrible* chicken Florentine. "Thanks," I said, realizing I'd meant it. I didn't want to be left alone with my thoughts.

Leland scrunched up his nose, pointing at the bottle in my hand. "Is that *gin*? You can afford to use aged Chateau Lafite's as mouthwash, yet you continue to drink gin?" He tskd in mock disappointment. "Where's the good stuff?"

I laughed in spite of myself, and Leland smiled in return. "In the kitchen. Second cabinet to the right of the sink."

"Can't you have a proper bar like normal rich people?" he asked, walking backwards.

"Bars are gaudy and send a bad message," I said, falling into our usual banter.

"What? That you're an alcoholic?" He opened the cabinet as I took up a stool.

"No. That I want people to stay long enough to share a drink."

"I hope *those people* don't include me," he said, reading the label on a bottle of scotch.

"No, you're always welcome, Leland." I left him to plate the food as I went to change, building myself up to eating the dish with a smile and keeping it down, too.

The phone on the bedside table rang. The concierge needed permission to allow an unlisted visitor up.

"Send him up," I said resignedly, after she announced my father's name. Perching on the end of the bed, change of clothes forgotten, I quickly ran through what his presence would mean.

The soft chime of the elevator sounded, and I hurried down the hall in time to see him step off as he surveyed what he could see of my home.

"Dad, what are you doing here?" I asked.

Glass shattered in the kitchen, followed by Leland's muttered curse, and my father's head swiveling sharply in that direction.

"I'm alright!" Leland called out.

My father brought his attention back to me, his gaze uncharacteristically unsteady. "Can't I want to be with my son for the holiday?"

"Ah, yeah. Of course. It's just I wasn't expecting you."

"Yes, well, I thought surprising you might be best."

In other words, he left me with no choice in the matter. He removed his coat, handing it off to me as if I'd asked for it. He wore a severe, dark suit underneath, reminding me so much of myself, of how similar we were. He peered over my shoulder, eyes widening before resuming their normal, unflinching state.

"Mr. Kincaid," Leland said, coming in next to me.

"I told you to call him Franklin," I said, because my father wouldn't.

"Yes, please call me Franklin," he echoed, shell-shocking me.

Leland scurried past with his head down, getting to his coat.

"You just got here," I said, now noticing the tension surrounding us.

"I, uh, forgot I had something urgent to take care of. Plus you two need to catch up." He mashed the elevator call button, tripping over himself to get inside. "By the way, I owe you a fancy tumbler," he mumbled, eyes downcast, before the doors closed.

Leland was anything but awkward, and I observed my father, wondering at the visceral reaction he'd stirred in my friend. Other than their initial introduction years ago, which was brief, they'd only ever seen each other in passing. My father said nothing, though, so I chalked it up to him being intimidating by simply existing.

"Can I come in?" he asked, gesturing to the home beyond the entryway.

I hung his coat and led him to the kitchen. "Hungry?"

"No thank you," he said, holding a hand up. "I won't be staying long. I'm aware I've intruded on you without notice. I wanted you to know I was in town."

You could have called.

"More importantly, I wanted to see you. I've...missed you."

I was grateful he couldn't see my expression as I poured the chicken Florentine into the trash. In all the years I'd known my father, he'd never verbally admitted to wanting to see me, or missing me. There was no question I was loved by him, but he showed his affection more by doing or being there when it mattered. And since Selene died, he hadn't done anything, and wasn't there much.

I understood why, and my own hidden guilt made allowances for the deterioration of our relationship. I never blamed him for how he chose to grieve, especially when unbeknownst to him, I'd played a role in the necessity of that. But until right then, I hadn't allowed myself to admit I missed him, too. I'd told Jasper I wanted my father to be okay, and maybe he was well on his way to being just that.

Speaking of Jasper... "How long are you staying for?" I asked, nervous about their paths crossing. I didn't want Jasper feeling ambushed. Didn't want him to think I'd set this up as a means to push him into facing things he wasn't ready to address.

"A while," he admitted, and then as if sensing my trepidation, he said, "I saw Jasper."

"You did," I said flatly, making it more statement than question. "How was he when you left him?" Because one doesn't walk away from an encounter with Franklin Kincaid the same. And because I already knew how he was before Franklin had gotten to him.

"In as bad a shape as you are. Though he doesn't hide it as well." About five feet and an island separated us, and although I'd lost the advantage of daylight streaming in through the windows, I'd never seen my father more clearly. Sorrow clouded his already dark eyes. And the aberrant slump in his shoulders expressed a weariness I'd never seen in him before, or one he'd never permitted me to experience from him. "I apologized," he said thickly, looking toward his feet uncomfortably. "And now I'm here to hopefully make amends with you."

It became apparent what this was, then, and I circled the island, holding an in-drawn breath before asking, "How much do you know?"

CHAPTER 24

Daniel

4 Years Ago

ENTERING MY OFFICE ahead of Jessica, anticipation buzzing through me, I instruct her to close the door as I take a seat behind my desk. She clutches three folders to her chest wearing a look of pride for a job well done. Once I settle in, she lays them out in front of me.

"The files you asked for, Mr. Ward."

I flip through them, almost forgetting she's there as a feeling of giddiness builds. "And what about the other information I requested?" I ask, doubling back through the paperwork in case I'd missed it. It has only been a few weeks since my initial request, maybe more time is needed.

"Waiting in your inbox," she said, smoothing down her pencil skirt as she waited for further instructions.

I boot up my computer and find her email, reading through the documents before leaning back, my steepled fingers hiding my smirk. "Print these out—only one copy, and bring them to me. Then delete all traces of this from your emails and wherever else you may have it saved. I'll do the same."

"I'll get right on it, Mr. Ward."

"And Jessica," I call as her hand meets the door handle. "This stays between us."

"Of course, Mr. Ward." Jessica's been with me for three years. She knows how I operate, and has more than proven herself trustworthy, but a little reminder never hurts.

"This all might be inessential anyway." I motion to the folders. "I'm about to serve Parker his biggest win yet. He'll have to see my worthiness then," I say smugly.

CHAPTER 25

Jasper

THE NEW YEAR came and went, and with it an abundance of changes. For one, Daniel and I had begun to grow apart. Not that we'd been growing together in the first place, but gone was the man who believed elaborate gestures were the only kinds of gestures worth making.

Last year for Valentine's Day he'd covered every surface in our apartment with roses. I'd gasped when I saw the invoice sitting on his desk a week later. This year the day rolled by with a text saying he'd be working late and couldn't do dinner.

We hadn't had sex in months, which was more than fine with me, but he'd stopped explaining it away with conflicting schedules and work exhaustion. It seemed he just didn't care anymore, and I felt it. I understood it. I was grateful for it.

Some days I'd catch him watching me with a look of disappointment, but then he'd quickly adopt a simulated smile before asking if I wanted takeout, or if I'd seen some missing item of his. His items never went missing.

It was the same smile he'd always worn, I realized, even while telling me he loved me.

"Are you happy, Daniel?" I'd asked one day out of the blue, finally ready to hear the truth.

"Of course, sweetheart," he'd said.

And there goes that smile again, I'd thought.

Leaving those ruminations behind for the moment, I dug through the paperwork on the coffee table for my phone, confirming I had an hour until Sofia arrived to go over our closing arguments on a case she'd come out of her fake retirement to help me with.

Daniel was away on business and wouldn't be home for a few days, so I'd invited her over rather than lugging everything to her place.

Something thumped onto the floor, and I peeked over the side of the table from my spot on the couch, to see Franklin's Christmas gift. He'd left it behind, along with my mother's final journal entry. The gift was still wrapped, the journal entry still sealed in its envelope.

While my conversation with Franklin had gone a long way, and I could feel repairs within me happening day by day, I hadn't yet unearthed the courage to deal with the heavy emotion I knew those two items would spur, especially since he'd hinted that even the gift had something to do with my mother.

"Merry Christmas," he'd said. *"Although I had little to do with the gift itself, other than hand-wrapping it personally."*

"I can tell," I'd said with a slanted grin, examining the wrinkled patchwork of paper held together by duct tape.

Every day without fail, I brought them out of hiding to keep me company as I worked, hoping one day I'd glance over at them and say, *"Today is the day."*

Knuckles rapped on the door, which wasn't a shocker since Sofia tended to be overly punctual.

"Hey, bestie," she exclaimed, holding up a bottle of champagne. I chuckled, moving aside to let her in.

She hung her coat then went to the fridge to store the bottle, as I stepped over file boxes and scattered sheets of paper to retake my seat.

"It's a mess in here," she noted, moving a stack of binders off the seat across from me. "Is Daniel going to keel over when he sees this place?"

"Probably," I said, looking around, then shrugging. Sofia laughed conspiratorially, and I joined in.

"Okay, Jasper Des Moines attorney at law, where are we?" She plucked an evidence folder off the table, thumbing through its contents.

"It's just Jasper to you," I said, affectionately. I'd started my own practice. I didn't have office space, or a steady influx of clients, or employees on payroll yet—because Sofia helped me for free. But my business had a name, and thanks to my best friend, I also had stationary with my firm imprint on it. It was a start.

We worked for a few hours, then came up for air and a glass of expensive champagne.

"Wow," I said, after my first sip, raising the bottle for inspection. "You splurged on the good stuff."

"Eh," she said, waving me off. "Hubby won it in a Christmas raffle at work. The thing's been sitting under the kitchen sink ever since. He's more of a Hennessey kind of guy."

Christmas. My gaze scanned the table, landing on the pen Cole had gifted me. His way of reminding me to follow my dreams, even if he couldn't be the one to remind me himself.

"I've got something to show you," Sofia said carefully, setting her glass on her coaster, then removing a magazine from her handbag. It was the latest issue of Modern Medicine Magazine. Cole graced the black and white cover, appearing pensive and shirtless, the letter X drawn over his heart in black sharpie. The headline read "Matters of the Heart."

I snatched it from her hand before thinking, my cheeks burning, but Sofia pretended not to notice.

I flipped through the pages when all I wanted to do was slobber over the cover image. That would have to wait for when she left. Hopefully, she'd forget the magazine on her way out.

"There's more shots on page sixty. The accompanying article starts on page sixty-eight." She topped off our glasses. "I don't see what having him oiled up with muscles on display has to do with the artificial heart, but it definitely draws the eye, that's for sure. Guess that's the point. Sell copies first, content later. He mentions Bystanders," she said.

"Does he?"

"Um-hm. Donations have been pouring in non-stop, too. We'll be able to start up the housing arm of the foundation."

"That's great, 'Fia." I tried to sound happy, and I was. Sadness lurked, too, though. I hadn't seen him since Christmas Eve, hadn't uttered his name unless it was to get myself off. Hadn't held a conversation involving him unless it was to make some excuse to Daniel as to why we hadn't hung out in a while.

Daniel still oversaw the team of attorneys assigned to Nexcom, but he wasn't as hands-on, even returning to Parker, Mitchell, & Ward's headquarters full time. It made it easier to avoid Cole. But I missed him. I missed him so much it hurt.

"Tell me," she said, staring into the bottom of her flute as if wondering where the contents had gone before pouring up the last of the bottle, "does he wake up looking like a GQ model? Or does it take a village?"

"Sadly, he rolls out of bed like that. You should see his father," I said, turning the magazine facedown on the table, hoping it'd ease the pain.

"Oh, I have," she said, then winced as if caught red-handed. "We met a couple times. Only briefly, really."

"It's okay, 'Fia. I don't expect you not to be friends with Cole." I sort of did, because of the whole if-I-can't-have-him-no-one-can thing, but I wasn't so far gone that I'd actually verbalize it. I had to deal with that irrationality on my own.

She'd never so blatantly mentioned Cole before. Not since we'd ended things. They remained friendly, I knew, but she was sensitive to my missing him, to me needing time to get my shit in order. I loved her for it.

"I think I'm ready to leave him, 'Fia."

She didn't waste words on asking me who. "For Cole?"

"No," I said. "For me."

"Now, that's something I can drink to." She tipped her glass to me.

We raided Daniel's wine cupboard behind the stairs, deciding work could wait for tomorrow.

"Oh this is good," Sofia said, twisting the flute in her hands, nodding appreciatively at the pink bubbly. "Why do you keep looking at that..." Her words petered off as she scooted to the edge of her seat, nearly tipping over as she stretched her neck in the direction of Franklin's present. Sofia narrowed her eyes on the shoddy wrapping job. "Don't tell me what it is," she said, fingering the duct tape.

"It's a Christmas gift from Franklin," I told her anyway.

"That's a gift?" she asked incredulously, then chased it with, *"Christmas?"*

"Yeah, I've been waiting to open it."

"Waiting for what, next Christmas?" She snort-belched a laugh, and I relieved her of her glass.

"That's enough for you," I said. "Whatever it is, it belonged to my mother. And I don't know. I guess I wanted to build up some emotional strength first, if that makes sense. Trying to work some things out on my own, let some things go, so by the time I get around to dealing with this, I'd be capable." I shrugged, knowing I hadn't articulated that well, or perhaps it was so silly a concept it couldn't be explained.

"I get it," she said. "As a mother, my main goal is to prepare my kids to face the world. I want them sure of who they are, and what they have to offer. I want their foundation unshakable, so that no matter what anyone says to them out there..." She pointed to the window. "No matter what circumstances they may face, they can never be broken in here." She tapped her head. "There's nothing wrong with preparing for the fight, Jasper. Although," she tacked on, "some fights can't be faced until you have all the facts."

I filled my cheeks with air, and then released it, setting the gift on my lap. "You're right." Building strength would only come *after* facing down my fears, not before. Thinking otherwise was just another form of denial.

"Do you need to be alone?" She made to stand.

"No," I said, taking in my big sister/best friend. The woman I'd hid so much from in the past. "No more keeping who I am from you."

"Well, you're gonna need a saw to get through all that tape, sweetie."

We laughed, and then I found the sharpest knife in the kitchen and got to work.

"It's a photo album," she said, coming to sit next to me.

"I've never seen this before," I admitted, caressing the black suede covering before forging ahead.

"Or a photo scrapbook may be more like it," she amended. Each sheet of cardstock contained a photo, with a trinket and handwritten note glued or stapled next to it. "Is that baby Jasper?"

"Yeah," I whispered. I couldn't have been more than a few hours old. I lay asleep, swaddled in my mother's arms, a blue cap over my head as we slept in her hospital bed.

"What does the note say?" Sofia asked, inching closer until our legs touched, excited to take this journey with me.

I read my mother's perfect script out loud, fingering my hospital ID bracelet. "'This is it, baby boy. The beginning of you and me. A bond no one can ever come between.'"

Next, I pointed to a photo of me kicking at the schoolyard grass. "This was my fifth birthday," I said with surety. I wore the new shirt my mother had saved to buy me. It was a red Thomas the Train shirt. "I remember because my dad had promised to pick me up for ice cream, but he never showed. I waited there alone for over an hour before the principal called my mom. She must have taken that as she approached from the parking lot."

I angled the book so Sofia and I could read the note assigned to it.

"'The first time I realized I didn't have the power to shield you from heartache, but that I could be your calm in the midst of life's storms.'" She'd attached the receipt for the three-tier ice cream cake she'd stopped at Carvel to buy on the way home.

"I remember she'd let me eat cereal for breakfast and dinner for the rest of the week. I thought she was being a cool mom, because I loved cereal, but she must have spent all the grocery money on that cake."

The next photo was of me asleep in front of Cole's locked bedroom door, my pillow underneath me and blanket drawn to my chin. A copy of the petition I'd created for the fountain in the park honoring Cole's mother had been folded and stapled to the cardstock.

"'What fighting for what you want and never giving up looks like. I couldn't be more proud,'" I read.

"Cole was a hard nut to crack," I said, remembering the days I'd camp outside his door until he'd let me in.

"Until he wasn't," Sofia ribbed, brows dancing. I kissed her nose and continued. "Is that Franklin?" she asked.

"Yeah, it is," I confirmed. "What's he doing?" I stared harder at the blurry photo. She must have taken it from a great distance, or maybe it hadn't held up with age.

"Looks like he's brushing someone's hair back. Could it be you?"

"Yeah. That was the week we'd moved into Franklin's home. I'd come down with something. The fever was pretty bad." I touched the wrapper from a cough medicine bottle taped to the page. "He must have looked in on me, not realizing he'd been spotted by her."

"'He took care of you when he thought I wasn't looking, and that's when it mattered most,'" Sofia read. "Your mom was a lurker."

"Apparently," I said.

"Do you think she ever caught you and Cole?"

"No. She wouldn't have kept quiet about that. And we were careful—until we weren't." *Until I wasn't.*

We spent hours going through the scrapbook of memories. Scrolling photos of Cole and me throughout the years. Family vacations, Easter egg hunts along the property, and even movie nights. She'd told a story of love, loss, gains, and even forgiveness. And I took my time explaining the symbolism of it all to Sofia. To myself, too, because I began to see things more clearly. Through the eyes of my mother. She loved me. *She still loved me.* Even in the end, because this type of love never died, not even when the heart did.

"I can't believe I've been running from this," I said, tugging the corners of the last photo until it pulled free. It was a Polaroid of me sleeping with my head in my mother's lap, taken the week before she passed away. Franklin had gotten her the Polaroid so she could have her photos instantaneously. We all knew what that meant.

Tacked to the photo was a picture of the Statue of Liberty. I'd drifted off filling her head with dreams of taking New York City by storm. It was mostly talk. She liked to hear me talk, and so I'd gotten in the habit of rambling about the most mundane things. She'd said she would miss me but had encouraged me to follow my heart. I'd held on to the part where she said she'd miss me, because it meant she'd still be around.

Sofia had read the attached note before I did, sucking in a breath and gripping my knee.

"I'll love and support you through anything, Jasper. Or die trying."

I closed the book and my eyes. *Those* were the words. Those were the words I'd needed to hear. The healing balm to my pain, the nurturing touch to my cold loneliness. She would've tried. Had she had the time to, she would have tried.

Franklin was right. I hadn't forgiven her. Until he'd said the words, I hadn't even known I was holding her death, my subsequent responsibility for it, and the loss of Cole against her. I hadn't realized I blamed her for it all. Because she wasn't perfect, because she'd made a mistake, and because she'd left before either of us could make things right.

The realization made me want to track down Cole and challenge every time he'd said forgiving was what I did best, because it was a lie, even if it was a blind one.

I needed to forgive her, and then I could forgive myself.

Sofia gave me some space, doing the dishes and returning the apartment back to normal as I sat with my thoughts. But nothing about this was normal. Nothing about what I'd chosen to do with my life was okay.

"Do you need me to stay?" she asked, sitting across from me again. "I can have hubby get dinner started."

"No, go," I said, waking from my stupor. "I'll probably do a little thinking then head to bed early." There was still her journal entry to grapple with, but it'd have to wait until morning.

"In the write-up, Cole talks about why the heart is important to him. You should check it out. Specifically the last paragraph." With that she kissed the crown of my head and left, the door softly clicking shut behind her.

I tore through the magazine, pausing to absorb the sexy shots of him first. I couldn't help it. I was starved for him. For any small glimpse of him.

I ran a finger over his chest as he reclined shirtless on a heart-shaped rug. The shot was taken from overhead, his hair strategically tousled as he gazed away from the camera's lens thoughtfully. The black and white color scheme contorted the blue of his eyes into a light, molten silver shade, causing lust and longing to slam into me like a sledgehammer.

The other intimate shots were more of the same. More muscles, more of his eyes searing into mine, more lust, more longing, more sledgehammers.

With a pounding heart and erection, I sought out the last page of the article, tracing a finger down its length until reaching the journalist's last question.

"So, this question is more of a two-fer. Is there anyone special in your life? Someone who's snagged your heart?—asking for a friend," she'd clarified, flirtation leaking off the page currently tearing under my grip. *"And why is creating a viable heart so important to you?"*

"There's no one, at the moment. Metaphorically speaking, I lost my heart, and in many ways I've been dead without it. I don't want that to be a literal reality for anyone, if I can help it."

CHAPTER 26

I SHUFFLED UNDER the spray of water, shutting my eyes and pretending it was rain, remembering when I stood naked and sated at Cole's balcony doors one night watching the ensuing rainstorm hungrily.

"One day, when the weather changes, when it's warmer," he'd said, sneaking in behind me and lacing our fingers together before pressing them against the glass doors. *"I'll fuck you in the rain, angel. I promise."* He'd proceeded to tap my ankle with his foot, asking me to widen my stance, and then taking me again while standing.

"The first day of summer," I'd said as he moved inside me. For no other reason than it was our favorite season, and the first day of any season had always felt symbolic to me. The act of leaving things behind as we moved on to something new. And nothing beat fucking under summer rain.

Slamming back into my body, leaving the recollection behind, I got to my toes like I had that night, one hand thrown out to the shower wall as I worked my cock with purpose, trying to recreate the feeling I always got with him. I yelled his name freely as I orgasmed. It was something, yet still unsatisfying.

Toweled off, I heedlessly blow dried my hair before dressing in dark jeans and a matching t-shirt, then headed downstairs to make my third cup of coffee for the day.

Sliding onto a stool at the island, I sipped cautiously as I waited for my laptop to start up, trying hard not to revisit the pity party I'd thrown last night. It had been a whole forty-eight hours since my evening on the couch with Sofia by then, and after burning the midnight oil the night prior to get my closing argument nailed down, I was left with free time to think and obsess over my mother's journal entry.

I'd given in. With Cole's favorite gin taking over my system, making me warm and soft and easily affected, I'd tackled the last of what I had of her.

"I can't sleep—and that's never been a problem for me. I'm ashamed of how things were left between Jasper and me tonight. Of how I handled the news about him and Cole. If I've learned anything from this bad heart of mine, it's that the last interaction is the one that counts, because another isn't promised. The last thing I said to him is what he'll remember most.

I've worked hard at motherhood. It wasn't always easy, but it was my most important and most prized job, and I wanted to get it right. I want to get it right. And now I'm lying here, unable to help but wonder if the thing I'd done last, the hurtful words I'd said last, will overshadow all the times I'd said and done the right things.

For the last twenty-two years I've been on the bench watching the game, waiting to be called onto the field to prove myself, waiting for some moment when I'd need to show them in a real way that when it mattered most, I'd have their backs. And when the time came, I failed them.

They're my children, and my children are in love with one another. There's no rule book for this. There's so many things that can go wrong, and I won't be here to help fix it. Where will that leave Jasper?

Death is coming for me. I feel it. No matter how much I smile and try to hide my physical pain. I see it in my dreams.

I feel it waiting in my chest. But after tonight, death isn't the thing I'm most afraid of. I'm afraid of not getting the chance to say I'm scared for all of you, but I'm sorry anyway. I am so very sorry.

The flood gates hadn't only opened, they'd been torn from their hinges and washed away with the stream of pain, anger, betrayal, and the sense of unworthiness I'd spent six years fortifying. And then I'd thought back to the night she died, to the words she'd mouthed to me.

"I'm sorry."

I'd smothered my scream into my fist as it hit me. She hadn't been sorry she didn't save me from Cole. She hadn't died believing he'd hurt me. She was sorry she hadn't handled the news better. Sorry she hadn't been what I needed when it mattered most. And she'd died trying to tell me that.

"I'll love and support you through anything, Jasper. Or die trying."

And then a brand-new pain attempted to creep into the space left behind from the flood, from the purging of the lies I'd told myself. I was finally getting what I needed, but she'd died without ever getting what she needed. I never got to tell her it was okay. That I loved her, that I understood her feelings on the subject of me and Cole, and that she and I were more than fine.

She could barely walk by then. The desperation she must have felt to get to me right away... Had she tried to call me first? I wouldn't have known. I was too overtaken by Cole.

Poisonous thoughts had begun to swell in my head then, stabbing like a hot poker.

It must have taken her forever to get to me.

It must have taken everything for her to get to me.

It was my fault.

In the end, it was still all my fault.

The yo-yoing of relief, release, blame, and the intake of fresh pain became dizzying, intoxicating in an unhealthy way.

"Stop it!" I'd shouted at the toxic voice in my head, but it remained vigilant, trying and trying to press against the barrier of affirmations I'd been slowly building up over the last month or so, destroying everything I thought I'd been working on.

I couldn't do this alone, I'd concluded, then. There were too many years of me beating myself into a bloody pulp to get over this on my own.

My home screen lighting up jarred me from thoughts of last night. I sipped at my forgotten coffee, but it had gone tepid during my musing. I shoved it aside and did a search for *top therapists in the New York City area.*

I thought back to how well adjusted Cole was before I'd gotten my hands on him again, and the blatant fear in his eyes the last night we were together, like he was terrified of spiraling to a time when he wasn't so adjusted.

"I can't compete with your pain, angel. Your wounds are too deep for my love to reach. Too deep for my love to heal. You have to find a way past it."

He'd chosen to save himself, and the decision wasn't easy, but maybe now I had the courage to do the same.

Ten phone calls and one last minute cancellation later, and I was running through the front door toward my first session, toward getting better. A welcome change from running away from it.

◆ ◆ ◆

I returned home excited, ready to share my day with someone, forgetting Daniel wouldn't be home for a couple hours, forgetting he wasn't the person to share anything with.

Quickly, without giving myself time to think, I gathered the scrapbook and journal entry into my satchel, and bolted through the door again. I should've probably waited for Daniel to get home, should've probably had "the talk" with him first, but I was more interested in providing Cole with a measure of peace, knowing the revelation of our mother's disapproval had to have weighed heavily on him.

Two trains and nearly an hour later, I was pushing through the hotel lobby, signing in and moving purposefully for the elevator bank. Knowing he hadn't removed my name from the approved visitors list helped relieve some of the fear-acid scorching holes through my insides as I made the journey up.

I'd been off the elevator three seconds when a sweat-slicked Cole came charging from the direction of his home gym, hair wet from a recent workout, dick caged to his inner thigh by his compression tights.

His eyes were hard as ice, breathing accelerated, chest pumping brutally. I didn't know what had him so riled up, or who he had expected me to be, but I wanted all of his menace let loose on me. All the barbarity and pain and the lust now boiling behind that stone cold stare... I wanted to be on the receiving and losing end of it all. My body clenched in agreement.

"Jas?" be breathed, the syllable rough as he worked on shifting gears. "What are you doing here?" He came closer, worry washing over his expression. He rested a folder I hadn't noticed he'd been holding on the foyer table. "You okay?"

"Yeah," I said, clearing my head and throat, thankful for the long coat covering my crotch area. My heart vibrated with missing him. "Sit with me." Too impatient to go any further, I moved to the wall and slid down, patting the space next to me. I pulled my satchel strap from over my head and reached in for the scrapbook. Cole shuffled over and took a seat.

"Why are we on the floor?" he asked.

I placed the book on his lap in answer. I explained every photo, read him every note, and waited as long as it took for him to absorb it all before moving on. Then I passed him the sheet of journal paper, and watched as his mouth moved soundlessly as he read it twice.

Cole stared ahead in a trance for so long after, I nearly checked for a pulse. I tucked the paper and book back into my bag and set it aside.

"She would've tried," I said, after a while. "You were right, Cole. About it all."

He sought out my hand and held it, and we did that for a while, just sitting, staring at the opposite wall, and speaking through touch.

"I had my first therapy session today," I said, and he whipped his head around to me, eyes wide, then growing cautious, as if he didn't want to give himself false hope. "I'm leaving him, Cole."

"You are?" he said with no emotion or inflection.

"I am," I confirmed, and he waited until he couldn't anymore.

"Jasper—?"

"Will you still forgive me?" I asked.

"Yes," he said.

"Will you secretly resent me for what I've done?"

"No, Jasper." He squeezed my hand. "I could never resent you for something you had a right to."

"Will you still have me?" Emotion clamped around my throat, making it hard to breathe, hard to wait in anticipation of his answer. "Do you still want me?"

"Yes," he said, as if it were the dumbest question in the world. "I'll not only have you, I'll swear to never let you go."

We were all fumbling mouths and overwhelmed hands after that, my layers of clothing meeting the floor as I helped him free of his tights. "I need a shower," he said, recapturing my lips with his teeth, a light fragrance of sandalwood and musk hitting my nose, triggering my salivary glands as his sweat transferred to my bare skin.

"I don't give a shit, Cole. Just *please* don't stop touching me."

"I need you on my tongue," he said, frantically pulling at my hair and humping me. "I need you on my tongue and down my throat."

"Fuck, Cole," I whimpered as he bit his way down my chest then lifted my balls, sniffing and licking me there, juggling the soft flesh in his mouth before cursing and sucking my cock to the root, drinking in the scent there.

"Hold yourself open," he whispered, spitting on two fingers and working them in me as I obeyed, panting, grip digging into the backs of my thighs.

Cole sucked my dick noisily, eyes closed in bliss as his fingers fucked me, then he ate my ass with a ferocious hunger as his hand took a turn with my cock, all while telling me how good I tasted, how warm my insides felt, how grueling the fucking would be once he got around to it. "Jesus Christ," he swore, wiping the wet from his nose with the back of a palm before diving back in.

"I need... Fuck me, Cole. Please," I said, trying my hand at asking nicely as I pumped my hips. I alternated between trying to ram my steel length further down his throat, and getting my ass impossibly closer to his face.

"Not until my stomach is pumped full of your cum, angel. It's been too long," he whispered to my cock, tilting it this way and that way, kissing it, caressing it lovingly, refamiliarizing himself with it.

It was all too much, and when his cheeks hollowed out on his way down, taking every inch of me again, the faint scrape of teeth against the sensitive organ, I came on a roar so loud it sent bells ringing in my ears.

Cole rose over me, heaving barbarically, mouth creamy at the corners, lips and chin sopping wet.

"Put your dick in me," I demanded, a fresh supply of blood already heading for my cock.

"On your hands and knees, angel," he said, and the way he handled his dick, like it was a weapon, made the order threatening. Cole disappeared from the foyer, and I writhed on the stiff, cold floor as I feverishly waited for him to return with the lube.

"Cole!" I shouted, slapping a hand to my ass, sending in a dry digit because I needed something plowing in and out of me immediately. "Shit," I whispered deliriously, and then the warm tip of Cole's cock poked at my left cheek as he positioned himself behind me.

My useless hand fell away, smacking to the marble as I begged through gritted teeth for him to get on with it. I was more than ready for the great breadth of his dick to deliciously widen me. I was prepared for the unconscionable long range of him to reach for my heart.

Cole made the process of preparation dirty as he worked two, and then three, and then four lubed fingers inside me while taking a palm to my ass cheeks, this time with the intent to stain me with his handprint. "Your hole's so pretty," he praised, as I chased his retreating hand.

"Cole," I growled, and then he was in me all the way, no warning, no build-up. "More!" I barked after yelling my surprise. My knees complained against the marble as I gave as hard as I got. No shyness. No games of innocence and virginity. No sweet, blushing submissive today. "Fuck me like you miss me, Cole," I whined at the back of my throat, needing him to do his worst. "Mark me, tear my flesh from my goddamn bones."

Cole fell over me, wrenching my head to the side by a fist full of my hair, slanting his mouth over mine and biting down, copper mingling with the taste of my cum. His thrusts turned explosive, violent even as he fucked me at a pace targeted to break me.

I welcomed the breaking, opened my doors to it, arched my back and flicked my ass backward to meet it with fucking delight.

"Take me, angel." His words were garbled, eyes flinty, dick making a point.

"I will," I said, teeth accidentally cutting into my tongue from the sheer force of him.

"Never leave me," he warned.

"Never," I promised, so close to diving off the edge again, my ass weathering the rippling of him inside of me, a sign he was close to coming undone, too.

"Who do you belong to?" he asked.

"You."

"Louder!" he shouted, turning up the dial on his war against my body. This wasn't lovemaking or fucking. This was mating, this was heat, this was a thirst being quenched after a long drought. It was anger, pining, pain. It was all those things, but also the washing away of it all, too. It was breaking ourselves down so we could build ourselves up into something new, something more. It was stakes being raised, claims being made, lines I'd drawn between us in the goddamn sand being erased. It was possession unleashed.

"You! Always and–and only you, Cole."

"Good. Now take that fucking ring off." Without breaking his rhythm, Cole brought me into a seated position on his thighs, holding me to his chest with a hand at my throat and the other on my hip. I twisted the band, getting it about halfway off when Cole impatiently said, "Keep fucking me. Keep up the pace." And then reached around to pop the ring off all the way, essentially declaring it null and void, sending it tumbling across the floor. "I'm the only one who shackles you now," he said, surprisingly gentle, the ongoing sex anything but.

"*Fuck,* I love you, angel," he said as he aggressively sent me back to my hands and knees right before his soul-cleansing climax tore free, baptizing the both of us, wiping our slate clean.

I plowed onto him harder, grunting with every backward thrust, clawing toward my own release as his refused to end without me.

A caged scream rumbled up my throat, jaw aching and throbbing in time with my pulsing hole as I opened wide and let the shout rip free. With balls tighter than a white-knuckled fist, I began to come without the help of my hand.

We were at the height of it all. The point of no return. When stopping now meant dying.

Wild horses couldn't tear me away from him. Nothing could. *Nothing.* Not now, now ever.

A storm could've blown through the windows right then, and we'd have kept fucking as shards of glass rained down on us. A war could have raged around us at that very moment, and we'd fuck to our deaths. Not even a fire burning through the building, scorching and tumbling the walls, burying us in its wreckage could've stopped the unbreakable reconnection we were forging. I'd have risked my life through it all to see things through.

"I love you," I said, fucking and coming and pledging my heart to him.

And then his elevator dinged, the doors parting as the band rolled to a stop on its threshold, as God decided right then to test my resolve, to put my sworn conviction to the test.

Daniel.

CHAPTER 27

Cole

I COULDN'T THINK of a better way to start my reckoning against Daniel Ward than to have him bear witness to my reclaiming of Jasper. To have him watch in abstract horror as Jasper's cum pelted the pristine floor, dirtying it up while I pumped him full to capacity from behind.

Even in Jasper's now frozen state, his pucker spasmed so tightly against my cock it made thrusting in and out exquisitely painful.

Daniel caught the closing elevator doors, using them for support as he blinked between both of us lazily, perhaps wondering if he were dreaming, if this were a nightmare, but his nightmare had yet to begin.

Jasper made some sort of wounded sound in his throat, a hand thrown out in Daniel's direction as if asking him to wait, asking for a chance to explain himself. Jealousy flared hot in my chest, and I dug my fingers harder into his hips to hold him steady as I wielded my pelvis and dick at him like a deadly weapon, gaining a sort of childish glee as Daniel's knees wobbled.

"Fuck," Jasper moaned, the sound a mixture of guilt and undeniable pleasure. Daniel stooped to pick up the discarded wedding band, then seemingly thought better of it as if disgusted by the idea. "Daniel, wait—"

"Do you want me to stop, angel?" I cut in, chin tucked to my chest as I stared down Daniel below my lashes, raking my tongue over my top teeth. My orgasm neared completion, but Jasper's hadn't, and that stroked every part of me. My ego, the animal residing in me, my heart... It touched and made all of it purr.

Jasper's body bucked at my question, clamping around me tighter, the wet smacking sound of our bodies clapping together disgustingly loud in the shocked silence. "No!" The word was all razor blades and fire clambering up his throat, never ending until his voice gave out.

Daniel had backed into the cabin of the elevator, so it could've been up for debate whether Jasper was asking me not to stop, or asking him not to leave.

But then Jasper whimpered, *"Sorry,"* as he began to rock back into me, seemingly out of his control, even as his forehead and hand lowered to the floor in devastation. Even as Daniel saw it all.

"That's it, angel," I cooed above the squelching sounds of my cock beating a path through his cummy hole. "Take every last drop of me."

The doors closed, sealing us off from Daniel, but not before I'd caught the look of victory in his eyes.

◆ ◆ ◆

"Fuck!" Jasper exclaimed, pacing the foyer naked, our semen cooling on the marble floor. "I did this all wrong. I do everything fucking wrong."

"Do you regret this?" I asked, getting in front of him and holding his head steady in my hands. "Do you plan on asking for his forgiveness?" I needed to know where we stood before revealing what I knew. I needed him to choose me before knowing Daniel was no longer an option.

"Yes, I plan on apologizing, and I hope like hell he can one day forgive me, because hurting him in this way was never the plan, Cole. Leaving him didn't mean I needed to eviscerate him first." He held on to my retreating palms, pressing them into the sides of his head, telling me to stay. "But no, I don't regret this. I choose you, Cole. No matter what, I choose you."

I nodded, satisfied for the moment. "Jasper," I said, unsure of how to prepare him for what I had to say next. I decided to simply come out with it. "Daniel knows. He's *always* known."

"What?" he asked, half listening and half in his head thinking up a way to make this right for someone so undeserving. "He knows what?"

"About us. About *all* of it," I said as his gaze flickered over my face wildly. I left him there with his confusion to grab the file off the table. "I had a private investigator look into Daniel a few months ago. I admit I was searching for anything that would encourage you to leave him." I held it to him, gesturing for him to take it as he stood there dazed. "Nothing came of it—or so I'd thought. Leland delivered that to me a few weeks ago. Everything the PI had compilcd, but he assured me he'd taken a look himself, and agreed there was nothing." I shrugged. "I was trying to get over you, so I stuck it in a drawer without opening it. Until today."

"Why today?" he asked, staring fearfully down at the closed folder in his hands.

"As my relationship with my father improved, I found myself missing you more," I admitted. "I don't know. I guess I went looking for something to reignite my hope again."

"And you found something?" he asked uneasily. He was being hit from all sides at once, and working on processing everything at once, too. A second ago it was Daniel's forgiveness he sought, and now he was essentially being told Daniel had gotten what he deserved.

"Not at first. It's filled with pointless receipts, aged itinerar-ies, old bank transfer details, and copies of emails so clean and aboveboard they sparkled under my desk lamp." I tucked my hands under my arms to keep from gathering him up into them. He needed the truth first. "But something kept nagging at me, and so I went back to the file again, and again, until I realized what it was."

Jasper swallowed, fortifying himself. If what I was saying was right, then everything had been a lie. An even bigger, more sinister lie than the one he and Daniel had been living as spous-es. It meant the lie had started years ago, well before he even knew Daniel existed. That had to cut bone deep. "How? How is that even possible? Who else knows? And—and *why*?"

"Open it, Jasper," I whispered.

Jasper riffled through the disjointed papers, failing to see how any of it fit with my accusation. "Are you sure?" he asked, tone hopeful.

I set the decorative vase at the center of the foyer table on the floor, and then laid out the breadcrumbs. First, the flight details from almost four years ago. Next, the airport car rental receipt, then the hotel suite booked for one night. And last, the printout from the five-figure wire transfer made to an unknown account the very next day.

Jasper started at the beginning. "Who do we know in Ne-braska?" he asked, pointing to the itinerary.

"No one. But we do know someone in Rocheport, and if Daniel couldn't get a direct flight into Missouri at that time of night, flying into Eppley Airfield would've been the next best op-tion. It's a five-hour drive to Rocheport from there. Less if the roads are clear." The car rental and hotel receipts were self-ex-planatory at that point, so Jasper worked on putting a face and name to our connection in Rocheport. "It has to be," I said, when he shot his head toward me, eyes enlarged with disbelief.

"Maggie?" he breathed. "Mom's friend?"

Maggie stayed in the pool house whenever she visited, and she was in town helping with Selene that week. "Think about it. She had to have heard the sirens when the ambulance pulled onto the estate. She must have rushed over," I explained. Jasper and I had been too consumed with grief to concern ourselves with prying eyes. Our relationship would've been evident, not to mention the state of my bedroom when the paramedics arrived, and how little clothes we'd managed to put on. It wasn't until they'd transported Selene's body into the back of the ambulance, and my father's headlights came into view down the drive, that we remembered we were supposed to be brothers, not lovers.

"And by the time my father jumped out of his car and ran over, Maggie was there. But maybe she'd been there all along." And she'd left after the funeral without ever saying a word about what she knew.

Jasper picked up the wire transfer confirmation next, homing in on the date.

"Less than twenty-four hours after he left Nebraska, the funds were wired," I explained.

"Almost two months to the day I was assigned as *his* intern," Jasper hissed red-faced, the sheet of paper disappearing into his fist. "Why didn't you tell me all this when I got here?"

"I thought you were Daniel. I had left a message for him to come here once his flight landed, then I called down and informed the concierge to send him right up. All that was forgotten when you arrived. I was lost in you, in us, in our mother. *Nothing* else mattered."

"Why?" he asked, perching on the edge of the pedestal table. "It doesn't make sense. Why go through all this trouble?"

"I don't know," I said. "To get to my father. Me. Daniel is nothing if not ambitious."

"It's been *years* since I met him, Cole."

"Yeah, but you weren't together for all of it."

"Shit," he said, as if having just thought of something else. "He'd asked me out once while I'd been an intern. I told him I wouldn't date someone I worked for."

"He must have been biding his time, then. Waiting for your internship to end while trying to work his way up on his own—or likely toying with someone else's life."

"Still, if it was all a ploy to use me, to get in with Nexcom, if he didn't really love me, how has he faked it all this time?" He averted his gaze as soon as the question landed, because pretending for years had been precisely what Jasper had done.

"It's not the same," I said.

"Isn't it?" he huffed.

"Only someone fucking diabolical could be capable of this magnitude of deceit."

His shoulders sagged. "Cole—"

"I don't care about his shitty childhood or his rich kid expectations, Jasper. We all have a choice between good and evil, right or wrong."

"And which choice did we make in all this, Cole?" he asked, taking in the cum and clothing painting the floor.

"Don't feel sorry for him, Jasper," I begged, knowing he'd likely do the opposite. I hated that he wanted to understand Daniel's motives more than he wanted to hate him for them. I hated that he saw even an ounce of himself in his husband's actions. I hated his aptitude for compassion, when all I wanted was revenge. And yet I loved him for it all.

A prickle of fear latched on to my heart. Would I lose him again? Was Jasper slipping through my hands? My breathing quickened as I drew so close to him, as I took hold of his hair, as a need to make this permanent, or to remind myself we were already permanent crashed into me.

"Cole," Jasper said, guiding a staying hand to my chest. "I'm yours, Cole. Nothing can make me go back on that. Nothing ever again," he amended.

"Prove it," I snarled, before assailing him with a frenzied kiss. I slammed him to his back, catching his wrists and locking them down on the table at either side of his head until he yielded. Once I was sure he'd no longer fight me, I lifted his legs, sending them around me.

"Cole, wait," he protested, trying to back off the crown of my cock now seeking shelter inside him, his hole still wet and slack enough to take me again.

"I can't." I pleaded for understanding, dragging him to me by his waist until his ass hung off the table and his hands shot out to grip the sides. Until I'd fully impaled him, buried balls deep and lunging rabidly in and out of his center, until he gave up and gave in, until my teeth were clamped viciously at his throat.

Sating my insecurities came first, getting answers from Daniel would need to wait.

♦ ♦ ♦

Jasper piled his clothes in his arms, irritated with my caveman behavior, but I didn't regret a thing. "I need to get cleaned up," he said, and I stopped him with a hand to his bicep as he passed me for the bathroom.

"No. You go with my scent on you," I said, immovable, reaching down to catch what leaked from him, and slipping a drenched finger past his lips as his nostrils flared in renewed irritation toward me this time. "Swallow." I removed my clean digit from the suction of his mouth in increments. "It's the least of what he deserves." Reminding him I wasn't the enemy went a long way, and he begrudgingly dropped his clothing to the ground before getting into them one by one. "I'll get dressed, too."

"No. I'll deal with him alone, Cole," he said, patience running thin. "Don't make me fight you, too."

"Mark drives us, and I wait in the car downstairs. It's the best I can do, Jasper."

We were dressed and driving through the night within minutes. We gave needy and clingy a whole new definition in the backseat. Mark's gaze through the mirror weighed on us, further darkening the interior like a shadow as we kissed, touched, and professed our love. We were so close, Jasper practically in my lap, but Mark maintained his professionalism, not raising a brow or saying a word. We no longer had to hide, so we wouldn't, not for anyone, and we both needed our minds taken off the impending confrontation.

We pulled in front of Daniel's high-rise, and I yanked Jasper's t-shirt down, exposing the barbaric hickey sullying up his pale neck, before sending him off with a death-defying kiss. "Hurry back."

Then I made calls as I waited, exploring my options for cutting Parker, Mitchell, and *especially* Ward loose.

CHAPTER 28

Daniel

4 Years Ago

LIGHT TAPPING SOUNDS on my open office door. I look up from the contract I've been mulling over to find Jessica shutting us in, a stack of files cinched under her arm.

"Is that what I think it is?" I ask, neatly arranging my paperwork to the side, capping and returning my pen to its holder, tweaking its position to my satisfaction.

"Yes it is, Mr. Ward. The top three candidates from the pool of interns." She places the manila folders in the space I'd cleared in front of me, then steps back, clasping her hands in front of her, shimmying in her heels from excitement. She makes an excellent co-conspirator.

"Well," I say, folding my hands on my desk, "you know the routine. Do the honors."

The best gift my father ever forced upon me was Jessica. He once told me to plot while the rest of the world slept. It is the one piece of advice I live by. I leave nothing to chance, and oftentimes, the little things are what make the biggest differences, which is precisely why while interns are no more than copy boys and errand girls to the other attorneys here at Parker Law, I view them as my ticket to the top. It's all about making connections, aligning yourself with the right people, setting up the playing field in advance. The world is my chess board. I control the pawns.

"The first candidate is Michael Waterbee. My amateur sleuth skills didn't get much of a workout with that one. The name pretty much speaks for itself."

"The cookie heir, right?" I ask, reading through his test scores and whatever other personal details we weren't privy to that Jessica was able to glean. She hums an affirmative, and I set the folder aside.

"Now, Abigail may come from humble beginnings," she warns as I peruse her file next, "but she runs in some pretty elite social circles, she's smart, and she's dating a professional quarterback's son—"

"Until they break up, as most young hopefuls do, and then he and his crew of silver spooners will leave her in the dust. Been there, done that, and failed, Jessica. No more charity cases." With one candidate left, and positivity waning, I don't bother opening it. I sit back in my chair, smoothing down my tie. "It seems the pickings are slim this year."

"I've saved the best for last," she says around a self-assured half grin, preparing to blow my mind. If only I were straight. We'd be an unstoppable match made in deceit.

With my enthusiasm now renewed, I open the final file, whispering the name at the top, "Jasper Des Moines," but it doesn't ring any bells. I angle my head at Jessica, waiting out her pause for dramatic effect. "Who is he?"

She pulls out the chair in front of my desk and takes a seat, crossing her legs, letting me know I wouldn't be getting the short answer. "The surname Des Moines didn't yield any paternal hits for him, but it did trace back to one Alexandria Des Moines of Austin, Texas, a poor baker's daughter, first generation immigrants." Jessica flicks a hand in a show of how unimportant Alexandria is to the grand scheme of things. "Alexandria gave birth to a son in 1951, Jasper Des Moines."

I glance at the date of birth on the sheet of paper in front of me and conclude we're speaking of an earlier Jasper Des Moines.

"Jasper Des Moines—the first, had a daughter twenty-nine years later, whom he named Selene Des Moines. Selene's grandmother and father died concurrently when she was seventeen. The former in a hit-and-run accident, the latter from heart issues.

"Less than two years later, Selene welcomed a son, out of wedlock, whom she named Jasper—after her late father, but she gave the baby *his* father's last name. Yorksman." Jessica sits up, and I lean forward in anticipation, completely engrossed by her tale.

"Eight years later, the Des Moines family name is wiped completely from future history when Selene marries, and then adopts her new husband's last name."

"Don't keep me in suspense, Jessica," I say.

"Selene Des Moines becomes Selene Kincaid. Jasper took on the Kincaid surname, too, but must have changed it to his mother's maiden name at some point."

Open-mouthed, I scan every piece of information in front of me. "I won't waste your time on stupid questions. There's only one Kincaid who'd matter, and I'm guessing you're smart enough to not waste *my* time giving me a history lesson that leads to John Kincaid the legendary Grand Central Station shoe shiner."

Peels of girlish laughter ring out, and I grin, impressed with myself. "No, sir. I'm referring to Franklin Kincaid of Nexcom Global. The richest man on American soil, the owner of one of the largest companies globally."

"Well done, Jessica. Call our PI friend. Get me everything you can on all three," I say, handing the files off to her. "No detail is too small. Have him cast a web out as far back as he can go. Any information that can be used will be. Put a higher priority tag on Jasper."

CHAPTER 29

Jasper

THE APARTMENT WAS eerily quiet, and I took in what I could see of it with nauseating disgust. The usual scent of bleach and pine were no longer reminders of home for me. The tolerance I'd built up for the ever-present toxic fumes, as well as the other toxins in my life, were now gone.

Daniel descended the stairs, not shocked to see me on his doorstep. He carried my duffle bag in his left hand, his wedding ring missing.

"I took the liberty of packing a bag for you. We can schedule a time for you to pick up your other belongings. I'm willing to make this divorce as swift and painless as possible, if only to preserve what Parker, Michell, & Ward have built with Nexcom." He'd pitched his tone perfectly. Not too sad, as to show strength, but not too businesslike, because he wouldn't want to appear cold and distant. He flinched at the sight of Cole's bruise on my neck, and he averted his saddened gaze at the mention of Nexcom, as if the reminder of Cole pained him, as if he couldn't bear to look me in the eye when speaking of the man I'd betrayed our vows with.

If I didn't know what I knew, this last vision of him would've haunted me forever. The guilt would've eaten me alive.

"How long would you have allowed this mockery of a marriage to go on?" I asked, stepping down into the living room, flinging my coat onto the wingback chair, enjoying his visual struggle with the disorder it created.

"Things weren't flawless," he said with the perfect hitch to his breath, "but I loved you—"

"You're not capable of love!" I tossed the folder onto the coffee table, receipts scattering everywhere. A sheet floated over to where he now stood at the end of the sofa. He squatted, picking it up, and then all pretenses fell away. It was like the sun incrementally lighting a dark cave. I saw him, then. I saw all of him. "Why?"

"Because I could," he said around a deviant smile. "Because they didn't think I had what it took. *None* of them did. But I showed them."

"You couldn't succeed under your own merit, so you decided to use me as your meal ticket?"

"Everything I've accomplished has been because of me!" he raged. "Everything I've suffered has been so—"

"*Suffered?*" I scoffed. "You've been in your element, Daniel. Even this, right now, has you oozing delight. You're happy we know. The game isn't the same without spectators, right?" Those hazel eyes I'd once found beautiful and inviting were now callous and cold. I'd once proclaimed that the arrogance he harbored in his slender limbs was a defense mechanism, labeling it "not the real him," but it was clear now it was the truest thing about him.

"I thought it'd be easy. Seduce you, gain your trust, get access to all your secrets, insert myself into whatever remained of your family tree," he said, as if sharing a brilliant plan with a friend. "You made my job more difficult than it needed to be with your damn *insufferable* martyrdom. So you fucked your stepbrother, *killing* your mother in the process." The stab was perfectly aimed, knocking me back a step, and his eyes shone brighter at the scent of my blood. "What I'd have given to trade places with you. What? Oh don't look at me like that, you've met my mother."

I choked down the rising bile. "Did you ever care for me at all?" Showing vulnerability to a narcissist wasn't the best move, but he couldn't hurt me any more than he already had, and there were certain things I needed to know for my own sake.

"That's rich coming from you," he said, but then for the briefest of seconds his mouth softened, reminding me of the Daniel I thought I knew.

"I did begin to develop feelings for you while I waited for you to open up. It wasn't love. I don't believe I'm capable of that emotion. But I thought maybe it might be nice to rule the world with someone. We didn't need love in order to dominate. Only you wouldn't get with the program." He chuckled darkly. "You wanted to ensure society's castaways had a fighting chance. That the lazy get a slice of my one-percenter pie." He tilted his head, considering me. "You became a challenge. A pet project. In many ways you were easy to influence. Even got you to shut up in public. But when it came to your career, you wouldn't give in, and I wanted to win. It kept me busy while I patiently waited you out. Until I had Nexcom in my hands, and Parker & Mitchell could no longer discard me." He reveled in his brilliance.

"You could have been great on your own, Daniel," I said, following his trajectory toward the bar. "Could've made an *honest* name for yourself."

"Are you not listening?" he snapped, dropping a few cubes of ice into his glass. "Everything that firm becomes will be thanks to me, and then when I leave them, taking all their contacts and high-profile clients, they will fall because of me too. And Jasper," he chided. "Honest men don't make great lawyers. Good liars do." And liars didn't come any better than Daniel.

"You've had Nexcom for months. We could've ended this months ago and spared everyone all this pain."

"Leave you? So your brother could be rid of me for using, and then casting you aside? No. I needed you to leave me. I needed you to plead my case to your brother because you were so consumed with guilt over having an affair, you'd have done anything to minimize the personal and professional damage to me."

"Affair?" I asked, caught off guard. Had he known Cole and I had been having an ongoing affair?

"Oh, did you think I believed that filthy performance I walked in on was an isolated incident? God, how could you be that stupid, Jasper? I practically shoved you into his bed!" He tossed back his drink, smiling through the burn. I needed a seat, but I refused to give him the satisfaction of seeing me buckle.

"The night Cole showed up here to what was supposed to be a romantic apology dinner. You said wires got crossed—"

"Yes, yes," Daniel said, his hand fluttering over his head. "I'd had Jessica call his insufferable assistant and reschedule our informal meeting. It was fun watching him squirm as I ran my hands over you across the dining room table."

"Jessica," I whispered. "Did you have her set Cole up the night of your partnership party? Did you have her send him to your office with that flash drive so he could walk in on us?"

"Of course. You don't think I'd actually have sex with you on the desk I sign contracts on, do you?" He shivered from the thought of it. I had found it odd, but I was filled with jealousy at having to see Leland stand so close to Cole all night, whispering in his ear, vanishing to the restroom... I'd have let my husband fuck me as some sort of asinine payback for my lover canoodling with his assistant and best friend.

"I had to have a whole crew come in and disinfect the place after your little tryst in there." He laughed at my stunned expression. "What? Did you think I didn't *smell* what had happened when I returned? I really should be insulted," he said offhandedly while pouring a refill. "But I'll blame it on your need to see the best in people, and all that smothering guilt you drag around like a security blanket. It blinds you. Makes you easy prey. I must say I expected more from your brother—or is it lover? But he was too obsessed with you to see me coming."

"Was sending me to Club Bale that night part of your grand scheme?" I asked, encouraging his rhapsody. If he wanted to hang himself, I'd happily provide the rope.

"Yes. And I take it you'd finally got what you were after that night. You stopped begging me to assault you after that. You are one sick puppy, Jasper Des Moines."

"What else?" I asked, more than happy to give him the stage to admire himself on.

Now on his second drink, he swiveled the contents around as he smirked evilly at me. It was the most effervescent I'd ever seen him.

"The morning he showed up at my door thinking I'd left him waiting in the car so I could fuck you. I really thought I'd need to replace my bed that day."

"You *heard* all that?" I flashed back to how erratic Cole had been. How he'd nearly taken me on the bed I shared with Daniel. How my use of our safeword had been more for me than him, because if I'd crossed that line, I knew there wasn't anything I wouldn't do. But I'd wanted him to take me in a way he hadn't before. At the peak of his possessiveness, where common sense didn't exist. I'd thought about little else for days after.

"I'd never been more disappointed in you," Daniel said with a sigh. "You choose that moment to grow a conscience and set a boundary."

"What else?" I snarled.

"Don't forget the empty gesture to drive four hours in the middle of the night to get to you. I bet he wiped the floor with you that night, huh? He's got 'savage' written all over him." He shook his head. "If I had a penny for every time you walked through that door with a speck of blood on your collar or a bruised lip..."

I instinctively licked the spot on my mouth where Cole often drew blood from. It never appeared any worse than a chapped lip, or a scorch from impatiently drinking my hot coffee. That had been how I'd explained it to Daniel.

Daniel paused halfway through another refill, the decanter suspended over his glass, as he couldn't wait to tell me more.

"The business trips were all him. Couldn't have planned it better myself. I misjudged, though," he said grimly. "The night of the Smithen brothers' Christmas party, when I removed your phone from your coat pocket, leaving it on the coffee table, and then guilt-tripped you into missing your *date* with Cole." He resumed filling his glass. "I hadn't expected him to reach the end of his rope so soon. I thought surely you would leave me for him before that happened. I guess the regret you carry for quite literally breaking your poor mother's heart was stronger than your love for him. What a shame, really."

"You son of a—"

"I grew bored of the game after that," he said, raising his voice to speak over me. "I already had what I needed from both of you. I no longer had to shower you with expensive overtures. And all you wanted was to be left alone to squander your life away on heartbreak. I didn't have anything—or anyone—better to do. So, why not?" He could've played this game forever, seeing each passing day as another day he'd won something, because after being made to feel like a failure all his life, winning was all that mattered to him now. He gave me a look. "Why are you looking at me like that?"

"I feel sorry for you," I whispered.

"Don't." And then as if he'd decided to do me a small kindness, he said, "Look, me not loving you wasn't your fault—"

"Clearly," I said, considering it was never about love. It was all about power, pawns, and control. "That blame belongs solely to your parents."

"Perhaps," he said. "But they're proud of me now." His joy was both childishly naïve and heartbreaking. "And pride trumps love." This time when he removed his wistful gaze from mine, the melancholy hidden there seemed genuine. Finished with his celebratory drinks, he set the glass down before strolling over to the window looking over the city like a conquering king, basking in his spoils of war.

I stepped closer to the front door before facing his back. "What do you think happens now, Daniel? How long will their pride hold up after you lose everything because of your lies?"

He turned, howling with laughter like the joke was on me. "Cole won't get rid of me. Not if he wants your little secret to remain just that. How long before word gets out, and all the gossip rags are talking about the incestual affair that took a sweet mother's life? Because you know how the tabloids just love a good true crime story. How long before the board goes apeshit, and looks to replace Nexcom's golden boy? All Cole has worked for will come crashing down. No artificial heart. No making amends for the life you two stole. Trust me. Men like Cole would never concede power for love." He gave me a pitying look.

A storm on a rampage blew in from behind me, edging me out of its path as it aimed for the man I somehow still found it in me to care for. Daniel whirled around in time to catch Cole's fist square on his jaw.

Daniel cried out, hitting the floor, a sound mimicking rolling dice on the hardwood planks meeting my ears. "My teeth!" he sputtered around a mouthful of blood. His utter disbelief would've been comical if the situation weren't so infinitely tragic.

"Your weakness, Daniel, is that you don't know what love is," Cole said, shaking out his injured hand. "You don't know what it feels like, what it makes you capable of doing, capable of withstanding." He placed a booted foot to Daniel's chest, pinning him to the floor. "Your ignorance will be your downfall, because there isn't a hit to me I wouldn't turn the other cheek for, no scandal I wouldn't face, no loss I wouldn't be willing to take for this man." He sent a thumb over in my direction, and I wondered how long he'd been eavesdropping outside the apartment door. "You can't blackmail me into compliance, Daniel. Because I'm willing to make the hard calls and light the dynamite myself." Cole was willing to blow his whole world up for me, and I vowed from that point onward to ensure that I was worth the trouble.

"Investors will pull out," Daniel promised as he squirmed under Cole's shoe.

"Let them," Cole dared as his phone pinged. He fished it from his pocket, reading a message before clicking the screen and turning it toward Daniel. Daniel's struggle to free himself renewed as he listened to the news report clip.

"This just in. Nexcom Global has severed all ties with their legal dream team, Parker, Mitchell, & Ward, amidst allegations of fraud, breach of contract, unethical business practices, and other criminal activities. An investigation into the firm will soon be underway, and we're being told they're currently moving into damage control with a press release of their own scheduled to go live shortly. But it looks like the man at the helm of all of this is newly minted partner, Daniel Ward. Our sources confirm..."

"Your hard drives are being seized as we speak," Cole said over the news report, allowing Daniel to stumble to his feet. "All your contracts will go under internal review. And I suspect even your cases won during your short stint as a litigation attorney will come into question."

"You can't do this," Daniel fumed, leering at Cole.

"Oh, but I can," Cole whispered, moving in for the kill. "It didn't take much for your assistant to blow the whistle." He allowed that tidbit to sink in. "Is that fear I see?" Cole said victoriously. "We're not just dealing with illegal background checks on interns, are we? What else have you been up to, Daniel?"

Daniel's cell phone had been ringing from upstairs non-stop since Cole charged in. The landline, too.

"Was it worth all this, Daniel?" I asked, coming to stand beside Cole, searching Daniel's gaze for the sliver of humanity I'd witnessed time and time again, the part I refused to believe was all an act. But either it was never there, or he'd lapsed into self-preservation, because only a vacant room lived behind his stare now.

"Look at you two," he spat, knocking into the window on his slow retreat. "Standing there so self-righteous. You think you're clean in all this?"

Daniel's underhandedness didn't absolve us of our role in his scheming, in the temporary success of it, however manipulated we may have been by him. I'd knowingly married a man I deeply cared for but wasn't in love with. I was an adulterer. And Cole was a man willing to take whatever he wanted no matter the cost. There were hard lessons to be learned from this.

"We merely lived up to your expectations, Daniel," Cole said, refusing him an ounce of sympathy. "We are the men you wanted us to be. Don't cry foul now. It's unbecoming of you."

No one got a free pass from Cole when it came to hurting me. There had been many boys before Daniel with missing teeth. I rested a palm on his forearm, letting him know enough was enough. We didn't share the same thirst for retribution.

"I gave you two unsaid permission to have your filthy affair." Daniel laughed mirthlessly as we turned for the door. "You could've left me for him. Things didn't have to get to this point, Jasper. But you mucked it up like you do everything else." The absence of his front teeth gave him a lisp, and blood dribbled down his chin, staining the front of his white shirt. He looked down at the mess and screwed his eyes shut as if pained by it.

"Don't, Cole," I said, holding him back from Daniel. "He's lost everything, and we've gained everything. The least we can do is give him the last word. It's all he's got left."

The phones rang in succession throughout the apartment, and Daniel had a wild look about him, fisting his chestnut hair before stomping over to the end table and hurling the phone at the wall. All while tossing insults at our backs as we exited.

"You have no proof! So I took a last-minute trip to spend the night with a woman, and then paid her for her time," he said, working out the spin he'd put on things, working on his defense. "I wouldn't be the first to do it. And Jessica," he scoffed. "You'll be hard-pressed to find any evidence that doesn't lead straight to her." He must have had her do all the dirty work, keeping his hands as clean as possible. "Who knows, maybe all this time she was in love with me," he said. "Or maybe, she's been working with you all this time to set me up. Yeah, that's it. You've been looking for a way to bring me down ever since learning I was married to Jasper."

I turned back to the apartment, holding up my phone and unveiling the voice recording app I had running, taking satisfaction in the widening of his eyes. "You've underestimated me for the last time, Daniel."

"This isn't over! You'll fucking pay for this!" He changed tactics when that didn't get a reaction from us. "If it's any consolation," he said, "if I were able to love someone, it would've been you."

That caught our attention, and we watched Daniel through narrowed eyes from the open doorway as we waited for the elevator. Daniel dragged his salacious stare over me, and I knew his parting blow wouldn't be good. I squeezed Cole's hand tighter, wondering if I was strong enough to hold him off Daniel a second time.

"Because no one takes a cock like you, Jasper." His bloody cocky smile said he'd thought he'd won, but Cole didn't give him the pulverizing he so obviously wanted. He gave him something even better.

"I'd answer the phone if I were you, Daniel," he said composedly as Daniel's cell phone continued to scream. "Might be your parents. I did you the favor of breaking the news to them. Didn't want the headlines catching them off guard."

Daniel went as still as death, the red coating his face harsh against the pale backdrop of his skin. We backed onto the elevator, and I pressed the button for the lobby.

"You're welcome," Cole said to Daniel, as the elevator doors closed.

♦ ♦ ♦

"What are you thinking?" Cole asked as we rode down. "Don't tell me you feel sorry for him?"

"Of course I do. But that's not what I was thinking. If it weren't for Daniel, we'd still be apart. I'd still be blaming myself for her death. I'd still be a poor reflection of who I used to be."

"So some good came out of his deceitfulness. So what." He shrugged his shoulders. "We don't owe him our thanks for it."

I nodded, lifting my chin at his directive, accepting a cum-fragranced kiss. "I was also thinking I could finally have a shower. Poor Mark must have been dying from the front seat."

Cole laughed into my mouth.

"You're such a fucking brute," I said.

"Does that upset you?"

"Occasionally," I said. "Like when I have a deceptive husband to tackle, and all you want to do is mark me and stuff me full of cum to prove to the world you own me."

"I was afraid. I wanted him to know who you belonged to. I wanted you to remember me, to *feel* me inside you as you dealt with him," he said, the mercilessness in his eyes replaced with something soft just for me.

I pressed my mouth to his lips, not with the intention to kiss him, but so he could feel my next words. So he could remember what they had once meant to us, and what they meant to me now. Halfway through our teenage mantra, he joined in, words shaking with deep emotion.

"I love you so much my heart hurts with it," we whispered together, and then repeated it as many times as it took for him to believe it. I had a lot of making up to do, and it would be my most important job from that day forward because I knew what mattered now. My love for him.

"I love you, Cole Kincaid," I said fiercely. "And you don't have to be afraid anymore. I'm not going anywhere."

EPILOGUE

Jasper

4 Months Later

I'D LET MY intern go early under false pretenses. Sure, tomorrow marked the first day of summer, and yeah, he was young, and it was Friday, and in terms of actual work—and not just setting up our desk chairs and ordering supplies, it was a slow day. It all made sense, but really, I wanted to be alone. I wanted to touch every inch of my new office space with my bare hands. I wanted to tap dance on the polished floors. I wanted to whoop into the air, and pray I didn't disturb anyone in the shoe store below me, or the office space on the floor above. And I didn't want to subject Leon to secondhand embarrassment while doing it.

Cole and I had gone full speed ahead after the debacle with Daniel broke. Not only within our personal lives, but professionally speaking, too. Too much time had already been wasted. No more second-guessing anything became our motto. I had a dream, and with him by my side encouraging me, and Sofia at my back pushing me whenever fear stalled me, there wasn't anything I couldn't do.

It also helped that I'd given in and claimed my trust, affording me the luxury of building my business when and how I wanted to.

"I did it," I whispered to myself with pride.

"Yes, you did," an equally awed voice said from behind me. Cole waited by the open door, and going by his breezy, reclined position, he'd been there for a while.

"I thought I was meeting you at the penthouse?" I chuckled, thinking about how mopey he'd gotten that morning when I told him he couldn't come with me to work. He'd taken the day off to come hang with me, but I wanted to do my first day alone. Well, there was Leon, but he didn't count.

"You were taking too long," he said, coming in and smiling at the walls and ceiling like a kid in a candy shop, like he hadn't seen it before. I'd turned down his offer to rent me one of the floors he had on reserve in the skyscraper that housed Nexcom. This space wasn't much, but I wanted to start small and watch myself grow.

"It's three in the afternoon," I said, "practically a half day."

"Speaking of days…" he said, drifting off, snatching me up and spinning us around. We ended up on the floor tussling and laughing like fools as I fought to get away from him. "I want to know all about your day," he said, helping me to my feet and forcing me against him. "I wanna know the size of your smile when you walked in here this morning. Which shrill ringer did you choose for the office phone line? What color pen did you use throughout the day? I wanna know your plans for the upcoming weeks. I wanna know where you're going to hang the *Casual Friday is Everyday* sign. I wanna know how full your heart is with joy right now, right this second. Tell me everything, Jas."

"Do you really want to know all of that?" I whispered, some insecurity behind sharing something as simple as my day still lingering from my time with Daniel.

"Yes," he said. "Except the joy part. I don't need you to tell me that. I already see it." He puckered his lips for a kiss, and I willingly gave in.

"How'd you get here?" I asked.

"It's nice out. I walked."

Being close to home was an added perk to this location. "How about we grab a soda and a pretzel and I'll tell you all about my day on the walk back. We need to head out of the city soon anyway if we want to beat the rush hour traffic."

Cole had kept the penthouse. Aside from the memories we'd already formed there, the amenities were fantastic, even though I often gave him a hard time about being spoiled. Our hearts belonged to our home outside the city, though. A white farmhouse with a three-car garage, infinity driveway, and a weeping willow tree in the backyard. It sat on ten acres of lush greenery, with maple trees forming an archway leading to the stables.

It was where we spent our weekends, where we planned to spend our holidays, and if ever we managed days we could work from home on the same day, we'd be doing it from there. We'd be calling out sick to lie in bed all day together there. We'd grow old together there.

We walked and talked as we ate, seamlessly maneuvering through and against the stream of pedestrian traffic, blocking out the sounds of irate car horns, avoiding potholes and bike messengers as we soaked in the sun and the smell of the subway system through the grates in the pavement. Mostly, we were excited about our upcoming break from all of it.

"Do you have something you want to say to me?" Cole hinted as we entered our lobby. Everything was *ours* now.

"Nope," I said, playing ignorant as I stepped onto our elevator. He'd asked me the same question that morning, and I knew my perceived lack of interest was driving him nuts.

I noticed the letter from the county clerk's office on the foyer table as soon as we exited the elevator. "Is that...?"

"Yes, Jasper," he said. "It's done."

I tore open the envelope, smearing a thumb over the word *filed* stamped below the letterhead. *It's over.*

Daniel had tried making the divorce difficult. Tried to use it as leverage to get Nexcom to drop their lawsuit against him. With the recording I'd made, we held all the power, but Cole conceded, because we wanted that chapter of our lives over with, and it was never about Daniel's money for Cole, and it was never about breaking him for me.

He'd lost his job, the integrity he never had to begin with, and his license to practice law. The scales were balanced.

"Mark just texted. He left the SUV with the valet for us," Cole said, kissing my neck from behind. "Let's go home."

♦ ♦ ♦

We pulled onto the property after six. and decided we wanted to ride while we still had a few hours of sunlight.

"What's today's date?" Cole asked nonchalantly as he drove the golf buggy toward the stables.

"June twenty-second," I answered, kicking my feet up and enjoying the sounds and scents of nature. Cole huffed but said nothing else.

The property had come with horses, and we'd kept the stablehand. He'd been with the family who sold the house for over a decade and was more than happy to work for us now.

I hopped out before Cole came to a complete stop, rushing over to speak with Ryan, giving him the rest of the day off. We wanted privacy, and I missed the process of tending to the horses.

Cole's frown righted itself as soon as he saw who waited inside the stables for us. "Lightning?" he gasped, opening her stall door and rubbing her neck down. "How the—" He stopped, looking through the steel stable grille into the adjacent stall. "Warrior?"

"Yup," I said, a jaw-aching smile splitting my face. "I had them sent over." We'd discussed making it happen, but I'd upped the timeline for this weekend specifically.

We readied the horses and rode out to the lake at the edge of the property, leaving them to graze while we relaxed under the shade of an oak.

"I know we're not supposed to dwell on the past—"

"Then don't," Cole said. "We can talk about it. We can reminisce. But we don't dwell there. We don't live there. Here is where we live." He held his arms out to encompass the beauty around us. "The here and now."

It was one of the first things we learned in couple's therapy. We'd needed it, because I didn't want my shit fucking us up any longer, and it wasn't as simple as willing it away. Plus, with all the headlines about our affair that "mysteriously" leaked, and the legal battle narrowly missed when one of Cole's more conservative investors decided they wanted no part of it, we needed to make sure our relationship didn't burn under the heat of public scrutiny. We were taking no chances with our love.

With the tree bark scratching at my back, I gazed toward the small opening in the dense patch of leaves, squinting at the ray of sun as Cole laid his head in my lap. "Think she's happy for us?"

"I think she's ecstatic, bursting with pride," he said confidently. I glanced down at him with gratitude, playing with the hair that curled slightly above his ears, getting lost in the way his pale blue eyes sparkled like shards of glass left out in the sun.

"What about Franklin?"

"What about him?" he asked, hands folded over his chest as he soaked up my affection. "He's okay with us. You believe that, right?"

I did. Franklin had been our biggest supporter when everything went down. As the former head of Nexcom Global, and as Cole's father, and my stepfather, his voice held weight, and he'd used it, stepping back into the spotlight to announce his approval of us. To stand by us, and against anyone who had a problem with us, making it clear the legacy of the company he'd built with his own hands came second to his legacy as a father. "Yeah, I believe it," I said.

"Come here," he whispered, towing me down by the nape. The kiss quickly advanced to something darker, hungrier, as it often did, and I found myself in a prone position, breaths sawing into the air as Cole scooted down my body to remove my shoes.

"Cole, we can't," I said, to which he ignored me, unlacing my other shoe. "Cole," I tried again, but his hands were now at his zipper, his cock so hard in his slacks, if I didn't get through to him before he hauled it out, we'd never make it back to the house tonight.

"I'm hungry. All we had were pretzels and Pepsi."

"Don't worry, angel. I'm about to feed you," he said, unwaveringly.

"We don't have lube!" I cried through laughter, shielding my eyes as he set his monster free. "We don't have lube," I said more seriously, because really, I had to get him back to the house in an hour.

I opened a slit in my hand, peeking out at the sound of a bottle cap opening. I pushed to my elbows. "You brought lube?" I fell back laughing hysterically. Of course he did. I'd never been so happy, so horny, so not willing to give in, or so in love as I was right then, living in our *right now*. And right now his hands were at my button-fly.

"Cole, listen to me," I spoke slowly, attempting to pierce through his lust-addled brain. My last resort would be to safeword him. "The sun is setting. I'd really like to enjoy it on horseback. Also, we don't want to have them out at night, do we? You can have me however you want for as long as you want when we get inside the house."

He rested on his haunches, jaw shifting on its hinges as he considered me. I fixed my hair, removing the golden halo effect, trying my best to not look like a meal. "Fine," he said, "we'll get the horses back, but then I'm fucking you in the stables." He stood, tucking his cock back into his pants.

"Cole—"

"You're wasting sunlight," he said, walking with a stiff gait to take his seat on Lightning before taking Warrior's reins in his hand. He clicked his tongue, and they circled until they were facing and waiting for me. "I fuck you in the stables, or I get down and take you right here on the grass. The choice is yours, Jasper."

"Is it?" I asked dryly, dusting my pants off and mounting Warrior.

The sky was orange with the dying sun by the time we arrived at the stables. We dismounted the horses, untacked and tended to them before leading them into their stalls. Cole worked with quiet determination, while I thought over how I'd get us to the house in the next fifteen minutes.

"So," I began, the rest of my words melting away at the sight of Cole stripping out of his clothes as he headed for a foldout chair, which sat atop a small patch of spilled hay.

"Get naked, Jasper," he said, settling onto the chair and letting his legs fall open as he worked lube up and down his cock, "and open yourself up." He dropped the bottle onto the hay at his feet.

"Can't we get to the house first?" I asked around the saliva pooling in my mouth.

"I promised to get the horses back before dark. I never promised you a cozy bed, angel." His hand moved a mile a minute, choking his dick as he shuddered in his seat.

I stripped, because I wanted him and because he wouldn't take no for an answer. I wouldn't have wanted him to, anyway.

Squatting in front of him, I fucked one, and then two fingers in and out of me until they entered and retreated without resistance, until I was begging for God, and until the twitch in Cole's cheek had its own heartbeat.

"Enough," he barked, as I went to insert a third digit. "I want the fit to be nice and tight."

I could've opened myself up with two fists and taking Cole's cock would've still been considered a tough entry. He patted his thigh, the chair rocking from the enthusiastic way he jerked himself off. "Is that going to hold us?" I asked, straddling him but still standing.

"I fucking hope not. Because if so, it means we're doing it all wrong," he said. He looked obscene sitting in the fragile chair, holding his shiny, olive-toned shaft with its purpling head up like a pistol, waiting for me to sink onto it. He made obscene look sexy as hell, though.

"That's it," he praised as I lowered onto him, sweat beading at my temples. "Take me like you always do, angel. Your hole was made for my cock."

I wasn't the only one feeling the effects of the careful consumption of his big dick. Freckles of perspiration bloomed along his Grecian nose.

Cole gave me no reprieve, as soon as he was deeply embedded in me, my nails digging into the skin of his shoulders, we were moving.

"Bounce on it, angel," he commanded, and with the help of his hands on my hips, I did just that. The chair squeaked, the rusty old screws were loose and complaining in their slots.

"Make yourself come," he said, after I'd been riding him and swearing into the sweltering heat around us for a while.

"No." I'd long forgotten why we shouldn't have been fucking in the first place. I no longer understood the meaning of time and how much of it we had left. "Not yet." I didn't want it to be over.

The chair collapsed, and we rolled over onto the hay, Cole now on top of me. "You asked for it," he sneered before folding me in half, my knees pressing at my ears as he pinpointed my prostate and attacked it ruthlessly.

"Fuck!" I yelled, as he peered down at me cruelly.

"Damn it, Jasper. I can't get enough," he said, breathing labored. "How can I make it enough?" He stared dreamily at his cock impaling me as I writhed, whimpered, and pleaded for a little relief on his assault on my body and senses. I was ready to touch my cock now. I needed to come, but the fear of coming while he continued to work me like this made me think twice.

"Please come," I panted. He leaned forward, and I released the fistfuls of hay I held to drag him closer to me.

This fucking felt severe, angry, out of our hands, and the faster he moved, the tighter I held on to him with my arms and my hole, making it hurt so damn good.

"You first," he said, hips snapping, pelvis slapping against my ass. With the type of depth his cock had achieved in this position, and the non-stop crashing against my nub, I couldn't have him in me after I'd orgasmed. Not this time. I wouldn't survive it.

He switched our positions, the transition making my head spin. "Now," he said, making it an order, giving me a hard spank on the ass.

"Again," I said, bracing my hands at either side of his head and riding him hard. He continued to spank me with one heavy hand, the sound ringing out in the stable, as he worked my cock with the other. I'd feel the sting of his hand for days. "Oh God. *Fuck.*"

"Faster, angel. Fuck my dick faster," he breathed. "Shit, Jasper. Do you hear the sounds we're making? Do you hear how wet you sound on top of me? I'll never grow tired of fucking you. *Never,*" he growled. I bit into his shoulder, coming, my scream passing between my teeth to be absorbed by his skin and the muscle beneath it.

"Oh, fuck," I whined, as he came right behind me, continuing to buck into me. "Wait," I begged.

"Almost...done," he gritted out, his release throbbing into me. He sat up, holding my waist to keep me moving on him. "I need to break your skin," he whispered before sinking his teeth into the area around my nipple and stilling as his orgasm completed. I held his head to me, encouraging his habit as I caught my breath. Hay clung to every part of us.

He eased back, staring drunkenly up at me, licking his lips.

"Fuck, you, Mr. Kincaid," I said weakly.

"Yes, you did." He laughed exhaustedly when I pushed his face away, not appreciating his snark.

Cole cleaned us with the hose outside, the cool water feeling great against my hot, punished flesh. We redressed and drove through nightfall to the house.

"Still nothing you want to say to me?" Cole asked as I opened our front door.

"Surprise!" Lights flipped on, and a gang of our friends and family jumped out from every corner. Sofia and her husband appeared from the living room to our right, Franklin popped out from behind the staircase, and running down the hall from the kitchen came Camille, who'd become the little sister Cole never had, and Leland, who I'd come to enjoy teaming up on Cole with, although some residual jealousy still lingered behind.

"You don't have to be threatened by me," he'd said once Cole and I were official.

"I'm a work in progress," I'd replied, but I suspected I'd always have a problem with anyone who thought they could love Cole, or know Cole as much as I did, didn't matter in which capacity.

Banners and streamers hung from the mezzanine, where Sofia's sons blew party horns and shook clappers.

"Happy birthday, baby," I said, kissing the dopey expression off his face. "You didn't think I forgot, did you?"

We had dinner, played games, had drinks, ate birthday cake, and gave heartfelt speeches. And to top the night off, Cole had gotten a call from one of his engineers. The prototype for the artificial heart was complete, which sparked another round of hugs and laughter.

At one point, I'd caught Cole standing outside our living room, smiling wistfully at our group as they botched charades, Franklin in particular—who weirdly couldn't keep his eyes off Leland.

Franklin had once been the person standing on the sidelines taking in his family as we played games. Now he was in the thick of it as his son took the opportunity to look on with pride. *Full circle.*

"What can I do for you?" I asked, closing in on him. "Anything. It's your day. Anything you want, anything you need, any way you want me," I said, lowering my voice. "All you have to do is ask." I'd spend the rest of my life giving him all of me, because I'd already spent too much of it not giving him enough. I'd love him fiercely. I'd fight every battle alongside him. And nothing or no one would ever come between us again. "What do you need? What else would make this day perfect for you?"

"I need nothing else, angel. Because everything we love is right here," he whispered, gazing at me through teary eyes.

"Everything," I echoed back. *"Everything."*

♦ ♦ ♦

"Angel!" Cole groaned from our bedroom as I slammed through the front door, kicking off my shoes and stripping as I dashed up the steps in the dark.

"I told you not to start without me!" I said, quickening my pace once I hit the upstairs landing. Wet slapping noises sounded down the long hall. My mouth watered and my cock hardened. *"Fuck,* Cole." My shoulder knocked into the door jamb as I used it for support.

Candles were lit in every corner of the room, the curtains pulled back on the balcony doors, letting in the moonlight. In the center of our bed, legs spread wide, feet planted, wearing a birthday hat, Cole lay panting, one hand gripping the headboard as the other one fucked his dick. Cum ran down the crease of his groin, making its way to his asshole. This wasn't his first round.

"You took too long. I—I told you...I—" His hips rose as he moaned, jerking himself faster. "Told you I needed you now, angel."

As much as we loved our tribe, by the end of the night we were craving our alone time. We'd offered everyone a guest room, but Leland had already pre-warned them what spending the night under the same roof with us was like. Apparently, we didn't know how to keep quiet.

Sending everyone off with more food and cake than they could carry, we didn't waste a second in tearing away our clothes and hopping into the shower. Then we realized we hadn't yet stocked the house with lube, or much of anything to be honest, and our only bottle had been forgotten in the stables.

I'd left Cole to set the scene in our bedroom while I'd raced there to get it.

"Don't come," I said, kicking out of my underwear and feeling oddly left out.

"Get your ass on my cock, angel," he said in warning. I straddled him, fingering lube into my hole as he upturned the bottle over his spit-slicked dick.

He held himself steady at the base as I swallowed him inch by excruciating inch to the halfway mark. I was still a little sore from earlier. Not enough to keep me from taking his cock, but enough to be concerned about taking him all the way.

I rode him cowboy-style, coyly pinching my nipples, and biting at my fingertip as I steadily moaned his name.

"Goddamn it, Jasper," he choked out, taking measure of my cock with his lubed hand. "I love how it curves right here," he said, applying pressure to the spot where it flared and nodded left. "I love this vein right here." He tickled a finger along the puffy vein on the underside, each word ripping out of him.

I slapped a hand to his chest as my legs began to tire and the sweat began to form everywhere.

"Can you take more of me?" he asked, letting me set and maintain the pace.

"I want to, but you're too big, Cole."

"Liar," he chuckled, licking a white bead of my precum from his thumb. The claim wasn't a lie, the insinuation it was a problem was most definitely bullshit.

"You love what a boost to my ego does for the fucking, don't you, angel?" he crooned as I brought my knees down to the mattress and let him slowly stuff me with the rest of his dick. I fell over him, my hands tightening on the railing of the headboard as Cole guided me with care up and down his erection.

"Hell, yeah," I said, my hair falling into my eyes. I freed one hand to gather up the cum pooling in the grooves of his stomach muscles. I sucked it off my finger and made a show of fucking my mouth with the digit, before subjecting him to a cum-flavored kiss.

"Are you close?" he asked frantically, squeezing my cock and jacking me off me with vigor. I nodded, eyes rolling to the back of my head. "Me, too." he said, air gusting in and out of his open mouth.

We were both there, right there, I could feel it, and I snaked a hand behind me, sending my wet finger straight through his asshole, crooking it, striking gold and finding his gland.

Cole bridged his hips on a feral shout, my one hand still on the railing the only thing keeping me seated as his cum poured into me. "Touch me, Cole," I begged. The shock had frozen his stroking hand. Two pumps later and I shot everywhere, a drop catching in his navel.

We were sweaty and sticky, but too tired to care.

"Right here," Cole said, pointing to the center of his throat. My nose rubbed as I circled my hips, and his dick spasmed inside me. I relaxed against him as he pressed down on my ass cheeks with both hands, ensuring his cock stayed put for as long as possible.

"Give me a few minutes to catch my breath. Then I'll lick you clean, angel," he promised, pressing and squeezing me between his palms. I grunted sleepily.

I hadn't realized I'd drifted off until Cole woke me up with a kiss. "Why are you still awake, birthday boy?" I asked, scratching his scalp. We laid on our sides facing each other with a thin sheet over us. The candlelight still flickered around us.

"It's four in the morning." He grinned at me. "Birthday's over."

I hummed, rolling to my back and stretching my limbs, feeling the sweet ache between my cleft. "Did you get some sleep?"

"Yeah."

"And *why* are we awake now?" I asked, confused, lazily blinking at him.

"Because it's raining," he said. I got to my elbows, staring through the bedroom deck doors.

"Yeah, it is," I said, plopping back down, "now let's go back to sleep." My nose sought out his throat. The knot there trembled from his silent laughter, and I drew back, suddenly more alert. "What am I missing?"

"I love you. And I can't believe I get to spend the rest of my life with you. It's officially the first day of summer, and it's raining, angel."

My smile was slow and shy as I recalled a memory.

"One day, when the weather changes, when it's warmer," he'd said. *"I'll fuck you in the rain, angel. I promise."*

"The first day of summer," I'd said.

"You didn't think I'd forget my promise, did you?"

"Never," I whispered with certainty. "Is this how it's going to always be?" I asked as he stood, tugged the sheet away from my body, and dragged me to the edge of the bed by my calves. "Will we always feel this lucky? Always love each other this hard? Always want each other this much?" Standing now, I traced the happiness on his face, emotions surging to a high intensity as the rain now hammered at the glass doors, begging us to hurry.

"How is it possible to love something this much?" I asked, trying to comprehend why my heart wanted and needed his so damn much. I felt suffocated by my love for him.

He gazed down at me, lost for words, eyes brimming with devotion. And that's when I noticed the platinum band on my finger. The one I'd pointed out in a jewelry store window we'd passed by during my last semester at Harvard. "I bought it the very next day," he said, a rare blush creeping over his neck. "I'd planned to give it to you, eventually, but things had worked out differently."

It was simple, like me. Nothing like the gaudy diamond band Daniel had gotten me. And it meant a lot that he could've afforded something fancier, but he'd gotten me what I wanted instead. "You've held on to this all this time?"

"I've held onto *you* all this time, angel."

"Is this real?" I asked. "Not the ring, but life, us, this moment." We'd dealt with so many obstacles in trying to love each other that sometimes it was hard to remember we'd gotten through it all. Hard to remember that we were allowed to be happy out loud now. And Cole never grew tired of reminding me. Of *showing* me.

"Oh, it's fucking real alright. And I plan on spending the rest of my life showing you exactly how real it can get. Remember what I told you yesterday? And the day before? And the day before that?"

I bobbed my head, words failing me.

"What did I say?"

"'This love is a forever kind of thing, angel,'" I quoted back to him. "'And I love you so much my heart hurts with it.'"

Out on the deck, Cole placed the lounger cushion on the stone pavers, then guided us onto it, making love to me as the rain commingled with our tears, purifying us. Making us whole.

Lies may have brought us back together, but love would keep us bound.

The End

Bonus Scenes
Click here for TEN bonus scenes from
Cole and Jasper's adolescent years!
https://cpharrisauthor.com/books#bonus-content

Pinterest Board
The Good Liar - Pinterest Board
www.pinterest.com/authorcpharris/the-good-liar/

OTHER WORKS BY C.P.

Visit here for all books/audiobooks by C.P. Harris
www.cpharrisauthor.com/books

FIND C.P. HERE

Website

http://www.cpharrisauthor.com

Newsletter

https://cpharrisauthor.com/#newsletter-signup

C.P.'s Patrons & Stalkers Reader Group

https://www.cpharrisauthor.com/subscriber-access

Amazon

https://www.amazon.com/stores/C.P.-Harris/
author/B088P988MF

BookBub

https://www.bookbub.com/authors/c-p-harris

Goodreads

https://www.goodreads.com/author/show/20305771.C_P_Harris

Instagram

https://www.instagram.com/authorcharris_?igsh=MWtjN-
Go1aDdiajcyOA==&utm_source=qr

ACKNOWLEDGEMENTS

To the usual suspects: My husband, my kids, my best friends, and my beta readers Irish, Layla, Heather, and Marley. Thank you all for the role you played in getting this book in shape.

A huge thanks to my developmental editor, Anette King. Not only are you amazing at your craft, but your constant positivity and belief in this book is something I'll never forget. You're stuck with me now.

And last, but not least, thank you to my proofreaders, Lori & Jill, who have been with me since the beginning. You're both rockstars. And to Kris Jacen for her help on *The Good Liar*.